Praise for *The Perfect Son*

"I thought I knew exactly where *The Perfect Son* was going and congratulated myself on working it out. But *The Perfect Son* had my head spinning 360 degrees. . . . Brilliant!"

—Sandie Jones, *New York Times* bestselling author of *The Other Woman*

"A powerful, unpredictable debut thriller about a mother's attempt to reassemble her life from the shards of tragedy. Lauren North's skillful narrative casts everyone as a suspect and keeps the reader guessing until the final, emotion-packed pages."

—David Bell, *USA Today* bestselling author of *Layover*

"A captivating, suspenseful thriller that draws you in—with a twist that will take your breath away." —T. M. Logan, author of *Lies*

"As satisfyingly intriguing and page-turning as you could possibly want. An emotional read—the end is a shocker!"

—Emma Curtis, author of *When I Find You*

"Beautifully written psychological suspense about the power of love after a life-changing loss. A sense of impending doom and foreboding gripped me from the first page. . . . The ending is stunning and powerful." —Mary Torjussen, author of *The Girl I Used to Be*

"A heartrending evocation of grief that packs a devious punch. It left me reeling."

—Lesley Kara, author of the international bestseller *The Rumor*

THE PERFECT SON

LAUREN NORTH

BERKLEY
NEW YORK

North

BERKLEY
An imprint of Penguin Random House LLC
1745 Broadway, New York, NY 10019

Library of Congress Cataloging-in-Publication Data

Names: North, Lauren, author.
Title: The perfect son / Lauren North.
Description: First edition. | New York : Berkley, 2019.
Identifiers: LCCN 2018058729 | ISBN 9781984803849 (paperback) | ISBN 9781984803856 (ebook)
Subjects: | BISAC: FICTION / Suspense. | FICTION / Contemporary Women. | GSAFD: Suspense fiction.
Classification: LCC PR6114.O7784 P47 2019 | DDC 823/.92—dc23
LC record available at https://lccn.loc.gov/2018058729

Corgi Books UK trade paperback edition / June 2019
Berkley trade paperback edition / August 2019

Printed in the United States of America
1 3 5 7 9 10 8 6 4 2

Cover design by Laywan Kwan
Cover image of cake by Max Oppenheim; image of Rose flowers by Elena Schweltzer
Title page art: Abstract Smoke Photo by Lifestyle Studio/Shutterstock
Book design by Elke Sigal

For my friend Kathryn Jones

THE PERFECT SON

CHAPTER 1

Monday, April 9

1 DAY AFTER JAMIE'S BIRTHDAY

There is a snippet of time, oh so short, when the morphine in my system begins to fade, but the pain is still fuzzy. Fuzzy enough for me to be certain of four things:

ONE—I'm in the hospital.
TWO—I've been stabbed.
THREE—You're alive.
FOUR—Jamie is missing.

Five minutes, is my guess. Five minutes where my heart is pounding with a force that makes my entire body jolt along with it. Five minutes where I know I have to do something. Our son is missing and I'm not sure anyone realizes this. I'm not sure anyone is looking for him. Five minutes before I become a prisoner to the pain that tears through my stomach like I'm being carved up from the inside out, and

I have to clamp my mouth shut not to scream out for you and the drugs.

It is in these five minutes that I realize Shelley is beside me. Her hand is clammy on my skin and I wonder how long she's been sitting in the plastic chair by my bed. I pull my hand away as my eyes shoot open and lock with hers.

"Tess. How are you?" She leans forward an inch and I catch the scent of her Chanel perfume. The smell triggers a memory of the last time I saw her, standing in our kitchen beside Ian, the knife from Jamie's birthday cake gripped in her hand. The only sound the split splat of blood dripping from the knife to the floor.

The inside of my mouth feels furry. Cotton wool in my cheeks. I can't find my voice.

"Do you want some water?" she asks, reading my thoughts in the way she always does, in the same way you do. There's a jug beside her and she pours water into a plastic glass and holds it up to me, but I shake my head, causing the pale blue walls of the hospital ward to spin before my eyes.

"Where's Jamie?" The words are shards of glass in my throat, but I force them out.

Shelley's head jerks around, a furtive glance to the three nurses at the desk by the far wall. "I'm sorry, Tess. Please, just concentrate on getting yourself better. You're safe here."

I'm safe? Safe from what? From who? Where's Jamie?

A bead of sweat forms on my forehead and tickles my skin as it rolls into my tangle of curls. The pain is waking up in the pit of my belly. My breath is shallow—in and out, in and out—as the searing hurt rises up to my chest.

"You did this," I whisper. "You and Ian."

Shelley shakes her head, swishing her smooth blond hair from side to side. "I only wanted to help you."

"Mark has been here. He'll fix this."

"Mark?" Something in her face changes. A split-second shift where her pupils dilate then shrink again. I've scared her.

"Mark is dead," she says, slowing down her words. "He died in January."

That's not true. Mark has been here. He's sat where you are sitting. His fingers have stroked the back of my hand, I'm sure of it.

She doesn't reply, and it takes me a moment to realize I've not actually spoken.

"Mark is . . . He's—" The pain is growing like a beast inside me, and all of a sudden I can't find the words or the certainty. You've been here, haven't you, Mark?

"Get some rest." She reaches out and squeezes my hand. "You'll feel better once you've had some rest and seen the doctor."

"I want to see Jamie." I try to move my hand away but I can't. "Bring him to me, please." My voice is pleading and desperate but I don't care.

"I can't do that," she says with another swish of hair. She smiles, but I see the fear lurking in her pretty green eyes. What are you afraid of?

"He's my son. You can't keep him from me."

Shelley squeezes my hand a final time before stepping away from the bed. "This was a bad idea. I shouldn't have come. I'm sorry, Tess."

I watch her talk to the nurse with the cherry red–dyed hair at the end of the ward. They both turn to stare and then Shelley is gone. Don't let her go, I want to scream. Jamie isn't missing. Shelley has him. I'm not sure which is worse.

Where are you, Mark? Jamie needs us.

The nurse bustles toward me. A voice from another bed calls out and she tells them "Just a minute" before reaching me and unhooking my chart from the end of the bed. She makes a note. About what? What did Shelley tell her? What is she writing down? I want to ask, but the pain is crippling me and I can feel the scream building.

A machine is beeping somewhere. Each piercing screech of noise is a screwdriver jamming into my skull.

"That's a good friend you've got there," she says in a strong Dublin accent.

She isn't my friend. She never was.

"My son—" I can't speak the final words.

"I'll get your next dose of pain medication," the nurse says, slotting my chart back into place. I desperately want to snatch it up and read her comments, but I don't. I can't. Everything hurts.

Only after the next dose has been pumped into my body and I'm sliding down down down into the murky depths of unconsciousness do I hear Shelley's voice.

"You're safe here."

Am I? Safe from whom? Where's Jamie?

My thoughts, like the pain now, are fuzzy, and I cling to what I know.

ONE—I'm in the hospital.

I try to remember the rest, but it's gone.

How did I get here?

How did it come to this?

CHAPTER 2

Transcript BETWEEN ELLIOT SADLER (ES) AND TERESA CLARKE (TC) (INPATIENT AT OAKLANDS HOSPITAL, HARTFIELD WARD), TUESDAY, APRIL 10, 4:45. SESSION 1

ES: Good afternoon, Tess. How are you feeling?

TC: Me? I'm fine, it's Jamie you need to worry about. I keep telling you he's missing and no one is listening to me. I told the other one—the policeman—the young one with the red hair who came to speak to me on the ward this morning. I think Shelley has him, or Ian. She knows something anyway. No one is taking this seriously. Please, Detective Sadler, tell me what exactly are you doing? I have to know what's happened to Jamie.

ES: The police are doing everything they can, Tess.

TC: They just have to find Shelley. She was here at the hospital yesterday, for God's sake. She knows where Jamie is. If I could just get out of here then I could find her.

ES: If you want to help, can you tell me what happened two nights ago? It was a Sunday. You were at home.

TC: Sunday was two days ago? Jamie has been missing for two days? Oh my God.

ES: What happened?

TC: It was Jamie's birthday. He turned eight. We were celebrating.

ES: Who was there with you? Who stabbed you?

TC: I (pause) I don't remember.

ES: What do you remember?

TC: I remember Shelley was there. I thought she was our friend. I thought she was trying to help us. She got on so well with Jamie. This is all my fault. Jamie is my whole world. If anything happens to him (cries).

NOTES: Session suspended due to patient distress.

CHAPTER 3

Monday, February 12

55 DAYS TO JAMIE'S BIRTHDAY

On the day you died, I lit a bonfire in the garden.

Yes, really. Your born-and-bred city wife finally adapting to village life. It was that pile of bloody sticks smack bang in the middle of the lawn that made me do it. How long ago had you trimmed the hedges along the road and left the debris in a forgotten pile (another job half-finished)?

It was before Christmas, I know that much.

Of course, I didn't know you were dead. Maybe if I'd stayed in the kitchen, scrubbing the grime from the insides of the cupboards and chatting along to Ken Bruce on BBC Radio 2, then I'd have known before the police knocked on the door. But I didn't because in that moment, on that morning, the sticks annoyed me more than the grime, and the day was dry—the sky a crystal clear blue—so I marched outside in my slippers with the matches and lighter fuel and the Sunday paper, and whoosh, up it went.

There was a moment of raw thrill. A moment when the crackling of branches and the smell unlocked memories of hot dogs and wobbly-headed Guy Fawkes dummies. A moment when I wished I'd waited for Jamie so he could see it. I had half a mind to dance around it, I was so blinking chuffed with myself.

Then the flames started licking the top of the stack, and gray smoke billowed out in dragon-like puffs. All of a sudden the smell was no longer nostalgic but scratching the back of my throat, and I was standing in soggy slippers in a snowstorm of ash. I dashed back into the house, shaking the ash out of my curls, laughing at myself and the stupidity of my devil-may-care moment, scanning the worktops for my phone so I could send you a photo.

I never did get round to texting you. Not that you'd have seen it. You were dead.

I try to remember what it felt like to laugh like I did that day, but I can't. The memory is of someone else now. Four Mondays is all it's been. Four weeks is a lifetime, it turns out. I wonder if you'd recognize me if we passed on the street. The life-of-its-own mass of strawberry blond curls is now limp and hangs scraggily down my back. I finally lost the extra baby weight too. It took only seven years and your death to do it.

Four Mondays. Four weeks without you.

A stream of sunlight finds its way through the lattice pattern of the window, illuminating diamond shapes on the kitchen table and the small box in front of me. I watch the diamonds hit the dark wood of the cupboard doors that hang wonky on their hinges.

I hate this kitchen.

How can a house this big have a kitchen so minuscule and gloomy? I miss the old kitchen. It's not the same tearing longing I feel when I think about our life, but it's there all the same—a quick tug, a flash of the gleaming white cupboards, smooth floors, and space.

My eyes fall to the box on the table, sitting beside a bowl of two soggy Weetabix I couldn't eat. The box is small and duck egg blue. *Fluoxetine* is printed in clear black letters above the rectangular label with my name on it: *Mrs. Teresa Clarke. 1 x 20mg tablet per day.*

The doctor made it seem so simple. *"It's not uncommon for grief to lead to depression, Mrs. Clarke. From the symptoms you've described, I would recommend a course of antidepressants. We'll start with three months' worth and then I'd like you to come back and see me. I would also like you to see a bereavement counselor."*

I wanted something to help me sleep, a drug that could pull me into nothingness without the nightmares, but he said I was depressed. I don't feel depressed. There are a lot of times when all I feel is cold.

You don't need them, Tessie.

Hearing your voice softens the ache in my chest, but like the play-dough Jamie used to love, the ache is putty and stretches across my body. I know you're dead. I know the voice inside my head isn't real. It's just me saying what I know you'd say to me if you were here, but it helps.

You don't need them.

You said that last time when I could barely get out of bed in the morning to take Jamie to preschool. You told me I could power through it, mind over matter—push the sadness and the emptiness away.

It worked, didn't it? You did get better.

Eventually.

The space behind my eyes throbs with the threat of tears. My thoughts are running away with me. I focus on the sounds of the house, on what is real. There are plenty of sounds to hear. The hot water pipes creak and bang, the wind in the fireplaces howls ghostlike into the rooms, the windowpanes rattle in the rotting wood. But these sounds are drowned out now by the noises of our son. Thud thud thud—his footsteps, heavy with sleep, make their way to the bathroom.

I imagine Jamie brushing his teeth, skipping over the gap in the middle where his bottom baby teeth used to be. Pushing his tongue against the tooth at the top, testing its wobbliness, and wondering if today is the day it will fall out. I'm sure he's grown too since you died. Me, I've shrunk. I feel so lost, so small, without your arm around me, but nothing can stop our boy from growing up.

Quieter steps now as Jamie moves back to his bedroom to finish getting dressed.

A minute or two ticks by before Jamie appears in the kitchen.

A rush hits me. Our baby boy is here. The relief laps in tiny waves over the pain squeezing my heart. Jamie is here. You are gone and my world has stopped, but Jamie is here. I still have a world.

"Morning, baby," I say.

Jamie slides into the chair across from me, where a bowl and a spoon are waiting for him.

I glance at the clock on the microwave. It's 8:35 already. Where did the morning go? "We're going to be late for school again. Sorry. I lost track of time."

A crease forms on his face. Jamie hates being late for school. He never used to mind. He never used to frown like that either. It's too adult on his seven-year-old features, but he's been doing it more and more when he looks at me, taking in the sallow color of my face and the dark smudges under my eyes.

His gaze falls to the box in my hand—the medicine I should take, but don't. I stand too quickly, dragging the chair legs against the ugly reddish brown floor tiles and dropping the box on top of the post pile beside the microwave. The stack of letters wobbles under the pressure of the new addition.

When I turn back, the concern is gone and he is a boy again, picking up the box of Rice Krispies and tipping too many grains into an empty bowl.

He needs a haircut, Tessie.

You always say that.

The blond curls, so like mine, are a tad unruly, but he scoops them away from his face so that the strands don't get in the way of those piercing blue eyes of his. Do you remember the midwife on the day he was born? She tutted at us, cooing over his eyes. *"They'll never stay that blue,"* she singsonged. But they have.

I'm putting off the haircut, but it's not for the same reason that I haven't opened the post or checked the messages on the answerphone. It's because the rest of him—the long legs, the square jaw, and the straight nose that ends in a point—is all you, Mark. And if his hair is shorter, then he'll look so much more like you. Besides, Jamie likes it longer. It's something to hide behind when his shyness gets the better of him.

"Have you got everything?" I ask. "Where's your jumper?"

Jamie shrugs, unable to speak with his mouth full of Rice Krispies.

"I'm not sure where it is either. Where did you leave it on Friday?"

"Don't know," he replies.

Frustration sweeps through my body. Anger is riding like a cowboy on its back, and the words fire out of me before I can stop them: "Jamie, for Christ's sake. Where is your bloody school jumper?"

He shrinks back, cowering at the anger in my tone, and now I feel shitty. Really shitty.

He hangs his head, slumping over his bowl, and a single tear rolls down his cheek. "Don't swear. It's rude," he whispers.

"I'm sorry," I blurt out, crouching beside his chair. "Mummy shouldn't have snapped, and I definitely shouldn't have sworn. You haven't done anything wrong. I'm just not feeling very well this morning, but it's not your fault.

"I'm sorry." I pull myself up, gnawing at my bottom lip. "I did some washing over the weekend. I'm sure I saw your jumper hanging up," I lie. "Eat your breakfast and I'll look for it."

Jamie nods and I know we're all right. As all right as we can be without you.

My slippers slap on the tile floors as I dash out of the kitchen and into the hall with the huge oak front door. I move from room to room, searching for the missing jumper. The dining room is first—the dark shiny wood of your mother's furniture sitting beside the whopping great fireplace, black with decades of soot. The furniture is the same coloring as the Tudor oak beams that stretch across the ceiling and down the walls.

No jumper.

I don't remember if I washed it. I don't remember if I hung it out to dry. It's another memory lost to the fog I'm living in.

I move across the hall to the living room that overlooks the garden and another fireplace; the Oriental rug with scorch marks dotted at the edges from years of spitting fires. I wanted to bin the rug but you wouldn't let me.

It suits the room, Tessie.

Maybe it does. I can't say I care much now. The black corner sofa from our old living room doesn't look right in here though, does it? It's too small, too modern, like the flatscreen TV on the glass stand. Perfect for the square living room in our Chelmsford semidetached, but not for here.

I expect to find Jamie's jumper in a discarded heap by the PlayStation, but it's not there and I keep on going. Along the hall and around the main staircase, to the rooms beyond: the library crammed with old copies of *Reader's Digest*; the other living room, or parlor—whatever it is—stacked with boxes. Half of them are filled with the things we haven't unpacked, and the other half with your mother's stuff.

Up the narrow stairs at the back of the house, I peer into the bedrooms. All but ours and Jamie's are filled with seventy-two years of your mother's life, and the dirt and grime of a woman who thought herself above cleaning.

She did go a bit doolally in the end.

An understatement if ever I heard one, but who am I to comment on mental health? According to the doctor, I'm depressed.

I check the bathroom. Gold taps, a cream suite, and aubergine tiles that stretch floor to ceiling, but no jumper.

I find it in Jamie's room. His bedroom is a mix of colors—red and blue Spider-Man bedcovers, green Ninja Turtle figures on the bookshelf, black and yellow Batman curtains, and the car rug he's had since forever that I can't bear to part with.

The jumper is hanging in Jamie's wardrobe. It smells of lavender fabric conditioner. I must have washed it and forgotten; hung it up on autopilot when I was thinking of you, of us.

"I found it," I pant, dashing back into the kitchen.

Jamie pulls the jumper over his head without a word.

"Ready to go?" I ask, looping my hair into a bun as I shuffle around the kitchen table to the nook by the side door where we keep the coats and shoes. Don't roll your eyes, but I'm still wearing a pair of your red tartan pajama bottoms.

Oh, Tessie. Really?

With the wellies and the long winter coat, it's not that obvious. It's only the school drop-off.

I know if I drove the few minutes down the lane to the village and the school, then I could stay in the car and wave Jamie in, and no one will see the pj bottoms, but I also know that I'm in no fit state to drive this morning. I'm in no fit state to walk either. My feet feel as though they are filled with lead, my legs with jelly.

The sun is a pale yellow but bright—a spotlight—and I squint, dipping my head and focusing my gaze on the road.

As the engine of a car roars by I have that split-second flash again, that heart-stopping what-if moment where I think about diving in front of the engine so we can be together. The feeling is gone so fast I can almost pretend it was never there. Almost.

I tuck my body nearer to Jamie, moving us both closer to the prickly hedgerows bordering both sides of the lane. The days of scooting ahead with his friends on the estate and waiting at every third lamppost are long gone.

I wish there were sidewalks.

"Stop, Tessie. Stop worrying," you said on Jamie's first day at his new school, and anytime in fact that I worried about all the things that might happen and all the things I had no control over, like sidewalks and plane crashes.

You took the day off and we all walked together, remember? *"It's the countryside,"* you said, nudging Jamie so that both of you were laughing at me. It was a laugh to say: Silly Mummy doesn't like walking in the road next to the cars. Silly Mummy would like sidewalks instead of bushes. Silly Mummy wants housing estates instead of rolling farmland thick with dark mud.

"Today, Clarke Tours will be taking you on a tour of the village on your journey to school," you said, making Jamie and me laugh with your silly tour guide voice. *"There is approximately a mile between our house and the church, Hall Farm and the old school building at the other end of the village, where I went to school before they built the new one on the estate. The old building is still there, but it's an accountancy firm now, I think. The village also boasts a post office, a vet's, a playground, and a new housing estate."*

"New?" I scoffed. *"Our Chelmsford house was new."*

"OK, so it's not brand-new, but new for the village. It was built in the seventies. The not-so-new estate runs parallel to the old road where the Tudor houses like ours are."

"And the cottages with hay for roofs," Jamie piped in.

"It's called thatch," I said, giving his hand a gentle squeeze.

"And if you're very lucky then I'll take you for a packet of overpriced crisps and a hot chocolate in one of the three pubs after school."

I rolled my eyes at Jamie's cheer and your boyish grin.

"Try an overpriced glass of wine," I said.

"I like your thinking, Mrs. Clarke. And if you're very good," you added, leaning so close to my ear that the heat of your breath tickled my skin, *"I'll let you kiss me behind the bus stop in the exact spot where I had my very first kiss. It was with a rather buxom girl by the name of Kerry Longston."*

"Oh, Mark." I laughed. You always made me laugh.

I catch the distant smell of a bonfire drifting in the wind. It's just a whiff, a trick of the mind perhaps, but it still tickles my lungs, and before I can stop myself I see the TV footage, I see the plane in the clear blue sky, I see the fireball. I scrunch my eyes shut as tears prick the skin beneath them. My breath comes heavy and fast.

A few more steps and we're around the bend and the smell is gone, replaced by the dewy, cold morning.

"Mum?" Jamie's voice floats in my periphery, distant and soft.

"I'm fine, baby," I whisper, the umpteenth lie of the day.

"Where's my book bag?"

"Oh." I stare at my hands as if I don't already know that they're empty. Where are Jamie's book bag and water bottle? I look at the empty hands of our son and just like that the anger is back.

"We've forgotten it," I hiss through gritted teeth. *It's your sodding book bag, Jamie. Yours. When are you going to grow up and take some sodding responsibility?* I shout in my mind, struggling to keep it inside, but it's still there in my loud sigh, and I sense Jamie's shoulders sag.

"Sorry, Mummy," he says in a voice so quiet I almost don't hear. The hurt inside threatens to pull me in two.

"I love you to the moon and back," I used to tell Jamie every day.

Jamie's reply was always the same. *"I love you to the sun and back a hundred times."*

It was never ever angry words and silence that we shared.

We turn around, back in the direction of the big white house with its black beams that sit a little wonky on the outsides of the house. Back to the L-shaped maze of rooms and cold and gloom. Back to the smell of the bonfire, and the memories it unleashes.

By the time we make it to school the playground is empty. The children have already filed inside. Jamie turns and disappears into the building, and just like that the anger from this morning is gone and all I feel now is the emptiness of the day dragging out before me.

When I look back at that first month without you, I wonder if I should've seen her coming. Like a siren, bright and blue, flashing in the night. If I hadn't been so wrapped up in you and the grief, would I have seen the path my life was about to take? The old Tess, the person I was before, screams YES, but the new one is not so sure.

CHAPTER 4

Monday, February 19

---

48 DAYS TO JAMIE'S BIRTHDAY

Happy birthday to me! Thirty-eight years old. When did that happen? Of course my birthday this year would fall on a Monday. That's five now, Mark. Five Mondays without you.

Happy birthday, Tessie.

At least it's cloudy today. A thick blanket of gray hangs low, trapping in the cold of the night and the frost shimmering like glitter on the brambles beside the road. I don't think I could've survived another clear-blue-sky kind of day, where airplanes leave those streaks of white cloud and I feel the injustice of it all like a savage beast in my gut.

So that's one thing at least.

Jamie caught me crying at the kitchen table this morning—big heaving sobs—which made him cry because he thought he'd upset me, which made me cry even more because I was being selfish and shitty.

"Don't cry, Mummy. Please don't cry," he said over and over as I held him tight in my arms.

By the time we both calmed down we were late for school, and I snapped at him for losing his school shoes, which were exactly where they should've been by the side door. And that set us both off again.

I asked Jamie if he wanted to stay home with me, but he said no. Monday is PE.

We arrived at school thirty minutes late, quivering, tear-streaked messes, the pair of us. At least the school has been lenient about the lateness. I've been waiting for the head teacher to grab me for a quick word, but the staff have kept their distance. I'm not sure if it's out of respect for my grief or fear over how I'll react, but either way I don't care.

It wasn't the best start to the day.

But it made me think—maybe I should take a tablet today. Just as soon as I'm home, just as soon as I've warmed up in a hot bath, I will. Maybe.

You don't need the tablets, Tessie.

Easy for you to say.

Here's what they don't tell you about grieving—you feel cold. Really cold. An icy chill froze my body in those first moments of knowing, and it hasn't left. Nowhere in the half dozen "Coping with Grief" pamphlets that have been thrust unwanted into my hands in the last month has cold been mentioned. It's all about the stages of grief: the denial, the anger, acceptance; as if I ever will accept it. The emotions are listed in bold and bulleted as if we, the bereaved, can simply tick them off one by one and come out the other side normal again.

By the time I'm almost home from dropping Jamie off at school, my teeth are chattering and I'm shivering all over. All I can think about is sinking into a scalding-hot bath. So I don't register the huge black Land Rover parked in the entrance of the driveway. Not at first anyway.

It happens all at once. I'm turning the corner, sidestepping between the car and the brick wall, cursing under my breath when my elbow catches the wing mirror, and then I see you and a rush like the wintry wind sweeps through me.

It's you. It's really you. You are standing in our driveway. Your half smile. Your head tilt. I love you. I love you. I love you.

For a split second everything is how it was. The darkness, the fog, the cold, it lifts and I smile. It was all a mistake. A terrible, terrible mistake. You're alive and I love you.

And just as quickly, in the very next heartbeat the feeling is gone. Reality hits with the same force as PC Greenwood's words: *"Your husband was on board . . . There were no survivors."*

It's not you. It's your brother. How have I never noticed it before—the similarities between you and Ian? It's in your eyes—deep brown and a perfect oval shape. I miss your eyes so much. I miss the way you cupped your hands around my face and stared at me with those eyes.

The hair is the same too. Ian's is shorter, more corporate, more suitable for his partner role at Clarke & Barlow Solicitors—but it's the same straight chocolate brown as yours.

"Hi, Tess," Ian says. He steps closer, crushing the final whisper of hope lingering in my imagination. Ian is not tall like you, but is my height, five foot ten, so that when he reaches me, his eyes—your eyes—stare straight into mine.

"Hi." I don't know where to look. I can't look into his eyes, so I pick a place to the right and stare at the white side door with black hinges that leads into the kitchen.

We hug—an awkward, weird kind of embrace where our feet stay rooted and we lean our bodies in. Ian never used to hug me on the few occasions each year when we saw him. It was always a little wave and an "Oh, hi, Tess," as if I was an odd cousin at a wedding that nobody wanted to invite.

We hugged at your funeral too. I can't remember if I started it or if Ian did, but we seem to be stuck with it now.

"I've been calling you," Ian says when we pull apart.

"Sorry. I've . . . I've had the flu," I lie.

"For a fortnight?" His tone is incredulous and I don't know what to say.

"Can we go inside and talk?" Ian strides to the open porch and side door without waiting for a response, leaving me trailing behind like I'm the visitor and this is his house.

My hands are shaking when I push the key in the lock. I'm not sure if it's the shock of thinking it was you standing on the driveway or the cold making them tremor, but either way I can't get the old dead bolt to shift.

"Here," Ian says, moving closer and waving my hand away from the key. "You have to lift the door a little as you turn it when it's cold like this. It's always been that way." The hinges of the door creak and whine as it swings open. Ian strides into the kitchen and I'm left on the doorstep wishing I didn't have to follow him in.

It doesn't seem to matter to Ian that he hasn't lived here for a good twenty years, he still treats the house like it belongs to him, like your mother is still alive and rattling around the place.

He's my big brother, Tessie. He means well.

Maybe, but he never stopped treating you like a stupid teenager, and me and Jamie like we were a temporary phase of your life.

You're just as bad. You never gave him a chance either.

I kick my boots off in the nook and pad into the kitchen in my woolly socks. The tiles freeze my feet. The heating has clicked off and the temperature inside is the same as the outside. Not that it matters. There could be a tropical heat wave in our kitchen and I'd still feel cold.

Ian leans against the worktop by the sink and the window that overlooks our driveway. He stares at the table and my and Jamie's half-eaten breakfast bowls. My Weetabix have bloated, congealing into one soggy mass. I catch Ian's frown, the disdain for the mess. He adjusts his tie and stands a little straighter.

"Here," Ian says. He lifts his hand and for the first time I notice the carrier bag he's holding. "I bought you some grapes, and some chocolate. I wasn't sure what you liked."

"Oh, thanks."

He looks disappointed and I wonder if I should be more grateful. Maybe you're right, maybe I never gave him a chance.

"That's really kind," I add.

"I'm sorry to ask this, Tess," Ian says, "but it can't wait any longer. The thing is, I need that money."

Money. The word pinballs in my mind. I should've known Ian didn't come to see me, or to ask after Jamie. He's here because of money. Money he says you borrowed from him.

"I told you, I don't know anything about any money."

"Have you looked at the accounts?" he asks.

"No."

He pinches the bridge of his nose and closes his eyes for a beat. You used to do that.

"I explained all this at the funeral," Ian says. "Mark told me you knew about it. He needed my inheritance from Mum, just for a few months while you sold the house in Chelmsford."

I swallow, and for a moment my teeth chatter together again. I don't remember much about the funeral. I remember the rain spattering on the stained-glass windows. The cold of the stone walls seeping through my coat and my dress, all the way to the block of ice already inside me. The rest is blank—a black hole, a deleted scene in my head.

"Tess?" Ian's impatience jolts me. His eyes seem darker in the gloom of the kitchen and I can't help wishing we'd stayed outside to talk—not that I had a choice in the matter.

"The Chelmsford house sold straightaway," I say. I turn my back on him and focus on clearing the bowls. Ian sidesteps away from the sink but doesn't offer to help. "We sold the house in Chelmsford and used it along with Mark's inheritance from your mum to buy out your half of this house and got a mortgage for the rest. It was all handled through your solicitors. I was with you and Mark in your partner's office when we signed all the paperwork. The money was transferred straight to you. You were there. So was Jacob Barlow."

"Yes." Ian nods and I have that sense of being treated like a child, of not understanding the simplest of things. "And then you borrowed some of it back."

"No, we didn't." The start of a headache throbs behind my eyes.

"I need that money, Tess." Ian takes a step toward me. He's so close that I can smell the citrus spice of his cologne, and I stop moving, bowls in hand. Something flashes in his eyes. Desperation, I think, or maybe frustration.

"Jacob wants to retire and sell his half of the solicitor's," Ian continues. "I have some of the money I need from a bank loan and savings, but not all of it. If I don't buy him out we'll be forced to sell into one of the umbrella companies. We'll keep the name and the office but we'll have to do everything by a tick box. All my hard work and my reputation down the drain. I know there's a death benefit from Mark's job, and a life insurance policy. He declared it all when you made your wills. You can use some of that to pay me back."

I grit my teeth, clamping my mouth shut before I can say something I'll regret. I hate how your brother knows so much about us. Things I don't even know. *"He's my brother, Tess. We need a solicitor and he'll give us a good rate,"* you said. *"Ian won't represent us. His partner can do that."*

But Ian still poked through our files, though, didn't he? He still read your will.

A flash of memory surfaces in my thoughts. Ian, sharp and composed in a black suit and tie, standing behind the pulpit and reading the eulogy he wrote. His words washed over me but I remember Ian spoke about a boyhood of climbing trees and swimming in the river. A life in this very house, a life before us that I knew so little about. Ian tagged Jamie and me on at the end as if we were an afterthought in your life.

"I . . . I haven't thought about the finances or any of that yet," I say. "It's still so soon."

"It's been over a month, Tess." Ian's voice softens. "I know you're grieving but you really need to get in touch with Jacob. He's been calling you too. You're the executor of Mark's will. Until you begin the process you won't have any access to his finances."

"And neither will you."

He has the decency to look embarrassed. "True. But I'm trying to help you. These things can take months to sort out."

I shake my head. "Hang on. How much are we talking about? How much did you lend Mark?"

"A hundred grand."

"What?" I splutter, dumping the bowls in the sink. A spoon clatters against the porcelain. It's so much money. An unimaginable amount to loan someone, isn't it?

Ian sighs, pinching the bridge of his nose again. "Mark said it was for improvements to the house and a new kitchen. It was only supposed to be until the extension on the mortgage came through. He said you knew."

"Does this look like the face of someone who knew?" I say, turning to Ian.

My question seems to throw him, but only for a moment. "Maybe Mark was sorting it out as a surprise then, I don't know. But I'm really sorry, I do need that money back," he says. "I can't wait much longer."

"Yeah, well, I need my husband back, and short of that I'm going to need the death benefit to tide us over for as long as it can."

Then what? I've been so focused on your death that I've not thought about money. How are we going to survive on the money from my tutoring? And that's if I even have any students to go back to. Ian's phone calls aren't the only ones I've been ignoring. The GCSE mock exams are coming up. Parents won't wait for me.

Is Ian right? Is there a life insurance policy? I try to remember the details of the wills we made. We were sitting side by side in the conference room, moaning about the bitterness of the coffee and planning where we'd go for lunch afterward. I didn't care about the rest. I didn't think it mattered.

I should've paid more attention. You should've made me pay more attention, Mark, instead of letting me live with my head in the sand and keeping all the little things to yourself. Like when your mother was dying of pneumonia in hospital and you told me it was a chest infection, nothing to worry about. A version of the truth but not all of it.

I was trying to protect you, Tessie.

Was I really that in need of protecting?

I didn't want you to worry so much. It wasn't good for you to be worrying all the time.

"Look, Tess," Ian says, dragging my thoughts back to the kitchen. "Like it or not, you are the only one right now who can begin the distribution of Mark's estate. I knew my brother. He wouldn't want this to drag on. If he was alive right now, he'd have paid me back already."

The anger comes from nowhere, rising up and surprising me as much as Ian. "How dare you," I hiss. Ian jerks back, my words a physical push. "How dare you say you know Mark. I knew Mark. I knew my husband. You two, you hardly ever spoke to each other, for God's sake. What would you know about what he did or didn't want?"

"We were brothers, Tess. We might not have spoken much, but we grew up together. I've known him a lot longer than you have. And if you knew your husband so well, why didn't he tell you about the money he borrowed from me?"

There's something knowing in his tone that I hate. As if Ian is holding something back. "We went over this at the funeral," Ian says again as if that will suddenly make things clear to me.

"You mean when you cornered me in the pews. Let me ask you a question—did it not cross your mind to wait a week, or even a day? You only live twenty minutes down the bloody road. Why did you have to talk to me about it at the funeral?"

The tears racing down my cheeks burn my skin with the same intensity as the anger scorching inside me. "I've lost my husband," I gasp. "He was the love of my life, you know?"

Something shifts in Ian's posture, and his voice when he speaks is quiet once more. "You're right. I'm sorry. I should've waited."

I nod, and just like that the intensity is gone and the darkness hits me again. "I'm not trying to be difficult, but I really don't know anything about a loan. Mark handled the finances. We talked about having a new kitchen at some point but we were going to save up for it. I'll look at the bank accounts, I'll get in touch with Jacob, I promise. We certainly haven't made any big purchases, so if Mark borrowed it—"

"He did, Tess. I wouldn't ask if I didn't need it right away. I didn't even want to lend him the money in the first place. It was only supposed to be for a couple of months."

"OK. I'll check the accounts."

"Thank you."

We stand in silence for a moment. Neither of us sure how to continue.

Jamie's coping fine, by the way, I want to say. You know, your nephew? I don't know why I'm so surprised he doesn't ask about Jamie. Ian has always been the ten-pound-note-in-a-birthday-card type of uncle. There's no point expecting him to be any different now.

"I'm sorry," he says. "Sorry this has happened, I mean."

"Me too." I nod and dab my fingers under my eyes, catching the next tear before it falls.

"I'll come back next week."

The way he says it, it sounds threatening somehow. Ian must think so too, because then he says, "I can bring some food. Let me know if you need anything."

"I'll check the accounts and let you know."

Ian nods. I can tell there's more he wants to say. Another push he wants to give. But my anger, my tears have rattled him, I think.

"Good-bye, Tess." He strides out the side door without a backward glance. The door catches when he shuts it, bouncing back open. I wait for Ian to shut it properly, but he doesn't. He's already gone, crunching his polished shoes across the gravel back to his Land Rover.

It's only when I reach the door to shut it that I see the flowers. Rich green stems wrapped in a rubber band, thick leaves and deep purple heads. Tulips. An entire bouquet of them—twenty at least.

There's no cellophane. No note. Just two rubber bands keeping the stems together.

Ian is reversing out of the driveway and before I can stop myself my feet are scrambling and skidding across the stones. He's almost gone, but I have to know. He's looking in the rearview mirror checking for passing traffic, only seeing me when the palms of my hands slam against his window.

Ian starts, surprised by my sudden appearance or the crazed look in my eyes.

"Did you leave those flowers?" I blurt out the question before the window has finished opening.

He shakes his head. "What flowers?"

"The ones by the side door. You didn't leave them?"

"No."

I stumble back and turn to the doorway, half expecting to find it empty, the flowers a figment of my imagination; but they are still there in the corner, half-hidden by a mound of dark leaves that have collected in the open porch. Did someone leave them while Ian and I were talking, or were they there when we arrived and I didn't notice because Ian was standing in the way? I don't know.

"Don't forget, Tess. Check the accounts, OK?" Ian calls as he eases the car onto the lane.

I give a meek nod and he's gone.

Who would leave me flowers? A bouquet of tulips for my birthday, just like the ones you gave me every year.

I'd ask if they're from you, but of course they're not.

CHAPTER 5

Hot water fills the bath with a gushing roar, causing the pipes beneath my feet to groan under the pressure. The mirror on the wall is now misty from the steam dancing in the air and running in lines down the window.

There are no bubbles in my bath. This is not a luxury, this is a necessity. I have to rid myself of the cold.

When the water is deep I turn off the tap, throwing the bathroom into silence. I'm just about to peel off my clothes when I hear it—a knock, knock, knock, in bursts of three, too persistent to be the pipes.

It's coming from the front door. Knock, knock, knock, pause, knock, knock, knock, pause.

I glance at the bath for a long second and consider ignoring the visitor. It will only be the vicar come to check on me like he said he would at the funeral. Or your brother again with some other tidbit of knowledge about you that I don't know. There's no one else it can be. In the four months we've lived here, I haven't made any friends.

Knock, knock, knock, pause, knock, knock, knock.

Whoever it is, they are not going away, and by the time I make it to the bottom of the main stairs the letter box is sticking up and a woman's voice is calling through the house. "Teresa? Mrs. Clarke? Are you there? Can you open the door, please?"

My heart hitches in my chest. Is it the police? Could something have happened to Jamie at school? I cross the hall in four strides and yank open the door.

"Yes?" The one word is shaky and breathless from the panic racing inside, but it's not the police. It's a woman with straight bleach-blond hair, cut above her shoulders, and bangs that sit above dark eyebrows.

She's smiling at me and I realize she's the first person to smile at me since you died. A real smile, one that isn't leaking with pity. It's the kind of smile that compels the recipient to smile back, but I can't. My face has forgotten how.

She's pretty. A girl-next-door type with a pale, smooth complexion. She's not much younger than me. Midthirties, I guess, but staring at the sparkle in her green eyes, and her perfect white teeth, I feel frumpy, worn-out. I am both of these things.

"Teresa?"

"It's Tess." I nod as a gust of wind rushes past me, blowing the front door out of my hands. The heavy wood slams against the inside wall hard enough to leave a dent in the plaster. I grab at the door, pulling it back and wedging my foot behind it, but the woman must think I'm inviting her in, because she steps into the hall.

"I'm Shelley Lange," she says, pulling off her coat to reveal a black V-necked jumper over a pair of skinny jeans. A gold oval-shaped locket sits below her collarbone on a delicate chain. The way she says her name, the way she's looking at me—smiling, but expectant too—it's as though her name should mean something to me. It doesn't.

I try to think but my mind is a white wall of nothing. The woman is slipping out of her suede ankle boots, and I still don't have the first clue who she is.

Her gaze scans the wall behind me, looking for a coat hook, I presume, because next she folds her coat in half and places it over her boots.

"We have an appointment," she says.

"Do we?"

She laughs, a proper laugh, right from the throat. Like how I used to laugh with the mums in Chelmsford, regaling each other with stories of nappy explosions and tantrums in the aisles of Tesco. I drop my eyes and pick at the skin flaking around my fingernails.

The mums on the estate sent me an orchid in a pink china pot when they heard you'd died. It's withering on the windowsill by the kitchen sink. If we'd still been living in the old house they would've been around all the time, bringing cakes and dinners by the trayload for Jamie and me.

They came to the funeral—Casey and Jo, Lisa and Julie. Even Debbie took the day off work. I'm sure they have a WhatsApp group about me. Messages pinging back and forth. Worried-face emojis. Whose turn is it to text Tess? Has anyone heard back? I will reply at some point. They want to know we're coping OK and I don't know what to tell them.

The woman in our hall opens up her handbag and pulls out a phone. Her bag is a black leather satchel with a thin strap she has looped over one shoulder. The bag is small and I find myself wondering how my bulging purse, filled with useless receipts and out-of-date membership cards, would ever squeeze into such a bag. I could fit two of her bags in the holdall I use when I go out.

She taps the screen of her mobile before reeling off my name, address, and today's date.

I shrug. "That's me, but I haven't made any appointments. Who are you again?"

"I'm Shelley. I'm a grief counselor. I volunteer with Grief UK in the Ipswich branch, as well as running a private practice. I was told you'd be expecting me."

"I'm sorry, I think there's been a mistake. I didn't call anyone."

"I might be way off base here, but you have the look of someone who's grieving. Am I wrong?"

"No, you're not, but I still didn't call you." My words are clipped and ring with an annoyance I don't mean to convey. All of a sudden I think of Jamie and how I snapped at him about his lost school shoes this morning.

My legs are weak and I long to sit down, but I don't want to lead this woman into the kitchen or the living room. I don't want to endure the hand-patting it'll-be-all-right speech, the time-will-heal-you bullshit. The same white noise I've heard so many times already. From my brother and his boyfriend at the funeral; from the many phone calls with my mum; from a woman who collared me on the way back from the school drop-off. Even the postman knocked on the door to impart some wisdom on the matter.

They're all wrong.

Shelley nods, businesslike, confident. "OK, let me call the office and see what's happened.

"May I?" she says, pointing her phone at the living room before striding inside.

I wait in my spot by the front door for a moment, listening to one side of a conversation about me. My head is spinning. Slow, looping spins—the final rotations of the roundabout in the playground—until I can't stand it any longer and trudge to the kitchen to sit down.

I'd like to say I had an inkling then, a shiver down my spine, a foreboding of what was to come, but I didn't. Not even the faintest whisper.

It's not your fault, Tessie.

Easy for you to say, Mark.

CHAPTER 6

"I just love your house," Shelley says a few moments later, running a hand over a dark oak beam as she moves along the hall and into the kitchen. "It's so oldie . . . like a smaller version of something from one of those historical dramas. I've always wondered what type of people live in old houses like this now."

My mind is slow, my thoughts clunky. Shelley's compliment may as well have been a question on quantum physics, and I'm incapable of reaching for a response.

"So it seems . . . um . . . your mother called us. I've just spoken to my colleague who took the call. They had a long chat. Your mum was worried about you, although she did say you'd agreed for us to visit, which clearly isn't the case. So I'm very sorry for the intrusion."

A memory of my mother's tearful good-bye flashes in my thoughts. Me standing in the doorway of the nook, shivering and numb while my mother's clawed fingers struggled to unravel a handkerchief and dab away the tears resting on her cheeks.

After two weeks of her hovering and the thump thud thump of her walking stick on the wood floors, I was desperate for her to leave, to just get in the taxi waiting too patiently on the driveway. Jamie was at the kitchen table, listening to who knows what on your old iPod. He was closed up, not speaking, and I didn't want him to feel shy anymore. I wanted Mum gone.

She was talking at me as I closed the door. Could she have mentioned the appointment then and I didn't listen?

Shelley pulls out a chair and sits across from me. At least I've cleared the breakfast bowls. The box of Rice Krispies is still out. The blue of the box is suddenly too bright against all the brown wood.

"Tess," Shelley says, her voice soft and coaxing. "We don't have to speak now if you don't want to, but it might help."

I shrug. "Now's fine." Better to get it over with.

"OK, that's good. How are you feeling?" she asks, leaning a little closer.

"Fine."

Shelley raises her eyebrows and fixes me with a look like a concerned mother talking to a child. A wave of sadness throngs through my body. I wish I had the energy to lie, to paste a smile on and nod, but I can feel tears welling in my eyes. Besides, something tells me this woman in my kitchen would see straight through me.

"It's my birthday today." I sigh.

"Oh, Tess. Happy birthday."

"I'm not sure there's much happy in it."

"How are you doing?" Shelley asks again.

"Not fine," I whisper. "Nowhere close."

"Your mum mentioned on the phone that you'd booked to see the doctor." Shelley's voice is soft and tentative. She's trying to tiptoe around my privacy, I can see that, but it's not working and I feel myself bristle. How much does she know about me? How much did my mum tell her? Everything, no doubt. "How did it go?"

"OK, I guess." My mind is no longer blank but flashing with memories of the past five weeks. The times I've snapped at Jamie for no reason. The weekend before last when my period started and I cried in the bathroom all day, forgetting to take Jamie to Liam's football birthday party that had been on the calendar for months. The hours and hours we've spent on the sofa together, eating oven pizzas and watching old episodes of *Scooby-Doo* because that's all I was capable of doing.

"Did the doctor give you any medication? Or suggest anything else?"

I nod and feel a single tear roll down my cheek. All I can think about is the scrunched-up frown on Jamie's face when he looks at me. Seven-year-old boys shouldn't have to worry about anything other than winning at tag and having friends. They especially shouldn't have to worry about their mums.

I focus on picking at the flake of skin hanging from the edge of my thumbnail. "He said I'm depressed. He gave me antidepressants, but . . . I don't feel depressed. I wanted something to help me sleep."

"Nightmares?"

My eyes shoot up. Shelley's smile is gone but her eyes are still sparkling. I wonder how she knows. "Just one nightmare. I'm . . . I'm in an airplane. I don't know where I'm going, but the plane isn't flying, it's sort of tumbling and spinning downward, and I know it's going to crash. There's smoke everywhere. Thick gray smoke coming from somewhere and it's stinging my eyes and hurting my lungs. There's luggage from the overhead compartments flying all over the cabin, and I'm trying to protect my head from the suitcases, even though I know the plane is about to hit the ground. Then I wake up and I swear I can still taste the smoke."

I gasp for air and feel something wild surging through me. It's the same heart-pounding, hopeless fear that I feel every time I wake up. And every time I remember you're gone.

"I lit a bonfire in the garden the day Mark died," I tell Shelley. "I didn't know Mark had died until later, but I guess the two are stuck together now—the bonfire and Mark's death."

I wait for Shelley to squeeze my hand and tell me that the nightmares will pass. Instead she stands. "Do you mind if I put the kettle on? I'm desperate for a cup of tea."

I almost don't hear her next question over the purr of water boiling in the kettle and the banging of one cupboard, then another as Shelley locates the mugs and the tea bags. "Do you want to talk about what happened?"

"Did you hear about the airplane, the one that crashed last month?"

"Oh God, the suicide by pilot? Of course I heard about it. I'm so sorry. I didn't know the details."

The wild something morphs into anger, thrashing out of me before I can stop it. "Why does everyone keep calling it that? It wasn't suicide. It was murder." The kettle has stopped boiling and my voice carries loud and angry in the silence. "That pilot destroyed my family. No one else on that plane chose to die. It . . . it was a mass killing. Murder."

"You're right," she says, opening the fridge and pulling out a bottle of milk. Her voice is even, controlled, next to mine. When she closes the fridge her fingers rest on a photo of Jamie—the magnet of his school photo taken before we moved, when his school uniform was bright red and his hair short, the curls stuck down with the gel I'd smeared on that morning. Shelley stares at the photo for a long second.

"This is your son." She says it like a statement, more of a comment to herself than to me.

"Yes. Jamie." I nod and feel the anger shrink back into its cave.

All of a sudden my throat feels as though it's being squeezed by an invisible hand and tears blur my vision. "Does it make a difference how? Would I be feeling any less . . . broken if it had been a heart attack behind the wheel?"

Shelley touches my shoulder as she places a cup of tea on the table in front of me. "I guess not," she says, sitting down again. "We had a son—Dylan. He was perfect in every way. A beautiful smiling baby, an energetic toddler. We always thought Dylan would be a footballer. He was kicking a ball before he could walk properly. Or a swimmer. He loved the water." She draws in a breath and fiddles with the locket around her neck before she continues. "He was two years old when he was diagnosed with a rare leukemia and four when he died. It was long and drawn-out. We'd spent half his life in and out of hospital. We knew he was dying, but it didn't make the hurt any less when it happened."

"Oh God." My hand flies to my mouth. "I'm so sorry," I mumble, feeling shitty again. Shitty because losing a child is worse than losing a husband. Even in my current state I know this. I would be nothing without Jamie.

"Thank you," she says. Our eyes meet and I feel something pass between us—some kind of shared knowledge of the rawness of grief. That's how Shelley knew about my nightmares. I wonder if she still has hers.

"It was four years ago this summer," Shelley continues. "I had lots of people who helped me through the grief in those early days. My sister moved in with us and took care of everything. She forced Tim and me—that's my husband—to eat and to get out of the house. It's why I started volunteering for the charity, and why I took a course and qualified as a grief counselor. I run my own private practice from a room in my home. The thought of going through something like that without my friends and family, I just don't know if I'd have survived."

A silence settles over us. Shelley blows on the top of her mug, changing the direction of the steam and reminding me of the bonfire. I can feel the scratch of the smoke in the back of my throat just thinking of that day.

"Do you have any family nearby?" she asks.

"My mum is an hour away. She lives on the seafront in Westcliff. She has arthritis and is very frail. She stayed here for a few weeks but the stairs were too much and I couldn't . . . I couldn't look after her on top of everything else. She calls me most days, but I don't always pick up. It's hard to tell her how I'm feeling when I know it'll only worry her, so I lie, or more often than not, I let the answerphone get it."

"What about brothers and sisters?"

"One older brother, Sam. He lives in Sheffield with his boyfriend, Finn. They're both hospital doctors and work all hours. Sam would come if I asked him, but I can't bring myself to. He's worked so hard to get where he is, and anyway, I don't know how it would help.

"Mark's brother lives nearby in Ipswich. He stopped by earlier to check on me—"

"That's good."

I pull a face. "Not really. We've never got on. I always got the impression he wasn't interested in me and Jamie. He isn't married and doesn't have children, and it's like he couldn't understand why Mark did want those things. Mark said I was worrying over nothing. He thought I was trying to compare Ian to my brother, Sam, and that the two weren't comparable. He thought the only reason Ian was cool toward us was because I was cool toward him."

"Ah. Maybe not the best person to go to for support then."

"Probably not."

"How about friends locally? Neighbors you can turn to?"

"We haven't lived here long. Have I said that already? Sorry if I have. We don't exactly have neighbors. I think an elderly couple live in the house nearest to us. I had, still have I guess, plenty of friends in Chelmsford where we used to live, but I haven't met anyone here.

"I used to say hi to a few school mums when I saw them in the playground at drop-off and pickup. We'd chat about the weather and school stuff. Nothing much. Then the plane crashed, and . . . well . . . look at me." I gesture at my clothes—a saggy T-shirt and a worn cardigan, bobbled and fraying at the cuffs. "You'd keep well away, wouldn't you? Anyway, I have to learn to cope at some point, right?"

Shelley nods and takes a tentative first sip from the mug cupped in her hands. "You do, but it's about baby steps, Tess. After my son died, I didn't wash for days. I couldn't bring myself to get out of bed, or get dressed. I just lay there feeling half-dead myself. You're up, you're wearing clothes, you're washing, you have milk in the fridge."

I'm crying all the time, neglecting Jamie—or, worse, lashing out at him, I think but don't say.

"No one is expecting you to be all right tomorrow or next week," Shelley continues. "And you shouldn't expect yourself to be either. At this stage in your grief, try to focus on achieving one small thing each day, rather than looking ahead to the future. Even if it's just opening a letter you've been putting off."

My gaze pulls to the post pile beside the microwave. I guess Shelley saw it too. It's not one letter I've been putting off, but all of them.

"Shall we go through them together now? I bet most of it is junk anyway. It might make you feel better just to get them out of the way."

I bite my bottom lip, torn between wanting Shelley to leave me alone and wondering if this woman with her sleek blond hair and shining eyes, who survived the worst tragedy I can think of, is right. Shelley takes my hesitation as acceptance and is out of the chair, scooping up the pile of letters before I can muster the energy to shake my head.

"I'll divide them into four piles. Ones that are obviously bills," she says, dropping a letter down with the red mobile phone logo on it. "Another for what looks like junk, a third for bereavement cards, and a fourth for everything else."

"Put the cards straight in the bin," I say. "I can't look at them. I don't want them."

"Are you sure?"

I nod. "I don't need reminding." Nor does Jamie, for that matter.

"How about I pop them all to one side? There may come a time when you find comfort in them," Shelley coaxes before sliding a few letters toward me.

I won't ever find comfort in those cards, but I don't tell Shelley that. My heart is pounding so hard inside my chest, and there is a gale-force panic whipping around my stomach. Most of this stuff is rubbish, so why am I so afraid to open them?

My hands shake but I reach for the first letter. The envelope is plain white with a window, and your name is printed inside. I watch Shelley working her way through one of the piles as the noise of tearing paper fills the kitchen. Her confidence reminds me so much of you, and there's a smidgen of reassurance in that, enough to make me slide my fingers under the lip and prize open the envelope in my hand.

The letter is from a car dealership, reminding you to book a test drive of their new Audi. It's rubbish, and all of a sudden I don't know why I allowed the post to mount up like this.

I reach for another envelope. This one is addressed to me.

I know the instant the letter is in my hands that it's from the airline. Their swooping dark logo cries out at me from the top corner. Tears fill my eyes, and even though every part of my being wants to drop the letter—never read the words—my gaze is fixed.

Dear Mrs. Clarke,

Please accept our deepest sympathies for the tragic loss of your husband . . .

My eyes skip forward.

Further to the Civil Aviation Authority (CAA) ruling: [. . . the copilot leaving the pilot alone in the cockpit without another member of the aircrew present, the CAA finds the airline named above negligent]

We are attaching two compensation forms—one for each passenger on your late husband's booking.

An involuntary noise escapes my mouth and I have to clamp my lips together to stop myself from crying out. How can they even think of sending compensation forms? It feels like a cruel joke. As if there is anything in the world the airline could give me to make it right.

Then it hits me. Two compensations. Two seats. Not one.

Who was the other seat for, Mark? I try to think back. Who were you going with? I don't remember if you told me. Someone from the sales team, I guess. I wonder for a moment if they had a family too, if they are being missed like you are, but then I push the thought away.

I can't think about all the other people who died that day. All the gory details are still being hashed out in the news, splashed across the front pages, but I've stayed away. I don't want to know. I don't want to share our grief with anyone.

"Tess?" Shelley says, reaching a hand out toward me. "Are you all right?"

I nod, fumbling with the letter and sliding it into the pocket of my cardigan.

"I can't do this," I whisper. "I'm sorry. I think I need to lie down."

"But it's done—look." Shelley smiles and waves her hands over the table. "It was mostly rubbish. Two bills that probably aren't urgent, and these three left—" She pushes them forward. "One looks like a bank statement and the other is from a solicitor's. I thought it might be to do with Mark's estate. And this is from the passport office. Feels like a passport."

I take the letters, tucking them into the pocket of my cardigan. "I renewed it just before Mark died. We were going to take Jamie to Spain in the summer holidays," I mumble.

Shelley reaches out and gives my hand another squeeze. "Well, the rest," she says, standing up and scooping up a pile of paper and torn envelopes, "can go straight in the bin. See, I told you it wouldn't take long."

"Oh" is all I can say as the lid of the silver bin in the corner shuts with a clang.

Shelley turns back toward me, reaching into her bag. For a moment I think she's going to leave, and I feel a trickle of disappointment. I don't want her to go.

But Shelley doesn't make a move for the door; instead she pulls out a spiral bound notebook from her bag. It's bigger than pocket-sized but not by much and the cover is thick cardboard and plain brown.

"This is for you," Shelley says, sliding the notebook across the table and returning to her seat. "It's to write things down in."

"Is it? Thank you." I brush my fingertips over the smooth cover. "What kinds of things?"

She gives a swish of her hair and sits back in her chair. "Whatever you want. Some people find it's useful to keep a diary. I knew one man who found writing a letter to his wife each night helped him grieve after she passed away, but it's really for you to decide. Even little things become hard when you're grieving. Use it to write a shopping list or a to-do list, if that helps."

"Thank you," I say again.

"You're welcome. I give one to everyone I meet through my work with the charity." Shelley pushes the cup of tea toward me and I wrap the warmth of it in my hands.

"Do you want to talk about Jamie?" she asks.

A fog creeps over my thoughts. It's hard to concentrate, hard to put the words together, but I try. I tell Shelley about how shy he is. Painfully shy. Running off to his room or the tree house in the garden whenever someone knocks on the door. Even when it was just my mum in the house with us, Jamie spent most of his time in his bedroom. But how once he's let you in, once he's accepted you, he blooms and is bright and loving and cheeky.

I tell her how much Jamie looks like you. The same nose, the same body, the same crooked smile. I tell her how he's a typical boy. Football and PlayStation and reading Horrid Henry books. I tell her how well he has settled in to the village school, how even though I wasn't sure I liked the house that much, or the village, and I missed my friends, seeing Jamie come out of his shell made it all worth it. I tell her how much we miss you.

Picturing Jamie helps. The fog drifts away and I have the strange feeling of having just woken up. I blink quickly, aware of the silence in the kitchen and Shelley sitting opposite me.

"Small steps, Tess," Shelley says later as she walks out the side door. "Remember, try one thing each day, however small, OK?"

I nod but don't speak. The hand is gripping my throat again and I can't find my voice. This woman knows how I feel, just like you always did, and there's a relief to that. No one will ever know me the way you did, but Shelley understands more than most, I think.

CHAPTER 7

IAN CLARKE

I really don't know why I'm here. Shelley is the one you should be speaking to, not me. I was trying to help Tess. What you need to understand is that Tess was in a right state after the plane crash. She wasn't coping, not at first anyway. I arranged all the funeral proceedings. I even spoke to the coroner in Essex and arranged the death certificate. I did everything she should've done. I'm not saying I minded, because I didn't. Mark was my kid brother, of course I didn't mind. I'm just saying, Tess wasn't capable of doing much of anything. Someone had to step in.

SHELLEY LANGE

When I met Tess for the first time I could see she really needed help. I should've given Tess the number of the charity at the end of our first meeting, but I gave her my mobile number instead. I think it was the photo of Jamie on the fridge that drew me to Tess on that first visit. He looked so much like my Dylan in that photo. I knew I had to help right then and there. I felt a connection to Jamie and to Tess. All I wanted to do was help.

CHAPTER 8

It's only when I wave off Shelley and her "Call me anytime" goodbye and lean against the huge front door that I think of the bath still waiting for me.

I twist the gold taps and refill the tub until the water is burning hot to the point that for a second or two it feels icy. The skin on my legs prickles, turning a bright red, but I sink into the water anyway and close my eyes.

Are you there, Mark?

Remember the day we found out you were pregnant?

I knew you'd bring that up. You always loved telling Jamie that story. I swear each time you told it I became a bit more crazy and you oh so heroic.

I will admit I was worried. I knew I wanted a family with you, children of our own, but we'd only been dating for three months. I hadn't even met your mother at that point. We weren't living together. Plus the hormones.

You said it would never work.

And it wouldn't have done. Us living apart. But you found us a family home. A perfect three-bed semidetached on a new estate in Chelmsford.

Not too far from the station for my commute to London, and close to the park and the shops for you.

Exactly. Lots of families, lots of friends. We gave Jamie the second bedroom, saving the box room for a second nursery, for the brother or sister I wanted so badly for Jamie to have.

And I asked you to marry me, Tessie. That was the best part of the story. Don't leave that bit out.

Ah, yes. Sweeping me off my feet and all the way to the registry office in the basement of the council buildings in Chelmsford. What a hero! I wore that white maxi dress from H&M and jiggled Jamie on my hip the whole time we were saying our vows.

Jamie had just started weaning, remember? He threw up orange gloop down your back just as we had our first kiss.

I loved how we started our marriage laughing. It wasn't grand or romantic, but it was us, our start, and we were happy. You always made me laugh. Even though we were complete opposites. Even if I was angry at you for being late home, or not picking up your clothes from the floor, or hiding yourself away with your computer and working on your secret project instead of spending time with Jamie, you always made me laugh.

Another voice fills my head: *"Can you tell me the whereabouts of your husband, please, Mrs. Clarke?"* The policewoman with the brown hair in a neat ponytail. PC Gemma Greenwood, as if I'll ever forget that name. Oh God, I don't want to remember, but it's too late.

I was at the kitchen table. PC Gemma Greenwood was sitting opposite me, but the other officer, the one whose name I can't remember, stayed by the sink. Her skin was the same gray as the bonfire smoke and her eyes were glassy with tears, as if it was she who loved you. As if it was her life that had been destroyed.

"Mark?" I asked as if I had more than one husband. *"He's in*

Frankfurt today. The computer software company he works for has an office out there. He'll be back tomorrow if you want to speak to him. Why?"

"I'm afraid we have some bad news."

My eyes shoot open. Suddenly I need to hear the tap dripping and see what is real. I stare at my body. A month of grief has slimmed me down, but it's not pleasant. My breasts are flaccid and sink toward my armpits. The skin around my belly button floats in the water. A half-empty sack, as if your death has removed a physical part of me.

I twist the tap with my toe and add more hot.

My thoughts pull to Ian's visit. The grapes and chocolate, a subterfuge I mistook for kindness. He only wanted to ask about the money you borrowed from him.

One hundred thousand pounds. The amount feels lodged somewhere in my mind as if I can't quite process it, imagine it. It's so much money, isn't it?

We never spoke about money. It's the way you wanted it, Tessie. I would've told you if you'd asked, but you never did.

Didn't I?

A memory surfaces. It was from early on, when I was pregnant. We'd just moved into the Chelmsford house and everything was new still, including us.

"Good news," you called as you walked through the front door.

"What?" I shouted back from the kitchen. I was stirring a pot of chili on the hob and trying not to splash sauce on the bright white tiles of our new kitchen.

"I'm moving into the sales team." You came up beside me and kissed my cheek. I remember the mix of aftershave and London grit that clung to your clothes.

"Sales?" I stopped stirring and leaned against the work surface, watching the excitement on your face and trying not to wince from Jamie's foot wedging under my ribs. *"But you're a programmer. You program stuff."*

I remember your laugh, deep and just a little strained, now that I come to think of it. *"Your technical knowledge of my job is astounding,"* you said, pulling open one of the doors of our American-style fridge-freezer and retrieving a bottle of beer.

"Ha-ha. You know what I mean."

"This is a great move. There's a commission structure, which means more money—"

"If you sell," I said. I remember wondering how long you'd been planning the change of job, how long you'd been keeping it to yourself. I told myself we were still new at this; we hadn't learned to share ourselves yet. It was later that I realized it was just your way. Keeping things bottled up, waiting until it was a done deal before telling me. I was the opposite, worrying about every little thing before it had happened.

"Who better to sell the software than the person who created it?" you said, gulping back a long mouthful of beer straight from the bottle.

"Oh God, is money an issue? I thought we'd be OK. I . . . I suppose I could put the baby into a nursery and go back full-time. If I have to—"

"Relax," you said, stepping close and running a hand over my belly.

"Sorry. It's just I hate talking about money and worrying about it all on top of everything else. I'm so nervous about the birth and . . ." And us, I wanted to say but didn't because we didn't ever talk about us and how we hadn't known each other that long.

"I don't want you to worry about it again, OK? All you need to focus

on is cooking that little monkey inside you and putting your feet up for the next four weeks. We've talked about your job before, and I meant what I said—you're not going back to that sweatshop of a school ever, OK?"

I remember the relief and the whispered knowledge that my offer hadn't been real. How could I have gone back to St. Luke's and be a mother? Teaching GCSE History had taken everything I had to give each week. St. Luke's might have paid better than most teaching positions, but the school was a high performer. Part-time and job shares didn't happen. The days were long and intense, and it had been hard to see how a baby would fit into that mold. Besides which, neither of us wanted Jamie to go into nursery full-time at such a young age.

"Will it mean more traveling?" I asked, trying to sound positive, trying to be happy for you. I rested my hand over yours, rubbing the hard bulge of my belly, and fought back a wave of panic.

"Maybe, but not a lot, I promise. This is good timing for us. The benefits are better. We all get private medical insurance and I get a company car and mobile phone. Plus it will take the pressure off our finances." You smiled, pulling me into your arms.

"OK." I nodded, breathing in the smell and the warmth of you. I didn't know we'd been under financial pressure to start with, but I didn't say anything. I wanted to be happy for you.

"It's going to be fine. You don't need to worry, Tessie," you whispered, using Tessie instead of Tess, like you always did when it was just us.

The memory drifts away and I sink deeper into the bath.

Maybe you're right, Mark. Maybe I didn't want to know, but I would've listened. I never wanted you to lie to me.

I never lied. I wouldn't do that.

Fine. You never lied. But you sugarcoated and you glossed over the details until it was your version of the truth. Did you think I couldn't handle it? Was I really that much of a weakling?

Tell me you loved me, Mark. Really loved me. Tell me our love wasn't a lie.

Oh, Tessie, you know I did.

CHAPTER 9

Transcript BETWEEN ELLIOT SADLER (ES) AND TERESA CLARKE (TC) (INPATIENT AT OAKLANDS HOSPITAL, HARTFIELD WARD), TUESDAY, APRIL 10. SESSION 1 (Cont.)

ES: Are you feeling better now, Tess?

TC: (nods)

ES: That's good. How are your pain levels?

TC: Better. The nurse gave me something. Sorry about before. I . . . I just want to find Jamie.

ES: We all do. That's why we're here—to find out what's happened to Jamie.

TC: Why are you talking to me then? Shouldn't you be interviewing people or out looking for Shelley?

ES: We're doing everything we can, Tess. But I need more information from you.

TC: I thought of something a minute ago, just as you came in. It might help.

ES: Oh?

TC: I don't think Shelley was working alone. I think she had help from Ian, my brother-in-law. Maybe they were partners in this.

ES: What makes you think that?

TC: There were times . . . (sighs). A lot of things happened to me that she couldn't have done alone. I keep thinking this is all about Jamie. I mean, it is, isn't it? That's why we're sitting here, but maybe it's about money too. Ian told me that he loaned Mark some money—a lot of money—and he needed it back. Is anyone checking my phone? I don't have it. Someone might call for a ransom.

ES: I'll make a note. I'm sure that's being taken care of.

CHAPTER 10

Wednesday, February 21

---

46 DAYS TO JAMIE'S BIRTHDAY

I wake with a start and blink in the darkness. My heart is hammering in my chest and for a moment I think it's the dregs of the nightmare shuddering through my body. Then I hear the sound again—the one that must have woken me—the crunch of gravel on the driveway. Footsteps.

Fear grips my body. It's the kind of fear that makes you realize that all those other times you thought you were scared, were just pretend.

This is real. It's the middle of the night. I'm alone in this giant bloody house, just me, and Jamie asleep down the hall, and there is someone walking around on my driveway.

I gasp for air and hold it in my lungs as I try to listen over the sound of my heart pounding in my ears.

Stop, Tessie. Stop worrying. It's just cats.

Cats? Come off it, Mark; since when do cats tread with the same force as footsteps? Human footsteps.

Or foxes fighting. This is the countryside, Tessie.

You don't need to remind me. I only need to open my eyes to know I'm not on the estate in Chelmsford anymore. There is no orange glow from streetlights here, no car doors slamming and people walking by on their way to town. The only noise is the low hum of the A12 a mile away and the hoot of an owl somewhere nearby.

I know I'm in the countryside, and I know what I heard.

I listen again, waiting to prove you wrong, but the silence of the night is deafening.

I told you—foxes.

I'm up and by the window before I can stop myself, half-naked in just knickers and one of your T-shirts skirting the tops of my thighs. Fear pricks my skin as I peer through the gap in the curtains, primed for any movement, any sound, but there's nothing but darkness.

I pad along the hallway and check on Jamie. He's cocooned inside his duvet, with only his mop of curls poking out the top. His hair looks almost white in the blue glow of the nightlight.

The creak of the stairs seems too loud in the silence as I make my way to the front door and check that it's bolted. Then to the nook and the side door. They are both locked. In the hallway I dither for a minute. What do I do now? There'll be no more sleep for me tonight, but I can't bear the thought of rattling around the house for five hours either, so I slump back into our bed for warmth as much as anything. I listen for any sound but all I hear is silence.

I can't even hear the wind in the fireplaces.

See—it was just an animal. A wild deer looking for food.

It was footsteps. I'm sure of it. Someone was walking on our driveway in the middle of the night.

An image of the tulips by the side door floats through my thoughts. No cellophane. No note. I threw them in the bin before the school pickup. I couldn't look at them, let alone put them in a vase, and I didn't want Jamie to see them and ask who they were from.

If Ian didn't leave them, then who did? I know no one in this village. Who would leave flowers like that without a note? And by the side door too. The front door is right there—dark oak, the centerpiece of the house, but we always use the small white painted door to the side that leads right into the nook and the kitchen. Who would know that?

Who would be walking around on our driveway in the middle of the night?

I close my eyes and feel my heartbeat slow. A deer, you say? Fine, a deer it is.

Somewhere nearby an engine strains for a beat and roars into life.

My eyes shoot open and the fear is back, pressing down like a force crushing my chest. There's a flash of white light in the crack of the curtains. Headlights. A car. I want to jump out of bed and see the driver, but I can't. The fear is a beast holding me down.

Last time I checked, deer don't drive cars, Mark.

CHAPTER 11

Thursday, February 22

---

45 DAYS TO JAMIE'S BIRTHDAY

I took a tablet this morning.

After lying awake half the night, listening to any and every sound and scaring myself silly with thoughts of someone breaking in and taking Jamie. After the milk bottle had dropped on the floor at breakfast and it had clattered and bounced on the tiles and spilled the last of the milk everywhere.

After I screamed at Jamie at the top of my voice for being so bloody careless and he hadn't flinched or told me not to swear. He just stared at me with steely blue eyes, prodding his tongue out against the tooth at the top that's about to fall out. After I came back from the school drop-off and cried. Pitiful fat tears that dripped onto the kitchen tiles I was supposed to be cleaning, until I was half drowning in self-loathing and guilt.

I took it quick. Like the time you ripped off the bandage above Jamie's eye when he was three. Remember?

Another hero moment. How could I forget?

He bounced off the sofa and caught his face on the corner of the coffee table, and he was wailing and hiccuping and bleeding all over the place. I called you at work all screechy and panicked, dithering over whether to phone an ambulance.

He didn't even need stitches, Tessie.

The plaster was huge though. A big white square with four sticky corners covering his eyebrow and half of his forehead. When the day came to take it off he wouldn't let me near it, wriggling and writhing at the slightest suggestion of teasing the plaster away. You plonked him in the bath and played Mr. Submarine Tickle Toes, and then right when he was giggling and slapping his hands on the surface of the water, right when his eyes were shut, you whipped the plaster off. Jamie didn't even stop splashing.

That's how I took my first antidepressant. I popped out a pill from its plastic casing and washed it back with a mouthful of water before I could question right or wrong or ask you what to do.

I had a shower and washed my hair. Lathered it with shampoo three times over. I put on jeans and a bra, a T-shirt and a jumper. I'm going to Tesco to buy food today. Not the oven chips, fish fingers, and pizzas—the dregs of the freezer—that we've been living on for the last month, but the real kind—onions, mince, mushrooms, tomatoes. I'm going to make a pot of Bolognese for Jamie and me, so we can have spaghetti one night and penne the next, then lasagna with the leftovers.

I'm going to try harder.

That's my girl, Tessie.

The supermarket on the outskirts of Colchester is busy. Busier than I expected for a Thursday morning. I find a space in the third row of the car park, and a trolley without a dodgy wheel. The air has a biting chill to it that stings the skin on my face, but somehow I feel warmer than I have done for weeks.

As I step through the automatic doors I weave around an elderly couple on their way out. *I'm OK,* I think. I'm slipping back into the old routine just like I slipped on my jeans this morning. I can do this.

Of course you can, Tessie.

I glance at the paper in my hand, the scribbled list I tore out from the notebook Shelley gave me. It's the first time I've used it, and seeing the clean lined page feels nice somehow. Shame to waste it on a shopping list, but I'm not sure what else to do with it. I don't need to write a letter to you every night when speaking to you feels so normal.

Shelley texted me earlier, just at the right moment when I was feeling so tired after cleaning up the milk and was wobbling over whether I'd make it to Tesco or not. It wasn't anything meaningful, just a—Hi Tess, it's Shelley. Just checking in. Call me anytime—but it helped. She signed off with a smiley emoji, and I felt her calm confidence in the air around me.

Somehow Shelley's text felt different from the well-meaning messages my Chelmsford friends have sent, as if Shelley knew just what to say at just the right moment. I replied with a thanks and a thumbs-up, then jumped into the car before I lost my nerve again.

I catch the earthy smell of roasted coffee beans drifting from the café and move toward the fruit and veg. *I can do this,* I tell myself.

It's the chocolate aisle where things start to go wrong. There's a display of chocolate Easter eggs, an entire row of every kind imaginable. I know Easter is still weeks away, but I also know that by the time it creeps up on me I'll be so wrapped up in thinking about Jamie's birthday that I'll end up doing a mad rush to the supermarket the day before and all the best eggs will be gone.

So I scoop up a Hot Wheels egg for Jamie. It has two racing cars as well as the chocolate, and a bright orange piece of track that will fit to the parts he already has. I add a Dairy Milk egg for me and some packs of mini eggs in case Jamie wants to do an egg hunt again this year. I lean against the trolley, pushing it forward and reaching for your favorite—KitKat Chunky. There's two this year. One has a mug with it, and one doesn't. It's only when I'm holding them both in my hands, wondering which one you'll prefer, that I remember you don't need an Easter egg. You're gone.

I drop the egg boxes, like a saucepan hot from the stove, and hurry away to the next aisle. Cleaning products line the shelves, but it's not them that I'm looking at, it's you, standing at the other end of the aisle, dropping a tube of black bin bags into a basket. Even from behind I know it's you. The edges of your brown hair are sticking out from under a woolly hat. I don't recognize the clothes—gray jeans and a navy jumper—but I would recognize your posture, your walk, anywhere, Mark.

And even though I know it isn't you, I still shout out as you disappear around the corner. I still sprint down the aisle with the trolley in front of me.

I find myself in the central walkway that cuts between the aisles, and suddenly there are too many people, too many shoppers and children in pushchairs, and I can't see you anymore. I race down pasta and world foods; jams and tins; the frozen section. I dart through the clothes, electrical, the shampoos; I scour the tills, but you're nowhere and then I can't breathe.

My legs weaken. My cheeks flush. Of course it wasn't you. I know that. My hands shake as I dig through my bag in search of my phone. I have to call you, just to hear your voice. Six words on a recorded message—"Hey, it's Mark. Leave a message." I don't know why I didn't think of it before.

I have to hear your voice.

There's a silence, then it rings. Except the voicemail doesn't pick up. Instead, someone answers. "Hello?"

"Mark?" A tornado is spinning in my head. You answered your phone.

"Tess."

"Mark . . . I—"

"Tess, it's Ian." His words are rushed, but the moment Ian says his name I register the clipped tone of his voice, the one you always teased him about.

"Ian? But I phoned Mark's mobile."

"I spoke to someone in human resources at Mark's office and they agreed to have his mobile number redirected to my phone. Just in case anyone called who didn't know about Mark's death."

"Oh." I hadn't thought to do that. I am barely capable of answering my own phone. But still I feel put out. Mark was mine, not yours, I want to say, but of course I don't. Even in my head the thought is childish and silly. "You didn't tell me."

"I spoke to you about it when we were arranging the funeral. Your mother was there too, and the vicar."

"Oh," I say again. I remember the meeting in our living room. The tray with the teapot, the cups and saucers, unearthed from a forgotten box at my mother's insistence. Apparently a visit from the vicar requires a saucer. I remember the biscuits on the plate that nobody touched, but I don't remember the conversation. Jamie had been in the garden playing in his tree house. I'd spent the entire time standing by the window watching the trees, terrified he'd slip on the wood and fall.

"Tess, are you all right? Why have you called Mark's mobile?" Ian asks.

"I . . . I thought I saw him. I'm in Tesco. It wasn't him, obviously, but I needed to hear his voice—" I stop talking and glance around me. A group of shoppers have huddled with their trolleys and are staring right at me. A member of the staff is with them. I've caused a scene.

"Where are you?" Ian asks. "I can come and get you and drive you home. You sound very upset."

My husband died and I've seen him shopping in Tesco. Of course I'm upset. For a moment I'm tempted to tell Ian where I am so he can come and take me home, but then he sighs and there's an impatience to it that makes my cheeks grow hot.

"No . . . no, thank you. I'm OK. I just wasn't expecting anyone to answer Mark's phone."

"I'm sorry, Tess."

"I'd better go." I hang up before Ian can reply and drop my mobile back into the depths of my bag.

The staff member breaks free from the group of shoppers watching me. She walks over purposefully and rests a hand on my trolley. She is in her late forties, I guess, with dark blond hair tied in a loose ponytail and foundation that sits between the lines around her eyes.

"Are you all right, madam?"

I nod but the tears are falling, streaming down my cheeks and I can't speak anymore.

"Do you want to sit down for a minute? I can get you a glass of water."

I shake my head. "No, I just want to get my shopping and go."

"Let me help you. What else is on your list?" She prizes free the paper scrunched in my hand and guides me down the aisles, finishing my shopping for me and only leaving my side to open my car door and usher me inside.

"Thank you so much," I say.

"Of course. Anytime." She nods and I think I see an unspoken understanding in her eyes. I wonder if she can see the grief written across my face, just as Shelley had. I wonder if she has lost someone too.

When I'm alone in the car I pull my phone from my bag again and scroll through my contacts until I find Shelley's number. My mum is waiting for me to call, my friends and Sam too, but right now I want to speak to someone who understands.

Shelley answers on the second ring. "Hi, Tess, how are you?" Her voice is breezy and bouncing, and I picture her smiling the same smile she had on my doorstep on Monday.

"I . . . I thought I saw Mark." My voice is almost a wail and finally I let the sobs take over.

"Oh, Tess," she says after a pause.

"I was in Tesco, and . . . and I swear it was him. He disappeared around the corner and by the time I made it to the next aisle he was gone."

"The same thing happened to me for a while too," Shelley says. "Any little boy with blond hair and I would be frozen to the spot. It still happens sometimes. When I'm least expecting it."

"Did you ever chase after anyone and cause a scene?"

"No. But I was holding Dylan in my arms when he passed away, and however hard that was, it gave me a closure that you haven't had. You never got to say good-bye. What you're going through is completely natural. It's normal to see the loved ones we've lost in the faces of others. After what you've been through I'd be surprised if you didn't."

I nod and wipe a hand across my cheeks. "Thank you. Sorry, I didn't mean to call you up and dump this on you."

"I'm glad you did. I'm glad you thought of me."

"I'd better go."

"Why don't you call me later when you've had a bit of time to process what happened and we'll talk properly?"

"OK, I will. Thank you, Shelley."

You died. It wasn't you. I hold the thought in my mind as I pull out of Tesco and drive back to the village.

That evening Jamie and I played a game of Parcheesi and ate spaghetti Bolognese at the table with the hum of the radio in the background. I didn't jump up and dance like a loon when a pop song came on like I used to, but it was progress. And after what happened in Tesco, I was pleased with myself.

Later, when I kissed Jamie good night, I said sorry for shouting at him over the spilled milk.

"Things will get better, I promise."

I meant it too. Really meant it.

Was it Shelley? Her words of, not comfort, but understanding. The feeling that she gets me like you always did. Was it Jamie? The gnarling guilt of my outbursts that no longer seemed to upset him? Or was it the medication doing its job? A combination, I suppose, but either way I felt better. Not great. Not normal, but better.

Of course I didn't know then that it was all for nothing. Friday rolled around and Denise from your office knocked on the door, and the two tablets I swallowed, the plans I made were all for nothing. I was right back at rock bottom.

CHAPTER 12

Friday, February 23

44 DAYS TO JAMIE'S BIRTHDAY

There's been a whisper of spring in the air today. The wind blowing across the fields had lost the sting of bitterness on the walk home from school, and the sun has clung on for that bit longer. So it's a while before I realize that the kitchen is shrouded in a dusky gloom. That darkness has won and I can barely make out Jamie across the dinner table. I stand up and flick on the light, scrunching my eyes shut against the sudden brightness. Jamie seems oblivious to the change.

"Not hungry?" I ask, looking at his plate.

He shakes his head.

I cooked too much pasta as usual, forgetting how it expands in the pan. It's hard to see a dent in either of our plates. Eating has become a clinical process, a conscious step. The sauce and mince tasted of nothing and every mouthful I forced down now lies heavily on the grief. I guess Jamie feels the same way. I can't remember the last time I saw him eat more than a few mouthfuls of anything.

"Right then. Toilet, teeth, and reading." I clap my hands, forcing a normal I know neither of us feels.

Jamie stays in his seat, his head bent, staring at his hands. Tears are pooling in his eyes and there's a wobble to his bottom lip. Seeing his hurt is a physical pain in my chest, and I wish I could take it away. I wish I could add it to my own and shield him from this grief we are living in.

"I miss Daddy too," I whisper.

Tell him something, Tessie.

I think for a minute.

"Do you remember the time we took you to London to see the sharks at the aquarium?" I ask. "You were only four. It was the summer before you started school. We took you up on the train for a special day out. And we went on a double-decker bus." I smile. "We climbed the stairs as it started pulling away and you were so desperate to sit at the front that you made Daddy ask the people sitting there to move. Then we went to . . . er . . ." The memory and my voice trail away. Gravel is crunching on our driveway. It's not footsteps this time, but car wheels, then the unmistakable thud of a car door.

Jamie jerks his head up. The tears are gone, replaced with wide-eyed panic.

All the months we worked on coaxing Jamie out of his shell, Mark. The drama workshops he hated that we thought would build his confidence.

And didn't.

He was getting better though, wasn't he? Remember the Christmas assembly when he stood up in front of the entire school and all the parents, and read his poem? Mrs. Banbridge, the head teacher, gave him a gold star sticker.

Of course I remember, Tessie. You were bawling your eyes out next to me.

I was proud, that's all. He never would've done that at his old school.

I told you it was a good idea to move.

Well, it was all for nothing now. Jamie's shyness has returned worse than before, and I can't bear to make it harder for him.

"Why don't you go and start your reading, and I'll see who it is."

At the faint tap of the door knocker Jamie scurries upstairs and disappears. I flick on the hall light and heave open the door.

"Hello," I say to the woman on the doorstep.

"Hi, Tess," she replies. "I'm not sure if you remember me. I'm Denise. I'm the personal assistant for the sales team. I worked with Mark."

She's vaguely familiar but it's only when she steps inside that I recognize her from the sea of faces at your funeral.

Upstairs, the floorboards creak and I hear the tap running in the bathroom.

"I was passing this way," she says, "and thought I'd stop by and see how you are."

"Oh . . . thank you" is all I can think to say as I close the door and try to smile at the woman in her smart gray trouser suit now standing in our hall. "Come in."

Denise is tall. Even in flat pumps she has to stoop her head of auburn hair under the exposed oak beams as I lead her to the kitchen. She has a round face and her makeup is thick and contoured, but it's not enough to hide the strain on her face when she smiles at me.

"Sorry to barge in uninvited," she says, her gaze fixing on our dinner plates. I wonder if she's a clean freak like Ian.

"No problem," I mumble. "We're finished anyway." I collect the plates and slide them onto the work surface by the sink. I wonder if she'll sit down, but she doesn't. I want to ask her what she wants. She isn't really here to check on us, is she? But every configuration of the question in my head sounds too rude to voice.

"Mark used to talk about you and Jamie all the time," she blurts. "He . . . he was so proud of Jamie."

"Oh." Is that true, Mark? You were always so worried about Jamie's school progress, his shyness, his lack of drive. It was one of the reasons we moved. A village school, smaller class sizes. Less disruption. *"It's like private school, but we don't have to pay for it,"* you said when I didn't want to leave Chelmsford.

Then all at once I see it—recognize it—the look in Denise's eyes. It's in the air too, seeping out of her like a bad smell. Guilt.

Denise isn't here to check on me, she's here to tell me something.

Oh God. What if she tells me something horrible, something about you that I don't want to know?

Stop, Tessie.

I can't.

I stare at Denise's face and the guilt and sadness. Questions flit through my mind. I want to ask her what she wants. I want to ask her who else died that day. Who else in the office was sitting beside you, the second seat on the plane. I want to ask if she knows what your secret project is—the one you wouldn't tell me about—but I don't, because Denise gets there first.

She opens her mouth to say something, then stops. Tears glint in her eyes, causing a shiver to race down my spine.

I shut the kitchen door, leaning my weight against it until the catch clicks into place. Whatever Denise has to say, I don't want Jamie to hear it. I don't want to hear it either and I have an almost primal desire to cover my ears and scream and scream until she leaves. Instead I turn my back to her and flick the switch on the kettle. "Cup of tea?" I whisper.

My hand reaches for the fridge to retrieve the milk. The magnet with Jamie's school photo on it has fallen off again. Kicked under the fridge when the milk bottle smashed, I bet.

"No thank you, Tess. I won't keep you. I . . . I wanted to tell you something at the funeral, but there didn't seem to be a right moment."

Acid burns at the back of my throat and my mouth fills with a metallic saliva. I flick off the switch on the kettle and plunge the kitchen into a loaded silence.

"The guilt has been eating me up inside. I've tried to come here so many times. I've been parked around the corner for the last hour trying to figure out the words to tell you this. The thing is . . . the event . . . the event in Frankfurt was canceled."

"What?"

Tears are dropping from her eyes, and when she speaks it's in between deep, wrenching sobs that make me want to yank the words right out of her. "An email went out first thing Monday morning from Frankfurt. Half the German office were down with flu so the trip was canceled. It was fine because the main flight wasn't until ten thirty. But then I remembered Mark was booked on an earlier flight than the rest of us.

"I phoned him straightaway to check he'd seen the email. He was about to board the plane. I heard someone in the background asking for his boarding pass, but I thought he heard me tell him he didn't need to go. I'm sure he laughed and said, 'OK,' but I was still at home packing and my phone signal was terrible. I kept breaking up. I thought he'd heard me but . . . but then I found out about the plane. It's . . . my . . . fault . . ."

I stare into the watery eyes of the woman in my kitchen. She stops sniveling and takes a breath in without releasing it. Denise is the reason you are dead. This woman is the reason Jamie no longer has his father.

"I don't understand. Why were the rest of the team on a different flight?"

Denise shakes her head and sniffs. "That's my fault too. Mark asked me to book the flights and I was really busy that day. I'd only just been promoted and I was struggling to keep on top of the workload. Everyone was asking me to book their flights and hotels for the trip, and I thought I'd done everyone but when I came to send out the confirmation emails I realized Mark's wasn't there. By the time I tried to book his flights the ten thirty was fully booked. Mark was really nice about it. He said he didn't mind going early and joked about it being a quieter flight without all of us on it . . ." Her sentence trails off and there's a beat before she speaks again. "I'm so sorry, Tess. If I'd only booked him the later flight in time or spoken to him sooner on that Monday he'd still be alive."

Denise's words hang in the air and I know she is waiting for me to tell her it's OK. She's waiting for my clemency. For a fleeting moment I wonder how she found out about the crash, how she knew you boarded the plane. Did I call your office? I don't remember. It's another blank space where a memory should be. Ian must have done it. He handled everything else.

"It's not your fault the plane crashed," I say. "Mark liked going to the office in Frankfurt. He probably would've gone anyway since the ticket was already paid for." It's not really true, but it feels like the right thing to say.

Denise nods, her posture softening as though my words have lifted actual bricks from her own shoulders and dumped them onto my own.

"It's not your fault," I whisper. It is. It is. It is. I grind my teeth together and bite down on my lip before I can snatch back my faux forgiveness.

"Thank you for telling me." I shuffle my feet to the nook and the side door and see Denise out. I can tell by the way she lingers in the doorway, her eyes flicking to the dinner plates and then back to me, that she's hoping for more. More from me? Or more relief from her confession? Maybe she is hoping to see Jamie, but I'm not about to let that happen. He's been through enough. We both have.

"Here's my number," Denise says, pressing a card into my hand. "In case you need anything. Call me anytime."

I nod and open the side door. Cold night air stings my cheeks. The kitchen light shining through the window illuminates a square of gravel on the driveway, but the rest of the drive, the rest of the world for as far as I can see, is black.

Denise hangs her head and steps past me. I'm about to shut the door when she turns and speaks. "I . . . I wanted to ask you—has anyone called you?"

"Sorry?" My tone is snappish, and I don't mean it to be, but I'm so tired now. What more can there be to say?

She shakes her head and steps away. "Nothing. It doesn't matter. Good to see you, Tess. I'm so sorry."

Denise strides into the darkness and I hear the beep of her car unlocking.

I shut the door and try to process Denise's final question. Something about a phone call. I let the thought go and think of you instead.

Oh, Mark. You didn't need to go. You shouldn't have been on the plane. If only you'd turned around and come home.

Stop, Tessie. It doesn't matter now.

It does, but I'm suddenly too tired to argue.

My hand trails the wall as I move through the house. A spinning has taken hold of my head—long, meandering loops that make me feel sick to my stomach and tired. Really tired.

I find Jamie facedown on his bed. The room is cast in a pale blue glow from the nightlight in the corner. From the doorway I can't make out his features but somehow I know he's crying.

"Jamie, baby?" I sit beside him on the bed.

He lifts his head and looks at me. Even in the gloom his eyes are startling, and glassy from tears.

"Oh, baby." He heard Denise's confession. Anger wends through my body. I'm not sure if it's Denise I'm angry at for off-loading her guilt, or Jamie for overhearing it, but I push my teeth together, waiting for the worst of it to pass before I trust myself to speak.

It's not Jamie's fault.

I lie down on the single bed, squishing my body against Jamie and the wall.

I'm sure there are things I should tell him, comforting words I should offer, but my mind is blank—numb. You shouldn't have been on the plane.

It's an effort to talk, and my words are as slurred as my thoughts. "I'm so sorry."

You'll get through this, Tessie. Just like last time.

You're wrong, Mark. This is nothing like before. Last time I was mourning a family we couldn't have—a brother or sister for Jamie. I lay in bed and cried and cried thinking of the family I'd always wanted. I worried so much, wondering why we were failing this time and what our lives would look like without the family I longed for.

You didn't understand. You thought Jamie was enough for us. You were right, but you were wrong somehow too. It wasn't about Jamie; it was about the picture in my head of days at the beach and Christmas dinners with children laughing and playing.

I couldn't see past it. I let the worrying gnaw at me until it was all I had inside. The worry worm, my dad used to call it. Did I ever tell you that? *"Oh, Teresa's worry worm is back,"* he'd say, opening up his arms and letting me scramble onto his lap when I was six, maybe seven. I'd dry my face on the sleeve of his shirt and tell him my worries about the waves swallowing our house, a hurricane blowing us away, a car crash, a madman, and a thousand other things.

The fears changed as I grew up, but the worry has always been the same.

I tried to hide it from you, Mark. I tried to bury the worry deep inside and I bit my tongue to stop the questions coming out and the fear from sounding in my voice. You saw it anyway. I guess it's why you kept things from me—a loan from Ian, your secret project. What else didn't you tell me?

This feeling, it isn't worry, it isn't like before. This loss is raw—an open wound, blood that won't clot, tissue that won't heal. I'm worried about things, sure, but it isn't all that there is.

Exhaustion is tugging at my thoughts and my eyelids are pulling closed. In the darkness I feel the fog creeping back until I see nothing but you.

CHAPTER 13

Saturday, February 24

43 DAYS TO JAMIE'S BIRTHDAY

The phone is ringing. Ringing and ringing—an incessant noise that pierces my sleep and drags me into the world.

I breathe in and peel open my eyes. There's an alien feel to my surroundings and it takes a beat for the hazy memory of cuddling in Jamie's bed to drift into my thoughts. I stare again at the room and recognize the row of Ninja Turtle figures on the shelf.

Slits of gray daylight penetrate the edges of the curtains.

"Jamie?" I call in a voice husky with sleep. "Jamie?" I shout this time.

"I'm on the PlayStation." His voice carries up the stairs.

"What time is it?"

He doesn't answer.

I stagger to the end of the hallway and to your makeshift study with the old desk you did your homework on as a boy. The room is icy-cold and I long to dive back under the covers in Jamie's room. Like the rest of the house, your study is still filled with the cardboard boxes from moving day. They are tucked up against the wall and stacked three high. Resting on one of the boxes is the cordless telephone sitting in its base, and I snatch it up.

"Hello?"

It's an effort to keep my eyes open, as if the air is filled with needles prickling my irises. I close them and feel myself drift again.

"Tess?" Shelley's voice jolts me back to the room. "Are you there, Tess?"

"Um."

"I've been trying you all morning. I was getting worried. You were going to call me to talk about what happened at the supermarket."

It takes me a moment to remember what Shelley is talking about. "What time is it?"

A gust of wind blows into the microphone, and I imagine Shelley on her mobile, walking somewhere.

"It's . . . twelve thirty," she says.

"Oh." Twelve thirty on a Saturday. Did we have plans today? I can't remember. Guilt jabs at me—a pin to a balloon—and I'm no longer floating in and out of sleep. I'm awake. "Sorry."

I haven't made any lunch or breakfast. I race down the stairs as fast as my legs will allow and poke my head into the living room. Jamie is engrossed in a football game on the PlayStation.

I cover the microphone and whisper to Jamie, "Have you eaten?"

He twists his face around and flashes me a brief smile, nodding his head before losing himself once more to the game on the screen. I can tell he's pleased with himself. For making himself his own food or for being able to play on the console all morning without interruption, I'm not sure.

The relief that he's eaten doesn't touch the surface of my guilt.

How could I have slept all morning? What if Jamie had gone outside? Run into the road?

"Tess?" Shelley's voice breaks into my thoughts again. "Are you all right?"

"I . . . I'm not feeling too good. I think it's flu." The lie seems garbled, even to me. I move an arm and rub my eyes. My muscles feel weak, overused, but from what I don't know.

"Tess, this is me. I've been where you are. Is this about thinking you saw Mark? What happened?"

"A . . . a woman from Mark's office came over last night." I lower my voice to a whisper and stagger from the living room and along the corridor to the kitchen. "She told me the event in Frankfurt was canceled. There was no reason for Mark to be on the plane." A sob shudders through my body and I drop onto one of the kitchen chairs.

"Oh, Tess, that's awful. I'm so sorry." There's a pause before she speaks again. "I'm coming over."

"You don't have to do that." The line is dead. She's gone.

I don't know how long I sit there for, in yesterday's clothes, with yesterday's dinner congealing by the sink, but my bare feet are numb from cold by the time there's a knock on the side door.

"Tess?" Shelley calls out.

"I'm coming," I shout, heaving myself out of the chair. It's only then, as I'm reaching for the handle, that I remember I haven't told Jamie. I'm not sure I've mentioned Shelley to him at all, in fact. He won't be happy, but it's too late to do anything about it now.

A burst of cold air blows straight through me as I open the door. Shelley is wearing the same tight jeans, with a red V-neck jumper this time. The winter coat and the suede boots have been replaced with a black silk scarf and a pair of black Converse trainers.

"Hey." Her smile is as wide as it was on her last visit, as if she is on my doorstep for a lunch date, a catch-up with an old friend, instead of here to help me pick up the pieces of my shattered life. "You look dreadful."

"Thanks," I say, and maybe because Shelley's energy is infectious, or maybe because she didn't tiptoe around how awful I look, I smile.

"Shall I put the kettle on? We can talk some more."

"I . . ." I shake my head. "I'm so tired." Tears flow from my eyes like a tap someone has forgotten to turn off. "You didn't need to come over. I'm sure your volunteer role doesn't extend to weekends."

"I'm not here as a grief counselor, Tess. I'm here as a friend, one I think you need right now. I understand what you're going through. So why don't you go back to bed for a bit or have a bath if you prefer? Get some rest. We can talk later. I've got some food in the car. I can make dinner. Leave everything to me."

Shelley slips out of her shoes, leaving them in the nook beside Jamie's, and steps through the kitchen. I'm about to trail after her and protest, to remind her how shy Jamie is, but before I have the chance I hear him talking. I follow the noise and stand in the living room doorway. Shelley is moving around the room, fluffing cushions and scooping up a pile of newspapers in the corner that have been there since forever.

"These are the controls," Jamie says. "X to pass and O to tackle." The way he's talking it's as though they're old friends instead of total strangers. There is no hint of the shyness he so often shows. I guess he feels it too—Shelley's energy and the way she understands without having to say anything.

Shelley looks up and smiles.

I want to join them. I want to flop onto the sofa and listen to Jamie's chatter, but I can't. There's a dead weight on my chest. I have to lie down. I have to sleep.

"Are you sure you don't mind if I go back to bed?" I ask them as a yawn takes hold of my body.

"We're fine, Mum," Jamie shouts back.

"Leave it all to me, Tess," Shelley calls after him as I'm already moving toward the stairs.

It's OK, Tess, I'm here.

You're not, though, are you, Mark? Your voice is really my voice.

Do you remember our first holiday with Jamie? We took him to Portugal, and he spent most of the holiday trying to eat the sand.

I remember.

All those waiters kept tripping over themselves to speak to you.

Hardly, but keep talking to me. I like to hear your voice.

CHAPTER 14

It's the sound of Jamie's giggling that pulls me back to consciousness. Our bedroom is dark. I stare at the curtains waiting for my eyes to adjust and see daylight, but it's not there anymore. How long have I been asleep?

There's a glass of water on the bedside table and I gulp it back in one. The liquid sloshes inside my empty stomach, leaving me suddenly nauseous as I stand and make my way downstairs.

I find Jamie alone in the living room. He's lying on his stomach, sprawled across the rug, legs kicking back and forth as his eyes scan the pages of a *Where's Wally?* book.

The lights are on and it's dark outside. I've lost all sense of time but I can tell by the puffy skin around his eyes that it's close to bedtime. I should tell him to get ready for bed, but it doesn't seem fair, considering the day he's had.

My heart aches staring at our son. Love—pure and raw—floods my body. The plane crashed and took you with it. It took a sledgehammer to my world, but I still have a world because of Jamie. I am nothing without him.

"Hey," I say from the doorway.

Jamie's legs stop midair and he looks up at me, wobbling that front tooth back and forth, back and forth.

"Are you OK? Sorry about today," I say.

"I'm fine. Shelley looked after me." Jamie's tone is matter-of-fact. His attention is back on the beach scene in the book and finding Wally's dog.

"What have you done today?"

"Er . . . played on the PlayStation—Shelley's really good. She beat me three times. We dusted, played football in the garden, cooked dinner," he says, rattling off the answer like a list.

"You cooked?" I gaze around the room and notice the clean floors and the smell of jasmine furniture polish. There's another scent: herbs and chicken wafting from the kitchen.

A proud smile spreads across his face. "Yep. I chopped the onion. Shelley is amazing. She let me use a proper knife. It was much easier than the baby knife you make me use."

"Oh . . . that's good." At least I think it's good. Good that Jamie has had fun and opened up to Shelley. Maybe not so good that he used one of the sharp knives I don't let him touch for fear he'll cut himself.

I'm about to ask another question, but voices in the kitchen stop me. Shelley's voice, and a man's voice too. Why is there a man in my house? What if it's the police? What if they have more bad news to give me?

Stop worrying, Tessie.

I can't, Mark. My heart is pounding in my chest and my mouth is dry.

"Stay here," I manage to whisper to Jamie.

Six long strides and I'm at the door to the kitchen. It's ajar but not closed. With a trembling hand I push it open an inch and peer through the gap.

In the kitchen I see three large church candles sitting on the worktop near the oven—the ones I bought after the power cut last winter. Shelley must've unearthed them from the larder cupboard, but it's not the flames slow dancing their light across the room that my attention is drawn to, but the nook and the open side door.

"You have to understand that these things take time. I'm not making any promises," Shelley says, her voice harder than I've heard it before. Her body is blocking the space in the open doorway like a gatekeeper, or a nightclub bouncer, going by her tone. So I can't see the person she's talking to.

"I'm not asking you to," the man says.

The recognition is instant. It's Ian.

Ian sighs and I picture him pinching the bridge of his nose. "I'm only asking you to give this to Tess. Look, why don't I come in for a minute—"

"Are you crazy? Have you not listened to a single word I've said? You need to leave now."

"OK, I'm going. Just give it to her, please."

"Fine."

Shelley slams the door shut. It's only when she turns the key and the bolt locks with a clonk that I breathe again, drawing in a long, shaky breath and push open the kitchen door.

Gratitude swells inside me, a warm bubble welling to the surface, and all I want to do is hug Shelley. She has saved me today in more ways than I can think about; saved Jamie too. She didn't give in to Ian's persistence. She knew there was no way I could cope with him this evening and she protected me like a lioness protecting her cub.

Shelley turns, stepping out of the nook, and jumps when she sees me in the doorway. "Tess," she gasps, throwing a hand to her chest. "You scared me. How long have you been standing there?"

"Not long."

"I just met your brother-in-law." Shelley runs a hand through her hair and smiles. "He's a piece of work, that one."

"Sorry."

"It's not your fault." Shelley pulls a face and moves to the oven. She lifts a lid, and steam billows out of a saucepan on the hob. The scent of chicken and tomatoes is stronger now and my stomach growls a long, hollow rumble, reminding me that I haven't eaten since last night's pasta. "I hope you don't mind me saying this, but he seemed a bit put out that I was here. I'm sorry you had to hear that."

"I think he's put out that I'm here to be honest. This used to be his mum's house, and he grew up here. Mark and I bought it when his mum passed away. Ian didn't say anything at the time, but I don't think he was happy about it. He still treats the place like it's his."

"Ah, yes, I got that impression."

"I'm sorry if he was pushy with you. He's like that with me too," I say.

"Don't worry. I'm used to bullheaded control freaks. I married one." She laughs as if she might be joking, but I'm not sure she is.

Shelley replaces the lid on the saucepan and reaches out her arms, pulling me into a hug. "How are you feeling?" she asks.

"Empty," I say, hugging her back for a moment before we both let go.

"Have you been taking your antidepressants?"

"They don't work. I thought I was feeling better but I'm not. If anything I'm worse."

"Well, when did you start taking them? They take at least seven days to kick in. It can be up to six weeks before they're fully effective. You have to keep taking them, Tess. It's the only way they'll help you. Didn't your doctor explain that to you?"

"Oh, I'm not sure. Maybe. I wasn't really listening." All of a sudden I feel like a naughty child. A silly, stupid, naughty child.

"Take one after dinner then, OK?"

"OK." I nod.

The kitchen is warm from the heat of the oven, and cozy in the candlelight. The window, black from night, acts as a mirror, making the gloomy place seem large and welcoming, as if it isn't our kitchen at all.

My eyes are drawn to the fridge door and the bare space where the photo magnet of Jamie should be. I can't remember when I last saw it. I clamber to the floor and rest on my hands and knees.

"What are you doing?" Shelley asks as I push my fingers into the small gap between the bottom of the fridge and floor. I feel the tickle of dust balls and crumbs and bits of who knows what, but I can't feel the magnet.

"I think I knocked the photo of Jamie off the other day. It must've got kicked under the fridge," I say, leaving out the part about the spilled milk and screaming at Jamie. I stretch my fingers further until the top of my knuckles press painfully against the bottom of the fridge.

"Leave it for now," Shelley says, resting a hand on my shoulder. "We'll get a spatula and flashlight and look later. Ian brought you chili," Shelley adds. I look up and she nods to a Pyrex dish on the worktop nearest to the nook.

"Oh . . . did he want anything else?" I ask, giving up my hunt for the magnet and dusting myself off.

"He wanted me to give you this." Shelley steps around me and picks up an envelope from beside the dish and hands it to me.

It's white, A4-sized, and there's no name written on it, no markings at all. I guess Ian was planning to give it directly to me.

"Dinner isn't for ten minutes," Shelley says. "Why don't you open it now and get it out of the way?"

"OK," I mumble.

Shelley ushers me toward a chair.

The old oak table has been cleaned and shines in the dim light. Cutlery and plates have been set at one end and so I sit at the other, not wanting to destroy Shelley and Jamie's work.

As Shelley busies herself with stirring saucepans I open the lip of the envelope and peek inside. There is one sheet of paper. *Renunciation of Probate* is printed in bold across the top of the document. Your name is on it, and mine too, and there's an orange tab at the bottom where I think I'm supposed to sign.

"Everything all right?" Shelley asks as she sits down beside me.

"I have no idea." I slide the paper toward her. "It's something to do with Mark's will."

There's a short pause as Shelley scans the document. "I'm guessing you're the executor?"

I nod. "We made them together. A joint thing. I was his and he was mine."

"Do you want to be executor? Because if you sign this then you can hand over the responsibility to Ian."

"Oh."

"I'm guessing by your face that you didn't ask for this?"

"No." I shake my head. "I didn't even know I could ask for it. Ian is a solicitor. He wants Mark's estate sorted out because . . ." I pause for a second, wondering how much to say before remembering that Shelley understands, and unlike Ian, she doesn't have an ulterior motive for helping me. ". . . Mark borrowed some money from Ian. Quite a lot. I didn't know anything about it, but obviously Ian won't get it back until I sort through our finances."

"Well, if you sign this, then it would mean you wouldn't have to deal with all the estate stuff. It's not an easy task. There's a lot of paperwork and following up with different companies and people. You can sign this form and not have to think about it anymore until it's all done."

"That's true." I nod. Shelley makes it sound so appealing, and a part of me wants to grab a pen and sign it straightaway.

"But . . ." Shelley prompts.

"But I'm just not sure how much I trust Ian."

"Ah, well, the thing is, you don't really need to trust him. Ian will be bound by law to follow the instructions in the will."

"True." I feel myself waver. "What do I do?"

Shelley smiles and reaches out to squeeze my hand. "You've had a tough week. Don't make a decision today. Think it over and see how you feel next week."

"You're right," I reply, relieved Shelley has made the decision for me, even if that decision is just to put something off for a few days.

I tuck the form in the drawer below the microwave. The drawer is overflowing with bits of paper and take-out menus we'll never use. I press my hand against the mass, squashing it down and forcing the drawer closed.

"Right," Shelley says with a wide grin. "I'll just wash up and then let's eat. You must be starving."

My stomach growls an answer and I find myself smiling when Shelley laughs.

"I'll take that as a yes," she says. "Back in two secs."

I lean back against the chair and close my eyes, allowing the warmth of the room to seep through me. I don't feel half as cold inside when Shelley is here.

When I open my eyes again Jamie is standing in the doorway, all wide-eyed and tired. His hair is sticking up at funny angles as if it hasn't been brushed for days. It hasn't.

"Has Shelley gone?" Jamie asks, his eyes scanning the kitchen.

"No, baby. She's just washing her hands," I reply, moving chairs and sitting down opposite Jamie, where the plates have been set.

His face breaks into a large grin and he slides into a chair. "Good."

"I'm sorry about today," I say to both of them when Shelley returns. "I'm feeling better, I think."

"I didn't mind. It was fun," Jamie replies, beaming at Shelley.

"It's fine, Tess." Shelley smiles too as she places a steaming casserole dish on the table between us. "You've had a setback, but you'll get there, I know you will."

"Thank you," I whisper. The two words don't feel like enough.

"I'm sure some food will help you to feel better," Shelley adds, scooping a large chicken breast onto my plate before adding a helping of carrots, mushrooms, and sauce until my plate is swimming in a light orange liquid. Then potatoes—white and fluffy and glistening with butter—and broccoli.

Jamie and I tuck into our food as if neither of us has eaten for a month. The casserole is delicious. Wholesome. The sauce salty and warm; the meat and vegetables tender. For a few minutes none of us speak, and the only sound is the clinking of our cutlery on the plates.

I try to think of something to say, something normal—a neutral territory—that won't lead back to thoughts of you, but my mind is blank. "This is lovely," I say in the end. "Perfectly chopped onions." I smile at Jamie.

Shelley laughs; Jamie too. The pair sharing a private joke from earlier, I guess, and the time they spent preparing the dinner. I want to ask what it is, but Shelley speaks first.

"Did I tell you I'm training to swim the English Channel?" she asks us.

Jamie and I shake our heads.

"I'm going to swim all the way from Shakespeare Cliff near Dover to Cap Gris-Nez in France. It's a crazy idea, especially as I was never much of a swimmer until a few years ago. But Dylan loved the water. He was a water birth baby, so he started his life swimming."

Shelley pauses for a moment and touches a hand to the locket around her neck. "After he died I found myself going to the local pool and just sitting on the benches in the humid heat and listening to the sounds of the swimmers and the children playing. Until one day I decided to actually swim, and now I swim almost every day. It's the one place I feel most connected to Dylan."

Something changes in Shelley's face, her whole body in fact, as if a light is being dimmed inside her. I can't begin to understand the energy and joy Shelley exudes from her every move, but I do understand the pain cutting through her body at the mention of Dylan.

"How far is the channel swim?" I ask.

"Twenty-one miles."

"Wow," Jamie says between mouthfuls.

"It works out as over a thousand lengths in a normal-sized pool. I'm building up slowly though so I don't get injured. I've got until August, so I'm not panicking yet, but I might feel differently when I start practicing in the sea in a few months."

"That's so amazing."

"Thanks." Shelley nods. "It's good to have something positive to focus my energy on. I'm raising money for a leukemia research charity and Grief UK. There's the Big Bash BBQ happening in the summer to raise money too. There'll be live music and a great raffle. You should come."

Jamie's head bobs up and down and he grins, staring at Shelley with wide-eyed awe.

"Maybe." I take another mouthful of food, but it's lost its flavor and tastes bitter in my mouth. My stomach hardens and I fight an urge to spit it back out. My eyes are flicking between Jamie and Shelley. Jamie has been so quiet recently, so withdrawn, but with Shelley he seems so much like his old self.

I should be relieved, happy even, that Jamie has found a friend in Shelley, just like I have. And I am, but I can't help wish Jamie would look at me with the same shining eyes and think I am amazing. The problem is that I'm not amazing, am I? I'm broken. You've broken me, Mark.

The tiredness hits like a punch and suddenly it's all I can do to stay awake. The gray fog is slinking over my thoughts.

CHAPTER 15

Transcript BETWEEN ELLIOT SADLER (ES) AND TERESA CLARKE (TC) (INPATIENT AT OAKLANDS HOSPITAL, HARTFIELD WARD), TUESDAY, APRIL 10. SESSION 1 (Cont.)

ES: Did Shelley and Ian know each other before they met through you?

TC: (Shakes head) Maybe. It's so hard to think straight with this pain medication. What are you doing to look for Jamie? You keep saying that you're doing everything you can, but what exactly are you doing? He's really shy. The officers looking for him need to know that. He could be hiding somewhere. Has anyone checked the tree house in the wood in our garden? It's not really a wood, more like a dozen oak trees and a few pine trees, but Mark built a tree house for Jamie really high up. The only way to see if someone is up there is to climb up or look out the window of the study. Jamie spends a lot of time there.

ES: How was your relationship with Jamie after Mark's death?

TC: (Pause). It was (pause) it was hard for both of us. Jamie was very quiet most of the time.

ES: When was the last time you saw Jamie?

TC: On his birthday.

ES: What happened?

TC: I think Ian was working with Shelley. I think that's where you need to focus.

ES: I understand, but first I want to focus on the events of two nights ago. Can you tell me what you remember?

TC: (Silence)

ES: Let's stop here for today. You should rest. We will talk again tomorrow morning.

TC: (Cries). Please find Jamie.

SESSION END.

CHAPTER 16

Sunday, February 25

42 DAYS TO JAMIE'S BIRTHDAY

The phone in my hand is slick from the sweat coating my palms. I stare at the display, willing it to ring. It doesn't.

Where are Shelley and Jamie?

What if they've had a car accident?

I don't know what to do, Mark.

Stop, Tessie.

I can't let anything happen to him.

My eyes flit between my phone and the window in the second living room, where the sky is turning all kinds of pink and orange. The room is only a little smaller than the main living room we use every day. Boxes and furniture are scattered across the floor. It's cold in here and smells of your mum's sickly perfume and the mold from the curtains I ripped down the day we moved in. But if I push myself against the wall in the far corner then I can look out of the window and see beyond the entrance to the driveway and half a mile down the empty lane.

Still no car.

I don't even know what type of car I'm looking for. What kind of car does a woman like Shelley drive? Something flashier than my dilapidated Ford Focus, that's for sure. Why didn't I notice Shelley's car?

I lean my forehead against the cold glass and feel it shift from my touch. Cool air blows against my face and I shiver, hugging my arms to my body. What is Shelley thinking? You can't say you'll be back at three and then not turn up, not answer your phone. She must know how worried I am. She knows Jamie is all I have left.

My heartbeat jitters at the noise of an engine. *Please be Shelley, please be them.* It isn't. The car—a red Nissan Micra—drives straight by.

I check the time again. It's past five now, Mark. Two hours late. That's not a "we got held up in traffic" kind of late or a "we lost track of time" kind of late. Over two hours is a "something's wrong" late. I can feel it.

I press redial on Shelley's number. Twenty-two is displayed in parentheses on the screen. Twenty-two times I've tried to call her. Twenty-two times it's gone straight to her voicemail.

What was I thinking? I let a woman I've only met twice in the space of a week take care of Jamie.

I know what I was thinking. I was thinking of Shelley's voice when she bounced through the door yesterday. *"I'm here as a friend, one I think you need right now."* I was thinking of how close I feel to her, this woman I barely know who sees my pain and isn't scared of it. And however crazy it sounds, I trust her, Mark. At least, I thought I did.

Should I call the police, or the hospitals? Should I drive off looking for them? Except what if they come back while I'm out?

Stop, Tessie. It's OK.

You don't know that, Mark.

I force my mind back over the last twenty-four hours. The memory is there, but it's patchy, like a moth-eaten coat, frayed and almost unidentifiable as the piece of clothing it once was. I remember the three of us eating dinner. I remember offering to tidy the kitchen and listening to Jamie's laughter carrying from the living room as he and Shelley played a game of FIFA on the PlayStation. I remember wishing it was me sitting beside Jamie, me making him happy.

I don't remember going to bed or tucking Jamie in—another chewed-up hole of a memory—but I must've done, because then the next thing I remember is breakfast and finding Shelley still in the house.

"I hope you don't mind, but I slept on the sofa. I didn't want to leave you feeling so low," she said, handing me a cup of tea and seeming more at home in my kitchen than I have ever been. "Why don't you come swimming with me today? A bit of exercise might be just what you need."

My gaze moved from Shelley's face—bright and pretty even after a night sleeping on the sofa—to Jamie, his expression bursting with excitement, his hands clasped together and waving prayer-like at me.

"I . . . I can't." I sighed, hating myself. "I feel so weak." The thought of a cold swimming pool and the physical effort needed to stop myself sinking to the bottom is too much.

Jamie's smile dropped. His bottom lip stuck out. "Can I go with Shelley? Please, Mum, please?"

"Of course." Shelley smiled at me. "How about I stop at the supermarket on the way back? I can get a few bits for the week. See you about three? Have you got a spare key? I can let myself in that way if you're sleeping."

"OK. Thank you. If you're sure?" I said as Jamie raced upstairs to grab his trunks and goggles and I riffled in the drawer by the microwave and found the spare key to the side door.

"If you're sure?"—that's all I asked. Three words. I didn't ask Shelley if she could handle a seven-year-old in the pool. I didn't warn her how quickly Jamie tires in the water, or check that she knew to watch him constantly. I didn't tell her not to let Jamie go into the men's changing rooms because he's too young to handle himself around strangers, and will probably drop his clothes in a puddle.

I didn't even ask Shelley which swimming pool she was going to. And now they're late and I'm all alone and worrying, always worrying. What if something has happened, Mark?

I check the time on the phone display. It's almost five thirty. Time to call the police. It's dark in the room, pitch-black, but if I switch on the lamp then I'll lose sight of the driveway and the lane, now barely visible in the last of the dusky light.

I'm just about to press the first nine when I hear the purr of a car engine pulling into the drive. I lean closer to the window and see Shelley behind the wheel of a white Mini with a black soft-top roof. Jamie's smiling face is visible in the back.

Suddenly I'm shivering all over with relief, and maybe anger too. What was Shelley thinking?

The anger is gone the moment the side door crashes open and Jamie's footsteps tap in the kitchen. "Mum," he shouts. "We're back. Can I play on the PlayStation?"

A gust of wind blows from the open side door as I race along the corridor, almost knocking straight into Jamie as I reach the kitchen.

"Hey, baby, did you have a good time?" My voice is shaky but I manage a smile.

He nods. His mouth is open a little and I can see his tongue touching his top tooth, wiggling it back and forth.

"Did you say thank you to Shelley?"

Before he can answer, Shelley bustles in with two bulging carrier bags in each hand. I step forward to help her and when I turn around Jamie is gone. A moment later I hear the familiar beep of the PlayStation powering into life.

"Was everything all right?" I ask, dumping a bag onto the worktop. A jar clonks from inside, and there's a frozen pizza sticking out the top. Pepperoni—Jamie's favorite.

"It was great. Just what I needed." Shelley's hair is scooped into a ponytail at the nape of her neck, and a few strands curl around her ears. Her skin is a shade paler without makeup, but her eyes are still large and vibrant and dancing with fun. "Once I got over how cold the pool was anyway." She laughs, giving a little shiver as she slides the rest of the shopping onto the mottled beige worktop.

I swallow back my frustration before I dare to speak. "It's just, I was expecting you back a while ago. I was starting to worry. You didn't answer your phone," I add, failing to keep a whine from my voice.

"Oh. I'm sure I said five-ish. I didn't think it mattered too much."

"Of course it matters," I snap, my voice rising loud enough for Shelley to stop riffling through the bags and look at me. "You said three. I was starting to panic. All these thoughts were racing around my head. I thought something had happened. I was about to call the police."

"Oh, crikey, Tess. I'm so sorry. I really didn't think you'd mind. You looked so washed-out this morning, I thought you'd be resting. But look, I'm here now." She takes my hand. Her skin is smooth and her hand seems half the size of my own, but it's warm and I instantly feel better.

"I'm sorry, I didn't mean to panic you," Shelley says, staring straight into my eyes. "I did try the home phone a few hours ago, just to see if there was anything in particular you wanted from the shops. When you didn't answer I thought you might still be sleeping. I couldn't leave a message because your answerphone is full, and then my phone battery died. I meant to tell you about your answerphone yesterday."

"Oh." I swallow back the tears threatening to fall. "Sorry. You're right. I'm overreacting. After all you've done this weekend, it's me who should be sorry."

"Don't be sorry. I've been exactly where you are, remember? The number of times I lashed out at Tim and my sister in those early days, well, it was a lot. I should've texted you or tried your mobile earlier before my battery died. I honestly thought you were sleeping, but let's put it behind us." She smiles. "I've got lots of food to keep you going. Why don't you get started packing these away and I'll put the kettle on."

Shelley's confidence, her breezy way, eases the knots strangling my insides. Jamie is safe. Nothing bad happened. It isn't Shelley's fault that I worry so much. I should've heard the home phone. I should've gone with them for a swim like Shelley suggested. Why didn't I? I could've just sat on the side and watched. I didn't even have to swim. Instead I spent the day shuffling around the house, my world in slow motion, lost in memories of us.

And now I'm not so sure Shelley did say three. Maybe she did say five. It's not as though my recollection of this morning is rock-solid. Maybe it was just a mix-up.

"Oh, talking of last night, I forgot to tell you," Shelley says, putting the kettle on to boil and grabbing two mugs from the draining board. "Your mum called your landline yesterday while you were asleep. I answered it so it wouldn't wake you. She's worried about you."

I sigh, sliding a tin of baked beans into the cupboard. "It's hard to speak to her right now. She wants me to say things are getting better, and I can't do that."

"I know. I explained that to her. We had a long chat actually. She spoke about how hard it was for her when your dad died, and how she wants you to know that she understands what you're going through."

"She doesn't." The words slip out. My fingers close around the handle of the cupboard door. I squeeze it tight before slamming it shut. "Sorry, I know that's an unfair thing to say, but she doesn't. My dad died at sixty-seven. It isn't the same."

"She's trying, Tess. There is no way to measure someone's level of grief."

I nod through a pang of guilt, feeling bad for not calling Mum, but resentful too. I know she doesn't mean to make me feel guilty for not calling her, but I do and it isn't fair. "I'll call her."

"It's OK," Shelley says. "I explained how you've been feeling and gave her my number. From now on she can call me when she wants to know how you're doing, and you can call her whenever you're ready."

My throat tightens. Relief and sadness mingled into one claylike lump. "Thank you."

"It's nothing. I'm glad I can help. If there's anyone else you don't want to speak to I can talk to them for you. Here, have a cup of tea."

Shelley slides two mugs onto the table and we sit down across from each other just like on her first visit to the house. So much has changed between us since then.

I don't know what I'd have done this weekend without Shelley.

"So how was the pool?" I ask. "Did you have fun?"

"Yes." Shelley smiles. "I don't normally swim in the afternoons on a weekend. There were so many kids there, splashing each other when they jumped in. It made me think of Dylan. He would've loved it. I miss him so much." She sighs, touching her locket. "Kids have so much energy, don't they? Dylan gave Tim and me so much love, but he also gave me a purpose. I loved being a mum. Sometimes I miss that as much as I miss Dylan."

I try to picture Dylan in my mind. I bet Shelley was an amazing mum. Full of fun and mischief. The kind of mum I used to be. I hope having Jamie in the pool with her wasn't too painful. Before I can ask, Shelley is out of her seat and washing up her mug. "I'd better head off before Tim sends out a search party for me," she says.

"Oh . . . OK." I don't want her to go. I don't want to feel alone, just me and Jamie in this big old house. "Sorry again for snapping at you . . . I—"

She waves her hands at me. "Don't even think about it. I'm glad to see you looking better. Text me later?"

"I will."

"I'll just grab my scarf," she says. "I think I left it in the living room."

Jamie's laughter bounces through the open door and he shouts a "Bye."

"Take care of yourself," Shelley says a few moments later. She leans over and gives me a tight hug and I feel her warmth against my body. "Small steps. Do one thing each day. OK?"

"OK."

"Promise?"

I smile. "Yes."

"And take your antidepressants. They'll help."

And with that Shelley is gone.

I wander through to the living room and curl up on the sofa, watching Jamie play his game. I catch the scent of Shelley's perfume lingering on the cushions. The house feels so much emptier now. Empty and cold, like me.

CHAPTER 17

IAN

It's not like I went round there all the time. I popped in about a month after the crash to see if Tess needed anything. She wasn't returning my calls and I was worried. After that, the next time I spoke to Tess was when she called me in a right state about thinking she'd seen Mark in the supermarket. In fact she didn't call me, that's right, she called Mark's mobile. She gave me some line about wanting to hear his voicemail message but I didn't believe her. She acted like she forgot that we agreed I'd redirect his calls to me. We spoke about it during the funeral arrangements and Tess thought it was a good idea.

SHELLEY

We grew close quickly. The second time I saw Tess was on a Saturday. I called her to check in. She'd had a tough week. The minute I heard her voice I knew straightaway she was in a bad way so I went to help her.

I probably crossed a line that weekend, but I understood Tess's grief and she needed someone there desperately. Tess was in a dark place at that point. She was zoning out a lot and had this faraway look in her eye. She didn't want to talk to her family so I offered to do it. It helped Tess a lot.

CHAPTER 18

Wednesday, February 28

39 DAYS TO JAMIE'S BIRTHDAY

I've picked myself up, Mark. "Propped myself up" might be closer to the truth. It feels like I'm teetering on the edge of a cliff in that middle place where my balance has gone but I'm not actually falling yet. Any minute I'll fall, I'm sure of it, and I'll be right back in the darkest hole, cold to my core and hurting too much to care, but for now I'm still on top of the ledge, and that's as OK as it's going to get.

I'm not sure how I crawled out of the hole, to be honest. Shelley helped of course. And Sunday became Monday and Jamie went back to school and I focused on taking my tablets and my one thing each day just like Shelley told me to.

On Monday I used the eggs Shelley bought and made pancakes. I poured the gloopy yellow liquid into the frying pan when I heard Jamie's footsteps on the stairs, ready to do the first flip when he appeared in the doorway. I was a bit out of practice and gave the saucepan too much force, sending the pancake across the room and landing on the back of a chair, drooping for a moment before slipping to the floor. Still, I made Jamie laugh, so it was worth it.

On Tuesday I cleaned the bathroom and ordered the Lego Star Wars *Millennium Falcon* Jamie wants for his birthday. I know he won't be eight for a while yet but I worried it would be out of stock or get lost during delivery.

Today I poked under the fridge with a spatula and scooped out all the dust and dirt. There was no sign of the magnet with Jamie's photo on it, but maybe it got knocked under the oven instead. Then I scrubbed the inside of the kitchen cupboards, something I'm quite sure your mother never did in the decades since she had them installed. I turned the radio on while I worked and listened to Ken Bruce on Radio 2. I even got a question right on "PopMaster." I made sure to turn it off on the hour and miss the news, just in case the crash was mentioned.

But cleaning the cupboards is not my baby-step task for today. I just did it to keep busy, keep focused. Today my baby step is Jamie. I'm going to do something fun for him just as soon as I've collected him from school.

I hurry down the lane to the village, clomping in my old winter boots with my coat zipped up to my neck and shielding all but my head from the bracing gusts of icy wind.

There's a tractor up ahead. A dark green monster of a machine pulling a flatbed with a huge hosepipe on the back. I keep going another few steps and watch the giant rubber wheels roll nearer before pushing myself right up against the edge of the lane and into the thorny bush. Even so, it's close when it passes. I could reach a hand out to touch it if I wanted. The noise of the engine is a roar in my ears and my legs wobble for a second.

A minivan is crawling along at ten miles an hour behind the tractor and in the back seat are two bored-looking children in their navy school jumpers, the same school jumper as Jamie's—and that's when I realize I'm late.

I jump from the hedge and feel the thorns tugging and scratching at the fabric of my coat. Around the bend, the redbrick walls of the school are visible now and I see Jamie's face searching for me. I reach out and wave my hand until he sees me.

"Sorry," I puff. "A tractor blocked the lane and I had to wait for it to pass. How was your day?"

"Fine," Jamie says and we start walking again.

"What did you do today?"

"Nothing."

"Really?" I ask with a playful nudge. "You must've done something."

"Can't remember."

"That's OK. I was thinking—how about we hop in the car when we get back and go to that indoor playground in Colchester? You loved it there when we went for the Halloween thing. You know, the one with those drop slides."

"Now?"

"Yeah. Why not?"

"I don't want to," he says with the same tone as if I've asked him to tidy his bedroom. He's cross because I was late, I know, but still I wish he was a little more excited.

"Oh . . . it's just I thought you might enjoy it."

"Is Shelley coming with us?" he asks.

"Er . . . no."

"Those places are for babies. I don't want to go."

"You liked it last time."

Remember that, Mark? He raced around the climbing frames for hours in that werewolf costume and we drank cups of weak tea from sticky tables and wished it was wine.

"I'm NOT A BABY," Jamie screams so loud I flinch.

"But—" I stare at our sweet amazing boy who has never ever shouted at me before and flounder for a reply. I stop and reach out for Jamie's hand, but he moves, throwing himself into a sprint and running down the lane toward the house.

"Jamie," I gasp.

The giant wheels of the tractor turn over in my thoughts until it's all I can see—those monstrous wheels rolling along the road and Jamie falling in front of them.

I break into a run as fast as my legs and my boots will let me on the stony tarmac. I can't let anything happen to him, Mark.

He's waiting for me in the driveway, red-faced and scowling.

"Jamie." His name comes out a shrill shriek as I gasp for breath and feel the tidal wave of panic hit me with a hot fury. "Don't ever run off like that. Do you hear me?" I stride closer, almost skidding on the gravel. "You don't ever run off, especially, especially on the lane. A tractor could've been coming round the corner. You know that."

"Go away," he screams at me.

I'm close to him now and before I know what I'm doing—before I can think—my right hand is flying through the air toward him.

I catch myself in time, thank God. My fingers swipe the air inches from his shoulder and I yank my hand back and cradle it in my arm as if I've burned it.

Jamie glares at me for a moment before spinning and running around the side of the house toward the garden and the tree house. He looks back just before he disappears as if he's expecting me to be chasing him, but I can't. Even if I wanted to, I can't. My legs are threatening to give way from under me and hot tears are forming in my eyes.

"Jamie, I'm sorry," I sob, my voice too weak to be heard by anyone but me.

What have I done, Mark?

It's OK, Tessie.

Never, never, never have I lashed out in anger before. Not at anyone. Not at you, and especially not at Jamie. I'm not even the type to honk my horn when a car cuts me off.

I didn't mean it, Mark. I was so scared when he ran off. I didn't mean to hit him. I wouldn't do that. I'd never do that.

I close my eyes, freeing the tears. A phone is ringing somewhere and it takes me a moment to realize it's coming from inside the house. I force myself to move, praying it's Shelley calling. She'll know what to do.

Sweat cloaks my skin under my winter coat and I'm panting as I wrestle open the bolt on the side door and kick off my boots. The ringing is louder now and I remember Shelley's comment about the answerphone being full.

I dash through the downstairs and into the dining room, snatching it up mid-ring. "Hello?" I say all breathless from my dash and my fight with Jamie.

The line is quiet.

"Hello?" I say again.

There's a click and the dial tone purrs in my ear. *They must have been hanging up as I answered and didn't hear me,* I think.

I'm all the way in the hall when it starts ringing again and I turn back and snatch up the receiver on the second ring.

"Hello?"

Silence.

I wait for a beat and listen to the sound of nothing. No heavy breathing, no dodgy signal, just nothing.

"Mark?" It's only when I whisper your name, when I hear myself say it out loud, that I realize what I'm thinking. I slam the phone into its cradle and stumble until my back hits the edge of the dining room chair. It's not you, it's . . . it's a stupid call center or a wrong number or a hundred other things. It's not you calling me.

CHAPTER 19

Thursday, March 1

38 DAYS TO JAMIE'S BIRTHDAY

People are screaming. So many screams. Men and women alike, wailing loud and shrill. The man two rows ahead of us struggles out of his seat and throws open the overhead compartments. I want to ask him why—why is he bothering? I want to scream too but I can't open my mouth, I can't move. An invisible force is pinning me against the chair, crushing the breath right out of me.

There is smoke pouring through the plane. My eyes are stinging and I can taste it in my mouth. More people leap from their seats and a suitcase flies down the aisle, slamming into the headrest of a nearby seat.

The window is a kaleidoscope of blue sky and green, then gray—the tarmac, the ground.

Any second now. Any second and we'll hit it.

My eyes shoot open and I gasp for air. My lungs hurt and I can taste the smoke of the bonfire I lit the same day you died. The top of my head throbs with every furious beat of my heart pounding in my ears.

I blink in the gloom. There's a moon out tonight and its pale silver light illuminates the shapes of the furniture and bounces off the giant TV in the corner. I must've fallen asleep on the sofa.

The nightmare clings on and all I can think about is how scared you must've been. How alone you must've felt.

It's another minute before my heart stops hammering in my ears and I hear the silence of the house. Outside an owl is hooting nearby. I stretch my arms up, my neck stiff, my eyes puffy and sore, and I remember I was crying.

I waited until Jamie was asleep. After he'd slunk into the house for dinner and we'd eaten leftover casserole in a stilted silence. I guess both of us felt a bit sorry and a bit more upset and pretended we were neither. I know I did anyway. I read him a story and kissed him good night before carrying myself to the living room and shutting the door so Jamie wouldn't hear me. I collapsed on the sofa and cried and cried until there was nothing more inside me.

The heating has clicked off by the time I sit up again. The house is freezing. I'm shivering all over and need to move. I'm not sure how long I've been here for, but it feels like hours have passed. I'll check on Jamie and wrap myself in our duvet for warmth. You can tell me the story of the night we met. Remember that, Mark? The housewarming party we both ended up at. Neither of us knowing anyone but Stacey.

Of course I do, Tessie. You were the most beautiful woman in the room. You always are.

Not anymore.

Jamie is fast asleep, and beautiful in the soft light of the nightlight. I'm just tiptoeing down the hall to our bedroom when the phone starts ringing—the sound is fire-alarm loud in the still of the night. I don't know what time it is, but it's late. A past-midnight kind of late. Too late for a phone call.

I rush along the upstairs hall all the way to the end by the back stairs and your study. I wanted you to take one of the downstairs rooms as a study. It's not like we didn't have enough rooms to choose from. I wanted this spare for a nursery, but you liked being tucked out of the way, overlooking the garden and the tree house you built for Jamie, and I couldn't tell you what I was thinking. I couldn't bear your eye roll, your "Not this again" comment if I mentioned the baby we were trying so hard to have.

I flick on the light. There's no lampshade, just a bare, dusty bulb casting a harsh light. The room is empty except for the old desk you had as a boy growing up in this house and one of your mother's old bookshelves—both are covered in a fine layer of dust.

There are three columns of cardboard boxes stacked neatly up against the wall. *Mark's study* is scribbled across the side of each one. Seeing your handwriting causes a stab of longing in my gut that shudders through me.

The phone is resting in its holder, propped on the nearest box, and I grab it, throwing the house into silence.

"Hello?" I say before it's even at my ear.

There's no sound, just like the calls earlier.

I hang up quickly and feel goose bumps prickle the skin on my arms. A gust of wind hits the window, rattling the panes and making me start. With the light on, the window is a black mirror. A shiver races over my body when I see my own frightened face staring back, and I flick off the light.

It takes only a few seconds for my eyes to adjust and the room to fall back into focus. Since the moon is out, there's just enough light for me to see and I don't feel so scared anymore.

The flashing red of the answerphone blinks into the darkness. Shelley's voice plays in my thoughts. *"I couldn't leave a message because your answerphone is full."*

I try to remember when I last listened to the messages, but I'm not sure.

I sink onto the worn carpet and press play, jabbing my finger on the volume button until it's as low as it can go. I don't want to wake Jamie.

"Answerphone storage full," an electronic voice informs me. "You have twenty-five new messages. Message one."

"Hi, darling, it's me." The frail voice of my mum seems to echo in the empty room. "I'm settled back in now. How are you? I know it wasn't ideal me staying in that house, but why don't you come and stay here instead? The sea air will do you the world of good. I don't like to think of you shut in that house all day. I love you so much, my darling. Call me anytime, day or night."

My jaw tightens with every word she speaks. No mention of Jamie. No thought of school. So typical of my mother to think about what is best for her. We can't just drop everything. I'm glad Shelley has spoken to her. I'm glad she won't be calling as much.

The message clicks off and another begins.

"Hey, Tess," my brother's voice speaks into the room, undoing the tightness in my chest. There is the bustle of the hospital noise in the background. "I'm grabbing a quick break and phoning for a chat. It's your birthday soon and I haven't spoken to you for a while. I need your help with yesterday's cryptic crossword in the *Guardian*. One word, five letters. The clue is 'old.' Give me a call when you can."

No mention of Jamie or asking how I'm doing, but Sam doesn't need to ask. It's there in his voice and in his excuse to call. Sam was the one who got me hooked on crosswords to start with, back when we were teenagers and being dragged on camping holidays we were far too old for. There is no way he didn't know the answer to his clue. It's a joke about my age and I smile. The answer is biddy.

I think about snatching up the phone and calling Sam, but something stops me, a barrier. I don't want to speak to Sam or my mum right now. They want to know I'm OK, but I don't have the energy to lie. Besides, it's the middle of the night. Sam will be working or sleeping, and calling at this time will only worry him more. I'll call him tomorrow. Maybe.

The next message clicks on and I push thoughts of my family to the back of my mind.

"Tess, it's Ian. I hope you're OK. Can you call me, please? I need to talk to you about the money I mentioned at the funeral."

Beep.

"It's Ian again. Call me, please, Tess. This is important." Each word is short and punctuated with impatience.

There are two messages from a secretary at Clarke & Barlow Solicitors asking to get in touch, and one from Jacob Barlow himself. I wonder if all solicitors are this pushy or if Ian is behind their persistence.

There's a call from a kitchen company I've never heard of, then more shaking pleas from my mother. The next call is a hang-up, and the next and the next and the next until I lose count. Whoever it is, they stay on the line just long enough for the recording to begin and then they're gone.

I turn my head to the side each time and listen to the silent message, trying to hear any kind of background noise, but there's nothing.

And yet, it's something, isn't it? Why is someone calling and hanging up? I shiver again and swallow hard.

I'll call the phone company tomorrow and see if they can do something. It's probably a malfunction on one of those stupid electronic messages telling me we're eligible for free loft insulation.

I skip them forward until the message from Shelley on Saturday morning. "Hi, Tess, it's Shelley. I thought I'd check in after our chat on Monday and see how you're getting on after yesterday. I'm free all day so give me a call when you get this, or I'll try again later. Bye."

Shelley's message is bursting with energy, and when it clicks off, the room and the house feel too quiet.

Then the phone rings again. It's siren-loud this time and I reel away from it, hitting my back on the wall.

Who is calling? This late at night, while I'm sitting right here next to the phone? Who would call me?

My hand hovers midair, my heart thuds in my chest, dragging back the fear, the panic of the nightmare. I close my eyes and see the gray tarmac and hear the screams in my ears.

I'm about to pick up when the answerphone beats me to it.

"Hey, you've reached Tess, Mark, and Jamie. We're not here right now, so leave a message after the beep." My tone is game-show-host peppy and sounds like a stranger's voice.

I hold my breath and wait for the silence, the hang-up just like the others, but this time there's a noise—a rush of wind in the microphone. This isn't a machine. Someone is there. Someone is calling our house in the dead of night.

"Mark, where the hell are you? We were supposed to meet an hour ago," a man's voice barks out with such force that I cry out before throwing my hands to my mouth as if he might hear me.

"It's been three months," he says, his words gravelly and laced with anger and intent. "You were supposed to have delivered by now. I told you at the start of all this that I'm not a patient man. Don't test me. We need to talk. Call me."

There's another rustle on the line, and from inside your study, half a meter away from where I'm sitting with my back against the wall, the window panes rattle inside their crisscross lead.

My body freezes. Is it the same gust? Is he outside wandering around our driveway? Was it his footsteps I heard when you told me it was a deer?

I hug my knees to my body and bite down on my bottom lip. I'm scared, Mark.

The answerphone beeps. He's gone. All I can hear is my own breath gasping in and out. My mind is racing as fast as my heart. Who was that man, Mark? What is he losing patience with?

I sift through my memories of your work parties, the colleagues I've met over the years, but none of their voices fit, and besides, why would anyone from your office call you? They were all at the funeral. They all know you died in the plane crash.

With a shaking hand I reach out and press play, jumping all over again when the man's voice growls in the silence.

I hug my knees tighter and close my eyes as I listen. The fog is creeping over me and my thoughts begin to muddle. I think of Denise, but I don't know why.

Who is that man, Mark? What does he want from you, from us?

CHAPTER 20

I should've dialed that call-back thingy that tells you the last number that's called when I had the chance. I should've let you buy the caller ID phones you wanted to get last year that I said were pointless. *"Why do we need caller ID on the landline? The only person who calls our home phone is my mum. We always use our mobiles."*

Of course, that was before we moved a million miles away from a cell tower and four bars of signal. Now we use the landline all of the time.

I'm not even sure why I want to know the number of the man who is losing patience, only that it's what you'd have told me to do if you were here. But I didn't think about it until this morning and by then Ian had called and left another message. He didn't mention the money or the form he wants me to sign; he didn't even sound impatient this time.

"Hi, Tess, Ian here. Er . . . your friend Shelley said you weren't feeling too good. I hope you're feeling better. I'm just on my way to work right now but I was thinking of popping by at some point. Let me know if there's a good time and if you need anything. OK, well give me a call if you feel up to it. Hope the chili wasn't too spicy. Bye."

I told you, Tessie. He's my brother. He means well.

And now the last number that called is Ian's, so the call-back service won't work. I'm trying the phone company instead. I can ask them the number when I tell them about the hang-up calls. If I ever speak to someone, that is. I've been on hold for ages, listening to the same Take That song over and over, and before that I was transferred twice, my call pinging from India to Newcastle.

"Mrs. Clarke?" someone says when the music stops. The voice is young and I imagine a spotty teenage boy working shifts in a stuffy call center on his days off from college.

"Yes."

"Good afternoon, my name is Paul. How can I help you?"

"I've just explained it all to one of your colleagues." I sigh, wishing I didn't sound so whiny and desperate. "I'm getting hang-up calls and I want them to stop. I think it's a call center or one of those recorded messages. I want to know if there's a way to block them, please? And also, there was a call made to the house at one this morning and I'd like the number." My heart flutters in my chest. Do I want the number of the man who makes my insides twist every time I think of his voice? No.

"Well," Paul says. "I can see from our computers that your husband is the account holder. I'm very sorry, but you're not listed as a named person on the account, so I'm unable to give out any information regarding your account. If you can ask your husband to give us a call and tell us it's fine for us to speak to you—"

"I can't do that." Oh God, I'm going to cry again. I can feel the tears and hear the rupture of emotion tugging at my voice.

"I'm afraid without—"

"He died," I sob, feeling pathetic and stupid for crying down the phone to some kid, some stranger, who doesn't care about me and my problems.

"I . . . I'm very sorry," he stammers in my ear.

There's a long pause and I picture the teenager scrambling for his script and finding the page about the death of an account holder. I'd feel sorry for him if I wasn't so busy feeling sorry for myself.

"So in that case, Mrs. Clarke, what we'll need you to do is send a copy of your husband's death certificate to an address I can give you, and once we've received it we'll be able to transfer the account into your name."

"Please," I say. "I just want the calls to stop."

Another pause.

"What I can tell you, Mrs. Clarke, is that we have a nuisance call system for all of our customers. If any call comes in from, for example, a double glazing company and you don't want them to call anymore, you hang up and dial 1572 and that company will go on a list of people who can't call you anymore."

"Thank you," I whisper. "That's all I wanted."

"Except . . ." he says, lowering his voice, "it won't work if the caller has a blocked number." The way he speaks, his tone, the slowness of his words, I know he's trying to tell me something. The calls I'm getting are blocked. The code won't make a difference. Damn.

"Mrs. Clarke?"

"Yes?"

"Do you have a pen and paper there? I'll give you the address to send the certificate to. Once we've put the account in your name I would suggest you call back. It may be that you decide to change your phone number."

"Right, yes, hang on." I dash out of the dining room and into the kitchen and grab the first thing I see—the notebook from Shelley. I'll change the number. That's what I'll do.

After the call I move through the downstairs, the notebook open in my hands, slippers scraping and slapping on the floors. I'm not sure what I'm looking for. Something to do probably. It's ten a.m. The day is stretching out ahead of me. Five hours of nothing until Jamie comes home.

The antidepressants must be working, because I don't want to lose myself in the fog today. There are so many boxes still to unpack. You were supposed to help me sort through your mum's stuff. You were supposed to hire a dumpster. *"It'll all be done by Christmas,"* you told me back in October when we moved. But it wasn't. You kept putting it off and now it's just me and the job is too big.

I guess I should speak to Ian. I'm sure he looked through the house soon after your mum died, but I can't just throw it all away without checking. What do I want with old ornaments and photo albums of your uncles and aunts and people I've never met?

I drop into a chair in the kitchen and sigh. The notebook is open on the table and I stare at the address from the phone company again. Your death certificate is stuffed in the drawer in the kitchen, buried amidst the take-out menus and the old phone chargers we'll never need. I can take a walk to the post office and get a copy to send off today, get some fresh air too.

My eyes fall to the window and I watch the rain rolling down the glass. Or tomorrow. I can do it tomorrow after I've dropped Jamie at school. My gaze moves to the draining board where our breakfast bowls from this morning are sitting, turned up and clean.

Panic shoots like bullets through my body. I don't remember washing them up this morning. Are they even from this morning? Or are they yesterday's? It has to be this morning. I wouldn't have sent Jamie off to school without any breakfast.

How can I not remember, Mark?

The blue cardboard box from the doctor's is sitting on the window ledge and I reach out to grab it. I can't remember if I've taken my tablet this morning. I usually do it first thing with my breakfast, but I don't remember breakfast.

My hands shake as I pop out a tablet and wash it back with a gulp of water.

It's tiredness, that's all. You've always been forgetful, Tessie. Remember when Jamie was four weeks old and you hadn't slept for days? You drove to the supermarket and forgot where you parked the car?

That was awful. It took an hour to find my car, and that was with the help of two shop assistants. I'd forgotten the car park had been full and I'd parked on the street nearby instead.

You're right. It's tiredness.

I flip to the back page of the notebook and draw a grid. The lines are wobbly but it will do. I write the days of the week down the side and put a tick in the box next to Thursday. I'll put a tick each day when I take a tablet; that way I can check back if I forget.

It feels good to take control of something, and I wonder what else I can write down. At the front of the notebook, underneath the address for the phone company, I write: *Hang-up calls. Who are they from? Call center or person?*

On the next line down I keep scribbling. I write the date and the time of the call from the man. Thinking about it makes the pen shake in my hand, but I carry on writing, adding the little things that don't make sense.

I continue to write: *Flowers on my birthday without a note—from whom? Owe money to Ian—where is £100K? What is the money for? Why did we need it? Someone walking around our driveway in the middle of the night.*

I look up and catch sight of the two white envelopes leaning up against the microwave—the ones Shelley left me to open after her first visit.

Before I can think too much about it, I pick them up and rip open the first one with such force that the letter inside tears too. It's a solicitor's letter. From Clarke & Barlow. At first I thought it had something to do with the form Ian dropped in at the weekend, but it doesn't.

Dear Mrs. Clarke,

RE: LAST WILL AND TESTAMENT OF
MR. MARK THOMAS CLARKE

Further to my voice messages left on January 31, February 8, and February 19, I am now writing to request that you contact our offices at your earliest convenience. As you are Executor of your late husband's Last Will and Testament, it is imperative that we arrange a meeting to discuss arrangements for the distribution of his assets.

Please call the number at the top of this letter to arrange an appointment.

Kind regards,

Jacob Barlow

The letter was sent weeks ago but it still causes a weight to drop inside me like a cement block. I barely have the strength to get through the day. I do not have the energy to handle your estate stuff.

I think about the form Ian dropped around at the weekend. Renouncing the job or whatever fancy word he used. Shelley made it sound so easy. Maybe I should sign it. I add a line to the notebook: *Ian wants to be executor of the will—I need to decide what to do!!!*

I move on to the second letter. It is from a bank but it's not a statement.

> *Dear Mr. Clarke,*
>
> *Thank you for your loan application dated December 18, 2017. We are writing to inform you that unfortunately you do not meet the requirements for a loan at this time.*
>
> *Regards,*
> *Dimitri Lipov*
> *Loan Officer*

The pen drops from my hand, clattering to the floor and rolling out of sight under the table.

What the hell, Mark? You applied for a loan and didn't think to tell me? I don't know why I'm surprised. You never told me anything.

That's not true, Tessie.

I force my mind back to mid-December, searching for any conversation we might have had about money, but of course there isn't one. You were stressed about work, you said, and I believed you. Late home every night, spending hours in your study, unable to sleep. Those whispered phone calls you thought I didn't know about.

First the hundred thousand pounds Ian says he loaned us, and now a loan rejection.

What did we need the money for, Mark?

Ian's words spin through my head. *"If you knew your husband so well, why didn't he tell you about the money he borrowed from me?"*

We didn't live extravagant lives, didn't drive flashy cars; we didn't take all-inclusive cruises in the Caribbean like some of the sales team you worked with. I thought we were doing OK.

I stumble up the stairs, the solicitor's plea forgotten. The loan rejection letter is gripped in my hand.

It's too much. The phone calls—all those hang-ups and then the horrid voice of the man, and now this.

Suddenly I don't want to think about it. I go into Jamie's room and lie on his bed. It's easier to be in here than in our room and the double bed with the side that's always empty.

I close my eyes and breathe in the scent of Jamie's bedsheets. Underneath the Spring Fresh fabric conditioner is Jamie's smell. Something soft I can't quite hold on to, but I breathe it in anyway and close my eyes.

The phone is ringing again. There's a wet patch on Jamie's pillow from my tears. I must've fallen asleep. Paper rustles when I move—the loan rejection letter is still in my hand. It hits me all at once—a baseball-bat wallop—pounding the events of the past six weeks back into my consciousness. Everything—the plane crash, the funeral, Shelley coming, Ian's money, the voice of the man on the phone—hits with a thwack and I'm wide awake.

The answerphone clicks on by the time I'm in the hall.

"Hey, Tess," Shelley's voice says as I reach your study. I quicken my movements and reach the phone before the next words are out of her mouth.

"Shelley, I'm here," I reply, pressing the phone to my ear and sinking back to the worn green carpet in the exact spot where I sat last night.

"Hey," she says again. "How are you?"

I pause for a second and think of the fear I felt last night, in this very spot, in fact. I want to tell Shelley, but it seems so unreal now, and I'm not sure what it all means.

"OK," I say in the end. "I'm not sleeping great, but I'm feeling clearer. Less fog, if that makes sense?"

"That's great, Tess. I'm so pleased. Have you thought any more about signing over the executor role to your brother-in-law? Might be a weight off your shoulders if you do."

I find myself nodding, although there is still something off about the whole thing that I can't put my finger on. "Maybe."

"Good. One less thing for you to worry about. Hey, did I tell you at the weekend that I'm planning to redecorate our living room?"

"No."

"Have you got your mobile there? I'll send you some colors. I need help deciding."

I hurry down the stairs with the phone in my hand and find my mobile. I move to the nook where I can get one bar of signal and sit on the floor.

Shelley and I talk for ages about mundane things—cleaning and decorating. I don't have the first clue about color schemes but I like that she asked. I like that she called.

"What are your plans for the weekend?" Shelley asks after we decide on Royal Berry—a deep reddish purple—and Frosted Steel—a light gray.

"I don't know." After what happened with Jamie and my suggestion of going to the indoor playground this week, I haven't thought about the weekend. Maybe the cinema.

"I'm free on Saturday. I could swing by after my swim and hang out for a bit."

"That would be great. If you're sure you've not got anything better to do?"

"Don't be daft. I want to see you."

We say our good-byes and when I hang up I feel so much better. The notebook is still open on the kitchen table. I close the cover and tuck it back beside the microwave. I don't want to think about the call anymore. The rain has stopped and it's time to get Jamie from school.

Jamie is quiet on the walk home. I gnaw at the skin on my bottom lip so I don't scream at him to talk to me, to tell me he is OK.

"Is there anything you want to do this weekend?" I ask.

He shrugs a response.

"Shelley's coming over on Saturday. I thought we could go for a walk along the river. What do you think?"

Jamie's face lights up and there's a bounce to his step. "Yessssss."

When he looks up at me his smile stings like the brightest sunlight in my eyes. I push the feeling away before it can take hold. It's good that Jamie has a friend in Shelley, someone he can talk to when he doesn't want to talk to me.

I'll bake a cake tomorrow, I decide. Not fruitcake, that was your favorite, but a lemon drizzle. Something easy.

CHAPTER 21

Transcript BETWEEN ELLIOT SADLER (ES) AND TERESA CLARKE (TC) (INPATIENT AT OAKLANDS HOSPITAL, HARTFIELD WARD), WEDNESDAY, APRIL 11, 9:15. SESSION 2

ES: Good morning, Tess. How are you feeling today?

TC: Is there any news? Have you found Jamie?

ES: Not yet. We're still trying to find out what happened.

TC: Oh God. Oh God, oh God, oh God. This is my fault. I never should've trusted her.

ES: Who shouldn't you have trusted?

TC: Shelley, of course.

ES: Tell me about your friendship.

TC: Um (pause). I don't know what to tell you. She came to visit as a grief counselor that my mum organized for me, but we became friends. She and Jamie became very close. We've spent a lot of time together over the last few months.

ES: Did Shelley spend a lot of time with Jamie?

TC: Some, yes, enough for them to become close. They seemed to have this unspoken bond. Jamie and I were both struggling with losing Mark. It was hard. I wasn't being a good mother. I thought it was nice for him to have someone like Shelley around. She has this energy that seems to just pour out of her, like she just walks into a room and a light switches on. I'm sure Jamie felt it too. Compared to me I think he found Shelley a relief to be around.

ES: Did you keep taking your antidepressants during that time?

TC: Yes. What's that got to do with finding Jamie? What has any of this got to do with finding my son?

ES: So in the buildup to Jamie's birthday you would say you were coping better?

TC: Yes. It's hard to remember everything that's happened. I was struggling with my memory. I still am. I'm not sure if it's the grief or maybe a side effect of the antidepressants, but it's like I can remember a memory of Mark from years ago word for word, like I'm watching it back as a film, but my memory of yesterday, last week, basically since Mark died, has holes in it. Sometimes little holes and sometimes the whole day is just black. So much has happened in such a short space of time.

ES: But you and Shelley developed a strong friendship during this time.

TC: (Sigh) Yes. I guess in part it was because I didn't have anyone else to turn to and in part because Shelley sort of pushed the friendship. It's hard to explain but it was as though her spending time with me and Jamie was something she needed as much as I did.

ES: What about your mum and other friends, and your brother? Why do you think you cut yourself off from them but formed a close friendship with someone you barely knew?

TC: (Silence) She made it easy to be her friend. She was so confident, like Mark in so many ways. She always seemed to know the right thing to say and got how I was feeling. Mark was good at that too. Like I said, Jamie was drawn to her. We both were. Of course, I didn't know at that point just how far she was willing to go to get what she wanted.

ES: Do you think Mark is still alive?

TC: (Shakes head)

ES: You told one of the nurses when you were brought in that Mark was still alive.

TC: Did I? Oh. I was in a lot of pain then. With the morphine I was on I probably said Elvis was alive too.

ES: So you don't think Mark is alive?

TC: (Silence)

CHAPTER 22

Saturday, March 3

36 DAYS TO JAMIE'S BIRTHDAY

The sun is out today. Its rays stretch through the house, lighting the corners—the gloom—in a way I've never noticed before. In the garden, daffodil stalks have sprung out overnight—at least a hundred of them—an army of green stalks standing to attention.

The air is cold and there's a freshness I haven't felt in the house or the village before. But I wonder how much of that is to do with the sun and how much is to do with Shelley. From the moment she strode through the side door this morning, her energy has infected us both. Jamie has been brimming with it all day, skittering around Shelley's feet and hanging off her every word. Always with a smile on his face, always big blue eyes wide, gazing at her. I've felt it too.

"Right, come on," Shelley says as she marches along the downstairs hall, past the main staircase to the parlor.

"Can't we sit in the garden and eat more cake instead?" I pull a face, half joking, half not.

Jamie gives a giggling squeal and Shelley laughs too. "Nope," she says. "We've done quite enough cake eating for one day." Shelley pats her flat stomach as she turns around and flashes me a grin. "At this rate I'll be sinking in the pool tomorrow."

It's as if we're off on an adventure, a bear hunt, a search for buried treasure. We're not, of course, but Shelley is making it feel that way and even I smile as I follow after them with a roll of black bin bags in my hand. The last thing I want to do right now is go through the boxes in the second living room. It was your job—the unpacking and the sorting. Half our stuff, half your mother's, dumped and forgotten since moving day. If I do it, then it'll be one more reminder that you're not here. I won't be able to pretend that you've just put it off for another week.

I was happy sitting in the garden with our winter coats zipped up, watching Jamie charge around the garden with his football. I was happy drinking cups of tea and eating giant slabs of the lemon cake I made and talking about nothing and everything. I didn't mention the phone call or the hang-ups though. I didn't mention my fight with Jamie either. The thoughts were there, but the words never formed. Shelley makes my fears seem so distant, and I couldn't bear to drag them to the surface.

It was Shelley's idea to go in. "It can't be doing you any good living in a house full of boxes," she said. "Let's make a start together now. It won't feel like such a big job once we've started."

I don't know how, but I found myself nodding along.

"You take those ones," she says as the three of us step into the parlor. She points Jamie toward a stack of boxes resting on your mother's floral sofa. "And I'll do these." Shelley steps up to a box and pulls at the cardboard top. "We'll make three piles. One over there"—Shelley points to the window where I stood last weekend waiting for them to come home—"for things we think are valuable or want to keep. Things we're not sure of can go over by that wall, and the third pile can be rubbish and go straight in the bin bags. OK?"

Jamie and I nod and we all get to work. I help Jamie lift out a vase. It's chipped at the top and there's green mold growing in the bottom where it hasn't been cleaned properly. "Rubbish," I say to Jamie and we share a smile.

We're about halfway through the job when Shelley finds the photo albums. I watch her from across the room, the walls shrinking in as she opens the first one. She's found the baby photos, I guess, by the look on her face. Tears shimmer in Shelley's eyes and she touches her hand to the locket around her neck, like she always does when she is thinking of Dylan.

All at once the mood changes; the sun goes in and the gloom is back.

"Mark did them," I whisper, hopping over the pile in the middle and reaching her side. I flick a glance over to Jamie. He's stopped unpacking and is playing with a set of wooden Russian dolls, opening the middles and lining them up before putting them all back together again.

I count the albums. All eight of them are there. Each one labeled with Jamie's age. *Jamie 0–1 years old* is written on a white label on the album in Shelley's hands.

I loved that about you, Mark. How you printed the photos we took every month and tucked them away in an album. You never forgot, never skipped a month. I wasn't allowed to look until Jamie's birthday. *"A special present for Mummy,"* you used to say to Jamie. *"For being the best, most amazing mummy in the world."*

It's another job I'll have to do myself. Another reminder that you're never coming back.

"They're . . . they're lovely," Shelley whispers. "You all look so happy." Shelley reaches for another album. *Jamie 4–5 years* is written on the label.

"I'd forgotten about them," I say as Shelley opens the pages.

"I used to look at the albums of Dylan every day, but now they feel so distant from the boy he would be if he was here."

I reach out and touch the dark blue cover, feeling suddenly protective over the contents. It isn't just Jamie in these photos, it's you as well, us.

Shelley sighs and places the album carefully in the box and shuts the lid. "You don't have to look now."

"It's OK. I think . . . I think I'd like to look at them, but maybe later. I'll put them upstairs for now."

I scoop up the box, displacing a layer of dust, which floats in the air and tickles my nose. My mind is full of Shelley's words and her own sadness over the death of her son. I'm halfway up the narrow back staircase when the phone rings. My body freezes mid-step, thoughts of Shelley forgotten. One ring, two ring, three rings and it stops.

I breathe and start moving again. I hate that it's another hang-up but at least it wasn't the man with his scratching tone. He hasn't called back since the other night and if it wasn't for the message still saved on the answerphone I'd wonder if it was a dream or a sick joke.

With the box tucked safely beside our bed, I head for the main stairs. Shelley's voice carries through the house. It's only when I reach the final step that I realize it's not Jamie she's talking to, but someone on the phone. The call wasn't a hang-up. Shelley answered it.

She's talking to someone in the dining room as I make my way down the main staircase.

"I'm sorry," I hear Shelley say. "Tess is resting right now."

There's a pause and I imagine the caller asking a question.

"She's doing brilliantly, all things considered. She's having ups and downs, more downs at the moment. . . . I know, but she has your number and she'll call you when she's ready."

It's Ian, I guess, taking a step and catching sight of Jamie hovering in the doorway of the dining room, wobbling his tooth with his index finger and waiting for Shelley to finish.

"You're a doctor, right?" Shelley says. "You must see this a lot. There is no single length of time or one way to grieve. However hard it is to understand, Tess doesn't want to speak to anyone right now, and it's important that you respect that and give her space."

Oh. She's speaking to Sam, not Ian. I rush forward to tell Shelley it's OK, that I can speak to Sam. Today has been a good day and I'd like to speak to my brother.

"Will do. Bye," Shelley says, placing the phone back into the holder as I make it to the doorway.

I'm too late. Sam is gone.

Shelley turns toward me, surprise playing on her face. "Tess, you made me jump again."

"Was that Sam?" I ask.

"Yes. He wanted to see how you were. I told him you weren't up to speaking to anyone right now."

"Oh . . . thanks."

She must see the disappointment in my face because then she says: "Was that the wrong thing?"

"No, it's fine," I lie.

"Sorry, Tess. It's just you've said a few times that you want your mum and Sam to leave you alone for a bit. I thought it might help for them to speak to me. Sam was lovely, by the way. He's just starting his shift, but you can always call him tomorrow."

"You're right." I nod. "Thank you."

"Why don't we stop for the day? You look shattered."

Jamie nods and sidesteps us both, pointing at the living room and looking up at me with pleading eyes. "Can I play on the PlayStation?"

"OK." I smile at our boy.

Shelley is right—I am tired, and what is stopping me from calling Sam tomorrow? Nothing.

I'm about to suggest we head back to the garden for more tea and cake, but Shelley beats me to it. "I'd better head off. My walls still need another coat of paint and I can't see Tim doing it."

"Oh . . . of course."

"Have you got any plans for Wednesday?" she asks.

"Err . . . no." I don't have any plans, full stop.

"I'm meeting a client in Manningtree. It's not far from here and I thought we could meet for lunch."

"I know Manningtree," I reply. "Mark took me there once just after we moved here. It's pretty."

"It is, isn't it? How about we meet at one thirty? I'll be done way before that but I've got a few errands to run. We can have some lunch and potter around the gift shops."

I think of next week and the empty hours stretching out before me. "That sounds great. Can we make it twelve thirty though?" I ask, thinking of the school pickup and not wanting to be late.

"Sure. I'll do the errands afterward."

Shelley lifts her head and smiles at me and I feel her warmth cascading through me.

"I'm looking forward to it already." I return the smile.

Later, when Jamie is sitting in bed, I squish up beside him and rest the photo albums, one at a time, half on my leg and half on Jamie's so the pages are lopsided. We look through the albums with silent tears rolling down our faces.

Every so often we smile though and laugh at something, like the shot of you dressed as Captain Hook for Jamie's fourth birthday party. A fake beard hanging off your face, hands on hips, shoulders back, and grinning at the camera with ten little boys and girls sitting on the floor bawling their eyes out because they thought you were a real villain.

It takes over an hour to go through them all, from that first photo of us in the hospital with Jamie cradled in my arms to the selfie of the three of us on Christmas day, in our matching Christmas jumpers, with the fairy lights on the tree glinting in the background making the photo seem somehow magical. That was the last photo you printed.

It steals my breath seeing those albums. It tears open the wound of us just that little bit more.

Oh, Mark. There were so many little things you did that made our lives so special, so full of laughter and love. How will I ever be strong enough to take on all of those things on top of everything else? Why did you get on the plane? Why didn't you get the message and come home?

I love you, Tessie.

I love you too.

CHAPTER 23

Wednesday, March 7

32 DAYS TO JAMIE'S BIRTHDAY

Manningtree is smaller than I remember from the time you took me for lunch last October. *"You know you can't drive to Chelmsford and back anytime you want to have your hair cut or see the dentist, Tessie?"* you said with a grin on the way back from dropping Jamie off at his new school. You took my hand, giving it a squeeze because you knew that I was worried. Would Jamie make friends? Would he be bullied? Would he cry himself to sleep every night for weeks, begging us to move back to Chelmsford?

"Let me show you the nearest town—Manningtree. It's pretty. You'll like it. It's right on the River Stour as it makes its way out to sea. Plus it's easier to park in Manningtree than the multi-stories in Colchester, and cheaper too. You can't get everything from Amazon and Tesco," you laughed.

"Almost everything though," I muttered, unsure whether I was annoyed that you'd found another excuse to avoid unpacking or pleased

to be spending the day together. The latter won me over, and when you pulled me into the crook of your arm and kissed my cheek I smiled.

I didn't like the drive to Manningtree though. One narrow twisty lane, then another, and you bumping the car onto the bank and into the bushes anytime we met a car coming the other way. I preferred driving on the A12 to Tesco, but lunch at the pizzeria overlooking the sailboats sloping to one side in the low-tide mud was nice.

"You'll get used to the lanes," you said on the drive home, and maybe I will, but today my hands gripped the steering wheel at ten and two, and I spent the entire time hunched forward in my seat, barely scraping twenty miles an hour, praying a 4x4 didn't tear around the bend ahead and send my little Focus toppling into a ditch. It didn't help that there was a car right behind me the whole way. I could feel the impatience of the driver at every break and turn.

I park in the main car park by the long concrete floodwall. It is chilly and a mist hangs in the air. Droplets of it cling to my hair, flattening my curls, and I pull my scarf closer to the bare skin on my neck.

It feels good to be out after two days hauled up inside with the rain a constant spatter on the windowpanes, watching the *Home Alone* movies with Jamie after school and doing not much else.

I should get out of the house more, out of the village. I see that now. The two trips down the lane to the school each day, the one trip to Tesco last week, and walking to the post office to send the letter to the phone company haven't been enough.

With the smell of the salty estuary sea carrying in the fresh wind, the house feels like a dark and depressing place. Maybe I'll walk along the river wall if there's time after my lunch with Shelley before Jamie finishes school.

The main high street is an odd mix of old and new. Quaint gift shops and tearooms, alongside a kebab shop and hairdresser's. There's a market across the road—half a dozen stalls selling cleaning products, fruit and veg, and women's clothes.

I turn right opposite the library with its white Georgian facade and find myself on a cobbled street that curves down to the wide, sandy banks of the river. Seagulls swoop and screech high above my head.

The café Shelley suggested for lunch is halfway down on the right-hand side, tucked at the end of an alley no wider than a doorway. If it wasn't for the handwritten chalkboard advertising homemade lasagna at the Honey Pot Café, I would've walked straight past.

I hug my bag a little tighter and glance over my shoulder before I step down the passageway and into a shadowed courtyard. There's a tattoo parlor dead ahead, and two businesses on either side. To my left is a small New Age gift shop with dream catchers dangling in the window above silver skulls and fat Buddha statues. The smell of the river is gone, replaced by the musky scent of sandalwood incense drifting from the gift shop. The Honey Pot Café is on the right.

When I step through the door, a bell tinkles above my head and I'm hit by the smell of fresh brewed coffee and bacon. The place is small, with a dozen tables covered in gingham tablecloths. The kitchen is at the back behind a long counter covered with cakes and scones and muffins and cookies. Jamie would love it here.

The heat from the oven and the steamy windows adds a coziness to the place, and it must be good food, because there's not a single table free.

"The breakfast rush is just finishing," a woman in a black apron says as she shimmies between the tables, carrying four plates heaped with all the trimmings of an English breakfast. It's your kind of place too, Mark. "I should have a few tables free in about ten minutes. Is that OK?"

I nod and check the time. It's only ten to twelve. "I'm early anyway. I'll come back."

"Grand," she replies, puffing a loose strand of hair away from her face as she turns and starts gathering empty plates from a group of workmen—decorators, I guess by their paint-spattered overalls.

Back in the cold courtyard I dither for a moment, racking my brain for a purpose, something to fill the next forty minutes. There must be things I need from the shops, but my mind is a blank page.

It's only when I'm out of the alley, with the gray daylight hurting my eyes, that I catch someone watching me.

CHAPTER 24

The figure is in a doorway across the cobbled road. At first it's little more than a shadow in the corner of my vision. And if it wasn't for the shiver traveling through my body, and the sudden jerking movement as the man backs out of sight, I probably wouldn't have noticed him at all.

Every part of me freezes. I don't breathe, I don't move. The last few seconds replay in my mind as my eyes fix on the now-empty doorway. Did I imagine it? There's a flight of concrete steps and a buzzer system on the wall. It looks like the entrance to flats or small offices.

Time passes, a few seconds, enough for my mind to start to question what I saw, and I catch my breath. It was a deliveryman or an office worker waiting for the door to buzz so he could go inside. That's all.

Except I'm not sure.

I give the pockets of my coat a pat as if I might've forgotten something and turn back in the direction of the alley. At the last second I whip around to face the doorway, expecting to see it empty, expecting this feeling tightening in my gut to be a figment of my imagination.

It isn't.

He's back, staring right at me. His face is just a shadow beneath a black baseball cap, but I feel his eyes on me and the scream building in my throat.

The man moves a fraction further into the light, a fraction closer to me. He's wearing black jeans and a dark hoody. He is staring right at me. I stagger back and he moves again, walking toward me. My old winter boots slip on the wet cobblestones as I turn and run toward the main high street. The alley is a dead end, the side street is empty, but if I can make it to the main road then surely I'll be safe among the shoppers.

My heart is raging like the hooves of a bull stampede inside my body but even so I hear his footsteps tap tap tapping on the stones behind me. Five paces, four paces, he's gaining on me and I burst into a sprint, dashing the final meters and half throwing myself into the passing shoppers, all the while expecting to feel the weight of a hand on my coat pulling me back.

"Watch it," a woman's voice shouts in my ear as I knock into someone.

I look up and see a young mother with a pushchair. One of her shopping bags has fallen to the ground and the toddler in the pushchair has dropped a packet of crisps, spraying the contents to the damp sidewalk.

"I'm so sorry," I gasp.

I force my gaze back to the cobbled street, but it's empty. I look around and around, scouring the street for any sign of the man. I can't see him, but I can feel his watching eyes tickling the hairs on the back of my neck.

I duck into a greeting card shop with helium balloons floating in the windows. I shuffle around and face the door before moving further into the shop. My eyes are glued to the street outside as I wait to see who is following me.

Where did he come from? How did he know I was here? Did he follow me from the village? I try to remember the make of the car behind me on the lane but I can't even be sure of the color. I think it was blue.

"May I help you?" The voice startles me like a prod in the small of my back. I yelp, dancing sideways, almost toppling over a rickety magazine display rack. My hands grab the creaking frame at the final moment and steady its base on the floor.

"Here, let me," the shop assistant says, stepping out from the counter and shifting the stand to one side. "I've been telling them for weeks that this thing is in the way, but no one ever listens to me."

The woman clasps her hands together and stands before me. There is a stiffness to the way she is holding herself that reminds me of my mother and I wonder if she's in the first stages of arthritis. Her hair is white and cut close to her scalp and the thick lenses of her red-framed glasses magnify her eyes so when she looks at me it's as though she might be able to see right into my thoughts.

"What'll it be?" she asks, like I might order a glass of wine and a packet of crisps.

"Oh . . . I . . ." My eyes move to the window and the empty street beyond, then back to the shop and the display racks stuffed with cards. "I . . . I need a birthday card for my son," I stammer, surprised I can speak at all.

"How nice. Well, our children's cards are over here," she says, striding deeper into the shop. "How old will he be?"

"Eight." I follow the woman, glad to be moving away from the window.

"Here you are then." She waves her hand over two rows of cards, more colorful than the others on display. "I'll leave you to have a look."

I flick a final glance back at the empty street before focusing on the display. The cards, like the shop itself, are dated. There are no character cards, no Star Wars or Spider-Man, nothing Jamie would like, but I stand and stare for a long time anyway, picking up each one in turn before sliding it carefully back into its slot, killing time.

My phone hums in my bag. I dig through the pockets and pull it free. Shelley's name flashes on the screen.

"Hi," I say in a whisper.

"Hey, Tess, I'm just parking. Are you in town yet?" Shelley's voice bounces in my ear.

"I'm in a card shop opposite the library."

"Are you all right? You sound weird."

"It's . . . I'm . . . I think . . . I mean I know—someone is following me."

"What?" Shelley gasps. "Are you OK? Are you hurt?"

"I'm shaken up." Scared out of my wits.

"Stay on the line and don't move. I'm a minute away."

Nausea tumbles in my stomach. I close my eyes and fight the urge to throw up.

"Should I call the police?"

"Wait until I get there. OK?"

I nod and inch toward the window so I can watch the street for Shelley. The phone is pressed to my ear and I can hear her breath in the microphone and the rustling sound of her movements. It reminds me of the man with the gravelly voice who called in the middle of the night. *"I told you at the start of all this that I'm not a patient man."*

Was it him following me? What does he want, Mark?

I brush too close to the shelves and knock into a display of sweets. A packet of Haribo drops to the floor with a crackle of plastic. It's when I'm bending down to retrieve them that I see the newspapers—knee height and spread out so that every front page is visible.

My breath catches in my throat and I make a noise, a yelp. Every newspaper, every single one—tabloid and broadsheet alike—has the same photo on the front page. I've seen the image before—watching the news on the TV in the hours, the days that followed the visit from the police. When I clung to every word about the crash, desperately praying they'd made a mistake. Got the wrong flight number, or found survivors.

I stopped watching when they showed the crisp white body bags lining the concrete beside the black, charred wreckage. There was no mistake, there were no survivors.

I've stayed off the Internet and Facebook, I've kept the TV channel on Jamie's kids' shows. I've hidden us away in our bubble of grief. But I guess somewhere in the weeks that have passed I assumed the news cycle had moved on to an earthquake or a political scandal. I was wrong.

My chest heaves up and down, up and down. I'm breathing, I know I am, but I can't seem to get the air in. My head is spinning. It's too hot. My scarf is too tight around my neck. The heat of the shop is suffocating me and I'm sweating under my clothes. The walls are closing in. I can't breathe. I can't think.

When I open my eyes the photo of the wreckage, the body bags, swims into focus and I read the bold lettering of one of the headlines: SUICIDE PILOT'S FAMILY FINALLY SPEAKS OUT.

Underneath is a smaller headline that reads: *Seven Weeks On the Parents of Philip Curtis Break Their Silence.* There's movement at the door and I cry out as I turn. It's the man in the black baseball cap here to get me.

I can't breathe.

"Tess, it's me," Shelley says, her voice loud and clear in my ears. I stumble back, knocking against the sweets again, and when I blink Shelley is standing before me in her black winter coat.

"It's OK, I'm here," she soothes, wrapping an arm around my shoulders and steering me away from the newspapers and out of the shop, only stopping when we reach a bench on the street.

"That's it," Shelley says. "Breathe. You're OK. You're having a panic attack. You're OK. Just keep breathing."

A panic attack? It feels more like I'm dying. My heart is racing so hard it feels like it's going to explode. My head is filled with helium and no matter how hard I try, I can't get the breath into my lungs.

It's another few minutes before I notice the rain drizzling on my face, soothing my hot skin. The day pulls back into focus—I smell the salt water in the air again and hear the cars moving on the wet road and the cry of the seagulls above my head.

The world has kept turning. I'm not dying.

"Sorry," I whisper, drawing in a long breath.

"Don't be sorry. Seeing those newspapers must've been a terrible shock."

"I . . . I thought they'd moved on to something else. I didn't think it was still news."

"It's not front page every day now, but it's still a big story. I'm sorry. It can't be easy seeing it."

"There was someone following me too." I sit up straight and look around. Shoppers are hurrying to get out of the rain. The street is quieter, the market stalls are packing up, and there's no sign of the man I saw in the dark hoody and baseball cap. "Do I call the police?"

"Are you sure they were following you, Tess? One hundred percent sure?"

"Yes." I nod.

"Can you tell me what happened?"

So I do. From the moment I stepped out of the alley until she called me.

Shelley slips her hand in mine before she speaks. "Is it possible that you saw someone by the building and they made you jump, and when they started walking, you freaked out and thought they were following you?"

"I . . . I don't think so. He was definitely chasing me."

"Did you see this person actually running behind you? Did they call out to you?"

I close my eyes and think back. I heard his footsteps, I felt him closing in, but I didn't turn back, I didn't see. "No . . . but—"

"I'm not saying I don't believe you, Tess. If you tell me that you're one hundred percent sure that someone was following you, then I'll come with you right now and we'll report it at the police station." She gives my hand an extra squeeze. "I just want you to think first about how certain you are. Maybe this trip was too much for you and you started to panic and imagined the worst."

My mouth is dry and it's hard to swallow as I process Shelley's words. I thought I was sure. My fear was real, I know that much, but Shelley's thoughts ring with a truth I can't ignore.

"I . . . I don't know. There was a car right behind me all the way from the village. Someone might've followed me?"

Shelley doesn't say anything. She doesn't need to. I can hear the waver of doubt in my voice. Lots of people use the lane.

"Shall we get out of the rain and get lunch?" Shelley asks. "Or do you want to go home? I can drive you and you can collect your car tomorrow."

I nod. "Thank you. I think I should go home, but I'm OK to drive. Sorry for messing up our plans."

"It's fine, Tess. I'm glad I was here to help you. I'm visiting my sister in Hertfordshire this weekend but let's arrange another trip together next week. I'll come with you from the start. Until then, stay close to home, OK? If this happens again and you're alone it could be much scarier for you."

Scarier than this?

Shelley is right about one thing—I wasn't ready to come out today. Driving on the lanes was too much. It felt so good to leave the village and be away from the house, but now all I want is to be back there, safe and protected in my bubble of grief. Shelley is probably right about the man I saw too, but the fear is still pumping through my blood. He was so close to getting me, I'm sure of it.

Shelley and I walk back to the car park arm in arm. We're both soaked from the rain. Shelley's mascara has smudged beneath her eyes and her normally glossy hair is damp and clinging to her head. She is still beautiful though.

"Thank you," I whisper as we say good-bye.

"It's what friends are for." Shelley smiles. "I'll call you later, and remember—no trips out. Wait for me to come with you," she says, hugging me tight.

When I'm home and the back door is locked and I feel safe again, I sit for a while at the kitchen table staring at nothing. Rain patters on the glass panes.

Was it real? Was that man with the hat pulled low and the dark clothes following me?

I reach for the notebook Shelley gave me and turn to a clean page before I write. The pen feels alien in my grip and my hands are still shaking with a jitter that makes the letters almost impossible to form. Almost.

Followed in Manningtree by a man in a black baseball cap, I write. *Could be imagination????? It felt real!*

I add the date and the time and stare at the words.

I wish I knew what it meant, Mark. I wish you were here to help me.

CHAPTER 25

IAN

I really had no idea what was going on with Tess. The first I heard of someone threatening her was from you. But I'll tell you this—my brother was always crap with money growing up. If someone was after Tess then that's the first place I'd look. I bailed Mark out more times than I can remember when we were teenagers. I gave him his first loan when he was twelve and he never paid me back. I offered to take over the probate of Mark's will because, well frankly, someone had to do it and it clearly wasn't going to be Tess.

From what I could see she was barely getting dressed most days. Personally, I've always thought it was a ridiculous idea for spouses to name each other as executors for each other's will. It's not something we encourage at Clarke & Barlow Solicitors. I'm surprised my business partner didn't point that out to them at the time. Tess was devastated, obviously, but the legal arrangements can and often do drag on for months. I didn't want Tess to wait too long. Credit card companies and banks don't generally care that much when someone dies. They still expect to be paid, and I didn't want Tess falling into arrears. She didn't listen to me though; she was too busy letting Shelley take over.

SHELLEY

We started seeing a lot of each other. I really believe it did Tess the world of good. She was feeling better. I was on my way to meeting Tess when I called her and she told me someone was following her. By the time I got there she was having a full-blown panic attack.

I should've taken her more seriously. I didn't know what to think. It's a horrible thing to say now, and of course I didn't say anything to her at the time, but I did wonder if it was her imagination getting the better of her. It can't have been easy living in that big old house.

If I could go back and do it all over again then of course I would've done something, but Tess didn't tell me everything that was going on. Maybe if she had, things might've been different. You have to believe me, I would never hurt Tess, and if things had been different, I wouldn't have hurt Jamie either.

CHAPTER 26

Transcript BETWEEN ELLIOT SADLER (ES) AND TERESA CLARKE (TC) (INPATIENT AT OAKLANDS HOSPITAL, HARTFIELD WARD), WEDNESDAY, APRIL 11. SESSION 2 (Cont.)

TC: I don't know what I think. It's hard sitting here knowing Jamie is out there somewhere. It's all in my notebook. I wrote everything down. My memory wasn't great, and I wasn't thinking straight a lot of the time. But even so, I knew something was going on. I didn't suspect Shelley at first but I knew someone was trying to scare me. There was a man who called me. He threatened me and Jamie. He said Mark was working on something for him and he wanted it back. I can still hear his voice in my head. It was horrible.

ES: Did he tell you his name?

TC: No. Oh God, what if it isn't Shelley who has Jamie? What if it's the man? He knew all about me and Jamie. Oh God. What have I done?

ES: Take a breath please, Tess. Let's try and calm down.

TC: Has that ever worked?

ES: What's that?

TC: Has anyone ever actually calmed down because someone told them to? Jamie is missing. I won't calm down until he is in my arms. Can you get an officer to get my notebook? If you just read that, then you'll see everything. I'm sure the answer is in there.

ES: The police have your notebook, Tess. They are looking at it right now. They are interviewing Shelley and Ian.

TC: What have they said? Do they know where Jamie is?

ES: Why don't you tell me your side of things? Starting with the night of Jamie's birthday.

TC: I need to know Jamie is safe first. I have to see him.

ES: Let's take a break.

TC: I don't need a break. Jamie hasn't been found. Jamie is still out there. How can we take a break?

ES: Tess, you've had a serious injury to your abdomen which you are reluctant to talk about. If you want to help us find out what happened to Jamie then you need to rest. We'll talk again later.

CHAPTER 27

Thursday, March 8

31 DAYS TO JAMIE'S BIRTHDAY

Something occurred to me this morning, Mark, as I watched Jamie dash into the school. Time is no longer the constant ticktock that it used to be when you were alive. In the daytime, when it's just me, and in the dead of night when I can't sleep and I listen for hours to the owl hooting for a mate, time grinds to a stilted crawl—a train drawing into a station.

But when I need to leave for the school run—no matter how many extra minutes I have—time seems to bound ahead of me like a dog chasing pheasants across the fields. Jamie is always the last one through the glass doors in the morning and the last one waiting in the school playground in the afternoons.

The minute I step back into the house and shut the back door I feel the shift in time, the cogs grinding down, but I won't let it beat me today. I'm going to keep busy.

I'm on my way to the parlor to finish sorting the boxes when the phone rings.

It's rung half a dozen times this week. Each time I'm frozen to the spot, holding my breath and waiting for the answerphone to pick up, waiting to see if it's him again. Each time my voice from before echoes through the rooms, the message starts to record, and then they hang up.

Today's call is no different.

Why? Who is at the other end? I wonder as silence fills the house.

I close my eyes for a moment and the image of the charred wreckage fills my head. I know I should carry on walking, carry on with my jobs, but instead I find myself in the living room with the TV remote in my hand.

Sky News appears on the screen.

An anchorwoman with glossy brown hair and the wrong shade of lipstick is staring right into me as she speaks: "A suicide note from the pilot of the Thurrock plane crash has been handed in to police."

Stop, Tessie. Don't watch it!

Too late.

I sit down, perching on the edge of the sofa.

An expert of some sort—a lecturer in aviation safety—is talking about the failings of the airline, but I'm only half listening. A picture is forming in my mind of you sitting down and clipping on your seat belt. The compensation letter from the airline flashes in my thoughts. It's still tucked in my cardigan pocket waiting for me to do something about it or throw it away.

"The plane left London City Airport on schedule and was on the flight path bound for Frankfurt, but we know from the cockpit recording," the lecturer says, his eyes moving between the camera and the anchorwoman as if he's not sure where to focus, "that the pilot sent the copilot out of the cockpit only a few minutes after takeoff, supposedly because he had a headache and asked the copilot to get him some painkillers."

"Is it normal practice for the copilot to leave the cockpit during takeoff?" the anchorwoman asks.

"No, it is not. Aviation Safety regulations recommend two people should remain in the cockpit at all times during the flight, which is why the CAA—the Civil Aviation Authority—ruled the airline to be negligent. Alarm bells should have rung for the copilot then as it would have been far simpler to call a member of the cabin crew into the cockpit and ask for painkillers from their medical kit. But as we know, the copilot didn't question the pilot and left the cockpit.

"Following the tragedies of 9-11, all cockpit doors were installed with a lock on the inside, which the pilot then used, giving him sole access to the aircraft controls."

"And we also know that the pilot—Philip Curtis—was signed off on medical leave by his doctor with stress," the anchorwoman continues, "just four weeks before the Thurrock crash. The flight to Frankfurt was his first flight back at work following his absence, leaving many people to speculate that Philip Curtis returned to his duties as a pilot with the intention of killing himself and all those on board. What kind of safety measures are in place with airlines to support the mental health of their employees?"

My heart is beating in loud rapid thuds in my ears. The anchorwoman and the lecturer are still jabbering on about negligence and suicide, but I know what's coming. A red banner flashes across the bottom of the screen. THURROCK CRASH UPDATE: PILOT SUICIDE NOTE FOUND is written in bold white writing.

My throat constricts, and tears blur my vision, but not enough to obscure the change in the screen and the amateur video footage now playing, just as I knew it would.

I blink the tears away and feel myself sucked like the last dregs of water down the drain, all the way back to that first Monday. The bonfire is smoldering in the garden and the smoke from it is still clawing at my throat. From the kitchen I can hear the whir of the kettle and the murmur of PC Greenwood talking quietly to the other officer, the one with the gray face and tearful eyes. A phone is ringing somewhere in the house.

Shaky footage starts of a young girl in a park riding her bike. Then the camera moves up to a clear blue sky. The image blurs as the person filming zooms in on an aircraft. It's flying low in the sky but climbing higher and higher, until it isn't. Until the nose of the plane dips suddenly and it's rocketing straight toward the ground. The video shakes as the plane disappears into a fireball of black smoke. The voice of the person filming is screeching out of the TV, but I block out the sound and think only of you, bent over in your seat with your warm hands wrapped around the back of your head. How scared you must have been in those final moments. Were we your last thoughts? The wife and son you'll leave behind?

It breaks my heart to think of Jamie watching this one day. I didn't tell him it was the pilot's fault. *"Daddy's plane crashed. It happened very quickly. He wouldn't have felt any pain"* was all I said. One day, when he's older, I'm sure he'll search for more answers. He'll find the footage of the plane going down and learn about the pilot's cruel and selfish actions, but I'll shield him from it for as long as I can.

The news anchor appears back on the TV, her lips touched up with more of the wrong color, and I'm back, almost eight weeks on. Almost eight weeks without you.

The camera zooms in, cutting out the expert, and leaving only the anchorwoman. "Up next, we'll be talking to two of the families of the

Thurrock crash victims and the lawsuit they are filing against the airline.

"Here is our main headline today: A suicide note from the pilot of the Thurrock plane crash has been handed in to police investigators. The letter was posted by Philip Curtis to a colleague in the human resources department of the airline and remained unopened until yesterday. Forty-five people were killed in the crash, including—"

The screen turns black, plunging the room into silence. I stare at the remote clenched in my hand. I don't want to know who else died that day. I don't want to share the grief.

I force myself to stand. Every part of my body is willing me to climb the stairs and lie on Jamie's bed, or sink into a bath, but I can't keep doing that. It isn't helping me, and it certainly isn't helping Jamie. Instead, I shuffle along the hall to the parlor and slowly, very slowly, I continue to unpack the boxes.

By midafternoon it's done.

CHAPTER 28

Saturday, March 10

---

29 DAYS TO JAMIE'S BIRTHDAY

Memories have been haunting me today, Mark. The ones from before you died that are still intact and running like old home movies in my mind, filling my head with laughter and joy. So after lunch I switch off the TV Jamie is slumped in front of and we put on our wellies and go out in the drizzly rain to the playground.

"Why isn't Shelley coming over this weekend?" Jamie asks. He skips ahead a little in his wellies and I let him. The lane into the village is so quiet. I guess people are tucking themselves up indoors, away from the heavy gray clouds and the rain in the air, but I like it. The feel of the droplets on my face, the chill blowing through me. I feel more alive outside.

"She's visiting her sister. I'll ask if she can come after school one day next week instead. Would that be OK?"

"On Monday?"

"I don't know when. I'll ask her."

He gives a huff-like sigh and steps ahead a little further. "I wish Shelley was here now."

So do I.

We're almost at the gate to the playing field when we find the puddle covering the entire width of the lane. It's too long to jump over so we wade through in our wellies. We're halfway in when I think of you beside me. If you were here right now, you'd scoop me up and pretend to drop me in the water and I would scream and Jamie would roar with laughter.

A sob catches in my throat but I swallow it back and jump—a little splash—but Jamie's giggles fill my head and I laugh too. I jump again, harder this time, causing water to spill into the tops of my wellies and soak my jeans, but I don't care because I made Jamie smile. I made him laugh.

We're giggling and jumping so much that I don't hear the car on the lane until the horn toots and I flinch, pushing Jamie to the side of the road and waving an apology as we step to the gate. The playground is just across the field. The bright red and yellow climbing frame looks out of place amidst the green of the trees and the bleak sky.

The Land Rover moves closer and stops. I recognize the black paintwork and tinted windows—it's Ian.

He buzzes down the driver's window and smiles at us. "Hey, I thought that was you."

"Hi," Jamie and I chorus.

"Puddle jumping, eh? Glad to see you feeling better."

The frown creasing his forehead says otherwise, but I don't bother to comment. Jamie tugs at my coat and looks at the playground with hopeful eyes. I nod and he's off through the gate, racing across the field to the zipline and the swings.

"I was just coming to see you," Ian says. "I've got a tool kit in the boot. I've got some WD-40 too. I thought I'd oil the hinges on the side door to stop it creaking for you and see if there are any other jobs I can do."

"Oh . . . erm, thanks, but that's OK. We're fine."

Ian doesn't look like he's come to do jobs. He's freshly shaved and is wearing a dark Ralph Lauren polo shirt.

"Do you want to jump in and I'll give you a lift back?"

I shake my head and motion toward the playground where Jamie is swinging from the monkey bars. "I think I might be here awhile."

Ian pulls a face as if I've just given the wrong answer in a quiz. But now that I'm out of the house I have no desire to go back. Maybe I'll take Jamie to the pub for hot chocolate after he's finished playing.

"Look, about the form I dropped off—"

"I haven't signed it yet."

"But you're going to?" he asks.

"I think so."

"That's good. I'm glad you're going to let me help you, Tess. I'm not trying to pressure you into signing it. I just wanted to give you the option, that's all."

I give a laugh. "You're not trying to pressure me, but you dropped off the form at the weekend when you could've posted it, and your solicitor's has left a load of messages telling me to call them. It kind of feels like pressure."

He shakes his head. His eyes soften a little and I think again how much like yours they are. "I wanted to drop the chili off to you. That's why I came to see you last Saturday. The weekends are the only time I have to cook. Didn't your friend tell you that? I'd hoped to talk to you about the form and let you know that I'm happy to help if you need it. I'm sorry if you thought I was being pushy. I'm more than happy for you to continue as the executor for Mark's will, Tess. I was only trying to help."

"Thanks," I mumble.

"How long have you known Shelley?" he asks.

A drop of rain hits my eyelashes and I blink it away. The change of conversation throws me. "Er . . . not long, I guess. Why?"

"She seemed quite protective of you the other day. She wouldn't even let me through the door."

Good, I think.

"Not everyone has your best interests at heart, Tess," Ian says then.

Maybe because of the sheer bloody ridiculousness of his warning, or because I'm still giddy from my puddle jumping, I laugh. "Don't you think I know that?" I say.

"Look, how about you get in the car and I'll drive you back? It's pouring down out here. We can talk properly over coffee."

He's right. The rain is no longer a drizzle but fat droplets bouncing in the puddle. Water is streaming from my hair down my face, and my coat is so wet that it's no longer waterproof.

"You're right. I'd better go," I say, stepping toward the gate. Jamie is on the zipline now, zooming back and forth, oblivious to the weather.

"Tess, wait." Ian reaches behind him into the back seat before opening the driver's door and stepping out beside me with one of those large white golf umbrellas in his hands.

He opens the umbrella and moves nearer so that we're both sheltered from the rain. I don't like how close he is.

"Tess, please. We can't keep having conversations like this."

"Why not?" I ask.

"What do you mean, why not?"

"I mean, you never bothered with me or Jamie, or Mark, for that matter, before the plane crash. The only reason you're bothering now is because you want me to sort out Mark's will and look for your money."

"That's not true at all, Tess."

"Isn't it? You've never liked me—admit it."

My words hang in the damp air. The only sound is the pattering of rain on the umbrella.

"What difference does it make now whether I liked you or not?" Ian says with a long sigh. "Not everyone is supposed to get on."

"Right." I'm not sure what I was expecting, but it wasn't an admission. "But you never tried to get to know me."

"You and Mark didn't give me a chance. The first time I heard anything about you was from Mum when she phoned me up to tell me that Mark had got a girl pregnant. When I met you, all you talked about was giving up work and having a family. What was I supposed to think? You saw Mark as your golden ticket to an easy life."

"Easy life? Does any of this look easy to you?"

"No, it doesn't. And for what it's worth, my first opinion was probably wrong. You and Mark clearly loved each other."

"But not everyone is supposed to get on," I finish for him.

Ian shrugs and I find myself fixated on his eyes, your eyes. "We're different people."

"So why are you here then? If you don't like me, then why are you bothering?"

Ian looks past me to the playground and Jamie, now standing on one of the swings and swaying back and forth, higher and higher. "You're the closest thing to family I have left. I want to help you. I want us to get on. It's what Mark would've wanted."

Tears swim in my eyes at the mention of your name. "I have to go." I back away until the rain hits the top of my head.

Ian stands for a moment as if he might follow me, but then he moves back to the car. "If you change your mind, give me a call," he shouts over the sound of the rain.

I hurry through the gate, breaking into a run for no reason at all except wanting distance from your brother and a sudden need to be near Jamie.

My head spins with Ian's words. *"You're the closest thing to family I have left. I want to help you."*

Does he? Why don't I believe him?

There has to be more to this than brotherly obligation, I'm sure of it. And there is no way I'm signing that form until I find out what it is.

CHAPTER 29

Wednesday, March 14

---

25 DAYS TO JAMIE'S BIRTHDAY

Tessie, remember our honeymoon in Scotland and the evenings in the little B and B when Jamie slept like a log and we cuddled up together trying to stop the bed creaking?

Please don't. Not today, Mark. I don't have it in me today.

Oh, Tessie. I thought you were getting better.

So did I. So did Jamie. I saw the disappointment on his face this morning when he walked into our bedroom already dressed for school and found me still in bed. It was awful, Mark. You should have seen the look in his eyes as he turned and left without a word. He despises me, my own son.

He loves you, Tessie. We both do.

Why would you? What is there to love?

I feel like I'm being pulled to the ground, weighed down by a hundred dumbbells. It's an effort to breathe in and out, to blink, to think. I don't even have the energy to cry.

What happened, baby?

Nothing. Nothing happened. The weekend ended. Monday came back around. Our eighth Monday without you. Day after day and it's the same hurt right in the center of my chest, the same fight to carry on. No end. No way out.

But not today. I can't fight today.

"Imagine you're the beach," Shelley said when I called her this morning, after forcing myself out of bed to take Jamie to school. "And your grief is the sea. Sometimes the tide will be high and it'll be all you see and all you feel. Other times the tide will be out and your grief, that pain, will feel further away. Not gone, but distant."

It was a good analogy but I phoned her for actual help, not a supportive chat. Plus I promised Jamie I would invite Shelley for tea.

"Can you come over later?" I asked.

"Sure," she said, and I could feel her smile all the way down the phone. "I have a few clients I'm meeting this afternoon. I'll swing by about five thirty. How about I bring a takeout? Anything you want."

"That would be great actually. Thank you."

We agreed on KFC. Jamie's favorite.

"KFC it is." Shelley laughed before hanging up.

The KFC family bucket had lost its heat by the time Shelley arrived. The chips were halfway between cardboard and soggy; the southern-fried chicken slimy with grease. Even Jamie didn't show his usual enthusiasm for his favorite fast food. He barely said more than a few words during dinner, and went to bed without any fuss.

Later when Jamie was asleep, Shelley and I slouched on the sofa and watched *Bridget Jones's Baby* with the rest of a mint Viennetta I dug out from the freezer balanced on a tray between us.

"Finally, someone who'll watch this film with me," Shelley says with a grin, licking green ice cream from the back of her spoon. "Tim won't go near anything the least bit chick flick."

I'm reminded then that Shelley is married. She has a job; she has friends too, I bet. Yet she's spending the evening with me. I guess I haven't thought about Shelley at all except for her visits to me. "How long have you been married?" I ask.

"Fifteen years. We had Dylan and were just at that point of talking about having another baby when he got sick. We decided to wait until we got the all clear from cancer before trying, but it never happened."

"I'm so sorry."

"Tim wanted to have another baby a few years ago, but I couldn't do it. The oncologist thought that the type of cancer Dylan had was linked to his genetics, and I couldn't go through it all again. Here—" Shelley reaches behind her neck and unclips her necklace. She fiddles with the clasp of the locket for a moment before it opens and she holds it out to me.

The photo inside is small and wrinkled at the edges from being pushed inside the case, but the image of Dylan is crystal clear. He is young in the photo—three, I guess. His blond hair is wet and sticking up as if he's just out of the bath or a swimming pool. He has Shelley's smile, I think, staring at the two rows of baby teeth. There's a gauntness to his face, hollow cheeks that should be chubby, but it's his eyes I find myself staring at. They are light blue, like the early morning sky in summer, like Jamie's. The thought lurches in my head. Dylan looks just like Jamie did at that age.

"This was just before the chemo when he lost all of his hair," Shelley whispers. "He was perfect in every way."

I nod but can't find the words.

"He'd be eight this summer."

Just like Jamie, I think again.

"It's funny, but I miss being a mother almost as much as I miss Dylan. Having someone to care for and love unconditionally. I'm not sure I'd call it a biological clock, but there is definitely something inside of me urging me to be a mother again. I want to adopt," Shelley continues. "It's not like there aren't kids out there in need of a decent home, you know?"

Shelley sighs and I can feel the hurt radiating like heat from her body. "Tim thought it would feel like we were trying to replace Dylan. He didn't think he could love a child that wasn't his. So we did neither. I have my job and my work with the charity, and Tim has his company and his golf club membership. We muddle along. Sometimes I wonder why we're still together, whether it would be easier to just run away and start again. I worry we're holding each other back from moving on with our lives. Sometimes I can spend entire days fantasizing about what Dylan would look like now, what kind of boy he would be, what fun we'd have had together. Other times I fantasize about adopting a child and moving far, far away."

"So why don't you?" I force myself to ask. My voice is shaky. I push the locket back to Shelley. I can't look anymore.

"Maybe one day," Shelley says. "That's what I keep telling myself. I'm still young enough."

A silence falls between us and I try to find the words to fill it but I can't.

"I'm sorry," Shelley says then. "I'm being insensitive. With everything you're going through, I shouldn't be talking about my marriage and wanting a child." The locket clicks shut in her hands and she fastens it at the back of her neck.

"It's OK," I say, although I'm not sure it is. Dylan's face floats in my thoughts. "I'm glad we have each other to talk to."

"What about you?" Shelley asks. "You didn't fancy more kids?"

The pain is instant and cuts deep into my chest, and suddenly Dylan is forgotten. "I did. We both did. I was so desperate for Jamie to have a little brother or sister, but it just never happened. It's one of those stupid things. I fell pregnant with Jamie instantly, but then when we actually tried, it never happened. I took it hard and blamed myself. We'd just decided to try IVF when Mark's mum died and we decided to move first. I was going to mention it again on my birthday . . ." My voice trails off.

Shelley lifts the tray of melting ice cream away and slides it to the other side of the sofa, budging closer to me until our shoulders are touching and I can feel the warmth of her body against my own. We watch the rest of the film in companionable silence.

"It's really coming down out there," Shelley says, stretching her arms up and arching her back as her words trail into a long yawn.

I blink and realize the end credits are rolling up the screen. I have the strange sensation of waking up from a doze, except I wasn't asleep. I glance at the window and watch raindrops trickling down the black glass in long snail lines. Every few moments a gust of wind rattles the glass inside the rotting window frame, blasting a spattering spray of raindrops against the pane and making me wish I hadn't been quite so hasty in ripping down the moldy curtains on moving day.

"I'd better go," Shelley says. "Tim will be starting to worry." She reaches for her phone and scrolls down the screen. "Or not," she mutters. "He's just texted me to say he's had a few too many drinks and is staying at the hotel by the golf club." There's a bitterness to Shelley's voice that I've never heard before.

I'm about to ask Shelley if she's all right but she gets there first. "Do you mind if I make us hot chocolates before I go? I could do with the sugar before driving in the dark." Shelley stifles another yawn as she stands and rubs her hands over her arms with a shiver. "I didn't realize how cold I was getting."

Shelley's yawn is catching. It sweeps over me and I feel the weight of exhaustion pulling me down. I'm desperate to crawl upstairs and drop into bed while I still have enough energy to move, but after all Shelley has done for us I can't say no.

"Sounds good," I say. "But let me do it."

"No, I'll go. You sit for a minute. You look beat."

I am beat, I think, slumping my head against the sofa.

Do you think I'll ever laugh properly again, Mark?

Of course you will, Tessie. You love to laugh.

I loved how you made me laugh. Nothing made me laugh like you did. And now you're gone. The film was funny, proper laugh-out-loud funny, but I barely mustered a smile. Right now, I can't imagine ever laughing again.

You will. Just give it time.

Shelley returns with two steaming mugs. She's fetched her bag from the kitchen and drops it down beside her feet as she slides onto the sofa and hands me the lion mug you bought me from the zoo that time. *"It reminds me of you,"* you laughed, nodding at my curls. I can hear your laughter in my head. I miss your laugh. I hug the mug of hot chocolate closer to my body, feeling cold to my core. I wonder what animal you'd choose if you could see me now.

"Tess, can I ask a favor?" Shelley says, blowing on her mug.

"Of course."

"Would you mind if I stayed on your sofa again? I wouldn't normally ask but I'm shattered and don't fancy driving back to Ipswich in that." Shelley nods to the window and the spatter of rain filling the silence.

"Oh . . . of course. I didn't realize how late it was getting. I shouldn't have kept you. I'm so sorry."

"Don't be sorry. It was my idea to watch the film. I think I needed a girly evening more than you did." She looks at me and I feel a pinprick of warmth inside me. I've missed having someone to spend my evenings with. Even if it is just one. "Tim and I haven't been getting on too well lately, which I guess is why he's staying at the golf club tonight. Every time we see each other we seem to argue. I don't fancy going home to an empty house. But if it's a problem—"

"No, of course it's not," I say. "I can unearth the spare bed from the boxes in one of the upstairs rooms."

"Oh, no, don't do that. Your sofa is perfectly fine; better than fine, in fact. Staying will save me part of my journey to the pool in the morning too. Thank you."

"Anytime. It's the least I can do," I say, glad Shelley is happy on the sofa. The thought of clearing space in one of the bedrooms makes my muscles ache, but I will do it soon. Maybe tomorrow, just not now, not tonight when I feel so tired. "I'll get some pillows and a blanket."

"Hang on," Shelley says. "I wanted to ask about last week and our trip to Manningtree. How are you feeling about what happened?"

I wonder if Shelley is talking about the man in the black baseball cap who followed me, or my panic attack in the shop, but I don't ask. What difference does it all make now?

The more days that pass, the more the moths feast on my memories, the less real it all seems. "I'm fine. I think you're probably right. I think it was just in my head."

Shelley nods. "It happens, Tess."

"I'll get you some bedding." I make a move to stand but Shelley's hand is on my arm.

"In a minute. Drink your hot chocolate while it's still hot," she says.

So I do.

CHAPTER 30

Thursday, March 15

---

24 DAYS TO JAMIE'S BIRTHDAY

I am yanked from the depths of sleep suddenly and unwilling. My eyes feel sewn shut. I listen for the noise of whatever disturbed me but there is only silence. Sleep is already dragging me back into its depths but somewhere in the deep fog I know something woke me.

The faceless man in Manningtree flashes behind my eyes and I force them open and stare out into the pitch-black room.

My fingers fumble for my phone. I squint against the bright light of the display screen until I register the time: 3:05 a.m. I should check on Jamie. I wonder if he's fallen out of bed like he did on his first night in this house, when he turned in his sleep, expecting to meet the wall of his small bedroom in Chelmsford and finding the floor of his new bedroom instead.

I feel dopey as I fumble out of the covers I'm twisted in and stumble to the floor. Goose bumps crawl like insects over my skin but the cold does nothing to shake the thick film of sleep.

The hall is swaying—a boat on choppy seas—one way, then the other. Except it's not the walls and the floor that are moving, it's me. I am the one swaying. I cling to the wall with both hands, planting my bare feet one after the other, fighting the vertigo that is pushing me downward.

I'm aware of a growing panic in the back of my mind. Something is wrong with me. But the thought is hidden behind a wall of thick fog.

It's only when I slump my weight against the doorframe of Jamie's room that I hear her voice and the soft, mellifluous lullaby she is singing.

Jamie's blue nightlight seems too bright against the black hallway as I push open the door and blink the room into focus.

Shelley is sitting on the edge of Jamie's bed. His eyes are closed but I can't tell if he's asleep or awake.

Shelley's face in the soft light is angelic and loving as she stares down at our son and starts to sing again.

> *"Your mumma loves you, oh yes I do*
> *I'll always be with you whenever you fall*
> *I'll pick you up, I'll help you out*
> *Never have a single doubt that your mumma loves you,*
> *oh yes I do*
> *Your mumma loves you, oh yes I do"*

The tune is enchanting and I'm mesmerized, dumbfounded by the sweetness. Then the words filter into my consciousness and I must make a sound in my throat because Shelley's head jerks around, her eyes no longer filled with love but with something dark and hateful.

The awareness is back—something is very wrong—but it is no longer hidden in the haze of sleep but staring at me with black eyes that make the room spin like a carousel before me. My hand fumbles for the doorframe but all I find is empty space and suddenly I'm falling to the floor and into a cloying darkness.

The next time I wake I am not dragged from sleep but clawing my way out of it. A heady dopiness cloaks my waking thoughts, making the memory of the night feel dreamlike.

My mouth is bone-dry and it hurts to swallow. I touch a finger to my lips and find them cracked and sore.

I look around me for a glass of water but all I see is my phone on the bedside table. Just then it vibrates against the wood. My arm feels achy and heavy as I reach for it and focus my eyes on the message from Shelley: Hey Tess, thanks again for letting me crash on the sofa. I had a really nice evening! Sorry to leave so early. I'm getting a swim in before work. xx P.S. You never told me you sleepwalked. I found you wandering the upstairs in the early hours.

She signs off with a kiss and an emoji of a grinning face with laughter tears sprouting from its eyes.

So it was a dream, I realize with a sigh of relief. I sleepwalked and dreamed the whole thing. I haven't done that since I was a child and my mum would tell me in the morning how she'd found me in the kitchen in my nightie. I wonder if it's the grief dredging up the old habit, or a side effect of the antidepressants.

The dopiness lingers all day, but at least the medication seems to be kicking in. Despite the strange headiness, I feel OK. I'll take feeling dizzy over the deep pit of despair I was living in yesterday. The pit isn't gone. It is still there, lingering on the outskirts of my thoughts as if I might lose my balance at any moment and fall back into the darkness, but right now I'm in the light.

Jamie is so quiet after school today, and more and more I wonder what he's thinking. I ask, of course, in every way I can think of. "How was your day? Are you OK? Is anything bothering you? What are you thinking about? Are you missing Daddy a lot?"

The answer is the same each time—a moping shrug accompanied with a sad sort of smile and a glance over his shoulder as if he can't wait to be somewhere else, anywhere else but with me.

He shut himself away in his room the minute we were home from school, and I find myself making excuses to go upstairs and walk past his closed door again and again. I guess I'm listening for crying, but it's not tears I hear coming from behind the closed door now, it's humming. A soft little tune that makes my feet stop dead and my mouth run dry. I hold my breath listening to the tune, willing myself to be wrong. Shivers travel in waves over my body. I'm not wrong.

I know that tune.

I remember the words too. I heard them last night. *"Your mumma loves you, oh yes I do."*

How does Jamie know the tune if it was just a dream?

I think of the hot chocolate Shelley gave me, the one she insisted on making. Did she slip something into it? A sleeping pill to knock me out? I try to remember if it tasted any different, but I can't. My memory of yesterday is patchy. Why did Shelley come over? Did I invite her? A scream swirls in my throat. I don't remember. I don't remember Jamie sitting with us. I don't remember putting him to bed. The only image in my mind is Shelley and the cold hateful eyes that turned on me.

That night I stare at the pages of my notebook, searching for the answer that I can feel is there. What am I not seeing?

I add several lines: *Jamie is more quiet than usual.*

Found Shelley in Jamie's room in the middle of the night. She was singing to Jamie. Why?

Guilt pricks my insides rereading my own words. After everything Shelley has done for me I shouldn't be questioning *why* Shelley was in Jamie's room. I should be asking *if* she was in Jamie's room. Right now I trust Shelley more than my own memories.

I see the photo of Dylan in my mind and try to imagine the helplessness she must have felt watching him lose his fight with cancer. My throat aches thinking of her loss. Four years on and she seems so strong. Will I feel that strong in four years' time? Will I have found a way to cope without you, Mark?

Of course you will, Tessie baby.

I can't see how.

I stare at the final lines on the page before crossing them out, running the pen back and forth until the ink is shiny and the paper worn.

CHAPTER 31

IAN

The whole thing was weird. This woman appearing out of nowhere and inserting herself into Tess's life. You really have to ask yourself why someone would do that.

SHELLEY

It was about a week later when I ended up staying the night again. There was a horrible storm. It hadn't stopped raining all evening. I knew the lanes out of the village would be flooded and I didn't want to drive home, so I stayed. Tess was fine with it and she'd been really down that day too. I thought it would help to have someone else there. I woke in the middle of the night feeling a bit spooked by the old house, so yes, I went upstairs to check that everything was all right. I don't know why, but I went into Jamie's room and sat on his bed for a while. It was a mistake, but that photo—the fridge magnet—Jamie looked so much like Dylan in that photo. I felt connected to him. I heard Tess on the landing. She was sleepwalking, so I put her back to bed.

CHAPTER 32

Transcript BETWEEN ELLIOT SADLER (ES) AND TERESA CLARKE (TC) (INPATIENT AT OAKLANDS HOSPITAL, HARTFIELD WARD), WEDNESDAY, APRIL 11. SESSION 2 (Cont.)

ES: Are you happy to continue now, Tess?

TC: Of course. It wasn't me who wanted a break in the first place. Is there any news? Have you found Jamie? What has Shelley said? Did she tell you she had a child who died? A little boy. He'd have been Jamie's age now.

ES: Someone will be bringing in your notebook shortly. Why don't we start now with Mark's plane crash. Can you tell me why he was going to Frankfurt?

TC: Why does that matter? You're here to find Jamie. The plane crash has nothing to do with it.

ES: This is a complicated situation we're in here, Tess. I think it would be prudent to start from the beginning with the plane crash.

TC: (Mumbles)

ES: Pardon?

TC: (Sigh) The beginning wasn't the plane crash, it was the day Shelley knocked on my door. She has Jamie. I'm sure of it.

ES: Humor me. What was the reason for Mark's trip to Frankfurt?

TC: (pause) It was nothing important. Some kind of away-day team-building thing. Mark moved from software programming into the sales team just before Jamie was born. There were a lot of motivational events. It was canceled. Have I told you that already?

ES: What was?

TC: The event Mark was going to. The people in Frankfurt had the flu. Mark didn't even need to get on the plane.

ES: There wasn't a special reason for this particular trip?

TC: I made a Batman cake.

ES: Excuse me?

TC: You wanted to know about Jamie's birthday, so I'm telling you. I made a chocolate sponge. Jamie hates plain sponge with jam, so I made chocolate. I cheated and bought slabs of black and yellow icing that you roll out. The yellow bat wings were a bit wonky but he loved it. I bought him the *Millennium Falcon* Lego set. It's huge. It will take weeks to build.

ES: What happened that day?

TC: Please find Jamie. He isn't safe. I can feel it.

ES: Who stabbed you, Tess?

TC: (Silence)

ES: Let's take another break.

CHAPTER 33

Monday, March 19

20 DAYS TO JAMIE'S BIRTHDAY

I don't know where the weekend has gone. Only that it has gone—a blur of playing in the garden, sleepless nights, and dozing on the sofa in the afternoons while Jamie watched TV.

We've not seen Shelley since the night she stayed over, but she's called me every evening.

The more we've spoken, the more certain I am that I was dreaming that night when I thought Shelley was in Jamie's room. She's our friend, Mark. She has no reason to sing to Jamie like that, no reason to stare at me with hateful eyes.

I only heard Jamie hum the lullaby once. In my dizzy exhausted state I could've imagined that too. Or maybe he heard the tune from me.

You've always been a bit of a hummer, Tessie.

Exactly. Most of the time I don't know I'm doing it.

I know. It drove me up the wall.

Sometimes when Shelley calls it's just for a quick "hi," a rundown of our days, and other times it's something more. Last night she told me about Dylan's cancer. How they'd had every diagnosis imaginable before the real one. Growing pains, anemia, rickets, flu. Weeks of doctors' appointments before X-rays were offered and the cancer found, the battle started. I could tell she was crying on the other end of the phone, and it made me cry too.

"I miss him so much some days, Tess. I'm supposed to help people who are grieving, but sometimes I want to tell them it won't get easier, it'll get harder, because you'll start to forget what they smelled like and the sound of their voice."

"Oh, Shelley," I said, because what words of comfort could I possibly offer?

"Hey," she said then, her voice bouncing once more. "I meant to say I've got a free morning tomorrow. I was planning to hit the pool and go food shopping on the way back. Why don't I pick you up and we can do a shop together? We can keep each other company."

I smiled down the phone. Trust Shelley to make it sound like I'm doing her a favor when really it's the other way round. I haven't left the village for over a week—since Manningtree and the man in the black baseball cap who almost grabbed me, and then in the shop when my lungs stopped taking in air. Every time I've thought about nipping to Tesco or even to the store in the next village, I've heard Shelley's warning in my head. *"If this happens again and you're alone it could be much scarier for you."*

"Good idea," I replied.

We were in Tesco for hours. Not that I minded. Shelley made it fun as always. We pushed our trolleys along, side by side, nattering away like two old grannies. Shelley ignored my list and filled my trolley with loads more than we needed, and enough vegetables to feed a football team.

"I think that's the best fun I've had shopping for food my whole life," Shelley says as the wheels of her Mini crunch on our driveway. The back seats are crammed with bags and there are more in the boot, half Shelley's and half mine.

"Me too." Jamie will be cross to have missed it, even if it was a trip to Tesco, which he usually hates. "Thank you. Do you want to come in for a cuppa?" I ask, trying to sound casual, trying to keep the desperation from my voice. I'm not ready to be alone yet.

Shelley glances at her watch and pulls a face. "I'd better not. I'm seeing a client in an hour. The poor man lost his wife of sixty years to Alzheimer's disease last month. I'll give you a hand getting the stuff in, then I'd better scoot off."

"Oh . . . OK." I nod, my voice betraying me.

"Tim is out tonight at some work thing. Why don't I come back for dinner and help you eat some of this food?"

"You don't have to do that. I'm sure you've got better things to do."

"Don't be daft." She reaches over and squeezes my hand and I feel her energy diffuse into my body. I stare at Shelley for a moment and take in her face and her smile, so full of kindness, and I'm absolutely certain that the other night was a dream.

"I want to," Shelley adds, opening the car door and letting the scent of dewy grass and freshness fill my senses.

"How are things with Tim?" I ask.

"The same." She sighs. "We're doing a very good job of avoiding each other at the moment. We need to sit down and talk our problems through, but I don't think either of us is ready for it, which is another reason why dinner with you tonight would be great."

"Ok. I'll make a paella for the three of us," I say as Shelley ducks her head into the back of the car and reappears with my shopping bags. Jamie will be so excited. He hasn't stopped asking when he'll see Shelley again.

Together, we lug the shopping to the porch and dump it down, two bags at a time. Ten bags in total. Shelley steps back to the car to shut the boot and I unlock the side door, giving it a shove with my shoulder until it opens.

The moment I step into the kitchen I know something is wrong.

It's subtle—the littlest thing—and if Shelley had been behind me chatting away, I probably wouldn't have noticed the kitchen door. The door I shut on my way out to keep the draft from the side door sweeping through the house. The kitchen door that is now wide open into the hall.

I freeze. The weight of the carrier bags digs into my fingers and I drop them to the floor. A glass jar hits the tiles with a crack, but still I don't move.

Someone has been in our house, Mark.

Flashes of memory strobe though my thoughts. I see the faceless man lurking in the doorway in Manningtree. Me running on the slippery cobbles. He was chasing me, I know it. I hear the gravelly voice on the answerphone, full of menace and threat, and feel myself huddled on the floor in your cold dark study. The weeks have dulled my fear, but it's back, digging its claws right into the pit of my stomach.

Stop, Tessie. It'll be OK.

I hold my breath, listening for any creak, any noise, out of place among the usual groans of the house.

"Tess?" Shelley's voice slices through the silence. "What's wrong?"

"Someone's been here."

"What do you mean?"

"Someone's been here while we were out. I shut the kitchen door and now it's open." Hearing the words aloud I realize how ridiculous I sound. But it's more than the door; there's a feeling too. Something in the air, the stillness of the house being disturbed, that I can't describe. And a faint odor I can almost smell.

"Right, let's walk through the house," Shelley says, giving my arm a nudge. "We won't touch anything, we'll just look and see what's missing."

"Should we call the police?"

"They'll ask what's been taken. We should take a quick look first."

"Of course." I nod and swallow the mounting fear.

We wander through the downstairs together, looking for anything missing. I'm looking for anything different too. Did I leave the cushion fallen on the sofa like that? Did I leave the dining room chair pulled out?

It's only when we reach the top of the stairs and turn onto the landing that I'm certain. Your study door is wide open, adding a chill to the upstairs. I can see all the way to the window and Jamie's tree house in the garden. I always shut that door.

"I didn't leave that door open either," I whisper. "The radiator is broken. I always shut the door or the whole of the upstairs gets cold."

My heartbeat hammers in my chest and I want to run and wait for the police, but Shelley pulls me forward.

The room looks like it always does. The boxes are stacked neatly against the wall by the door, the phone balanced on top of the first box. The bookshelves are still bare. Dust is floating in the room like a miniature snowstorm.

"Has anything been taken?" Shelley asks.

"I . . . I don't think so." My eyes are fixed on the boxes. Something isn't right. They are pushed up against the wall, just as they were the last time I came in here, but something is different. Then I see it—the writing isn't there. Where is your swirling handwriting that reads *Mark's study*?

"The boxes," I cry out. "They've been moved."

"Are you sure?"

"Yes."

"OK. Take a look through them and see what's missing. I just need to call my client to tell him I'm running late, then we'll call the police."

I nod and sink to my knees.

I pull at the lid of the first box and realize how futile this is. How can I tell what's missing when I don't have the first clue what was in them to start with?

The box is filled with papers and programming manuals. It's a mess. Everything is jumbled up and it looks like a recycling bin, but maybe you left it that way. Right on top of the pile, lying there like it's waiting to be discovered, is a glossy yellow folder. The words *Life Insurance Policy* are printed in blue across the front.

Ian's words ring in my ears. *"I know there's a death benefit from Mark's job, and a life insurance policy. He declared it all when you made your wills."*

I back out of the room and shut the door, breathing hard and wishing I hadn't opened the box. I know you're not coming back, Mark, but the policy makes it too final somehow. I'm not ready.

The walls of the hallway push toward me. My breath catches in my throat in short suffocating gasps. A dizziness spins in my head. I can't lose it again. I can't. I race down the main stairs to find Shelley. But she's not in the house. She's outside the side door, standing in the porch.

Her back is to me and she's talking on the phone. I'm about to step away and let her finish when she speaks.

"What did you think you were doing?" Shelley says, her voice hissing into the phone. "Are you purposefully trying to mess this up? Because if you are, then well done, you're doing a great job."

I've never heard her speak like this before. Her tone is sharp, each word punching the air.

Who is she talking to? Not a client, surely.

"Stay away from her. Do you understand? . . . I can't talk about it now."

Shelley ends the call and I back away from the door, tripping on the shopping bags and sending an apple rolling across the kitchen tiles.

"Was anything missing?" Shelley asks as I'm collecting the spilled fruit. There's a residue of the anger to her voice and I spin around, feeling guilty for listening, but curious too. Her porcelain skin is flushed a pale pink.

Who was she talking to? And who was she talking about?

"Huh? Oh, I . . . I couldn't tell. I'm sorry to mess your plans up this afternoon. Was your client OK about the delay?" I ask, hoping my question will prompt Shelley to explain the phone call I overheard.

"Oh, I couldn't get through, so I've sent a text, but it's fine, Tess," she says, her voice softening. "Come sit down for a second." Shelley points to a chair, and I do as I'm told. She takes my hand and looks right at me with her green eyes.

"When we walked through the house," she says, "I checked the front door and all of the windows and they were all shut and locked. Was the side door definitely locked when you came in?"

"Yes. I remember unlocking it. It's not an easy door to open."

She nods. "I'm just wondering how someone might've got in? And what they wanted when there's nothing missing."

"You think I'm making it up?"

She shakes her head, swishing her blond hair from side to side. "Not on purpose, but I think our minds have a way of playing tricks on us. You've been through so much, Tess. It's natural to feel scared and to worry about being alone."

"I'm not scared. I mean, I am but that's because there have been other things happening."

"What things?" Shelley frowns beneath her bangs.

I hesitate, suddenly reluctant to tell her, but I have to. Shelley is the only one I trust. She'll know what to do. "There have been hang-up calls to the house every day and . . . a man left a threatening message on the answerphone. Here, I'll show you—" I leap up and head to the dining room.

"Tess, it's OK, I'm not doubting you," Shelley calls after me.

She is, but I understand why. I'm not sure I believe me half the time, but the answerphone message exists, and now that I've started telling Shelley, I'm desperate for her to hear it.

"Just listen," I say, pressing play on the machine.

There's a beep and the room is filled with the sound of the electronic voice: "You have no new messages."

"What?" I jab the answerphone again and the same message plays.

"It was here." Tears blur my vision and my voice drops to a whisper. "It was."

Could I have deleted it without realizing? Maybe Jamie fiddled with the buttons and deleted it by accident.

"Tess," Shelley says.

I shake my head. "It's OK. I know. I'm letting my imagination get the better of me."

It's a lie for me as much as for Shelley. The answerphone message was real; so was the faceless man in the baseball cap. Someone has been in this house, and they may not have taken anything but they were looking for something. I'm sure of it. Maybe it was the intruder who deleted the message.

But if I try to tell Shelley all this it will only make her worry more. I have to figure this out for myself.

"I think I need to lie down," I say. "You'd better get to your client anyway."

"Are you sure, Tess? I can stay."

"I'm fine, honestly. I've not been sleeping, that's all."

"Call me if anything else happens," Shelley says in the doorway, hugging me tight. "It will be OK. I'll see you later."

I nod and shut the door, bolting it from the inside. Then I dig in my bag for my phone and find a local locksmith. They're coming first thing tomorrow to change the locks. Part of me knows Shelley could be right, but there's another part of me that knows I shut those doors. I walk through the house again, smelling the air as I go. If I'm sure the door was locked, and nobody broke in, then that means someone let themselves in.

Who has a key to this house, Mark?

You did, of course, but that has been burned to smithereens. And I do. Shelley has one too, but I know it wasn't her, because she was with me in Tesco. Who else?

We didn't change the locks after we moved. This house belonged to your mother; it's where you and Ian grew up.

Ian must have a key. It must have been him. But why?

CHAPTER 34

Shelley texts me at six p.m.: Accident on A12. Stuck in traffic.

By the time she arrives, bottle of wine in hand, the paella is overcooked and Jamie is already in bed reading a book.

"For you," she says, handing me the white wine. "After the day you've had I thought you might need it."

"Thank you." My fingers touch the green bottle. The glass is cold on my fingertips and I imagine the tang of citrus on my tongue and the heady hit of alcohol to my head.

"Fancy a glass now?" Shelley raises an eyebrow and grins.

"Er . . ." I pull a face. "I want to, but I don't think it's a good idea. I'm barely hanging on as it is. I doubt drinking wine will help."

"You're doing brilliantly, Tess," Shelley says, wedging the wine in the fridge between two packets of cheese and a bag of spinach. "We'll have this another time."

"Thanks."

Shelley turns, her eyes finding mine. "Are you all right? Has anything else happened since I left? I've been so worried. I wish I hadn't left you."

Me too, but I shake my head. "I'm fine. It was probably my imagination running away with me."

I don't believe it but it's easier to pretend than to tell Shelley that I think it was Ian. I need to figure out what he is up to before I tell her, I decide, thinking of the doubt on Shelley's face when I tried to show her the answerphone message. The one I'm now sure Ian deleted.

Shelley opens her mouth to say something more but for once I get there first. "I hope this will be OK." I motion at the pan on the stove filled with heaps of yellow rice and meat and vegetables. "I've made too much. We'll be eating it for weeks."

"It smells lovely, and I'm so hungry it could taste like cardboard and I'd still eat it," she jokes.

"Hey, what are you saying about my cooking?" I reply and we both smile.

"I'll just go wash up quickly." Shelley moves toward the door and slips into the hall.

The paella has stuck to the pan and it seems to take forever to scrape it off and stir it around on the low heat. Shelley hasn't returned by the time it's ready again. I don't know what makes me go looking for her instead of just calling through the doorway, but I do.

I find Shelley upstairs, creeping out of Jamie's room.

"What are you doing?" My voice is low, barely above a whisper, but Shelley jumps and turns to face me.

"Oh, I . . . I didn't mean to intrude. I'm sorry, Tess. I thought I heard something."

I push past Shelley and peer into Jamie's room. Jamie's bedside light is on and he's flicking through his *Where's Wally?* book. He looks up at me and smiles a beautiful smile.

The anger disappears and I realize how rude I must've sounded. "Sorry." I sigh. "It's just I'm a bit overprotective right now. Today has been a challenge."

"It's fine, Tess. Completely natural. I should've asked first."

She rubs my arm and tears leak from my eyes. I'm so fed up with crying, Mark. I wish you were here right now.

Me too, Tessie. I love you.

"Come on," Shelley says, "let's go eat. Oh, before I forget," she adds as I follow her down the stairs. "Your mum wanted me to tell you that she's thinking of you and that she loves you."

"Thanks. Maybe I'll give her a call tomorrow."

There's a pause before Shelley speaks. "That's a really good idea. I'm really pleased you're feeling up to speaking to your mum. I know how draining it can be reassuring loved ones when you're the one who needs reassuring."

"Oh" is all I say. Shelley is right. Speaking to Mum will sap my energy, and I know I'll feel guilty when I hear her voice. I used to visit every few weeks. Help around the house and take her out for lunch at a seafront café she likes. I don't even have the capacity to think about how she's doing, how she's coping without my visits. "Maybe next week," I add.

I should call Sam too. I can't remember the last time we spoke. I know my family are worried about me but I don't know what to tell them.

Shelley squeezes my hand. "I'm here for you, whatever you need, OK?"

I nod and we sit down to eat.

Later, when Shelley has gone and the house feels like the loneliest place in the world, I wrap the duvet around myself and write in the notebook: *Someone came into the house. Nothing taken. Were they looking for something? Did they find it? Will they come back? Answerphone message deleted—who did it? Why?*

I flick back through the pages and try to add meaning to my notes, but all I find are more questions. The hang-up calls have stopped, I think. The man hasn't phoned back. I wish I knew what it meant, Mark. I feel like the answer is here, in the pages, but I just can't see it.

Stop, Tessie. Go to sleep now, baby.

Remember last summer when we camped in the garden with Jamie? The tent was too big for our garden in Chelmsford. Jamie was so excited he didn't fall asleep until after midnight. But we stayed awake even longer, whispering quietly to each other. Making plans. I miss making plans with you, Mark.

CHAPTER 35

IAN

It was impossible to get through to Tess when Shelley was there all the time, whispering in her ear. I even wondered at one point if she'd moved in with Tess. It was frustrating. Anyone in my situation would've felt the same. There was no way Mark would've wanted things to drag on like they did. The probate needed to be started and instead Tess was walking around the village in the pouring rain.

Clearly things were not right, but I didn't know who to talk to about it. Her mother is an old bat and lives miles away. She has a brother somewhere, I seem to remember, but I didn't have any contact details for him and I couldn't exactly see Tess giving me his number. The only friend I knew of was Shelley, and considering she was the problem, I wasn't going to speak to her about it. I thought things would sort themselves out. Obviously with hindsight I would do things differently, but the fact that it was Jamie's birthday was irrelevant.

SHELLEY

After that Tess started doing better. She was getting dressed and taking care of herself more. She was far from OK but there were definite steps in the right direction. She was opening up to me and seemed so much more with-it than when I first met her.

We spoke all the time. It meant something to both of us. There was one awkward moment when I went in to Jamie's room again while Tess was sorting out dinner. I didn't think she'd mind. I was only in there for a moment, but she did mind—understandably, she's protective of him. I should've asked first. I thought I heard a noise, that's why I went in there. But we got over it. The next time I saw her we were fine. I was the person she called when she was in trouble, so obviously she trusted me.

CHAPTER 36

Thursday, March 22

17 DAYS TO JAMIE'S BIRTHDAY

The locksmith couldn't fit new locks. "They come as standard, you see," he said yesterday morning, turning up half an hour late for the appointment, not that it mattered to me. I wasn't going anywhere.

He was a squat man with more beard than hair on his head and skin a touch too red to be healthy. "Give me any door and I can offer you ten different lock types, but not for the listed buildings like this. Grade two listed, isn't it? Sixteenth century? It's a different lock size, ergo I don't keep them in the van, ergo I'll need to order and come back. Should be a couple of days. When is a good time?"

I told him anytime and resisted using the word *ergo* in my reply.

So when the front door knocker clanged against the oak and echoed through the empty house, jolting me from my doze on the sofa, I thought it was the locksmith back with the right-sized locks, or the postman with the new PlayStation games I ordered for Jamie's birthday.

It was neither.

"Hey, sis." Sam grins from the doorstep as I heave open the door.

"Sam," I yelp and smile all at once, before throwing myself into his arms. A dam breaks inside me and before I can hold it back I'm sobbing great gulping sobs in his arms.

When I pull away I see Sam is crying too and it makes me love him all the more.

"I'm so sorry this has happened to you, sis," he says. "I should've come sooner. I should never have left after the funeral. I'm sorry."

I wipe my fingers under my eyes. "It's OK. I'm doing OK, honestly I am."

"How?" His eyes are wide and watery and remind me of Jamie's.

I close my eyes and hot tears trickle onto my cheeks. "There are highs and lows," I whisper, thinking of Jamie's silence and his shrugged responses to my questions. I push the thoughts away and think of splashing in the puddle instead.

"Still weight lifting, I see," I add a moment later when it's clear that neither of us knows quite what to say next. I pinch one of his biceps, tight against his T-shirt. His jeans are fitted and his shoes smart. I guess Finn's style sense has finally rubbed off on Sam.

As I usher Sam into the hall I find myself glancing toward the empty lane and the fields beyond it and closing the door a little too quickly.

I turn my focus to Sam. He has changed so much since moving to Nottingham. He's not the beanpole with blond Einstein hair that he was when you first met him. Now his hair is shaved close to his head and he is broad-shouldered and muscular. But to me, Sam will always be the big brother who told me ghost stories at bedtime and showed me how to rub dock leaves on my skin when I fell off my bike into a ditch of stinging nettles.

"Still forgetting to brush your hair, I see," Sam retorts, flicking at my wayward curls.

"What are you doing here?" I ask.

Sam holds up his empty hands in a theatrical shrug. "If Mohammed won't come to the mountain, then the mountain will go to Mohammed."

I smile and shake my head. "I think it's the other way round."

"Anyway," Sam says, dragging out the word, "you weren't answering your phone, so I thought I'd take you out for lunch."

"So you just drove four hours for a sandwich?"

"Pretty much. It was that or have Mum keep phoning the hospital every day telling me how worried she is about you."

"She's not?" I pull a face. A needle of guilt pricks my stomach. "I'm sorry. She's been phoning my friend Shelley too."

"I know." He raises his eyebrows, mirroring my expression. "Grab your shoes, we're going out for lunch."

"I've got stuff here we can eat."

"I didn't really drive four hours for a ham and pickle sandwich, Tess. I fancy a burger. There's a restaurant in the village, isn't there?"

"Yes. It's at the top of the hill, bordering the next village. We'll have to drive."

"OK then, let's go."

"Give me a few minutes," I say, racing up the stairs to change out of the leggings I've been wearing all week.

"Don't take too long. I have to be back on the road by two," Sam calls up the stairs.

"Oh." Jamie will be disappointed. He barely sees Sam as it is.

"How's Finn?" I shout down, raking a brush through my hair.

"I'll let you know when I next see him properly. We're on different shift patterns at the moment. We pass on the doorstep for about five minutes every day, one of us on the way to work, the other to bed."

"I'm ready," I pant, running down the stairs a few minutes later and finding Sam sitting on the bottom step.

"Passable." He smiles. "It's good to see you."

Tears build in my eyes again and I nod. "You too." All of a sudden I'm glad Jamie is at school and it's just me and Sam. I don't have to carry the conversation along and pretend to be coping better than I am. I don't have to be a mum. I can just be me, whoever that is.

The restaurant is quiet and we choose a table in the corner by a long glass window that looks out to the gardens. Huge cowhides hang on the walls beside metal sculptures of birds and other creatures.

Sam orders the burger—a towerlike mountain of bread and meat with French fries in a silver pot on the side. I have fish and chips. The portion is huge but I eat until my stomach hurts. In between mouthfuls we bend our heads over the Sunday cryptic crossword that Sam produces from his pocket like a child with a stash of secret sweets to share.

I try my best to work through the clues. But my thoughts are clogged—a blocked sink—and the answers trickle out in between conversations about Mum, and about Finn and Sam and their life in Sheffield. We stay on safe ground in the restaurant. Neither of us mentions you, or how Jamie and I are coping, and I'm grateful for that.

"It's been so good to see you," I say as we step out into the cold afternoon light, my stomach aching with the addition of so much food. "You didn't need to come all this way."

"Yes, I did." Sam drops his arm around my shoulders and steers me to his car. It's an old Volvo, racing green with rusted dents. "You're an amazing woman, Tess. After what you've been through. . . ."

I nod but say nothing. My throat is aching and I feel the tears threatening. We've had such a nice lunch, I don't want to cry now. I clench my teeth together until the feeling passes.

"Will you come and see us soon?" Sam asks. "Might do you good to get out of the village for a week."

"Did Mum put you up to saying that?" I narrow my eyes but smile too. "She said the same thing."

"No, but I can see why she would. Rattling around in that old house all the time, it can't make things any easier."

"I . . . It's hard going out alone right now. The other week I had a sort of panic attack in a shop. If Shelley hadn't been there I don't know what I'd have done."

For a second I wonder if I should tell Sam about the man who chased me and the person who came into our house when I was out, but I don't. Shelley has been by my side this whole time and even she doesn't believe me. I picture her now, standing in the dining room doorway when the stupid electronic voice told me my messages were all gone. Her face said it all. And if she isn't sure, then what chance have I got of convincing Sam?

"It's Jamie's birthday in a couple of weeks," I say instead, turning my gaze toward the village and farmland below. The river has burst its banks and spilled out across the fields in one giant lake.

"I know," Sam says from behind me. "Will you be all right?"

"I guess so. It'll be hard." A stone settles in my chest thinking of Jamie's birthday without you. "I'll invite Shelley over." She'll make it more of a celebration than I ever could.

Sam doesn't reply but I sense he wants to say something, and I turn to face him. "What?" I ask.

"Look, don't shoot the messenger here, OK?"

"What?"

"It's just, remember that bloke that was hanging around Mum after Dad died?"

"Of course I do. He wouldn't leave her alone."

"You made me have a man-to-man chat about his intentions toward her." Sam pulls a face that makes me smile. "And it turned out he'd been in love with Mum for years and was desperate to step into Dad's shoes. Mum was horrified when we told her. She thought he was just being a good friend."

"So? What's that got to do with Shelley?" I feel myself bristle.

"Probably nothing. Look—I'm glad you've got a new friend helping you right now, but I just want you to be sure she's not after something else, that's all. You could be a wealthy woman now, Tess, and I don't want anyone taking advantage of you. Don't you think it's odd that she's asking Mum and me to call her rather than you? We're your family, you know."

"Only because I asked her to," I reply.

"Are you sure about that?"

"Yes." The truth is I can't remember, but if it was Shelley's idea to speak to Mum and Sam for me, then it was only because she was trying to help.

"OK then, but I'm still going to call you, whether you pick up or not."

I smile and we hug, long and tight. "I will answer, I promise. You don't need to worry. Shelley is a good friend, that's all. She doesn't want to fill Mark's shoes," I try to joke. "Ian gave me the same warning, by the way."

"Ian, Mark's brother?"

I nod. "He's been hounding me to get Mark's estate sorted out.

Apparently Mark borrowed some money from Ian and now he needs it back." A shiver travels over my skin thinking of Ian. I'm sure it was him who came into the house when I wasn't there.

"Would Mark have done that without telling you?"

I shrug. "Maybe. I'll figure it out."

"You will let me know if you want to talk about it or need help?" Sam asks, opening his car door. "I'm here for you, Tess. Please say you'll think about coming up to Nottingham for a visit?"

"Maybe in the summer. Let me get Jamie's birthday out of the way and we'll put a date in the diary."

Sam nods but I can tell he's still worried.

"You'd better hit the road," I say.

"Get in then."

"It's OK. I'll walk back."

"Are you sure?"

"It'll do me good." I'll walk slowly and take the long way around the village, and then it will be time to collect Jamie from school.

"Take care of yourself, sis."

"Thanks for coming," I say.

Sam jumps into his car. The engine whines for a moment before starting. As he pulls away he makes a phone sign with his fingers as he passes. I nod and wave and start walking.

On the walk into the village I think of the crossword questions and the feeling of the answers being just out of reach. My mind wanders to the notebook I keep beside the bed. The pages are filling up, but the harder I try to understand, the more questions I seem to have.

I can't keep living in the dark like this; I have to try to find the answers. Starting with the boxes in your study and why Ian was looking through them.

I didn't touch the boxes this afternoon. I had a dozen reasons, a dozen excuses, why tomorrow would be a better day to start. Maybe I was putting it off, or maybe seeing Sam wiped me out. The long walk back from the restaurant didn't help. I'm not exactly fit at the moment.

After school I let Jamie play on the PlayStation until his eyes went bleary. We picked at the leftover paella and watched *Tom and Jerry* episodes that were older than I am. I went to bed straight after reading to Jamie, cocooning myself up in my duvet and letting my eyes pull shut. It was the first night I've gone to bed without you that I thought I might actually sleep.

I was wrong.

CHAPTER 37

The phone rings. Right when I'm in that place between wake and sleep and I think it's a dream. The trilling noise rolling in my unconscious, prodding me, scaring me—another nightmare to add to the rest. But it's not. I open my eyes and blink in the darkness.

My hand flails on the covers, patting your side of the bed for my phone. When the display lights the room in a green-white glow I see it's not even nine o'clock.

I tilt my head and listen for a message, expecting and hoping it's Shelley, but there is only silence. Another hang-up. A slow fear trickles through my body. There is no way I can fall asleep now.

I thought they'd stopped, Mark.

It'll be a call center, Tessie. Mum complained all the time about them ringing all hours of the day and night, remember?

I guess.

I struggle out of bed and pad down the stairs, flicking lights on as I go. I need water and mindless TV to take my mind off the call and the fear now trickling through me. There must be a predictable action film on one of the three hundred channels we have access to. Or some kind of reality show. Anything with chatter and noise and life.

I'm in the kitchen gulping back a glass of water when the phone rings again. I don't move. I count the rings all the way to four and let the answerphone pick up. If it's Shelley, I'll answer.

"Tess?" His gravelly voice steals my breath. "I know you're there, Tess. I can see you in the kitchen. Pick up the phone."

The menace in his tone chills my blood as much as his words. He can see me. He's outside. I leap to the nook, expecting the side door to fly open. My slippers skid on the tiles, but I reach the door and check the bolt with shaking hands. It's locked. My heart is hammering hard enough to explode in my chest.

"Don't worry, Tess. I'm not coming in today," he says, his gravelly laugh carrying into the kitchen. "I just want to talk. Pick up the phone."

I move quickly past the window, my eyes scanning the driveway for movement, but all I see is darkness.

"Pick up," he barks again when I make it to the phone in the dining room.

My whole body is shaking. All I want to do is run up the stairs as fast as my legs can carry me and barricade myself in Jamie's room. But I can't. Our baby boy is sleeping in his bed and there's a man outside our house. There is nowhere to run.

"Who . . . who is this?" I stammer, pressing the phone to my ear.

"You husband has something of mine."

"Who is this?" I ask again in a voice stronger than I feel. I jerk my head to the dining room window. Can he see me? I step into the hallway and sink to the cold floor.

"I need it," he says.

"I don't know what you're talking about."

There's another croaky laugh. "I think you do, Tess. Your husband has got himself into a world of trouble and I think you know exactly what I'm talking about. Mark was working on something for me, and you're going to get it and give it back to me."

"I . . . I don't know what it is. Mark never talked to me about his work. I can't help you."

"You're a smart woman, you'll figure it out. You wouldn't want anything to happen to that darling child of yours."

"Leave my son out of it." The words tumble out at the same speed as the tears rolling down my face.

"Don't worry, I have no intention of hurting anyone." The malice in his voice says otherwise.

"I . . . I don't know anything. I swear I don't know what you're talking about."

"I'm sure you can figure it out, Tess."

"How do you know my name?" A scream forms in my throat, lodging against my larynx so every word is a fight to get out.

"I know everything about you. Now be a good girl and get me the file before my patience runs out."

"But—"

"No buts, Tessie." He drags out my name for several seconds before there's a click and the line is dead.

I drop the phone and shrink all the way to the floor until my cheek presses against the wood. The house is spinning and all I can hear is my breath dragging in and out. I can't get the air in, Mark. I can't breathe.

Stop, Tess. You can.

I can't.

Blotches of black creep across my eyes.

I can't breathe.

I'm going to die here.

You're not, Tessie. Remember the first time we met, at Stacey's housewarming party? You wore that black top with the glitter on it and

I was still in my suit. You asked me if I was the real estate agent who sold Stacey the house, and I asked if that was your chat-up line.

Keep talking.

There were too many of us crammed into a tiny living room and the music was so loud, the walls were vibrating. We found a quiet spot in the garden and talked all evening.

I knew the moment I saw you that it was something special.

Me too, Tessie. I felt it too. I was supposed to fly to Portugal the following Friday for a golf weekend with friends. I canceled the trip so I could see you instead.

I remember.

My breathing changes—each inhale takes a little longer. I sit up, cradling my head in my hands until the spinning stops.

I can still hear his voice, Mark. He called me Tessie. Why did you tell him that? You're the only one who has ever called me Tessie, and only when we were alone. It was ours and no one else's.

Do I call the police? He said you were in trouble, Mark. Is it the kind the police would ask about? The newspapers are still desperate for news about the crash. If they find out that one of the victims was breaking the law, they'd splash your photo over the front pages, drag you in the mud, and Jamie and me along with it. I can't do that to Jamie. I have to figure this out for myself.

I crawl on the floor, the wood hurting my knees as I move to the stairs. My body is shaking from the words of the man whose name I still don't know. I grab the banister and pull myself up.

I reach the study and flick on the light. The first box is sitting wonky, the lid not quite shut from the last time I looked in it.

I still don't know what I'm searching for, but I have to look, and properly this time.

His voice echoes in my head. *"I know everything about you . . . Mark was working on something for me."*

"But what?" I ask the empty room.

A hard drive? A USB stick? Whatever it is, if it's in this house, then it has to be in one of these boxes.

I leave the first box, the one your life insurance policy is in, and take the second one instead. Piece by piece I unpack each box, making piles of books, and papers, and computer equipment. There are several CDs, but they are all labeled, dating back years ago to when you were in college.

The threadbare carpet has disappeared by the time I open the final box, the one with your life insurance in it. This one is more personal. There are mortgage statements from the house in Chelmsford, and utility bills, bank statements, and insurance stuff for the house. No hard drives or USB sticks. Nothing I can find that would store a file on it.

The yellow life insurance policy folder is in one hand, the bank statements in the other, and I stare at the empty boxes and the mess. There is nothing here; nothing that the man could want anyway.

I shiver and switch off the light before stepping back to our bedroom and the warmth of our duvet.

Bank statements first, I decide, pushing the yellow folder out of sight under my pillow as if the tooth fairy might come along and whisk it away for me.

It's time to find Ian's money and why you needed it in the first place. It has to be connected to this man and his threats.

I cover the bed in a sea of paper. Every page looks the same, with neat, typed lines, double sided, two columns of numbers on the right—money in, money out. The joint account is simple enough. You put money in at the start of the month and the balance trickled down with each tank of petrol and food shop. I had the money from my GCSE and SATs tutoring going in too but it wasn't much—£60 each week, sometimes less.

There are a few odd purchases I don't recognize at first. Sanchez's for £65; £20 at a bespoke jeweler in Chelmsford. I grab my phone and Google the businesses, remembering as the page loads that I went out for dinner with the Chelmsford mums for Julie's birthday last September. The evening doubled as a farewell party for me. I bought Julie a pair of earrings as a birthday gift. It was a different lifetime from the one I'm living in now.

Money in. Money out. Amazon, Tesco, petrol. Repeat. Repeat. Repeat. There are no answers in these statements, just a realization of how mundane my life was, and how separate you kept your finances. Aside from putting money into it each month, you didn't use the joint account for anything other than the odd family dinner out and utility bills.

But if my life was boring, yours was too. Your personal account is no different. There's one entry in the money-in column each month. The amount varies each time, which makes sense, I guess. Commissions paid on top of your basic salary paid directly to you before transferring a chunk of it into the joint account. I wonder why you did it that way, why you didn't have your salary paid directly into an account for both of us to use. It's as though you wanted to keep me separate.

I stare at the monthly salary amount. It's more than I thought. We skipped, hell, we jumped right over so many stages in our relationship when I got pregnant with Jamie. We never did the weekend away, the meet the parents, the first fight, not until we were all in anyway. I'm not sure if discussing each other's salaries counts as a relationship stage, but either way we hopped right over it.

Your expenditure column is as boring as mine. There are tiny payments at coffee shops, and higher amounts in pubs. A round or two bought on a Friday night. Seventy pounds spent in December in the shop where you buy your shirts. I remember you bringing them home in an oversized paper carrier bag.

There are some cash withdrawals too, but never for any startling amounts. You always liked to have cash in your wallet, unlike me, who put everything on a card.

There is nothing out of the ordinary. There are no answers here; no sign of Ian's money either.

I told you not to worry, Tessie.

Not to worry? What about the man who for all I know is still standing outside our house? How can you tell me not to worry?

I flop back onto the pillow, sending paper floating to the floor. There's a crinkling noise beneath my head and I remember the life insurance policy. I close my eyes and reach until my fingers touch the folder.

There's no point putting it off any longer.

I open the folder at the same time as I open my eyes, scanning the words until I find what I'm looking for.

POLICY AMOUNT: £2,000,000

I blink, forcing my gaze to refocus and look again. Surely it's two hundred thousand, not two million? It's startling. It's unbelievable, in fact. It's enough to pay off the mortgage, it's enough forever. It's enough to pay your brother without breaking a sweat.

Two million, Mark. How is that possible? I feel like I should've known. It must have been mentioned when we made our wills. I wish I'd paid more attention that day. I really didn't think it mattered. I didn't think we'd need them.

I'm not sure what I'm supposed to feel—relief? I'll never have to work again. I'll never have to worry about money, which I guess was why you did it. But every penny is a reminder of what we've lost—you, me, and Jamie. There is no amount that can make up for losing you, Mark.

I had to try though, Tessie. I couldn't have you worry all the time.

Oh, Mark. What good is money if Jamie's life is in danger? Whatever this man wants, I don't have it.

I snatch the notebook from the bedside table and flick through the pages. The answer is here, I'm sure of it. I stop at Ian's name, circled in shiny black pen. Where is his money?

My phone is still gripped in my hand. Before I can think too much about it I call Ian's number.

"Tess, hi," Ian says. His voice is groggy.

"Sorry, did I wake you?"

"It's fine." There's a shuffling in the background and I picture him sitting up in bed. "Are you OK?"

"Yes . . . I just . . . I've got our bank statements in front of me."

"Good," he replies. I wonder how much self-will it took him not to add "about time too."

"But I can't see any sign of the money you lent Mark."

There's a pause.

"Ian?" I say.

"I'm here. Maybe there's another account."

"I don't think so. I've gone through all the financial stuff and there are only statements for two accounts going back since before your mum died. You said it was after that, didn't you?"

"Um."

"Do you have the account number Mark gave you?"

"I wrote a check."

"Oh."

"It wasn't the first time I bailed him out. Mark was . . . He was a good person, but with money . . ." Ian's sentence trails off.

Is that true, Mark? I stare at the bank statements strewn across the bed and the floor. If you were so bad with money, then where is the debt? Where are the credit card payments? Where is the proof?

"Tess," Ian says. "Can I make a suggestion?"

"What?"

"Let me put my forensic accountant on the case. He helps me with my clients and tracking down money. You can give him all the statements and give him the authority to act on your behalf, and he'll do all the work. He'll find any other accounts Mark had. He can find any debt in Mark's name, as well as any pensions he's got that'll be yours now. Leave it to someone whose job it is. You don't need this stress in your life, Tess. I should never have been so abrupt with you at the funeral. I'm sorry. I . . . I was upset too, and it was easier to focus on the money than . . ." His voice trails off and I'm glad he doesn't finish talking. "I'm sorry. I hope you understand."

"I'll think about it," I say, although I don't mean it. If I decide to look further into our finances, then I'll hire my own forensic accountant. I know Ian is your brother, Mark, but I don't trust him.

"And Tess?"

"Yeah?"

"Have you found Mark's life insurance policy?"

"Yes. Why are you asking?" The question flies out without any thought. I picture the kitchen door wide open and the scent of something I couldn't quite smell.

"I just wanted to make sure you have it, that's all," Ian says.

"Did you know the amount?"

Another pause.

"Mark told me he didn't want you to worry about money," Ian says by way of an answer. "Look, I know this is difficult for everyone, but the world keeps turning. Mark has made sure you were well cared for financially. I keep banging on about it, but please, Tess. It might be a weight off your mind if you at least talk to Jacob and start the process."

I have that feeling again, the sense that Ian is holding something back from me. I picture the boxes the wrong way round and the policy document sitting so perfectly on top. The smell in the air, faint, like . . . like the lingering scent of a man's cologne.

I gasp.

"Tess, are you all right?"

I called the locksmith to change the locks. I suspected it was Ian, but I didn't know for sure until now.

"Tess?" Ian's voice whispers in my ear and I jump.

"It's late, I should go." I hang up quick before Ian can say anything more.

I drop my phone onto the covers and pick up your life insurance policy instead. It would be so easy to dial the 0800 number at the top of the yellow folder, cash in the policy, pay off the mortgage. Even move house. Get something smaller with a fenced-off garden and windows that don't rattle at the slightest breeze.

But there'd be no tree house for Jamie. There would be no feeling of you in every room, and I'm not sure either of us is ready to give that up.

I pull the notebook toward me and start to write.

CHAPTER 38

Transcript BETWEEN ELLIOT SADLER (ES) AND TERESA CLARKE (TC) (INPATIENT AT OAKLANDS HOSPITAL, HARTFIELD WARD), WEDNESDAY, APRIL 11. SESSION 2 (Cont.)

ES: Hi again, Tess. Would you like a glass of water before we start?

TC: No thank you.

ES: How is the pain?

TC: OK. Have you got any news? Do you know where Jamie is?

ES: We're trying. You said earlier that someone had been in your house and taken things. Is that when you called the police the first time?

TC: No.

ES: What did you do then?

TC: (Pause) I changed the locks. It was Shelley's idea not to call the police. She made me think that no one would believe me, that it was all in my head. But it wasn't.

ES: You must've been scared to be in your home?

TC: Not all the time. Not at that point anyway.

ES: But later you were scared?

TC: Yes.

CHAPTER 39

Saturday, March 24

---

15 DAYS TO JAMIE'S BIRTHDAY

Today I woke up angry. Furious, in fact. Angry with you for dying. Angry with that vile, evil man who called me Tessie. Angry for being scared. Angry because there is something going on, something not right, something you didn't tell me.

The locksmith came back yesterday and changed the locks in the front door and the side door. He handed over two sets of shiny new keys, but still I found my feet padding across the kitchen tiles, checking every hour or so that the door was locked.

So I woke up angry and shitty today, and Jamie was quiet. He stayed in his room playing with his Legos all morning. I made sandwiches for lunch that neither of us touched, and when Jamie left the table he forgot to take his plate to the sink. He's seven, and seven-year-olds forget, and normally I don't care and do it for him, but I was grumpy so I said: "Jamie, come back and put your plate by the sink, please."

He already had his coat on and one welly boot. He stopped and stood up very straight before he spoke. "I'm going to my tree house. You can do it."

The anger boiled over, the words flying from my mouth loud and fierce without a moment of thought. "Jamie, you will get back here right now, and *you* will put your plate by the sink."

Jamie's tongue stuck out, pushing the tooth at the front that still hasn't fallen out, swinging it back and forth as he narrowed his eyes and glared at me. I was just about to snap at him again when he moved, stomping through the kitchen in his one welly boot, trailing dried mud across the tiles.

"Thank you," I mumbled, my teeth clenched together as Jamie lifted his plate from the table.

Except he didn't take it to the sink, he gripped it in one hand and threw it like a Frisbee. He was halfway out the side door before the plate had even smashed.

He aimed straight for me, and he was damn close too. The plate missed me and hit the cupboard with a clonk before bouncing off the worktop and smashing on the tiles.

"I wish Shelley was my mum," he shouted, disappearing into the garden before I could respond.

Shards of china covered the kitchen. Splinters of white lodged in the grout between tiles, larger chunks shot under the oven, and one piece jumped up and fell inside my slipper.

I dropped to my knees and cried gut-wrenching sobs, angry, loathsome tears. We'd been doing so much better, Mark. I haven't been snapping over every little thing. I thought we were OK, but we're not. Nowhere close.

I hated myself in those minutes. I hated who I'd become—a mother who screams at her child over nothing. I hated you too, just so you know.

Oh, Tessie. I'm sorry.

His final words turned over and over in my head. He didn't mean it, I told myself. He only said it to hurt me. Mission accomplished.

I didn't understand until I was on all fours sweeping up the last of the plate and the crumbs and the mud how bad things were between Jamie and me. I thought back over the past weeks of our lives. The times we cried together on the sofa, the time on the walk back from school when he shouted and I almost hit him. Almost. Then there are the snippets of normal when I tried really hard, when we played Parcheesi and jumped in puddles and Jamie was OK.

I realized then that I needed to do something fun no matter how much it hurt, no matter how exhausted I felt. I had to do it for Jamie. He was feeding off my mood. When I was sad, so was he. When I was angry, he lashed out.

He needed to laugh; we both did. So later, after I'd pulled out the fridge and swept up the decades of dust and dirt and the last bits of china, after I'd pushed it back without finding Jamie's magnet photo, after dinner when Jamie had disappeared into his bedroom, I flicked on the TV and called upstairs. "Jamie?"

"Go away," he shouted back.

"*You've Been Framed!* is on. I'm doing the ironing if you want to come down?"

There was a silence before I heard the creak of his bedroom door and the thud of his footsteps on the stairs.

I didn't say anything about the plate. I didn't say anything at all. I just moved your mother's old standard lamp from the parlor to the living room. The lampshade is straight out of Miss Marple's era—burgundy with a fringe dangling down over a twisted, dark wood stand—but it gives a nice light to iron by.

Then I scooped up the pile of ironing from the utility room. God knows when I last touched the ironing. It's been weeks and weeks. Almost ten weeks, in fact, but I don't want to think about that right now. Like I won't think about how creased Jamie's school uniform must have been over the last few months. It didn't even cross my mind to iron his shirts. Thankfully it's been so cold he'll have kept his jumper on.

With the living room door shut and the rest of the dark, cold house forgotten, the soft lamplight makes the room feel cozy for the first time, but maybe that has more to do with Jamie's howling, boyish laughter bouncing off the walls.

Remember that laugh, Mark? The one with gasping breaths and sighs and giggles before something sets him off again.

"Oh no." Jamie giggles, covering his eyes and splaying his fingers to peek through. "Why would anyone do that?"

I look at the TV and watch someone climb onto a low roof during a windstorm. Tinny canned laughter echoes in the room. It's obvious what's about to happen, but still Jamie's body is shaking with giggles.

There is something awful about a seven-year-old boy laughing at other people's misfortune, but I don't care. I didn't know I missed Jamie's laugh and the joy it unleashes inside of me, like warm summer evenings, like seeing old friends. I didn't know I missed it. You're the one who's gone and yet so much of Jamie and I were lost that day.

Then something moves in the corner of my eye. It's brief. A flash of light from the garden when it should only be darkness. But it's enough for a shiver to run over my skin and my smile to disappear. I move away from the ironing board and step to the window.

Chilly air creeps through the single panes. It's pitch-black, like I'm standing nose to nose with a black mirror. I can see the reflection of the light from the lamp and the sofa and Jamie watching TV. I can see my face—jutting cheekbones I don't recognize and hollow eyes staring out.

CHAPTER 40

I freeze, not daring to breathe. The phone cuts dead on the fourth ring just before the answerphone would've picked it up.

The only part of my body moving is my eyes, straining to one side to get a better look, to verify what my pounding heart already knows—there is someone in my garden, someone watching us.

The thought spurs me into action and I race through the hall with my slippers slapping on the floor. The house is as dark as the night outside and my hip knocks painfully against the side of the table but I don't stop. My sole focus is on the side door that I'm sure at any moment is going to burst open and the man in the black baseball cap will be in our house.

I reach for the lock with shaking hands. It's locked. I locked it. Relief floods my body. I gasp for air and will my heart to stop beating so quickly so I can figure out what to do now.

How secure is the house? How strong is the new lock on the side door? Should I grab Jamie and make a run for the car? Who is out there? Watching and waiting. And why? It has to be him, doesn't it?

"I have no intention of hurting anyone," he said. But he'll scare me half to death though.

I wish I was braver. I wish I could throw open the side door and march out there with a torch and a hammer and swear at the night and the man in my garden watching us. There is something a little familiar about that thought, and I realize it's because I did that once, not long after we moved. There was a God-awful noise in the garden, like two people fighting. You were still at work, Jamie was asleep, so I strode out into the night, swinging the beam of the torch this way and that until I saw the glowing eyes of two foxes, startled from their fight by my presence. I threw back my head and laughed and told them to keep the noise down as they darted away.

Where did that person go? And if I'm not that person anymore, then who am I?

I move quickly back through the house to the living room.

The credits of the show are moving across the screen and Jamie is grinning up at me.

"Time for bed." I force a singsong voice and switch off the TV.

He nods and disappears upstairs.

"Love you," I call up to him, swallowing back the tears.

"Love you too," he calls back.

Only when I'm sure Jamie is in bed do I turn off the living room light and grab the phone from the dining room and call the only person I can think of.

"Shelley," I say, whispering her name before she has a chance to say hello.

"Tess? What is it? Are you OK?"

"There's a man in my garden." I feel the fear, the adrenaline, in my stomach. I take a step into the darkness of the living room, keeping the phone and its white light pressed to my face as I inch sideways to the window. "He's by the trees, underneath the tree house."

The light is gone but there's a pale crescent moon in the sky and with the lights off I can just see the shadow of a figure moving behind the tree.

"Oh my God," Shelley gasps, her voice mimicking my own and dropping to a whisper. "Call the police!"

"Oh . . . OK. I didn't think," I reply, feeling stupid.

"Tess, hang up and call the police. Don't answer the door to anyone but them. I'm not far away. I'll get there as soon as I can."

I hang up, my fingers shaking so the buttons take longer to press than they should. Shelley is right. I need to call the police. I have to tell them everything. I have to keep us safe, Mark. Whatever happens, I have to protect Jamie.

Suddenly it's real. There is a man in our garden, leaning against one of our trees casual as anything, watching the house, watching Jamie and me. Hearing Shelley's panic rams reality down my throat and I'm stumbling over myself to get out of the living room.

I sit on the bottom step of the stairs and call the police. It's never as quick as they make it out in the movies. It takes ages just to give my name and address and tell the operator what service I want. The minutes tick by and all the while I wonder if he's still out there watching. The man who called me last week and chased me in Manningtree—it has to be.

The operator is cool, no-nonsense. "And you're sure it's a person?"

"Yes. I saw a torch or a phone light."

"Are you alone?"

"Yes . . . I mean no, my son Jamie is here, but he's only seven."

"Is the house secure?"

"I think so. I checked the doors and they're locked."

"OK, we're sending a unit to your address now. It's a busy night, so it may take some time."

A banging echoes through the house and then Shelley's voice shouts, "Tess, it's Shelley."

"What was that noise?" the operator asks.

"It's just my friend Shelley."

"Was she the person outside?" There's a note of doubt in the operator's voice now. An "are you wasting police time?" tone.

"No, no. I phoned her when I saw someone and she offered to come over."

"Right. Lock the door behind her and a unit will be on its way soon."

"Thank you."

I hang up and dash through the house, desperate to make sure Shelley gets in before the man can get to her.

When I yank open the door Shelley's eyes are wide as if she's as spooked as I am. Her nose is running and she looks frozen.

"Are you OK?" she asks without moving from the doorstep. "You took so long to get to the door I started to think something had happened, and I forgot to bring the spare key you gave me."

"Sorry. I had the police operator giving me twenty questions." I motion her in but she doesn't move.

"Good. You called them." She draws in a breath and shoves the sleeves of her black jacket up to her elbows as I try to pull her in and shut the door and bolt it tight. But Shelley isn't budging from the doorway. "Have you got a torch?" she asks.

"What for?" I dig behind the rack of boots for the clunky orange one I know is lurking there from trick-or-treating in the dark last Halloween.

"I'm going to look."

"What? No. The police said we should stay inside and lock the doors."

"There's some Peeping Tom leering away in your garden, Tess. Scaring you half to death. I'm not just going to sit here and let him get away with it."

Then before I can protest, before I can make her see sense, she's snatching the torch out of my hands and flying into the darkness. A shudder races through my body, and I slam the side door shut and lock it again.

I dash through the house, back to the dark living room. The circular torch beam is bouncing along the ground and swinging up, scanning the tree line ahead as Shelley approaches. I follow the beam of light to the trees. My heart is pounding in my ears and I hold my breath waiting to see the figure emerge, but there's nothing there now.

A minute passes before Shelley turns to the window and shrugs. I'm at the side door by the time she's trudged across the lawn. "I didn't see anything," she calls out, flicking off the torch as she nears the door.

My heart is still hammering away and I bite my lip to stop myself calling for her to hurry up and get inside.

"The wind is really blowing out there now though. Maybe it was a branch swaying in the wind," she says, stepping inside and pulling off her ankle boots, which are covered in a rim of mud. She must have really poked around in the trees to get them so muddy, and now I feel bad, bad and grateful.

"Maybe. Sorry, I didn't mean for you to drive all the way here. I just needed to hear a friendly voice."

"I was glad to get out. Tim and I had another row. I went for a swim to clear my head and got your call as I was leaving the pool." Her voice cracks.

I flick the switch on the kettle and motion for Shelley to take a seat.

"It's nothing new," she says, dabbing a finger under her eyes. "After our chat the other night, it got me thinking about adoption again.

I want a child so badly, Tess. I don't mean a baby, but a child. I want to be a mother again. So I asked Tim to consider fostering a little boy or girl. That way, if it doesn't feel right then we can back out, but Tim wouldn't even talk about it. He basically said I was being selfish for not wanting to have another baby of our own." Shelley touches the locket around her neck, running it back and forth on its chain.

I can see Dylan's photo clearly in my mind. That blond hair sticking up. Those bright blue eyes.

"That's horrible," I mutter. I forget the kettle and slide into the seat beside her. Thoughts of the man by the tree have been swept aside, along with my fears.

I can't shake the image of Dylan from my mind. He would be nearly eight now, just like Jamie.

"Ha! It gets worse." Shelley pulls a face—an upside-down smile. "Then he said, if I wasn't going to give him another child, then he'd go out and find someone who will. And . . . and I know he means it, because I found out last week that he's had an affair with the receptionist at the golf club."

"Oh my God, why didn't you say anything? What a bastard," I say. "Sorry, I know he's your husband and everything—"

Shelley waves her hand at me. "Don't be sorry. He is a bastard, which is what I called him as he slammed the front door."

"What are you going to do? Will you . . . will you try adopting on your own?"

"I think I have to, Tess. I want to be a mother again, with or without Tim. We've been clinging on to our marriage as a way to remember Dylan. Maybe starting again would be healthier for both of us. I'm never going to forget Dylan." She touches her locket, the smile gone, and for a moment I see a woman half destroyed by grief. For a moment I see myself in Shelley's face. "But I think I want to find a way to move on a little bit."

"You're welcome to stay here anytime," I say. "I will unearth the spare bed from the boxes one of these days."

"Thank you." She smiles then. "But Tim and I have been avoiding each other long enough. We need to sit down and talk properly. We won't be able to iron things out one way or another if I—"

"Oh shit, the iron." I leap up and dash into the living room.

I flick the switch off at the wall and yank the plug from the socket. The iron hisses a puff of steam. "Sorry," I say, forcing a small laugh as Shelley follows me to the living room. "I forgot to turn it off earlier."

Shelley flicks on the main light. I feel suddenly exposed, thinking of the man outside, but he's gone now, I remind myself. Shelley's eyes fall to the ironing board.

"You don't need to be doing that now, Tess," Shelley says, her voice slow and soft as if she's speaking to a child.

I follow her eyes to one of your shirts resting on the pile, along with a few of my tops and the last of Jamie's school shirts.

"Oh . . . no." I shake my head. "This is the first time I've touched the ironing since Mark died. I wasn't going to iron Mark's shirts . . . I wasn't going to . . ." My voice trails off.

"OK." Shelley nods but I can tell she's not sure.

"I haven't ironed anything for weeks. I haven't felt up to it. But I did tonight. It was nice." I think of Jamie's laughter filling the living room.

"Yes, but Tess, are you sure you're OK?" Shelley touches my arm.

"Apart from seeing a man in the garden, I'm absolutely fine." I try to smile.

"I'll make the hot chocolates then," she says.

I realize then that I haven't told Shelley about the plate Jamie threw at me. I could tell her now, but something stops me. Hearing about Shelley's argument with her husband has distanced my own fight with Jamie, and I don't want to dredge it up again. I feel the same about the phone call last night. I'll wait for the police to arrive. They need to know too. I can't carry on like this for much longer, Mark.

The hot chocolate Shelley made warms my stomach and coats my thoughts in a sickly treacle. It's hard to think straight. Exhaustion is weighing down my limbs. I'm so tired. There was someone in my garden, I tell myself over and over, but the memory of it seems more like an obscure notion than reality.

When the police arrive I try to concentrate on what I'm saying, but my thoughts are muddled and my words don't come out right. The two policemen ask question after question and I struggle to understand, let alone answer. "Where were you standing when you saw someone in your garden? Did you notice what the person was wearing? Has anything like this happened before?"

I want to tell them about the phone call last night—the man and his threats—but my tongue is suddenly too big in my mouth and my thoughts are jumbled, like one of Jamie's plastic puzzles with the sliding tiles all in the wrong place. I know what the picture should be, the words I want to use, but I can't figure out how to move the pieces in the right way.

"You mentioned your son is in the house, Mrs. Clarke?"

My eyelids are heavy and the fog is pulling me away from the living room.

Shelley is saying something about Jamie, but her voice is muffled.

We traipse upstairs—the two policemen, Shelley and I—and poke our heads into Jamie's room. The nightlight is on and Jamie is twisted in a ball in his covers, his head halfway down the bed.

One of the policemen asks a question about Mark but I'm too busy trying to shut Jamie's door and shush them to listen properly.

My memory is hazy after that. The police leave and then Shelley guides me to bed, promising to check on Jamie one last time before she goes. At least, I think that's what happened. I can't remember. I can't be sure.

CHAPTER 41

Sunday, March 25

14 DAYS TO JAMIE'S BIRTHDAY

It's only the next afternoon, when I shake off the pillow smothering my thoughts, that I think about Shelley's visit and how quickly she arrived last night.

The phone call to the police operator seemed to take a long time, but it can't have been more than ten minutes. Ten minutes from when I hung up the phone with Shelley and dialed 999. It would take me longer than that to find my car keys and put my boots on.

She said she was just leaving the swimming pool, but even if the A12 was empty, which it never is, it would've taken longer than ten minutes.

It doesn't add up. I slide my feet into my wellies and head to the garden. I walk the same route around the house as Shelley took the previous night. The grass is wet and the earth feels sodden with the week's rain. I can still see the boot prints of the officers from when they searched the garden, trampling through the daffodils.

At the tree house I stop and stand exactly where I saw the person last night. I can see straight into the living room. Even from this distance I can see Jamie hunched forward over the PlayStation controller and the TV screen displaying the dark world of his *Minecraft* game. From here I can see the study, and Jamie's bedroom too.

I give a sudden shiver and I'm about to step away when something bright on the ground catches my eye. I drop down to my haunches and run my fingers over the leaves until I find it—a button. A shiny silver button.

I recognize it straightaway. It's from Shelley's jacket, the one she was wearing last night.

The logical part of my brain knows the button could easily have fallen off when Shelley was checking the garden last night, or the other day when we were gardening, and yet, I think again to how quickly she arrived, how cold she looked on the doorstep, and how strange I felt after drinking the hot chocolate. Just like the last time Shelley made me hot chocolate.

Suddenly the lullaby—Shelley's soft voice—is turning in my head. *"Your mumma loves you, oh yes I do."*

The last time I drank the hot chocolate Shelley made I could barely walk to Jamie's room in the middle of the night. I could barely stay awake. The day after, my mouth was dry, my thoughts clunky, just like today. I thought it was a side effect from antidepressants, but what if I'm wrong?

I turn on my heel and run back to the house, kicking off my wellies at the door before racing upstairs to our bedroom and my notebook. I scramble through the pages. There are more than I remember writing, but I find the page with Shelley and add a question: *Is Shelley drugging me?*

The thought is obscene. Shelley is my friend. And yet I run the nib of the pen around and around the question in a dark circle.

It wouldn't be difficult. A few over-the-counter sleeping pills mixed into my drink when I'm already so tired.

I try to remember the argument I overheard after our shopping trip last week and Shelley's cutting words that were so unlike the friend I know. *"Are you purposefully trying to mess this up? Stay away from her,"* I thought she said.

We spent so long in Tesco that day. I thought Shelley did it to help me, but I can't shake the convenience of it all. The one time I leave the house that week for any longer than the school run and someone goes into the house. I'm sure that someone was Ian, which means Shelley and Ian are connected somehow.

It feels too far-fetched to even consider, but then I think of the disbelieving looks that passed between the officers, and how keen Shelley was for me to call them, as if she wanted them to doubt me.

What is going on, Mark?

CHAPTER 42

IAN

I didn't see Tess in the weeks leading up to Jamie's birthday. We may have spoken on the phone a few times. I can't remember where I was on Saturday, the twenty-fourth of March, but I was probably in The Tavern in Ipswich. I normally meet friends there on a Saturday night. I'll give you their names. I'm sure one of them can confirm I was there that night.

It's ridiculous to suggest I was trying to scare Tess. Why would I want to stand in her garden in the freezing cold? I know she thinks I wanted the house back, but I genuinely didn't care that they bought it. I'm quite happy in my waterfront apartment, thanks very much.

SHELLEY

I really didn't know what to believe that night when Tess called me. She was very distressed and was convinced there was a man in her garden. When I got there, I went outside to look because I thought it was Ian. I thought Ian was trying to help Tess at first, and I did think handing over all the probate stuff to someone who knows what they're doing was a good idea, but I didn't like the way he was pressuring Tess about Mark's will and their finances. Whether he was owed money or not, it really wasn't any of his business what Tess did or when she did it.

When the police officers arrived it was awful. Tess started acting all weird, like she was drunk. She could barely speak. I guess you've got the report. They searched the outside and we all went up and looked in Jamie's room. PC Higgs and PC French were very understanding but I'm not sure they believed Tess. I know I didn't at that point.

CHAPTER 43

Monday, March 26

13 DAYS TO JAMIE'S BIRTHDAY

For once I'm early picking Jamie up from school. There are no other parents here yet, and all the children are still tucked inside finishing off their schoolwork before the bell rings, signaling home time.

I sit on a brick wall by the teachers' car park and draw in a breath, relishing the silence and peace and the buttery yellow sun on my face.

The brightness hurts the backs of my eyes but I don't turn away. It's nice to be out from the gloom; it's nice to be early. I glance behind me, back toward the lane. A car is passing, slowing on the bend. Sunlight bounces off the window and I can't see the driver, but I feel them watching me and I turn quickly away.

There's something church-like about the school with its old burned red bricks and arched windows. Even the triangular porch that ends in a point in the middle of the building looks like a steeple. There's a cockerel weather vane that sits on the highest spot on the porch roof and creaks in the breeze.

I wonder if they use the slim red door in the porch? Or do the children always come and go through the glass reception area that's been built on the side with two wide double doors?

I imagine Jamie sitting at a desk somewhere beyond the worn brick wall. I imagine him concentrating on his looping script writing. To me it's just a sentence but to Jamie it's a long list of things to remember: words on the line, comma in the right place, speech marks, expanded noun phrases, a full stop at the end. He's just like you, Mark. He prefers math.

A light breeze, like a breath on my neck, makes me shiver, and with it comes the feeling of being watched again. I shift position on the wall and scan all around me but I see no one. Then a movement catches my eye and a woman appears at the glass doors of the school. She pulls it open and moves in my direction. She's wearing a long black knitted cardigan over a lilac shirt and black trousers and wraps the cardigan around herself as a gust of cold wind travels across the farmland, creaking the weather vane.

She has jet-black hair that reaches her jutting collarbone. She's painfully slim and her forehead is lined as if she's in a constant state of concern. "Can I help you?" she asks, throwing a look back to the doors, where I see another face peeking out from behind the reception desk.

Her question seems odd and makes me smile. They clearly don't recognize me, but then I'm usually late, and usually my hair is scraped back and I'm in welly boots and your tartan pajama bottoms. With my hair down and a pair of jeans on, is it any surprise they don't realize I'm Jamie's mother?

"I'm just waiting for Jamie. Jamie Clarke." I smile and fumble in my coat pocket for my phone and blanch at the time. "Oh." It's only two p.m. School doesn't finish for another hour. I'm not so much early as completely bloody wrong. No wonder the reception staff are worried. "I . . . I'm so sorry." I shake my head. "I've got myself in a right muddle with the time, haven't I? I didn't mean to alarm anyone. I'll come back in an hour. Sorry."

Suddenly I'm not smiling but fighting back tears of embarrassment, which makes me want to cry even more. I only got the pickup time wrong. I read two thirty instead of one thirty on the clock on the fireplace in the living room. A simple mistake. No harm done, but it feels like a big deal. After everything that happened last week and at the weekend, it feels like a very big deal.

"Better to be an hour early than an hour late, I guess." I laugh, but the sound is a choking cough of a thing, and when I stand up, the woman jumps back as if I'm an escaped mental patient.

I stride out of the school gates and back to the lane.

The woman is calling after me, but I quicken my pace. Wind stings the heat of my face and the hot tears now rolling down my cheeks. I'll apologize to Jamie's teacher at pickup. She can pass the message on to whomever I've just run away from.

My mobile is vibrating in my pocket and when I look at the display Shelley's name is on the screen. I hesitate. I want to answer and tell her what an idiot I've been. I know she'll say something silly that will make me laugh. But I still don't know if I can trust her.

Then I think of Shelley's large grin when she swept through my door with a KFC bucket, and the time before that when she looked after Jamie because I couldn't. *Shelley is my friend,* I tell myself, pressing accept.

"Hey, Tess." Shelley's voice bounces in my ear.

"Hi." I cross the road and tuck myself close to the bushes as I make my way back down the lane.

"You sound like you're out somewhere," she says. "Is now a good time?"

"It's fine. I was just . . . out for a walk," I finish. I'm not sure why I don't tell Shelley what happened a minute ago. My own stupid embarrassment, probably.

"Ah, that sounds nice. I've been stuck in my office seeing clients all day," Shelley says. "How are you? I meant to call you yesterday, but . . . well, things with Tim and me aren't great. He moved out yesterday."

"I'm so sorry, Shelley. You could've called me."

"Thanks, I know, but you're going through enough as it is right now, and I'm fine, honestly. I think it's been a long time coming. But look, are you OK? Has everything been all right after the other night? You kind of shut down when the police arrived. I think you were in shock."

"No, it's fine. I'm fine."

"Good." She sighs. "That's a relief. Anyway, I was wondering what you had planned for the Easter weekend. The weather is supposed to be nice."

"Is it? Oh, I'm not sure. I haven't thought about it."

"Why don't I pop by on Saturday and we can do something? Even if it's just sitting in your garden stuffing ourselves with chocolate."

I smile and am about to tell her that Jamie would love it when I hear something in the undergrowth ahead, a muffled cough and a rustle of leaves. I hold my breath, my gaze flicking one way, then the other. I can't see a face but there are plenty of places to duck out of sight along the lane.

"Tess, are you there?" Shelley squawks in my ear, her voice suddenly too loud as I listen to the silent landscape.

"Yes, sorry," I whisper. "That sounds great. I have to go." I hang up but keep my phone gripped in my hand as I quicken my pace.

Someone is watching me. The muscles in my legs pull tight and my eyes grow wide, stinging against the bright daylight. I stop moving, waiting, praying, for a bird or rabbit to dart across the road so I can laugh at myself and carry on. Except it isn't a bird that moves, it's the man who followed me in Manningtree.

He's up ahead by the track opposite the house, the one where you fell off your bike when you were a kid and got the scar on your chin. I must be fifty meters down the lane, and there's no way I can make it to the house before him. Saliva builds in my mouth and I swallow hard.

He takes a step into the road and turns to face me. He's wearing the same clothes as before—a dark hoody and black jeans—but this time there is no baseball cap, no shadows to lurk in, and I can see his face clearly. His skin is pale and sags around small, watching eyes. His nose and lips are thin too, as if all his features are too small for his face. His hair is black and thinning and his body is slight beneath his clothes. He looks nothing like the burly thug I pictured when I first heard his voice on the answerphone, but it doesn't change the terror gnarling my insides.

I don't know how long we stand like that for—me frozen to the spot, wishing for a tractor to trundle around the bend and squash the man dead, and him waiting patiently for what I suppose is the inevitable. There is nowhere to run except back up the lane. How far would I get before he caught me?

He smiles as if reading my thoughts. His lips part and my breath catches in my throat waiting for him to yell his threat at me. He starts to speak but I can't hear over the sound of blood rushing in my ears. He stops suddenly and turns away. There's a movement on the lane behind him. It's not a tractor, it's a cyclist decked out in red Lycra.

The man jumps to the side just as the cyclist swerves and brakes and the pair collide. Both men are talking in tight angry voices as they pick themselves up from the tarmac, but I'm not listening.

I turn and run back in the direction of the school. There's a gap between the hedges on the left that I've never noticed before. Without thinking, I dart through it. The path beneath my feet is slick with mud from last week's rain and I slip and skid, moving as fast as my boots and my fitness will allow. The path slopes upward between two fields, where the earth is black and deep divots run in lines from one side to the other. Sprouts of green litter the field with the first shoots of a crop.

The mud hardens as I clamber onward. At the top of the fields I twist around to look behind me, but my foot slips and I hit the earth so hard that the impact ricochets up my spine. I turn onto my back and lie for a second, the wet ground against my head. I close my eyes and check for any damage. I'm bruised, I know that much, and a tiny, sharp stone is embedded in the skin of my palm, but nothing is broken.

When I sit up to catch my breath, the lane seems far below and there's no sign of the man. I'm alone up here. I stand and step carefully this time, down the path and back to the road and the school, where Jamie will soon be waiting for me.

Who was that man, Mark? What does he want from me?

I picture his face and those little ferret eyes and think again how little he resembles the image I attached to the voice on the phone. He said something to me just before the cyclist came round the bend, and now that I think about it, I'm sure he said, *"Mrs. Clarke?"*

Not Tess.

Not Tessie, but Mrs. Clarke.

CHAPTER 44

Transcript BETWEEN ELLIOT SADLER (ES) AND TERESA CLARKE (TC) (INPATIENT AT OAKLANDS HOSPITAL, HARTFIELD WARD), WEDNESDAY, APRIL 11. SESSION 2 (Cont.)

ES: The threatening phone calls—

TC: What about them?

ES: Someone was following you. You believe someone came into your house while you were out. And then there was a man's voice on the phone telling you that he was going to hurt you if you didn't get what he wanted—

TC: And Jamie. He threatened Jamie too.

ES: I see. And yet you still believe Shelley is the one behind what's happened.

TC: She is. I'm telling you she is involved somehow. I should've seen it coming. She (pause) she drugged me. Twice. It was some kind of sleeping tablet, I think. I think she did it to keep me out of the way so she could spend time with Jamie.

ES: Why did you continue to spend time with Shelley if you suspected something was wrong?

TC: I don't know. I really don't know. I had suspicions, but every time I started to think about it, something else would happen or Shelley would say just the right thing and I'd convince myself I was wrong. She charmed us somehow. She used Jamie's feelings for her to get what she wanted. She knew I'd do anything for Jamie. And Jamie loved spending time with her. She's really good at this football PlayStation game he's obsessed with. Shelley wants Jamie and Ian wants the money. If you get my notebook then you can see for yourself. I figured everything out. The answer is in my notebook.

ES: Why don't you just tell me?

TC: It's hard to think straight. That's why I wrote it all down. What are you doing to find Jamie? Take me through it step-by-step please, Detective. Every one of your officers—where have they been? Who have they spoken to?

ES: We're looking into everything. Do you know a man named Richard Welkin?

TC: (Nods)

CHAPTER 45

Friday, March 30

---

9 DAYS TO JAMIE'S BIRTHDAY

There is a hurricane moving across the North Atlantic. Hurricane Bethany. It's about to hit Scotland and Northern Ireland. It won't get as far as the South East but the strong winds are pushing a warm front across the rest of England. A balmy seventy-eight degrees Fahrenheit on Good Friday—the first day of the Easter holidays—that nobody was expecting.

We are on our way back from the village playground, and as I slip-slap along the lane in my old Birkenstocks the temperature reminds me of that first August with Jamie when he was four months old. Jamie and I spent almost every day on a picnic blanket in the park with the other mums on the estate, eating sausage rolls and drinking sticky Pepsi turned warm and flat in the sun.

Pepsi, was it? I thought it was prosecco.

Only sometimes.

You'd come home from work and we'd share a bottle of chilled white wine and move the kitchen chairs into the garden so we could drop our feet in the paddling pool.

I seem to remember nappy rashes and teething too, Tessie.

I know, I remember those bits too, but this strange warmth reminds me of the good summer days.

We got married on one of those hot days, didn't we?

We did. See, it was idyllic.

I wonder if the Chelmsford mums will be meeting in the park this weekend and whether Jamie and I should go. I thought they were my best friends—Casey and Jo, Lisa and Julie, and Debbie when she wasn't working. But I've only seen them once since we left Chelmsford, and that was at your funeral.

They couldn't be bothered to visit you.

That's not fair. They've tried to keep in touch. Texts have come through from one or the other of them almost every day asking if I'm OK and if I fancy popping down to Chelmsford for lunch or dinner, or feel up for visitors at the house.

I haven't replied. Sometimes I think our friendship existed around proximity and children. Their friendship will carry on without me, other women will come and go, my spot will be filled by someone who lives closer.

If I go to see them, they'll want to talk about you, and I don't want that. They might ask me why I don't move back to Chelmsford, and I don't have the answer. I've thought about it, of course. I'd be closer to my mum, I'd have my friends again, it would be easier for tutoring if or when I decide to go back, and I'm sure Jamie would settle back in to his old school eventually.

But he's happy here. He loves the garden and the house, he loves school, and the days of nagging and bargaining with him to put his school uniform on in the mornings are gone. I think he's as excited about going back to school after the Easter break as he is about his birthday.

I do want to do something nice this weekend though, something normal. I want to get out of the house. I'm jumping at every creak of a floorboard and I can't answer the phone again, in case it's him. It's rung a few times and each time I've been frozen to the spot, unable to breathe.

It's why we came out. A trip to the playground and the meadow behind the new estate. Jamie had hoped to see a friend from school but the playground was empty so we're on our way home to the tree house instead. I should've arranged some playdates before the end of term but I forgot and now it's too late. When Easter is over I'll make more effort to be on time for school and chat to the other mums. I'll make more effort to be normal for Jamie.

The bushes along the lane have been cut back. Bits of nettle leaves and twigs litter the tarmac and I hop over them to avoid stinging my bare toes. An old estate car rattles past and I move Jamie and myself to the edge, grateful to whomever chopped back the brambles for the extra space on the road.

Jamie hasn't spoken much these past few days, but the heat has improved both our moods. He is quiet but not sullen. Just thoughtful, I guess. When another car passes, coating my senses in the tang of diesel, I feel only annoyance. The sudden burst of adrenaline, the what-if-I-jump thought isn't in me today. Will it be back tomorrow? I don't know, but for now I'm enjoying the brief sense of summer that hurricane Bethany has brought to the village. There will be no bonfires in the air this weekend, only barbecues.

"There's supposed to be a storm hitting in a few days," I say to Jamie as we reach our driveway. "It's the tail end of the hurricane. After that the temperature will drop and it will be cool spring days again."

He shrugs a response, his feet already inching away from me in the direction of the tree house. "If it's warm tomorrow though, shall we go to the beach at Frinton?"

Jamie smiles up at me with his big blues eyes. He prods his tongue against the wobbly tooth, testing its movement as he considers my suggestion. Then he nods before turning away and sprinting across the lawn.

I watch him disappear and feel suddenly alone. I hurry around the side of the house and sit on the lawn, listening to Jamie talk to himself. I don't want to be in the house by myself, and I don't want Jamie to be alone in the garden.

Tomorrow's trip will be good for both of us.

CHAPTER 46

Saturday, March 31

8 DAYS TO JAMIE'S BIRTHDAY

The weather is glorious. We wake up to bright sunshine and clear skies. It takes almost an hour of digging around in the garage to find the beach bag with the buckets and spades. Jamie and I are both wearing last year's faded summer clothes—a red T-shirt and denim shorts for Jamie, and me in an ASDA George dress with spaghetti straps that keep falling down my shoulders.

Dregs of last year's sand rustle in the beach bag when I chuck it in the boot, and I feel a sudden pang, a void inside I can't fill. Last year we all went to the beach together. The three of us—a family.

The time we went to visit your mum, I bet.

Probably, but I don't want to think about that today, or you, in fact. With a deep breath I force the sadness away. I've made a picnic of Jamie's favorite foods for the beach—jam sandwiches, Party Rings, and Monster Munch—and I remembered pound coins for parking and ice creams so we don't have to traipse half a mile to the nearest cashpoint. I made pancakes for breakfast and didn't drop them on the floor; the car is packed up and ready to go. I want to make a new memory today. A good one.

We're in the car about to pull out of the driveway when Shelley's white Mini pulls in.

"Shelley." Jamie's voice bounces with joy. He waves from the back seat.

Shelley grins and waves back and I feel something drop inside me. I forgot I'd made plans with Shelley. She turns off the engine and jumps out of the car wearing white cotton shorts and a yellow T-shirt. Her legs shimmer with a faint tan and show none of the stretch marks and blotches of my own legs.

Seeing Shelley makes me think of the notebook and her name written in it over and over. I think of the button I found by the tree and the hot chocolates she insisted on making, the eyes of hate staring at me from Jamie's bedroom, and the lullaby that I still find myself humming.

The thoughts flash before my eyes—snapshots of something just out of reach, but whatever it is, it's not enough to override the relief I feel seeing Shelley, the warmth I feel knowing she's come to see me, that I matter to her, to someone.

I wind down my window, kill the engine, and smile. "Hi."

"I was on my way to the pool and thought I'd see if you wanted to come for a swim, but you look like you're off somewhere." She leans closer and when I glance in the wing mirror I see Jamie pulling a silly face at her.

"We're going to Frinton," I announce like it's a holiday to Hawaii. "I've got buckets and spades and a picnic."

Shelley looks surprised but then beams. "What a great idea," she calls as she jogs back to her car. "I'll follow you."

I want to shout back, tell her I'm sorry I forgot we had plans and it's just me and Jamie today, our day, our new memory, but Shelley is already in her car, and Jamie is whooping in the back seat, making the car jig about.

It'll still be a good day, I tell myself, ignoring the disappointment curdling in my stomach with my breakfast. I'll still be present, and Jamie will enjoy it, which was the whole point anyway.

A warm breeze blows from the sea and lifts the hair from my neck as Shelley and I lug the picnic and the beach bag down a flight of uneven concrete steps. I can taste the salt in the air, the smell of the beach and my childhood. I have beach towels tucked under my arm, threatening to drop at any moment, and my arms are full and aching to be empty.

"Do you think we'll need the cricket set and the tennis bats?" Shelley asks.

I laugh and turn my face to the sun. "Sorry. It's the bag I always take to the beach. I never think to look in it and decide what we'll need or not. I just grab it. There's probably still the inflatable ring in there Jamie used when he was a toddler."

The tide is out, leaving a long stretch of soft yellow sand that darkens near the shoreline. It's not yet ten and the beach is still quiet, with only a few families scattered here and there and dog walkers throwing sticks and balls into the sea for their dogs to fetch.

We find an empty stretch between two groins. The dark wood fences slope all the way to the sea and make me feel as though this beach, this patch of sand, these waves are ours and only ours. The feeling doesn't last long and by the time we've rolled out the towels another two families are setting up their own areas on the beach.

There's a boy about Jamie's age among the families and before I've even unpacked the spades and buckets, Jamie is barefoot and racing across the sand with the boy and his football.

The void inside threatens to peel open again watching how grown-up Jamie is. He would never have run off to play like that last summer, or even a few months back. It's another reminder of how content he is living in the village. Suddenly I'm glad Shelley is with us, glad I have someone to talk to, a friend while Jamie is busy with his.

"Is it too early for lunch?" Shelley asks from the towel beside me. She puts her hands to her flat stomach and dips her head back. Her hair is glowing white in the bright sunshine. "I thought I was going swimming so I didn't have any breakfast."

"How about a Party Ring?" I rustle in the cool box and pull out the thin blue pack of biscuits.

"Oh my God, Tess. These used to be my favorite biscuits in the whole world." She laughs and rips them open, eyeing the different-colored rings as if she's choosing an exquisite dessert instead of a sugar-filled biscuit with a hole in the middle.

"What else have you got in that box?"

"Pickled onion Monster Munch and jam sandwiches."

She throws her head back, and her cackling laugh carries across the sand and right out to sea. "You're hilarious, Tess."

I smile and glance over to Jamie, wondering if he wants a biscuit. The football has been forgotten. Instead he's kneeling in the wet sand near the shore with the boy and a girl who I guess is his sister. Three heads are bent in concentration, and they appear to be digging between puddles of sea water, creating an elaborate maze of rivers. Jamie is using his hands to scoop out the sand and I bite back the urge to call out to him to grab a spade, or to take one down to him and join in. He'll hate me for interfering.

Shelley and I sit in a comfortable silence and watch the tide draw slowly in.

"Are you all right about you and Tim separating?" I ask.

Shelley sighs. "I think so. We haven't spent time together properly for years. I'm so used to being on my own that it doesn't feel any different. I texted him earlier to check he's OK. We got to a point when we stopped celebrating Easter and Christmas. It was just too hard to celebrate them, you know? But I still wanted to make sure he was all right.

"I'm sure I'll be angry one day about his affair, but right now I feel indifferent. Maybe it's shock that he'd do this to me after everything we've been through together, but I feel like it's been the push we both needed to end things."

I nod and stare at the rhythmic motion of the waves. Every day is hard without you, Mark, and I know Christmas will be even harder, but with Jamie here we'll celebrate somehow, I know we will.

"Fancy a swim?" Shelley asks, lifting her sunglasses and wiggling her eyebrows at me.

I laugh. "Are you kidding? The sea will be freezing."

"It'll do you good."

Shelley stands up and wriggles out of her shorts and T-shirt. She's wearing a simple black swimming costume that highlights the dip of her waist, and the curves too. I'm wearing an old tankini underneath my dress. The elastic has gone from the bottoms and I can feel them sagging around my bum.

I make a face and start to shake my head but then Jamie is racing up the beach and swiping his goggles out of the bag. He's grinning at Shelley as he strips to his swim shorts.

"Come on, Mummy." Jamie's squealing voice carries up to me as he races toward the water. *He wants me to be with him,* I think with a burst of love. And why not? It can't be any colder than the ice I've felt inside me these past months.

New memories, I remind myself, leaving my dress bunched on the sand and jogging after Jamie and Shelley.

The sea burns my skin with cold. My feet are numb before I'm even up to my knees, and I'm already stopping, preparing to turn back, but Jamie has jumped all the way in and Shelley is just ahead of him, drawing her arms up and over her head in long, smooth strokes. I wade further in until icy waves lick the skin around my navel.

Go on, Tessie. Remember who you used to be.

I sob as I drop in the water. Tears are pricking the edges of my eyes, but I kick with all my might and swim forward until my body and my mind are numb and I no longer feel the cold.

"I told you it would do you good." Shelley laughs, swimming up beside me.

I shake my head, my teeth chattering too much to speak.

The beach seems a long way off now. Jamie hasn't followed us out as far and is jumping in and out of the waves, his shouts and laughter carrying in the breeze.

I force my arms up and out of the water in long sweeping arcs and swim after Shelley. I'm sure my crawl is nowhere near as elegant as hers but it feels good to be moving. We swim lengths, back and forth in line with the groins on our stretch of beach. Every other stroke my head swings to the side and I clock Jamie splashing in the waves. My arms tire quickly and I begin to slow, increasing the time between each stroke and the glance at Jamie.

Then he disappears.

I stop swimming, choking on a mouthful of salty water that stops me shouting out. My eyes scan the sea and the beach, but he's nowhere.

Where's Jamie? The question presses down on me as if the water is squeezing me tight. I lurch forward and force my arms and legs to move. The numbing coldness makes every desperate movement feel sluggish but I kick as hard as I can, my head jerking left and right, willing Jamie's blond hair to bob out of the water, but it doesn't.

I reach the spot where I last saw him and stand. The water isn't as deep as I thought. It's only up to my knees. I turn and spin with soft squelchy sand beneath my toes, looking everywhere.

"Tess?" Shelley shouts out.

Then out of the corner of my eye I catch a glimpse of Jamie on the beach and feel the weight lift as I breathe again. He must have run out when I wasn't looking. I wade out of the water, shivering as warm air tickles my skin.

"Are you OK?" Shelley asks, following me onto the dry sand.

I smile and shake my head. "Yes, sorry. I just thought . . . Oh, it doesn't matter now. Let's have some lunch."

CHAPTER 47

By midafternoon, the river maze Jamie built with his new friends is swallowed by the sea and hazy gray-yellow clouds blow over our heads. The day is still warm but the sun is now circled in an eerie pinkish ring that makes the sky feel wrong somehow, and I can't help but keep staring upward.

Shelley follows my gaze. "It's sand from the Sahara apparently."

"What is?"

"The yellow in the sky. It's sand blown in from the hurricane. It's a bit apocalyptic if you ask me."

I nod but say nothing. The truth is, I feel it too. The sense of something coming, not a foreboding but an end, an answer. The pages in my notebook are filling up. My own cryptic clues. Where will they lead? I can feel the answer, like a word on the tip of my tongue.

The family with the two children are packing up to leave and Jamie races up toward me and plonks himself down by my legs. His hair is a mess of crazy curls, a shade darker from the sand and the salt that's dried in it. He's smiling from ear to ear, and when I stare into his crystal-clear blue eyes I realize we're going to be OK, he and I.

There is joy ahead for us still. It won't be the same without you, Mark, but it will be something.

Jamie lifts his foot and stomps on a sandcastle I made. He laughs and so do I. "I think we'll be bringing half the beach home with us," I say, reaching forward to brush dry sand from Jamie's legs.

Jamie shrugs and when I turn back to Shelley she is staring at me with wide eyes and a face so pale I wonder if she's ill. She glances at Jamie, then back to me. Jamie sticks out his tongue, making a silly face, but Shelley isn't smiling now, she isn't pulling faces. She looks emotional.

"You must miss him so much," I say, thinking of the son she lost. It never occurred to me how hard it must be for Shelley to see Jamie and me together. I feel a twinge of shame.

"What?" Shelley blinks, staring for a long second at Jamie before focusing back on me. "Oh . . . every day." She swallows, and tears glisten in her eyes.

"Of course. I'm sorry. That was a stupid thing to say."

"No, it wasn't." She shakes her head and smiles. The sadness shifts and the Shelley with the grinning face who knocked on my door nearly two months ago is back. "How are you feeling, Tess? Everything OK?"

"Um." I nod. "I guess." It seems as though her question has another meaning that I can't decipher. I pause and think of the menacing threat of the voice on the phone, the man in the lane, the secret project, the figure in the garden, someone in our house, eyes watching me, the loan from Ian you didn't tell me about. The questions and clues I'm so close to answering. I think of the days I couldn't get out of bed, and the days I cried and cried. I think of Jamie sitting beside me in the sand and the perfect day we've had.

"I think I'm still a bit shaken from the other night, but I'm getting there. It's like you said—low tides and high tides," I say, staring out to the sea where the color is dark, almost black. "I've been sorting some of the finances out."

"That's good." She's looking at Jamie now and it's clear from the expression on her face that she's missing Dylan. I run the sand through my fingers and I think about Shelley's son and her desire to be a mother again.

The thought unnerves me and I stand suddenly just as a gust of wind sprinkles us with salt water. The sea is inching up the beach. The place where the family were sitting before is underwater now, and I watch a forgotten spade bob in the waves.

"We should go," I mumble, throwing things into bags and looking around for my flip-flops.

The weather turns quickly. By the time we've packed up and made it to the cars the sky is as dark as night, and a strong wind buffets against the open driver's door. Jamie is in the back seat, his eyes half-closed.

"Thanks for today," Shelley says.

"I'm glad you could come. It's been fun. I certainly won't be forgetting that swim for a while."

Shelley smiles but there's something off about her expression and I wonder if she's still thinking of Dylan. "Tess?"

"Yeah?"

Rain spatters in fat drops from the sky.

"I'd better go. I'll call you later," I shout over a rumble of thunder, diving into my car and starting the engine before I get soaked through, before Shelley can say whatever it is she wants to say.

Jamie is asleep before we've turned off the coastal road. I glance at the sea a final time. Dark green waves are smashing and frothing against the groins. It's hard to believe it's the same sea I swam in today. Rain is pattering down on the windscreen and I flick on the lights and wipers and head for home.

CHAPTER 48

It's not yet four p.m. but the sky is inky black with storm clouds by the time we're almost home. Jamie is still asleep and the only noise is the squeak of my windscreen wipers and the roll of my tires on the wet road.

Dread is turning like sour milk in my stomach at the thought of the dark house, the empty rooms, the ringing phone. Will his gravelly voice be waiting for me on the answerphone? Will I smell the odd cologne again? I shiver and flick the indicator, turning off the A12 and onto the country road that winds down into the village.

I'm so busy worrying about the house that I don't hear the rev of the engine at first. It's like the 4x4 comes from nowhere—a huge monster of a thing with a metal grille as high as my back windscreen and tinted don't-mess-with-me windows that drives up close behind me. It's like it was waiting by the turning for me.

It looks like a Land Rover or something similar, but it's too dark to be sure.

I stop breathing. Panic is clenching every muscle in my body and roaring in my ears. It's him, I'm sure it is. The man in the black baseball cap with his menacing threats. *"I know everything about you, Tess."*

I'm scared, Mark.

It'll be OK, Tessie. I promise.

Every part of my being wills my foot to hit the accelerator and race away, but I can't give in to the mounting fear with Jamie asleep in the back. Instead I hunch forward, my hands gripping the wheel as I peer ahead for any sign of another car and help, but the road ahead is empty.

I ease off the accelerator, praying the monster behind me will whip into the other lane and fly up the road, praying he's just an impatient wanker wanting to get by, praying I'm wrong.

But I'm not wrong. The 4x4 slows too, closing the gap between my boot and his silver grille until my entire rear window is blocked by its huge mass. It's so close that I can't see it in my wing mirrors.

The purr of his engine is reverberating through the metal frame of my car and I'm sure at any moment he will simply tap the accelerator and run us off the road without a moment of thought.

He flicks his lights from low to full beam. Two spotlights brighter than the sun fill my car's interior with piercing light. I yelp from the pain hitting my eyes and the sudden blindness of it. The road ahead has gone. All I see is white light. I shove the rearview mirror away and the rebounding light out of my eye line.

Shit, shit, shit.

"You wouldn't want anything to happen to that darling child of yours."

A hysteria grips my body, my mind blanks, my foot slams the accelerator. My little car gives a whining strain, lurching forward before picking up speed and flying along the road. The 4x4 is keeping pace just inches behind me, the full beams of his headlights blaring straight through my windscreen and lighting the road ahead better than my own could ever do.

I ignore the road sign warning me to slow down—sharp turn ahead—and take the corner into the village too quickly. My wheels skid on the wet road, sending me careering into the path of a car driving on the other side of the road. I brake hard, scrunching my eyes shut as my body yanks against the seat belt. The engine grinds, then stalls.

A horn blast fills the air, from the 4x4 or the car in front, I don't know. I open my eyes and blink in the sudden darkness. I twist around and check on Jamie. He's rubbing his eyes, stunned and sleepy but not hurt. I stare into the dark rearview window. The 4x4 is gone. The road behind me is empty.

The car in front reverses back a meter before maneuvering around me. As it draws level a woman buzzes down her window and I think she's going to check that I'm OK but instead she shouts, "You stupid cow. You could've killed us both if I'd been five seconds further up the road."

Tears are blurring my vision. I want to tell her about the monster trying to run me off the road, but my mouth is flailing silently and she pulls away with an angry shake of her head before I can find my voice.

"What happened, Mummy?" Jamie asks. His voice sounds young and sleepy and makes my chest ache.

"Nothing, baby. I gave myself a fright, that's all. We're in the village. We'll be home in a minute," I reply, restarting the car and driving slowly away.

Later, when the sand has been washed away and Jamie is absorbed in the PlayStation, I dial the 0800 number on your life insurance policy and tell them you've died.

What happened on the drive home was a warning.

If I can't find whatever it is that the man wants, then maybe he'll accept money instead. He can have it all. I have to keep Jamie safe.

I add the time and date to my notebook and write: *Chased by 4x4. Land Rover?*

I'm skimming back through the pages when a message buzzes on my phone. It's Shelley: Did you get home OK?

My blood runs cold and I shiver. Five words. A concerned friend asking an innocent question, except where is the energy that seeps out of her usual texts in the same way it seeps out of her? The—*Thanks for a great day, I'm shattered!*

I picture Shelley's face as she stared at Jamie and me on the beach. I thought it was sadness, I thought she was thinking of Dylan, but now that I'm looking back, could it have been jealousy?

I scrawl Shelley's name down beside the words *Land Rover* and slowly connect the two with an arrow.

CHAPTER 49

IAN

I was having drinks with friends on Saturday the thirty-first. It was a birthday celebration. Like I said, I had no reason to want to scare Tess, and there are a lot of Land Rovers in this part of the world. I really think you need to be speaking to Shelley about this, not me.

SHELLEY

I really wish Tess had confided in me about the other things that were going on—the threats and the car chasing her. Maybe I'd have done something sooner and we wouldn't be sitting here.

I knew something was wrong that day at the beach. I should've done something about it right then and there, but the storm came in so quick and then I think I convinced myself I was mistaken. I was going through a difficult time as well, which didn't help. My marriage was ending and I wasn't myself. The thing is—this is terrible—but I was jealous. I kept looking at the little magnet photo of Jamie and imagining it was Dylan, and I felt so connected to Jamie and to Tess, but I never meant for anyone to get hurt.

CHAPTER 50

Sunday, April 1

---

7 DAYS TO JAMIE'S BIRTHDAY

I've lost Jamie's Liverpool F.C. shirt—the one we got him for Christmas that cost a fortune. He wore it for a week straight, remember? I had to sneak it out of his room after he'd fallen asleep and wash it overnight so he could wear it the next day.

And now I've lost it. It's not in the wash basket. It's not on the washing line. He's not wearing it now.

I stare at his open wardrobe and riffle through his drawers but it's not there. *Maybe I've put it away with my clothes by accident,* I think, heading to our bedroom and pulling open both doors of the wardrobe so I see not just my tops and the dresses I don't wear anymore, but your things too. Your suits and shirts and the jumpers you like to hang up.

My feet feel suddenly rooted to the carpet as I gawp at your clothes. I'll have to clear them out at some point, but not yet.

I keep staring, my eyes unable to pull away. Something isn't right.

There's an empty space at the bottom of the wardrobe where you keep your walking boots, and an empty hanger too. I can't see the gray Aran knitted jumper I bought you for your birthday in November.

My throat starts to throb and I sink to the carpet and find Shelley's number on my mobile. I keep hoping I've made a mistake. I haven't. There is nowhere else your boots or jumper would be.

It rings twice before she answers.

"Have you taken things from the house?" I fire out the question before she has a chance to distract me, before I can start second-guessing myself.

"Hi, Tess, how are you?" Her voice is bright but there's a falsity to it. It's too high. "I was just thinking about you. You didn't reply to my text last night."

"Have you taken anything from the house?" I ask again, remembering her text and the lights of the 4x4 blinding my eyes.

"What?"

"You've been in the house so much, and I wondered if you'd taken anything?" My tone softens despite the hurt in my throat. My nerve is slipping.

"What's going on, Tess?"

I sob and try to swallow but I can't. "Things are missing from the house."

There's a silence before Shelley speaks. "What things?" she asks, her voice hesitant.

"Stupid stuff." My fingers brush the smooth cotton of one of your shirts before I peel myself from the floor and move to your study to check on Jamie out of the window. He is shuffling around the tree house, talking in the animated way he used to talk to you when he was regaling you with tales of his lunchtime football matches.

A flicker of worry worms its way through me, dislodging the

missing clothes from the forefront of my mind, as if I only have the capacity to worry about one thing at a time. I probably do.

"Tess?"

"Sorry." I shake my head and move through the upstairs to Jamie's room. "I'm still here."

"What things do you think are missing?"

She doesn't believe me. It's not just the words she uses, it's the tone as well. Still bright, still kind, but there's something else there too—pity.

"I'm trying to figure it out." I give a shaky sigh, and suddenly I'm not accusing a woman I barely know whose motives I wonder about late at night. Instead I'm talking to my friend Shelley who has listened to and understood me since the moment she turned up on my doorstep.

Jamie's wardrobe is still open. I stare at the hook on the inside of the door where his rucksack should be, the one we bought him for the camping trip we never got to go on.

I pull at his clothes drawers with my spare hand, yanking them all the way until they reach the end of their cheap plastic runners and drop to the carpet. My eyes gaze over the drawers. They are all full. Faded T-shirts from the summer below long-sleeved tops. Jumpers, jeans, stray socks not in their pairs, and underwear of every color.

"Jamie's Liverpool football shirt is missing. It's his favorite." I try to remember when I last saw it. He was wearing it when we went to the playground last week. I'm sure of it. "And his rucksack and his Spider-Man pjs are gone."

"Tess—"

"There's more." I cut her off before she can tell me it's in the wash or under the bed, or that I'm just a crazy widow who's losing things, losing it. "There is some of Mark's stuff missing too. His walking boots are gone, and the jumper I bought him for his birthday. He wouldn't have taken them with him on a business trip," I add before she can ask.

"And you think I've taken them?" Shelley asks with an even tone as if she's asking me if I want milk in my coffee.

"I . . . You've been here." My spine tingles, my body reacting to the surfacing memory. Two weeks ago, after the trip to Tesco with Shelley, the house felt strange. The boxes in the study had been moved around. How could I have forgotten? Why hadn't I checked the rest of the house more carefully?

"Tess, I'm worried about you," Shelley says.

"I'm so sorry," I splutter. "Ignore me. I'm being jittery and stupid. It's the house." I'm babbling now and my cheeks are flaming with heat. "I need to get out more." I attempt a laugh but it sounds hollow.

"It's fine," she says, and I can feel her worry vibrating down the phone as if it's a physical thing. "Look, why don't we go shopping in Ipswich next Saturday? My friend Mel invited me. Her daughter will be coming too. Indra. She's seven."

"Er—" I wonder what Jamie will think of a shopping trip the day before his birthday. His worst nightmare normally, being dragged from shop to shop, but maybe if he's on the lookout for a few extra birthday presents and he knows Shelley will be there, he won't mind so much. And he'll have someone his age to talk to.

"Come on, it will be fun," she says. "And let's face it, you could do with a few new clothes." She's teasing me now and I can't help but smile looking down at the fleece I've had since forever. It used to be the deepest navy but has faded to a gray-blue. It's covered in tiny bobbles.

"Um . . . I guess."

"Do you want me to come pick you up? I normally go for a swim first thing Saturday anyway, so it'll be on the way past."

"OK. Thanks."

"Oh, gotta go," she says cutting my last words off. "See you Saturday."

"Jamie will love it," I say to the silent phone.

Emptiness consumes me. I lay my face against Jamie's car rug and cry for a while.

Oh, Tessie.

It's Easter weekend. I should be spending time with Jamie and hiding eggs for an egg hunt. And I will in a minute. I just need a minute.

Remember when Jamie grew out of his first baby onesies? You cried packing them away into a bag for the loft.

It felt like I was losing a part of him. It still does every time I sort through his clothes. My fingers run over Jamie's drawers. They need sorting. I bet half this stuff doesn't fit him anymore, although thankfully his growth spurt seems to have tailed off.

I'm just slotting the final drawer back into place when the side door crashes open.

"Mum?" Jamie's voice shouts through the house. His feet stomp on the kitchen floor.

"Take your shoes off," I call back.

"Oh," I hear him say to himself. I picture him striding backward to the side door and kicking his wellies off, leaving them strewn across the nook and in the way of the side door.

"I'm hungry. Can I have my chocolate?" he shouts. I smile and pull myself up and wipe my eyes.

"Have you seen your backpack?"

"Er . . ." I can sense his mind calculating an answer as if the truth might get him in trouble.

"Is it in the tree house?"

"Yeah," he says.

We meet on the stairs. His face is sheepish but there is sadness there too.

"It doesn't matter," I say softly. "I just wondered. Wash your hands and we'll play a game of Parcheesi."

He nods and disappears into the bathroom.

I head for the nook, surprised to see Jamie's wellies sitting on the boot rack. I jiggle the handle of the side door back and forth, checking it's locked. I'm pleased and sad all at the same time to see that Jamie thought to lock it when he came in. He must've picked up on my constant checking of the doors.

I try to remember when I last saw your things. Was it after the time someone had been in the house? I don't know.

I can almost understand Ian prying in your study, his desperation for the money, and the warped older-brother belief that he has a right to look through your will and take over as executor.

But why would he take your clothes and boots? And Jamie's things too. It doesn't make sense.

CHAPTER 51

Thursday, April 5

---

3 DAYS TO JAMIE'S BIRTHDAY

The thing is, even though I was jittery and jumping at every creak in the house, it still floored me when the man who chased me in Manningtree walked around the side of the house and into our garden.

I was pegging out the washing, my mind on the two chocolate sponges baking in the oven for Jamie's birthday cake. I was thinking about popping to the shops, and in my head I was listing the things I needed. Party Rings, chocolate chip cookies, blackcurrant cordial, bread, milk, a helium balloon.

It happens all at once. The crunch of feet on gravel and my mind blanking—the shopping list gone. I drop the towel and turn toward the house and there he is—the man—walking, no, striding toward me.

I gasp.

Fear presses down so fast and so hard that my legs buckle and I almost fall. I right myself at the last second and scramble back, thankful Jamie is playing up in his room and not in the tree house. The man is in different clothes today—a white short-sleeved shirt and suit trousers—but he is still the person with pale sagging skin and thin greasy hair who chased me on the cobbled street, the same man I saw on the lane waiting for me.

"Mrs. Clarke?" he says.

"What . . . what do you want?" My chest hitches so my words come out in a whispered inhale.

Color seems to drain from his face and his skin is now almost translucent in the sunshine. "I wanted to talk to you."

I sidestep around the washing line, adding a barrier between us, even if it is just a few towels.

Fight or flight? Flight. I could make a run for it, along the side of the house and around to the garage and the driveway, get to the lane, get help. Except he'd simply go back the way he came and get there first, and who's to say there would be help coming anyway.

The side door is open and my phone is in the kitchen. Even if I ran and made it, he could go right inside and grab Jamie.

Fight. My eyes drop to the lawn, searching for a spade or a trowel, anything in fact that I can use as a weapon, but there's nothing.

"Mrs. Clarke? Tess, can I call you that?"

"I told you on the phone, I don't know what Mark was working on. I don't have whatever it is you want."

He frowns and rubs a hand against his cheek. "Sorry. I don't understand. We've never spoken on the phone."

"Yes we have. You left that vile message on my answerphone and we . . . we spoke last week, or the week before." I can't remember the day now, only the fear. Why is he pretending not to know?

The muscles in my shoulders pull taut, my hands bunch into two tight fists. Fight.

"Leave," I screech. "Get away from me. I'm going to call the police." The anger erupts—hot lava into my blood. I grit my teeth and feel the heat flood my body. "LEAVE," I scream again.

"I can't do that," he says, shaking his head and causing two lines of tears to fall from his eyes. "I'm sorry, but I have to talk to you."

There's a pause. Me hunched forward, panting, ready to fight for my life and Jamie's too, and him, shoulders heaving up and down as more tears break free.

"What do you want?" I ask again, the anger fizzling just a touch, just enough for his mumbled Birmingham accent to register in my thoughts.

I am absolutely certain that this man in my garden followed me in Manningtree. I am absolutely certain that this is the same man I saw standing on the lane waiting for me. But all of a sudden I'm not so sure he is the same person on the phone who called me Tessie.

The man seems to crumble then as if his bones have disintegrated inside and there is nothing to keep him upright. He drops forward, hands on knees, crying loudly. I could run right past him and into the house, lock the door, call the police, and I don't think he'd notice.

But I can't keep running from him, from everything, or it will never stop.

"What's your name?" I ask, taking a step closer.

"Richard Welkin," he says, drawing in a shuddering breath. He looks up and seems to realize he's sitting on the ground. "I'm so sorry, I . . . I work at the airline." He swallows, his Adam's apple jutting out.

"Oh." This doesn't make any sense.

"Could I speak to you for a moment, please?"

"Out here," I say. "You have to stay right where you are. I'm going to go into the kitchen and get my phone. I'm going to dial 999, and if you move or say anything I don't like, I'm going to press send."

He nods and something like relief seems to settle on his face.

I wait another moment and then I run toward the house, keeping my distance as I go past him, just in case this is all a trick, a way to lure me close enough to grab. He doesn't move though, and when I reach the nook, I slam the side door closed behind me and bolt the door.

The smell of burned chocolate fills the air and I remember the cakes. I pull them out and rest them on the hob. There's a dusting of black on the top of the sponge and they're both slanting where they've risen wonky in the oven. But I think they'll be salvageable if I trim off the tops.

"Jamie?" I call up the stairs.

"Yeah?" he calls back.

"Stay in your room, OK? Don't come out until I tell you."

I grab my phone from the side and press 999 on the keypad.

When I step back into the bright daylight, Richard is exactly where I left him on the grass. He has stopped crying and is staring into the distance.

I think about sitting down too, but think better of it and remain standing, just in case I need to run.

"Why have you been following me?"

He clears his throat. "It might be easier if I tell you about myself and then we'll get to that. You see, I worked for the airline, in the human resources department. I was midlevel management, so I made some decisions myself, but not many. One of my jobs was to handle the paperwork and the interviews for employees when they returned from sick leave." The words come out like a well-practiced speech, like I'm not the first person he's said this to. "It was my job to talk to Philip Curtis—the pilot—"

"I know who he is." I will never forget the name.

"You've probably heard on the news by now that Philip was signed off work for four weeks with stress and depression. The flight to Frankfurt was his first flight back. I was supposed to interview Philip the day before he returned to work. He came up to my office for the meeting at five p.m. . . ." Richard's voice cracks and he shakes his head.

"We were supposed to talk for thirty minutes at least. We have an established protocol for supporting employees who are experiencing mental health issues. I had a checklist to go through. It had things like 'Is the employee exhibiting signs he may not be ready to return to work?'"

The sun is pressing down on my head and I feel suddenly weak. I don't know what this man wants, why he is here, but I don't feel scared anymore. I feel sad. I drop to the grass and sit down.

"And I didn't do it," Richard says.

"What? Why not?"

He blows out a puff of air. "There is no reason. I just didn't. I looked at Philip and he seemed fine to me. He was smiling, and we joked about the weather. So I patted him on the shoulder and said something along the lines of 'We're short-staffed for a flight tomorrow. It's yours if you want it,' and Philip looked at me. I'll never forget that look. It was like I'd given him a gift, and I remember congratulating myself on how I'd handled it. Like he'd been dreading the interview and I'd just made it easy for him.

"I left the checklist on my desk and I was going to tick through it the next day. But—" Tears form in his eyes again, and when he speaks, his voice is squeaking with emotion. "I'd given him a gift, all right. I'd given him a way out, you see. I've thought about it a thousand times, and I think when I offered him the flight to Frankfurt he knew then what he was going to do and it's my fault. I didn't clear him properly and I gave him that flight."

Cold runs over my skin. Oh, Mark. You really really shouldn't have died.

"Why have you been following me?" I ask.

"I was fired, of course. There has been talk of criminal charges being brought. No less than I deserve. Philip sent me his suicide note, thanking me for my help. I'd gone by then so the letter sat unopened on my desk for a while. Before I left I stole a copy of the passenger manifest, and I've been visiting all the families and apologizing the best I can and owning up to my part in it. The crash was preventable. It should never have happened, and that's something I will live with for the rest of my life."

"But—"

"You were hardest, Mrs. Clarke," Richard continues, preempting my question. "Every time I came to do it, well, I saw you and I . . . I couldn't."

I think of Jamie with his bright blue eyes and crazy blond hair. Our baby boy who will grow up without his father.

"The first time I came here, you were just pulling out of the drive and I followed you in my car to a town."

"Manningtree." I nod.

"I was going to talk to you, but then you ran away."

"And you waited on the lane that day, when the cyclist knocked into you."

"Yes," Richard says.

I look past Richard to the garden and the trees. This is Denise all over again. The handing over of guilt, the confession. I can't tell him it's OK, because it's not. And it never will be.

"Was it you in the garden that evening a few weeks ago?"

His face falls and I have my answer. "I . . . I was only there for a minute. I didn't know you'd seen me. I wanted to see if you were in and I was going to knock on the door, but I chickened out and tried to call you instead. I really didn't mean to scare you."

"Well, you did. A lot." My hand tightens on my phone. I want to call the police and get those two officers back here. I want to show them it was real, but what purpose would it serve? "How many times have you tried to call me?"

"A lot. I . . . I realized I couldn't do it face-to-face, so I thought I'd phone you instead, but that didn't work either. I heard your voice on the answerphone and you sounded so happy. I started phoning just to hear it. I think a part of me was trying to convince myself that you were still happy."

I shake my head. "How can I be?"

"I'm sorry. I'm so so sorry." Richard drops his head to his knees, the sobs shaking his body once again, but I feel no sympathy for him.

"I should call the police. You know that, don't you? You've been following me, calling my house. You've trespassed on my property and scared me out of my wits."

"I never meant to do that. I'm sorry."

"Stop saying sorry. It's meaningless." I stand up and stare down at him, forcing myself to think back over the days and days since you died. All the things that have happened, the pages in my notebook. Finally I have answers. Some, at least.

"So you never spoke when you called me?" I ask. "You didn't know my husband?"

Richard shakes his head and sniffs, and I believe him.

"What kind of car do you drive?"

"A blue Nissan."

"Did you follow me in a car any other time after Manningtree?"

"No."

Not all the answers, then. Just some. The hang-ups, the feeling of being watched. The man in the garden.

"Please leave now and don't come back. I never want to see you again."

Richard doesn't move. Not at first. He just stares up at me with his pathetic, beady eyes. I unlock the screen of my phone and allow my finger to hover over the call button. It's enough. Richard pushes himself up and walks quickly away.

Maybe one day I'll feel sorry for Richard and the burden he will carry with him forever, but after everything he has put me through, I don't think I will.

CHAPTER 52

The man in the black baseball cap—Richard—who I thought was trying to grab me in Manningtree, who stood in my garden in the dark and watched us, who called the house and hung up dozens of times, he is not the same person who called me Tessie.

The thought stuck in my mind as I washed up the cake tins. It was still there like a pin pricking my brain all the way through the evening. But it is only when Jamie is asleep and I'm sitting in bed with the notebook resting on my lap that something clicks.

There's one line written on the second page: *You didn't have to go!*

Denise's name is written underneath it, and it's only when I see it that I remember her parting question as I was trying to shut the door. *"Has anyone called you?"* she asked.

I picture her face and the dark pencil-drawn eyebrows. Her eyes were wide, her lips tight, as if she might've been scared. But of what?

I throw off the covers and pad barefoot down the stairs, holding your pj bottoms at the waist to stop them from falling down. I don't bother turning on the lights, and I use the torch on my phone to guide me.

I dig through the drawer with the take-out menus and phone chargers. I'm sure I put her card in here. I find it slipped between my address book and a Thai take-out menu and punch the number into my mobile.

The kitchen floor is freezing cold. It's seeping through my feet and into my body, and I shiver.

Denise answers on the third ring. "Hello?" she says, her voice hesitant as if she hadn't wanted to pick up at all.

"Denise, it's Tess."

"Oh, hi, Tess. Is everything all right?" There's a shuffling in the background and I hear a door closing.

"Yes. Sorry. I was thinking about . . . er . . . Mark's work stuff, and I wondered if you could help me with something."

"Now?" She sounds surprised. No, it's more than that; she sounds uncomfortable.

"I just have a few questions, and you did say I could call you anytime," I add, pushing at her guilt.

"Yes, sorry, of course. What can I help you with?"

I pause, suddenly unsure how to word what I need to say. "Do you know if Mark was working on something secret?"

"What do you mean?" she asks.

"Something . . . something that might have got him in trouble. Something he wouldn't have wanted people to know about." Something that would make a man call in the middle of the night and threaten Mark, threaten us.

There's silence on the line. I pull the phone from my ear to check that I've still got a signal.

"I can't talk now." Her voice is so low I barely hear. "I'm sorry. I need to call you back."

"Why? What can't you talk about?" I ask, but it's too late; she's gone.

What the hell, Mark?

I shiver again and stare at the blank screen of my mobile. Even in my panic I thought Denise would laugh off my question. I thought she'd reassure me there was nothing to worry about. Instead there is something, and she wouldn't tell me, or couldn't tell me. I think of her whispered response. She sounded scared.

I pull up my call log and try her number again. Denise might be scared, but so am I, and I have Jamie to think about.

It doesn't ring this time. Instead an electronic voice asks me to leave a message. I don't.

A sudden flash of light fills the kitchen. Headlights from a passing car. Except it doesn't pass; it pulls onto the drive. I gasp and drop out of sight from the window, crouching to the cold tiles. My hands shake as I pull up the keypad, ready to dial 999.

A car door slams. Footsteps crunch on the gravel. I stare at the side door and bite down on my lip until warm, metallic blood trickles into my mouth.

Is it Richard back again? I told him to leave us alone, but maybe he didn't listen.

The footsteps pass the window and reach the side porch. Knuckles rap against the wood.

Knock, knock.

I breathe shallow breaths, wobbling in my crouch and placing a hand to the tiles to steady myself.

Knock. Knock.

"Tess?" a voice calls through the door.

Knock. Knock.

It's not Richard, it's Ian. I reach a hand for the counter and I'm about to pull myself up and open the door when I hear the sound of keys—a jangle first as he finds the one he wants, then the click of metal on metal as he pushes it into the lock.

He thinks I'm out. He's trying to let himself in. My eyes grow wide, the cold air stinging my pupils.

Ian leans against the door with a thud and wiggles the key. He doesn't know I've changed the locks. He swears under his breath and tries again, and all the while I stay in my crouch less than three meters away from him. The muscles in my thighs burn, crying out for me to move. It was him who was in the house that day. I knew it, Mark.

The key clinks, then jangles again. He's giving up.

Then the home phone rings again. When the answerphone beeps I think it'll be Ian telling me to call him, but it's not, it's Shelley.

"Hi, Tess, it's Shelley," she says, her voice dancing through the house. "Just checking you're still on for Saturday. I found out today that my pool is closed for repairs until eight, so I won't be at yours until ten. Hope that's OK. There's a nice Italian next to the Buttermarket shopping center. I've booked us for a late lunch. We have to hit Debenhams first. They're having a one-day half-price sale. Oh, and your mum phoned me again. She says she's been leaving you messages too. Call me when you get this."

She signs off with a cheery "Bye," plunging the house into silence.

A moment later, Ian's shoes crunch on the gravel and his car door bangs. The engine purrs, headlights fill the kitchen, and he's gone.

I am alone once more.

I dash through the house and dive under the covers of our bed. With the light from my phone, I scribble the date and time in my notebook. Then I write: *Ian tries to get in. It was him in the house last time!!! I still don't know who is threatening us or what he wants??? Denise wouldn't speak to me. Why not? Is she scared?*

CHAPTER 53

Transcript BETWEEN ELLIOT SADLER (ES) AND TERESA CLARKE (TC) (INPATIENT AT OAKLANDS HOSPITAL, HARTFIELD WARD), WEDNESDAY, APRIL 11. SESSION 2 (Cont.)

TC: Richard Welkin was the man I saw in Manningtree who chased me. Shelley tried to convince me it was in my head, but it wasn't. He'd been watching me for weeks and phoning the house and hanging up. I thought it was the same man who's been calling me with threats, but it isn't. Richard worked for the airline and wanted to tell me that he thought the crash was his fault. That's why he was following me and hanging around the house. He said he was too scared to knock on the door.

ES: Do you think it was Richard's fault?

TC: Yes. I think it's a bit Denise's fault too. That's Mark's personal assistant. Have I mentioned her? She messed up Mark's flights.

ES: Why do you think Richard was scared to knock? Was he following all the families of the victims from the crash?

TC: I wondered the same thing. He said I was the hardest person to talk to.

ES: Why?

TC: I don't know. I guess he must've seen me and realized how much of a mess I was.

CHAPTER 54

Saturday, April 7

1 DAY TO JAMIE'S BIRTHDAY

The high street is busy; heaving, in fact. Solo shoppers, groups of teenagers, couples holding hands, children, parents, and push-chairs all weaving in and out of each other. There's a sense of desperation in the air, like it's one hour before closing time on Christmas Eve. The noise, the sheer chaos of it, is a jackhammer next to my head. I thought I wanted to get away from the stillness of the house and the village, but now I crave that silence.

We pass a busker—a teenage girl with a guitar and a nose ring. Her blond hair is dreadlocked and streaked with purple and blue. I expect something grungy when she opens her mouth but her voice as she launches into a Robbie Williams song is soft and angelic.

Jamie's feet slow as he stands to listen, transfixed by the girl.

I stop too. Her voice isn't just in my ears, it's permeating my body, like she's injecting her words, her thoughts, right into us.

My hand nudges Jamie's back, urging him on and catching up with Shelley two paces ahead of us.

We reach the sandy-bricked town hall, standing grand among the discount shops. I jump at the sound of a voice shouting and spin toward the noise. It's just a man with a stall of dried fruits heckling passersby.

In the pedestrianized square outside the town hall a group of older teenagers are sitting on the back of a bench with their feet resting on the seat. One of the boys has short, spiky hair and a tattoo of a gun on his neck. It's an old-style pistol like something from the Wild West. I stare at the detail of the ink on his skin and feel an undiluted fear that threatens to cripple me.

I want to take Jamie home now before the boy with the tattoo pulls out a real gun and kills us, before a car turns into the pedestrian zone and mows us all down, before the wall of a shop front gives way and covers us in bricks. Or a bomb. A terrorist attack. A madman wielding a container of battery acid.

Shelley moves beside me and squeezes my arm as if she senses my discomfort. I need to get a grip. I'm being paranoid and jittery. It's Ipswich high street, for God's sake, not a war zone. Yet I can't shake the vulnerability—an itchy wool jumper—covering my skin. I can't shake the feeling that Jamie and I are in danger here, that something terrible is about to happen, and I need to take Jamie's hand tight in my grasp and run far away from Shelley and all these people.

I'm sure Jamie feels it too. He didn't say a single word on the drive into town. Just stared out of the window from the back of Shelley's Mini and watched the world pass him by. He'll be eight tomorrow, Mark. Our baby boy is turning eight. It doesn't seem possible. He's so grown-up now, and at the same time he's so young.

Thoughts of Richard are still weighing on my mind and I'm desperate to tell Shelley about his confession, but Jamie hasn't left my side since she arrived this morning and I don't want him to hear.

"Mel," Shelley shouts, releasing my arm and standing on her tiptoes. She waves across the shoppers.

A woman with shiny black hair dashes over to us, with a girl trailing behind.

"Hey." Mel throws her arms around Shelley. "It's been too long."

Mel is wearing a white linen jacket and a pair of black skinny jeans that cling to her stick-thin legs. There's a glamour to both her and Shelley. It's in the heel of their boots and the cut of their jackets and the way their hair is sleek, their makeup subtle but there nonetheless. Suddenly I feel too hot and frumpy in my winter coat and foolish for blow-drying my curls and digging out a skirt and a pair of tights that didn't have runs.

"Tess, this is my friend Mel. We met at a baby group when Indra crawled over and stole the train Dylan was playing with." She laughs, and her eyes are bright and dancing. "Mel, this is Tess." Shelley doesn't expand on how we know each other, and I'm grateful for that.

"Hi," I say to Mel, pulling my cheeks up wide into what I hope is a happy face rather than the awkward grimace that it feels like. There's something familiar about Mel and I wonder if or when we might've met before.

"Hi, Tess. Nice to meet you. This is my daughter, Indra." She turns to Indra. "Say hi to Tess."

Indra is a younger version of Mel, with the same O-shaped eyes and sharp features. She's wearing a faux fur jacket over a black T-shirt which skims her belly button. Her long, dark hair is twisted into two plaits that dangle down her shoulders.

Indra looks up at me and lifts her hand in a brief wave. "Hi," she says, showing a large gap in the center of her mouth where her two front baby teeth used to be.

My smile softens. "Hello."

I turn to introduce Jamie but he's already stepped out from behind me and is whispering something in Indra's ear.

Jamie looks up with cheeks flushed red and gives a sheepish wave to Mel. Mel must sense his shyness because she plays it casual and doesn't say anything. Instead she smiles at Jamie and then at me as Jamie and Indra set off into the hordes of shoppers.

Only when we're moving do I glance at Mel out of the corner of my eye. It takes a long second for recognition to hit me, and now it's my face burning crimson thinking of the afternoon a few weeks ago when I perched on the redbrick wall waiting for Jamie to finish school. The receptionist who came out to talk to me with concern drawn on her face was Mel.

"I think we've met, actually," I say, hoping to make light of my embarrassment.

Mel nods, her black hair bobbing up and down. "I was just thinking that myself."

"It was outside the school the other week. I was early." I shake my head. "Sorry for dashing off. I was so embarrassed. My timekeeping has been dreadful recently." My throat tightens and I change the subject before Mel can ask why. I wonder if Shelley has told her about Mark. "I didn't realize you worked at the school. Are you a teacher?"

"I'm a receptionist." Mel flicks a glance to Shelley. There's a look on Mel's face that I can't read, and I wonder if I'm talking too much. "But I don't actually—"

"Mum," Indra cuts in, making the one syllable word into three. "Can we go to Claire's?" Indra and Jamie are already inching closer to the shop.

"Debenhams first, OK?" Mel nods. "You need some new clothes before we spend any money on accessories in Claire's." Mel tugs at Indra's top, pulling it down and receiving a scowl from her daughter.

Indra tucks her hands into her pockets, one arm looped with Jamie's as the pair walk ahead once more. I've never seen Jamie with a girl before, and the sight of them together makes me smile. He's always gravitated toward boys his own age, but he seems so content arm in arm with Indra.

"I sometimes feel like I've kept that bloody shop afloat over the last decade, the amount I've spent in there." Mel smirks, jabbing a finger at Claire's as we pass.

I fall into step with Mel and Shelley and try to keep up with the rapid-fire conversation they're having about a mutual friend. Every few steps one or the other glances over to me, trying to include me, I guess, but it doesn't work. I just feel watched. Jealousy grates my insides. Not just for Mel and Shelley, but for Indra and Jamie too.

You were my person, Mark. The one I always wanted to talk to first. I let my old friends slip away after we met. I didn't need them anymore. I had you, and now I have no one.

There's a blast of heat from above our heads as we step through the doors of Debenhams. Red banners are hanging down from the high ceilings and the staff are wearing red T-shirts. Both have the word SALE across them in large white writing.

The shop floor is busier than the street outside and people are budging me left and right on their way in and out of the doors. Shelley and Mel are drawn as if by magnets to the perfume counter, and I follow them.

It's too busy.

Too noisy.

I can feel the panic return, swooping through me.

Something is about to happen, like I'm hurtling toward danger without the first clue what it is or how I can stop it. My eyes are glued to Jamie and Indra as they weave around a pushchair to the makeup stands.

Shelley turns toward me. "Here, smell this?" She thrusts her wrist to my nose. The overbearing musky sweetness of the scent stings my eyes.

"It's the new Chanel. I might get some." Shelley is talking in a wistful sort of way. "You know, make a change."

Mel leans in and says something and they both laugh, but I don't listen, I don't hear. Someone is tapping my shoulder and when I turn around, it's Ian.

"Tess, hi." Ian looks beyond me to Mel and Shelley.

"Hi," I reply, my mind spinning. It's no coincidence that he is here, surely? Is he following me?

"Hi," Shelley says, moving closer. I catch the perfume on her wrist again. Sweat tickles my upper lip. The heat of the store and the caustic scent of the perfume counter are scratching at my lungs.

"Hello." Ian nods at Mel, then Shelley.

"This is Mark's brother, Ian. Ian, Shelley and Mel," I say, waving a hand between them.

"We've met," Shelley says, without any hint of her trademark grin.

"Thanks for your call the other day, Tess," Ian says, sounding strangely formal. "Can we talk privately for a few minutes, please?"

No is what I think, but Ian's eyes—your eyes—are imploring, and I find myself nodding.

"Do you want me to come, Tess?" Shelley asks, holding my arm as I try to move. She shoots a look at Ian.

"It's fine. Can you keep an eye?" I nod to Jamie and Indra. Indra is dabbing purple glitter gloss on her lips, making Jamie giggle.

Confusion crosses Shelley's face for a moment but she nods before shimmying through the people until she reaches the makeup counter and Jamie.

I follow Ian toward a space by the windows, but my eyes keep drawing back to Jamie. He's looking up at Shelley with such adoration, such love, that my chest pulls tight and I gasp.

"Tess?" Ian's voice is sharp, swiping at my thoughts, and they're gone. "Tess," he says again, "are you all right? You seem distracted."

"I'm fine." I hug my arms to my body and try to focus on Ian. "What are you doing here?"

"I was worried about you," he says, stepping closer. "I came by the house the other night to check on you. I was worried you might've . . ." His voice trails off.

"Killed myself?" I pull a face.

"Well." He shrugs. "But you weren't in."

Yes I was.

"There's something I need to tell you." Ian shuffles his feet and finds a spot on the floor to focus on.

He's nervous.

A young couple bustles past us, their hands loaded with bags. I catch the glint of a diamond on the girl's ring finger.

"Can we go somewhere quiet? Please, Tess. I really need to talk to you. It's about the money."

Part of me wants to go, wants answers, whatever they might be. But I hate how Ian has turned up like this. I might not have answered the door the other night, but it doesn't mean we couldn't have spoken another time. He didn't need to track me down while I'm on a shopping trip with Jamie.

"I do want to talk about the money," I reply. "But now isn't the right time. Let's meet next week. We'll go for coffee." *Somewhere neutral,* I think. "Or I'll come to the offices. I need to meet with Jacob anyway."

"Oh," Ian says. "I thought I—"

"I'm Mark's executor. I'm going to sort it out. I told you, I just needed a bit more time."

Ian says something, but my focus has moved back to the crowded shop.

"Are you listening to me?" I hear Ian ask.

I can't see Jamie. Shelley has disappeared too.

I dart forward and it's me now pushing through the shoppers, knocking people's bags with my shoulders, ignoring the tuts as I fight to reach Indra.

"Hey, where's Jamie?" I ask, stepping up alongside Indra.

She jumps and looks up at me. Gloss shimmers on her lips, but her eyes are blank as if she doesn't know me, as if we didn't meet twenty minutes ago, as if she hasn't been walking arm in arm with my son.

"Indra, where is Jamie?" I ask, slowing down my words. My fists bunch together and I have to fight the urge not to shake her.

Indra looks around before taking a long shuffle back and around me. I'm scaring her, I realize, straightening up and spinning around and around, my eyes scouring the shop for Jamie.

He's nowhere.

"Is everything OK, Tess?" Mel asks, appearing beside her daughter.

"Have you seen Shelley?" I keep turning, faces and bodies blurring. None of them are Shelley or Jamie.

"Er . . ." Mel looks casually around the store. There's no urgency to her glances, none of the panic I feel building inside me.

Shelley has disappeared. So has Jamie.

Stop, Tessie.

I can't, Mark. I can't let anything happen to Jamie.

Then it clicks—the pieces falling into place, the answer to the final cryptic clue—the thought I was trying to reach before Ian started talking to me. Shelley doesn't want to help me, she wants a son to replace Dylan. She wants Jamie. All of a sudden my head is filled with Shelley's voice. *"I miss being a mother almost as much as I miss Dylan . . . I want a child so badly, Tess."*

The shop spins before my eyes, or maybe it's me spinning. Where are you, Shelley? What have you done with Jamie?

"There she is," Indra shouts, flinging a finger toward the bag section.

I weave and push through people to get to Shelley.

"Oh, hey," she says. "What do you think?" She holds up a brown handbag, with a shiny gold buckle.

"Jamie." My voice is a strangled hiss. "Where's Jamie? You were supposed to be watching him."

"I . . ." Her eyes dart around the shop floor, her expression the mirror of my own panic. She hasn't taken Jamie, but she has lost him.

Suddenly they crowd around me—Mel, with Indra hugging her side, and Shelley and Ian. They are a wall blocking my view of the shop and the front doors.

What if Jamie is back on the street? What if someone takes him?

Stop, Tessie.

"Tess?" Ian raises his eyebrows and frowns. I can't tell if it's concern or irritation furrowing his brow but I don't care. Go away, I want to scream at him. "What's wrong?" he asks.

My legs feel suddenly weak. "I can't find Jamie," I whisper, staring unblinking at the faces of the shoppers who've stopped to stare, then looking back at Mel and Ian again. They stare back with pitiful confusion as if I'm speaking in a different language. Sweat dampens my skin beneath my clothes, and my breathing becomes short and gasping. Why is no one helping me?

"JAMIE?" I spin around. More shoppers stop and stare but I don't care. "I've lost my son," I shout out.

Shelley moves first, pushing her way to the front of the shop to check the street.

"JAMIE," I shout again.

A woman with a tight perm places a hand on her chest and backs away as if I've just told her I'm wearing a bomb under my coat. What is wrong with these people? "He's seven," I shout. "He's wearing a . . . a blue jacket and jeans and he has blond, curly hair."

My heart is pounding so fast I can't breathe through the force of it.

People start to move and look around the floor as if he might be sitting by their feet, as if I've dropped an earring.

"Tess?" Ian's voice is low and firm and I know he's going to tell me to calm down. How can I?

It's an effort to speak. A lightness floats across my eyes but I push it away. "Stay here," I shout to them as I move deeper into the shop. "I'll go look upstairs."

"Jamie?" I call out, running up the escalator. My foot slips and my left knee smashes into the metal grille of the step in front. Pain sears across my leg and there's a trickle of wet seeping through my tights.

Shelley is shouting my name and I glance back, willing Jamie to be by her side, but he isn't. She's near the front doors talking to a security guard with a walkie-talkie.

Jamie has to be somewhere.

When the escalator nears the top, I strain to see through the glass barriers, praying I'll catch a flash of Jamie's blond curls or hear him shout. "Jamie," I call again, pushing past a couple ahead of me to reach the second floor.

CHAPTER 55

The upstairs is quieter. Piano music is playing softly and in complete contrast to the urgency gripping my body. I have to find Jamie.

"Have you seen a boy up here?" I ask a man wearing a red T-shirt. He's carrying a box, which he drops to the floor when I stop him.

He shakes his head and starts to say something, but I don't have time to listen.

I turn a corner from bedding into household and there he is, right at the back of the shop, running a hand over a long black telescope. Our beautiful boy with his head of blond curls that need a trim.

I burst into tears, and when Jamie turns I see the tears on his cheeks too.

"I thought I'd lost you."

Jamie smiles and gives an apologetic shrug. He wandered off and got distracted by the telescope that looks up at the stars. He doesn't need to tell me why. I understand. He's thinking of heaven or wherever you are.

We stand in silence for a few seconds, staring at the telescope together. It costs almost five hundred pounds, but for a moment I'm so relieved I almost scoop it up to buy. But my hands, my whole body in fact, are shaking, and one thought overwhelms the rest—I have to get us out of here.

"It's OK." I give a weak smile and hold Jamie's hand as the escalator descends and Ian, Shelley, and Mel come into view. With a stab of guilt I see Indra crying too, but none of them are looking my way.

Ian has his back to me, gesticulating wildly at Shelley, but I can see Shelley's face clearly. It's stony and cold and she's snapping at Ian. "Don't tell me what I need to do. I'm handling it. I told you."

"Are you though? How exactly?" I hear Ian growl as we step from the escalator.

"These things take time. You can't just rush in," Shelley hisses.

"Either you do something or I will," he says as we reach them.

Mel elbows Shelley and the three turn toward us.

"Hey," I say, biting my lip as fresh tears swim before my eyes. My face flushes thinking of my outburst. "I found him."

They stare—Mel, Shelley, Ian—openmouthed, their faces almost sheepish, as if I've caught them out.

Then it hits me, punching the air from my lungs. They know each other. Shelley and Ian. I stagger back, stepping on the foot of a passing shopper.

What other reason can there be for a heated argument? Strangers don't argue like that—venomous and angry. It was not a "you stole my parking space" kind of bickering between strangers.

What exactly is Shelley handling? The question sends a queasiness turning in my stomach.

"Tess," Shelley says. "Let's go somewhere quiet."

I shake my head and step away. "No. Leave us alone. All of you." I wave a finger between them.

I throw my arm around Jamie and guide him from the shop.

We catch the bus home. The number 93. A rickety double-decker with its heater on too high and the stink of petrol fumes wafting in through the open windows. We sit upstairs right at the front and watch the world go by together, Jamie lost in his thoughts, and me in mine. Later I pull out my notebook and flick through the pages, reading every word, touching my fingers against the bobbled pen marks like it's braille, like I can feel the answer I cannot see.

Ian and Shelley know each other. What does that mean?

I try to remember the conversation between them that I overheard on the doorstep when I thought Shelley was protecting me. And the argument I overheard after our trip to Tesco together. Could Shelley have been talking to Ian?

It's funny how someone came into the house then. As if they were waiting for me to be out of the way for long enough. Other than the ten minutes to school and back twice a day, I hardly leave the house. It was Shelley's idea to go shopping. She picked me up too, when I could easily have driven myself. We were out for hours, dawdling around Tesco.

Have I got this whole thing upside down? I thought Shelley was being kind to me that day, but maybe she was just killing time, keeping me away so Ian could look through our things.

If I take Richard out of the equation, what is left? The threats from a voice on the answerphone, Ian and his money, things missing from the house.

Are Shelley and Ian working together? What do they really want, Mark?

CHAPTER 56

Transcript BETWEEN ELLIOT SADLER (ES) AND TERESA CLARKE (TC) (INPATIENT AT OAKLANDS HOSPITAL, HARTFIELD WARD), WEDNESDAY, APRIL 11. SESSION 2 (Cont.)

TC: Have you spoken to Shelley's friend Mel? Maybe she's helping Shelley. Maybe she has Jamie.

ES: How well do you know Mel?

TC: We met once—well, twice actually, but only once properly. Shelley took Jamie and me into Ipswich for a shopping trip on Saturday. So much has happened. It feels like a long time ago. There was something off about the whole thing. It was like Mel was watching me, assessing me—they both were. Then Ian turned up out of the blue and it was like the three of them knew each other.

ES: Did they?

TC: They didn't say as much, not at first anyway. Ian wanted to talk to me privately, so I left Shelley in charge of Jamie. She didn't watch him properly and he wandered off to the second floor to look at a telescope. I panicked. I guess I might have overreacted, but Jamie is everything to me. Shelley knew that. She should've stayed with him. After I'd found Jamie, we came back downstairs, and Shelley and Ian were arguing.

ES: About what?

TC: I don't know, but it definitely felt like they knew each other. They stopped the second they saw me. I'm sure it's all connected. Ian and the money and Shelley and Jamie, Mark and the threats. It's all connected somehow. If I could just get my notebook. What has Ian said?

ES: Let's stop here for now. Your mother will be here in a minute.

TC: My mum? Why?

ES: You were stabbed, Tess. The hospital found her contact details and phoned her. She's on her way right now.

TC: Oh. I wish you hadn't.

ES: Why?

TC: (Shakes head)

ES: I have your notebook. I'll bring it to you.

TC: Thank you.

CHAPTER 57

IAN

After the time I found Tess in the rain, I didn't actually see her again until the shopping center. Tess stopped taking my calls, which I bet was Shelley's idea. So I went to see her last week. She wasn't home, or at least, she didn't answer the door. I heard her phone ring and a message from Shelley saying that they were going into town on the Saturday. So I went along to see if I could find them. I've made mistakes, I'm not denying it. But when I went to find her in Ipswich, it was so I could make things right.

What happened in Debenhams was all the proof you need that Shelley was in way over her head. I needed to step in, and I did. But I tell you one thing—I had no idea it was Jamie's birthday until I turned up at the house.

SHELLEY

There wasn't time to stop and think about what I was doing. My judgment was clouded, I know that now. I let my own personal problems and the connection I felt to Jamie get in the way. I just kept thinking of the unfairness of it all. I'd lost Dylan, and Tess still had Jamie. It wasn't fair.

The shopping trip was awful. That's when I knew I had to do something. Things got out of hand, and that was my fault. I never should've invited Mel and her daughter, Indra, along. I think in the back of my mind I wanted someone else there to keep an eye on Tess. I didn't trust my judgment around her. I have no idea how Ian knew we would be in Debenhams, but he couldn't have chosen a worse time to show up. When Tess flipped out about losing Jamie, Ian was shouting at me that it was my fault, and maybe it was. I should never have told Ian to meet me at Tess's the next day. I should've gone alone. If only I'd gone alone, maybe none of this would have happened. I'm so sorry.

CHAPTER 58

Sunday, April 8

JAMIE'S BIRTHDAY

Denise calls first thing while I'm wobbling on one of the kitchen chairs, trying to hook up the "happy birthday" bunting across the cupboards.

I jump down and snatch up my mobile.

Jamie's presents are piled on the table, wrapped in stupidly expensive Star Wars paper. I have a few extra gifts in the car, along with the helium balloon. I'm saving them for later when we have cake.

Before I answer the phone I listen for any sound that Jamie is awake yet, but all I hear are radiators clanging.

"Hi," I say, pressing the phone to my ear.

"Hi, Tess. I'm so sorry it's taken me a few days to get back to you."

"I've been phoning you," I say. "Every day, in fact. What's going on?" I ask, stepping to the window and staring at the driveway. "What couldn't you talk about the other night?"

"I'm so sorry about that. It threw me when you called out of the blue. Hearing from you really upset me and brought the crash flooding back. I've already had so much time off work. I haven't been sleeping. I was just starting to feel OK when you called, and I panicked. I didn't want to think about it anymore. I know that's not fair, and I'm sorry."

It isn't fair. Denise's grief is nothing compared to mine. I want to shout at her for being so selfish, but if I do that then she'll probably hang up and I'll never have the answers I need.

"It's OK," I lie. "So do you know what Mark was working on? I know he had a secret project but that's it."

Denise sighs, her breath rattling in the phone. "Mark and two of the programmers were setting up their own company. They wanted to go it alone. They asked me to come with them and run the office, which is how I know about it."

"Oh." Something sinks inside me. I sit on the chair I was balancing on a moment ago. This isn't what I was expecting to hear. "So why all the secrecy?"

"It has to be secret so the company won't find out."

"Why not?"

"They'll fire us. They'll think we're stealing clients, which actually we are."

"Did you need money to start the business? A hundred grand?" I ask.

"No," Denise replies. "It is still in the planning stages, but the upfront costs were minimal. Peter Yang and Toby Gordon are the developers. They were planning to work from their homes to start with, and Mark was going to travel to clients. It was just a website they needed and some marketing, and they were planning to put that together themselves."

"I didn't know anything about it," I mumble, feeling embarrassed that you shared this secret with your PA but not with me, your wife.

"He didn't want you to worry," Denise says, her words suddenly rushed. "Honestly, Tess, he felt really bad. He told us all how he was planning to tell you after the trip to Frankfurt. He just wanted one more client on board to be sure it was all going to work."

"Oh. Thank you," I say, and I mean it too. I hate that you didn't tell me things, Mark, but I think maybe I get it. You were always trying to look out for me and stop me from worrying. You hated it when I worried, like it was your fault, your personal challenge to stop me. I should've told you all along that's impossible. I'm a worrier; I'll always worry. Keeping things from me wasn't the answer.

"Was there anything else?" Denise asks.

"Could Mark have taken on any extra work by himself?" I think of the rasping laugh of the man on the phone and the thing he wants back. "Some kind of programming job or anything like that?"

"I don't think so," Denise says. "I mean, it's possible, but I'm sure he would've told us. Peter is the software king. Mark hasn't been in the development side of things for years. Most of the technology has moved on, so it would've been a steep learning curve for Mark to jump back into programming."

"Oh." I hadn't thought of that.

"They're still calling it CYG Systems. Clarke, Yang, Gordon. We all miss Mark so much."

"Me too," I say.

"I should probably go," Denise says. "There's a management meeting this—"

"Wait, Denise. There's something else. You asked me if anyone was calling the house. Why did you ask me that?"

"Oh. Yes, I got a call from a weird guy. He was fishing around, calling the team and asking about Mark and you and Jamie."

It's him. The vile man with his threats. It has to be.

"I thought he might be a journalist at first," Denise continues. "I didn't want him harassing you. But then he said he was from the airline and got really upset. I'm sure he told me his name. It was . . ." Her voice trails off, but I know exactly who she means.

"Richard." I sigh.

"Yes," Denise says. "Sorry, has he been in touch? I should've just told you about him when I asked, but I thought he might've given up."

"It's OK. I'd better go. It's Jamie's birthday today." I hang up before Denise can reply.

My mind is whirring. You were setting up a new business. That was the secret project you didn't tell me about. More answers, but not the ones I was looking for.

I'm about to get my notebook when Jamie slinks into the kitchen in his pjs.

"Happy birthday!" I shout. My voice shakes but I paste a grin on my face and push the questions away. I must focus on Jamie today.

Jamie smiles and slides into the chair, eyeing his presents, then looks up as I launch into your song. All four verses . . . *"squashed tomatoes and stew."* I dance around the kitchen, hopping from foot to foot. Jamie laughs at my silliness and so do I. It's all wrong without you, but I don't stop.

CHAPTER 59

After breakfast when the presents were all opened and wrapping paper littered the floor, Jamie ran up to get dressed before going out to play in the tree house like it was any other day.

I stayed in the garden too. Partly to be near to him and partly because the house felt darker today, emptier. Outside the sun was high in the sky and dandelion yellow. Every so often white fluffy clouds would swallow the sun, and the air would cool a notch.

"Are you sure you don't want to do something special today?" I shouted up at one point, running a hand over the rope ladder and wishing he'd invite me into his world. "It's not too late."

"I'm fine" were the words that drifted back.

I leaned against the rough bark and listened for a while to Jamie's nonsense chatter and the sound of his little metal cars being driven across the wood.

"Is Shelley coming?" he asked later when it was almost time to go in, almost time for cake and a tea of crisps and jam sandwiches.

"Not today, baby."

Shelley called last night, over and over until I couldn't escape the buzz of my mobile and the trilling of the home phone. I blocked her number and unplugged the landline. I should've done it weeks ago. I'm no longer pacing the house waiting to hear it ring.

I don't know who is threatening us or what they want, but one thing I am sure of is that Shelley wants Jamie.

I flick the radio on the moment I step through the side door and into the kitchen. Every few minutes the signal crackles but the murmur of voices and music fills the kitchen with life. I shut the door into the hall as if the radio voices are ghosts that will float away into the bowels of the house and we'll be left with the stillness again.

Within minutes Jamie and I have eaten our way through a pack of chocolate chip cookies and buried the kitchen table under a dozen clear plastic bags of gray Legos in every shape and size imaginable. The instructions—a two-hundred-page manual—are open in front of us on page one. Jamie's head is bent in concentration and his tongue is sticking out, wiggling the tooth back and forth like a pendulum.

He's put his new Batman pajamas on over his clothes. They're too big and his hands keep disappearing inside the sleeves every time he reaches for the next Lego piece.

"Ah." I jump up, my chair scraping the tiles. "I left something in the car. You carry on. Ten more minutes and we'll have cake." I smile and it doesn't feel fake like it did this morning.

A pang of pure love digs into my chest. "I love you, Jamie."

I grab the car key and throw open the side door, ready to dash out in my slippers and retrieve the helium balloon. The sky above the fields is the color of pink cotton candy, and if it wasn't for Shelley standing right in front of me, with her hand lifted ready to knock, I would've beckoned Jamie over to see it.

"Hi. Your phone isn't working," she says on the doorstep, peering over my shoulder to look at Jamie.

"I unplugged it. Too many call centers," I lie.

"Your mobile isn't working either." Shelley narrows her eyes at me. There is no dancing joy or laughing grin tonight. Her jaw is tight, her lips a straight line.

I shrug.

"You ran off yesterday in such a hurry, and I wanted to make sure—"

"I'm fine. It's just . . . it's Jamie's birthday today . . ." My voice trails off and I wedge my body into the gap in the door, closing off her view of the kitchen and the cake and the celebration we're trying to have.

There's a part of me that wants to scream at her to leave, to slam the door and bolt it tight. Another part of me wants to tell her I know everything. I want to tell her to give up, because I'll never let her take Jamie away from me. Not ever.

Except I can't find the words. The Shelley I see in the pages of my notebook, the one I fear in the small hours of the night when I can't sleep, the one who drugs me with sleeping pills and sings lullabies to Jamie, the one I blocked from my phone and vowed never to speak to again, is somehow disconnected from the woman on my doorstep with her bleach-blond hair, the baby blue V-neck jumper, and the girl-next-door face.

Standing before me is my friend who pulled me back from the ledge of my grief, who came to my and Jamie's rescue when no one else was there. I don't know how I would've survived without her friendship. This Shelley saved me, and I don't want to slam the door in her face. I want to burst into tears and throw myself into her arms.

There's a scraping of chair legs on the tiles behind me, and I don't need to turn around to know Jamie is grinning ear to ear, desperate to show Shelley his new gifts and share his birthday celebrations with her.

So I ignore the siren screeching in my ears, I ignore the dread twisting knots in my stomach, and I step back, opening the door to let her in. Not just for Jamie and the happy dance of his feet thudding softly on the kitchen floor, but for me too. Shelley's energy will make it a real celebration. We can light the candles on his cake and sing "Happy Birthday" and it won't be fake, it won't be false cheer we'll feel.

"I just have to get something from my boot," I say, trying to shuffle past her.

Relief relaxes the muscles in her face and she smiles a little. "I'll get it. You're not wearing any shoes." She plucks the key from my hand and turns on her heel before I can stop her.

When Shelley returns, her face is drained of color and pure white against the colors of the sky. The balloon is blustering behind her, desperate to be set free, and she looks so distracted that for a moment I think it will fly out of her hands and be lost to the pink sunset.

Then I see the shadow and hear the extra crunch of footsteps on the driveway. Shelley is not alone. Ian is walking a pace behind her, his face dark and scowling. He's wearing a shirt with no tie and black jeans. There is a day's beard growth on his face. It's the first time I've seen him look even a little ruffled.

I step back, a shiver racing over my body. "What do you want?" I stammer.

"May I come in for a minute, Tess?" Ian asks.

I shake my head but he's already at the porch and bundling through the door with Shelley by his side. He strides into the kitchen, leaving Shelley in the doorway. Her eyes are wide. "I'm sorry," she whispers.

I throw a glance behind me. Jamie has picked up one of his presents from this morning—the driving game for his PlayStation—and is studying the back cover, avoiding Ian's gaze and the sudden addition of his uncle at his birthday.

Ian is standing by the sink with his arms folded. He seems to be staring wide-eyed at the piles of Legos on the kitchen table as if hypnotized by them.

"You're working together, aren't you?" I say to Shelley, nodding to Ian. "You're trying to scare me into giving you Mark's life insurance, and take Jamie away from me."

"How about we all take a seat and talk," Ian says. He raises his eyebrows at Shelley, sending her a signal I can't decipher.

I falter and Shelley steps into the kitchen, knocking the balloon against me as she passes.

"Look what I got," Jamie singsongs to Shelley. "Bet you won't be able to win at this one."

Shelley doesn't reply, but lets go of the balloon. The weight at the end of the ribbon drops to the floor with a clatter. The 8 bobs up and down for a moment, its top scraping against one of the dark beams and making Jamie laugh.

"Mum, can I set my new game up?" Jamie asks, his voice loud with excitement. For once Jamie is too distracted by his gifts to notice the mood, the tension crackling in the air, too happy to see Shelley to ask why Ian is here. He hasn't even noticed Shelley's silence.

I nod. "Of course. Then we'll do the cake." Just as soon as I've gotten rid of Ian and Shelley.

It's only after Jamie has skipped out of the room that I see Shelley is crying. Two perfect streams of tears leaking from her eyes. It's the first time I've seen her properly cry and it makes me want to cry too. I look away.

I turn to Ian and raise my chin a little before I speak. "I don't know why you've come, Ian, but you're not welcome here. I have found no proof that you loaned Mark any money. I think you're lying to me because you want to get your hands on some, maybe all, of Mark's life insurance. You keep saying that you're trying to help me, but that's not true, is it? You're trying to trick me. Both of you are."

I stare between them and feel the walls pushing closer. Their faces are both drawn tight. Have I caught them out at last?

"Tess—" Ian begins.

I hold up my hand and cut him off. "You came into the house when I was out, didn't you?"

Ian says nothing and I know I'm right.

"You . . . you are not welcome in our lives anymore," I say. "Tomorrow I'm going to contact a new solicitor and make sure you don't get a penny of Mark's money. I . . . I'm going to file a restraining order too. I never want to see you again."

My breathing is fast, like my heart thumping in my chest. I feel empowered and scared all in the same beat.

Ian shakes his head. "You need help, Tess." He looks to Shelley and another message passes between them.

Shelley nods. "This has to stop." She waves her hands across the kitchen.

"You're just as bad." I shake my head, talking fast and low so Jamie doesn't hear. "Do you think I haven't noticed you controlling me with all of your 'kind' little comments? 'Oh, poor Tess, best not go out without me. Poor Tess, let me speak to your family for you.'"

"Tess, I never—" Shelley starts to speak but I cut her off.

"Manipulating me when I'm at my lowest. I heard you on the phone after we got back and Ian had been in the house. You were speaking to each other, weren't you? I heard you arguing."

"That's not true," Shelley cries out.

"I want you both to leave now, or I'll call the police." I move around the table to the cake, sitting ready on the oven top. The plate is smudged with black marks from the icing, but the cake itself is not a bad effort. The sheet of pre-bought black icing is hiding the slope of the chocolate cake where it rose wonky in the oven. I've cut out the bat symbol in yellow icing. The wings are a little jagged in places but the eight yellow candles are hiding the worst of it.

The jangling of cutlery fills the silence as I yank open a drawer, pull out the first knife I come across, and slam the drawer shut. The carving knife in my hand is far too efficient for slicing through sponge but I'm too angry to riffle through the utensils to find the cake cutter.

I should never have let them in. I push the Legos to one side to make space for the cake and the knife on the corner of the kitchen table. I was stupid to see Shelley as two people. There is only one person standing before me, and any pretense that we are friends is gone.

Neither of them moves. It's as though they're waiting for me to say something. I don't need to look at Shelley's face to know she is crying still. Is she sorry for her part in this? Sorry I've found out? Or is it another angle for her to manipulate me with? She might have lost her son, but she's not having mine.

"Please, Tess, sit for a minute," Shelley says, throwing a pleading glance at Ian. "We need to talk. Ian's right. You need help."

"You'd like me to think that, wouldn't you?" I say, grabbing the box of matches from the window ledge. My fingers fumble in the box for a moment before I grip a match and scratch it across the box.

"Oh, Tess, no." Shelley reaches for my hand and the matches but I shrug her away. Does she think I'm going to burn the house down now?

The flame hisses and speeds down the stick. I touch it to each of Jamie's candles and blow out the match before it singes my fingers.

"This is ridiculous," Ian says.

"That's what you've wanted all along, isn't it?" I say to Shelley, ignoring Ian's comment. "To make me out like I'm a mental case and need help. Make me so reliant on you that I can't think for myself."

Shelley shakes her head. "No. That's not true."

I laugh, a short "ha," and shake my head. "I thought I was going crazy, you know, but that's exactly what you wanted. Who did you get to call me? And how did he know to call me Tessie?" I point the question at Ian.

"This isn't what Mark would've wanted," Ian says.

All of a sudden there's a shift in the air and it's them together against me. The walls of the kitchen are closing in.

"I don't need help and I certainly don't need you to tell me what Mark wanted. He wanted me, he wanted Jamie. He wanted us to be happy." The words unravel growl-like from my mouth. I slam the box of matches down beside the plate and the knife, upending a pile of Legos. A piece flies across the floor, adding to the anger crackling—wood on the bonfire—inside me. I can taste the smoke in my mouth as I turn to them. "I want you to leave." My voice is suddenly loud and bounces across the small kitchen.

"Tess, please listen to me," Shelley says. "Jamie isn't—"

I don't hear her final word. I don't need to. Happy—that's what Shelley was going to say—Jamie isn't happy. But I don't hear because Jamie is standing in the doorway. His face is dark, his tongue pressing so hard against the tooth at the front that it's protruding outward at a horizontal angle. Anger is pulsing out of his body, the same anger I felt just moments ago.

My indignation crumbles to ash as I stare into the piercing blue eyes of our son.

"Jamie." My voice quivers. "It's OK. Shelley and Ian were just leaving. Then we'll have cake." I wave a hand to the candles. The eight tiny flames are standing tall. Two blobs of wax have already rolled onto the cake and smudged the icing.

"No," he says. The one hollow word echoes in my head.

"Bloody hell," Ian mutters.

"Tess, look at me." Shelley's voice is almost a shout, but I can't pull my focus away from Jamie. His hands bunch into two tight fists and his piercing blue eyes narrow on the carving knife. I follow his gaze and no longer see a knife to cut his birthday cake—I see a weapon.

"This has to stop," Shelley says. There is a warning in her voice that finally drags my eyes away from Jamie and the knife. Shelley's face is tight, her eyes wide with panic. This is exactly what she wanted, isn't it? To drive Jamie and me apart.

"I want Shelley to be my mummy," Jamie says, his voice soft and childish like he's three again and asking for his teddy. "I hate you."

"Jamie . . . I'm sorry." I gasp, fighting for breath as his words cut into me. "I'll do better. I'll—"

"TESS," Ian bellows, making me jump.

There's a split second of silence and somewhere in the background I can hear a George Michael song on the radio.

I don't know who moves first, but the second ticks by and in the very next one we are scrambling for the knife—Jamie, Ian, and me.

Jamie reaches for it at the same moment I do.

Shelley is screeching, "Stop it, Tess. Stop it, stop it, stop it." And I'm trying, but then Ian is grabbing for the knife and reaching right over Jamie to get it. A pressure squeezes my body. Ian's hand is almost at the handle, but so is Jamie's. I can't let Ian get it. What if he wants to hurt Jamie? I leap forward. Too fast, too far. Jamie's hands are on the handle, Ian's too.

I'm moving too fast. I try to right myself but it's too late. The blade slides right into my stomach with the same ease as the cake it was intended for.

Oh, Tessie, oh no.

Your voice is distant, crackling like the radio.

The pain is hot and scorches a path out from my stomach over my entire body and I stare at the O shape of Shelley's face, and Ian's too as he stumbles back.

CHAPTER 60

Panic swirls like a tornado inside me. The knife is sticking out of my stomach, half in, half out. I can't bear to look at it, but I can't look away either. I reach for the handle and yank out the blade. Warm stickiness soaks through my top as the knife drops to the floor with a clatter of metal.

I clutch my stomach and feel blood ooze through my fingers.

"Jamie." I sink to the floor, clenching my teeth through the pain crippling every muscle in my body; forcing myself to sound calm against the panic clawing to get out.

He's just out of reach, standing over me in his new black and yellow Batman pajamas.

I hear their voices—Shelley's and Ian's. They are talking to each other or maybe to me and Jamie, but the only noise in my ears is the ragged inhale and exhale of my breath and the drumming of my heartbeat.

This isn't happening. This isn't happening. I repeat the words over and over in my head as if saying them enough times will undo the last few minutes—the last few months—of my life. A wave of pain crashes through me, returning my focus to the wound, the blood, the knife. I raise my voice and allow the desperation to ring through it: "Jamie!"

Jamie's eyes are wide and the clearest blue, like the sky on the day you died.

My hand shakes with the force of an electrical current, and even though every movement causes an inky fog to float in the corners of my eyes, I stretch my fingers out toward him. He stumbles back to the doorway and disappears.

My breath catches and an ugly, guttural noise escapes my throat.

Ian's voice comes fast and low and when I look up I see a mobile pressed to his ear.

"Oh, Tess," Shelley cries out. "Hang in there."

She picks up the knife and I watch droplets of blood run from the blade down her hand. Shelley puts the knife in the sink and crouches to the floor beside me.

"Hang in there," she says again, but I don't think I can. The blood is flowing out of me too fast. I can feel a puddle already cooling around me as my body collapses to the tiles.

"You can't take Jamie away from me." I force the words out.

Then darkness takes over my vision and all I can think is: *If only I'd chosen a smaller knife; if only I hadn't trusted Shelley; if only I'd been a better mother, then I wouldn't be about to die.*

CHAPTER 61

Transcript BETWEEN ELLIOT SADLER (ES) AND TERESA CLARKE (TC) (INPATIENT AT OAKLANDS HOSPITAL, HARTFIELD WARD), WEDNESDAY, APRIL 11. SESSION 2 (Cont.)

ES: So, Tess, I have your notebook here. Would you like to look at it?

TC: Have you looked at it?

ES: Yes.

TC: So you know then.

ES: Why don't you take a look?

TC: Fine.

ES: Tell me what you see.

TC: I see it all. Don't you? Look, here are the dates and times of the threatening calls, the times I was followed by Richard Welkin, although that's not part of it. The clues are all here. Ian snooping in the house and all of his lies. And look, here's Shelley's pages. She was desperate to replace Dylan. She told me so many times how she wanted to be a mother again. She separated

from her husband. She drugged me so she could have Jamie to herself and pretend he was hers. All this time she made out like I was the one who was struggling to cope, and maybe I was, but so was she. She wanted to take Jamie away from me. And both of them trying to make out like I'm crazy, like I need help.
(KNOCK AT DOOR)

ES: Excuse me.
SESSION PAUSED.
SESSION CONTINUED.

TC: Was that Shelley at the door?
ES: Shelley has been helping the police to answer some questions they have about you and this notebook.
TC: She's working with him. Can't you see that she wants to take Jamie away from me?
ES: The reason Shelley knocked on the door just now was to tell me your mother has arrived. Are you happy to see your mother now, Tess? I think it would help you to have her here for the next part of our session.
TC: I guess.
TC: What do you mean "session"?

CHAPTER 62

Wednesday, April 11

I flick through the pages and stare at the scratches of black pen. Every single lined page is scribbled and scrawled on. Front and back. There are holes in the corners and in the middle, with ink blotched around the edges where the pen has torn through the page, but it's all there and now that I'm staring at everything that has happened to me, to Jamie too, I can't believe I didn't act on it. I should've gone to the police straightaway. The minute I heard that first answerphone message, I should've taken Jamie out of school and gone to stay with my mum like she suggested.

I told myself I stayed for Jamie because he was happy in the house and at school. But he wasn't happy. He was quiet. He barely said a word when I was in the same room as him. No, I didn't stay for Jamie, I stayed for me, because being in that house made me feel close to you, and because I had Shelley there, pulling me back from the depths of my grief.

I have so many answers now. I know Shelley wants Jamie. I know it was Richard following me—all those hang-ups scaring me—and

I'm quite sure the voice on the phone was a trick by Ian and Shelley to keep me feeling vulnerable and needing them.

But the only question that matters now, and the one I don't have the answer to, is where is Jamie?

The lines of writing blur before my eyes. I can't think straight. My head hurts and the inside of my mouth feels fuzzy. The pain in my stomach is a dull throbbing that pulses outward. I shift in my chair and wince at the sharp stab of pain now slicing through me.

There's movement outside. A shuffling of feet and the thump thump of a walking stick on hard floor. There is a porthole window in the door and I can see Sadler's large frame blocking the window. Why aren't they coming in? What is he saying to my mum? My cheeks burn red and I pull at the scratchy fabric of my hospital nightie and the dressing gown wrapped around it.

There's a window beside the door with blinds shut tight. The blinds are gray venetian and seem to be trapped between two panes of glass. There is no string dangling down, just a switch to press. It seems like an overly complicated system for a hospital room. My eyes travel around the rest of the room as if I'm seeing it for the first time.

There is a low pine coffee table, boxed in by a sofa on one side and two armchairs facing each other. There are no shelves or pictures. The walls are painted an off white and someone has gone to the trouble of stenciling a rich green vine across one wall. There are pastel-colored flowers dotted on the vine. It's pretty, but again seems an extravagant choice for a public hospital.

I trudge back over the blur of memories from the last few days. Jamie's birthday was on Sunday. What day is it now—Monday? Tuesday? Time has lost all meaning.

There was the day I woke up after surgery on the ward with the

Irish nurse. I try to remember the name of the ward, but all I can remember is the smell of boiled vegetables at mealtimes and the incessant beep of the machines when the drips ran out.

There was a nurses' station at the end of the ward and only six beds, I think. There was a woman beside me with a white bandage wrapped around her head. The recovery ward from my surgery, I guess.

I remember being dragged in and out of sleep. In and out, in and out, and I remember asking for more morphine and a young doctor with a stethoscope around her neck telling me I was being weaned off the stronger painkillers.

Then I woke up and I wasn't on the ward anymore. I was in a private room and the nurses were wearing green instead of blue. Was that this morning or yesterday?

The police interview has dragged on for what feels like months. I've been evasive, but then so has he. Why can't he tell me what they are doing to find Jamie?

A panic is trying to escape from inside me—a caged beast rattling the lock. A memory flashes before my eyes: the scramble of bodies for the knife. Jamie reaching it, then Ian and me. The feel of the blade slicing into my stomach.

The door swings open and I catch sight of a bright lime-green wall before Sadler's bulk fills the doorway. His beard is scraggly, with more gray than black. He is tall with graying hair, and thick-rimmed glasses are in front of his brown eyes. He is wearing black suit trousers and a pale blue shirt, creased from a long day.

I notice the stoop the moment he walks forward. It seems to start halfway down his back as if his spine is angled like a boomerang. An injury on the police force, I guess, or the remnants of a childhood illness.

Sadler holds his arm out and my mum shuffles in, her walking stick jabbing at the thin carpet tiles beneath her feet. I can tell straightaway that it's a bad day for her, a day when the arthritis is winning, and I feel a sting of annoyance at Sadler and the hospital staff for making her come here.

"Mum," I croak, surprised by the ache in my throat and the tears building behind my eyes. I've missed her, I realize, and yet I wish she wasn't here.

Mum tilts her head up to Sadler, and he nods before she moves closer.

"I'm going to get us some tea and biscuits," Sadler says, before stepping out of the room and closing the door.

Mum shuffles forward around the coffee table to the sofa. The armchair is nearer and I wonder why she doesn't just sit there, but I don't ask because I'm too busy staring at the coffee table. My mum's leg is leaning up against it as she moves by, but the table doesn't budge. I sit forward, ignoring the pain that makes me bite down on the insides of my cheeks, and spy the bolts hidden on the inside of the table legs, pinning it to the floor.

"I'm so sorry," Mum says, busying herself with a handkerchief she has balled in her hand.

"I'm the one who's sorry." I sigh, suddenly tired. I wish for the fog to take me away, but for once it doesn't come. "You shouldn't have been dragged into this. Was your journey all right? Did the police bring you?"

Her forehead furrows. "The police? No, love, Shelley brought me."

"Shelley? What did she tell you, Mum?" I sit upright, my wound searing with a sharp pain worse than when the knife first went in.

"She told me . . . she told me . . ." My mum's voice is shaking, like her hands, and I desperately want to move to the sofa and tell her it will be all right, but I can't, because I don't think it will be.

"Look, there isn't much time." I glance at the door and lower my voice. "You have to get me out of here. I think Sadler—that police officer—is working with Shelley. They know each other somehow. I think he knows where Jamie is and they won't tell me."

A noise rattles in my mum's throat, like a hushed whimper.

"Don't get upset, please." My exhaustion morphs to frustration. "Please, Mum, focus on what I'm saying. I know you're upset, but we don't have much time. We have to get out of here and find Jamie."

"I should've done more when you stopped answering the phone. I told Sam something was wrong. . . ."

"It's not your fault." I shake my head, wishing she would shut up and listen.

"Tess, I'm here for you, but you have to listen to what Dr. Sadler is saying."

"Doctor? He's not a doctor, Mum, he's a detective. See, he's lying to us both."

The door opens and I jump, stretching the muscles in my stomach and causing another wave of pain to radiate from the wound in my belly. There's a craving in my mouth; it's buzzing around my head too. I'm desperate for the morphine to take me away from the pain and from this room.

Sadler appears with a male nurse I've not seen before. The nurse is short with a shaved head and is carrying a tray of cups and a plate of chocolate digestive biscuits. There's an A4 brown envelope tucked under Sadler's arm.

He's moving to the armchair where he's sat for all the hours we've been talking. The nurse is sliding the tray onto the table. The door is swinging shut behind them, but just before it closes, for a split second, I see Jamie.

It is just a flash of blond curls and his galloping walk as he keeps up with the nurse walking beside him, but it's Jamie. Our baby boy is here.

My heart is racing, pounding in my chest. It's making my wound throb so hard I think the stitches will burst at any moment, but I saw him, Mark. I saw Jamie. He's OK.

The door clicks shut and I turn my gaze to Sadler. He is staring right at me, studying my face.

"You should've told me." I close my eyes for a moment and sigh. How long has Jamie been here? "You should've told me," I say. "You should've told me you'd found Jamie."

Sadler nods but doesn't reply. Instead he turns to my mother. "Mrs. Garfield, I've been recording these sessions and I'd like to continue doing so now, with your permission, please."

"Yes." Mum's voice quivers as she pulls at her handkerchief again. I have a sudden desire to snatch it from her hand and throw it to the floor. It's me who should be upset. It's me who was stabbed, me who's trapped in here. Mum should be out there trying to help Jamie.

I stare at Sadler. In the armchair his stoop is hidden, but even sitting, his large frame dwarfs the room. Sadler's face is unreadable. We've talked for hours, for days, and yet we've made no progress. Why didn't he tell me Jamie was safe? "Who are you?" I ask. "I know you've told my mum you're a doctor. Why didn't you tell me you'd found Jamie?"

"I am a doctor, Tess. I'm a psychiatrist. You assumed I was with the police, but I never told you I was. I allowed the assumption to continue so you would trust me enough to talk to me."

"What?" I shake my head. "I don't believe you. Mum, don't listen to him."

"Teresa, please."

My eyes shoot to my mum's face. Her eyes are watery and pleading and her hands are shaking so much that the walking stick in her hand is jerking from side to side.

"Why have you brought my mum here? Surely you can see she's in pain?"

"I am very sorry for any discomfort I've caused your mother, Tess, but when I spoke to her on the phone yesterday and explained the situation, she was more than willing to come."

"Well, perhaps you could explain it to me then."

"Certainly." He nods.

"And while you're at it, you can explain why Shelley is wandering around free as a bird when I'm the one stuck in here. You can explain to me where that nurse was taking Jamie." I nod at the door and the corridor beyond. "When can I see him?"

"Why don't we all have a cup of tea?" Sadler leans forward and pushes the cups to the edges of the tray and in reach for all of us. The liquid is creamy brown and steaming and makes me think of the hot chocolates Shelley made for me. Is Sadler trying to drug me now?

CHAPTER 63

"You told me you were a police detective." My teeth are clenched so hard it's a fight to get the words out of my mouth. "This whole time I thought you were a policeman. If you're a doctor then where is your stethoscope and white coat? I thought you were here to help me find Jamie."

"I'm not that kind of doctor, but I am here to help you, Tess. I never told you I was a detective. You assumed, and I didn't correct you. I wanted you to talk to me. I wanted to understand the depth of your illness. I'm sorry for your distress but I saw your assumption as a necessary omission of the facts."

"What illness? What are you talking about?" My voice bounces around the room. I swallow. My throat is dry and sore from talking and crying.

"I believe you've suffered a psychotic breakdown, Tess, brought on by grief and depression."

My mouth drops open. I want to protest but Sadler's words are a brick wall in my thoughts. Psychotic breakdown? How can he think that? Sadler must be working with Shelley and Ian. Maybe the man is threatening them too. It's the only explanation.

"Please," I whisper as Mum's shoulders begin to shake. Why did they drag her into this? I force myself to calm down. Sadler wants me to be angry. They want to prove their theory right. They want to prove I'm an unfit mother so they can take Jamie away from me. "Please, I just want to see Jamie."

My mum leans forward in her chair and covers her face with her hands, mottled and clawlike from the arthritis.

"Tess," Sadler says, drawing my attention back to him. "I have Mark's death certificate here. It was retrieved by Shelley when she collected your notebook. If you wouldn't mind, I'd like you to have a look at it for me."

Tears are blurring my vision and leaking down my face. I reach out and take the envelope in my hands. The lip is creased from where it's been opened before but the glue is still tacky as I peel it open.

The paper is thick and it has the symbol of a crown top and center. *Certified Copy of an Entry of Death* is printed in bold at the top and your name is typed in neat Times New Roman.

I brush a finger over the letters of your name. I told Sadler that I hear your voice. That's why he thinks I've gone mad. The thought makes me want to laugh out loud, but then I really would seem crazy. This is what all the fuss is about. They think I'm deluded about your death.

Relief, like a gust of cold wind from the fields, breezes through me.

"I know Mark is dead," I say.

"Can you remember any more details about the trip he was going on when he died?" Sadler asks.

"It was a work thing. A team-building session. The head office was in Germany. He went there all the time. I don't know why you keep asking me about the trip. There was nothing special about it."

Sadler shifts forward in his chair before speaking again. "I want you to really think, Tess. I called Mark's company and I spoke to Denise. I believe she came to visit you and you've spoken on the phone since."

"Yes, Denise came to see me about a month after the funeral." I nod, leaning back in my chair. The envelope is sitting on my lap and I fiddle with the lip, pushing it down and using the last of the stick to seal it shut.

"She told me about the trip. It wasn't just a normal trip at all, was it?" he asks.

"I don't know what you mean. But look, this is all a big misunderstanding. I know I told one of the nurses I saw Mark in the hospital, but I was on a lot of drugs and in so much pain. I know he's dead. I've not had a breakdown or whatever you called it."

"Tess." Sadler places his empty cup back on the tray. "What I'm going to ask you to do now is going to be very hard, but I need you to try for me. OK?"

"OK." I really don't know what he thinks will be hard for me. I've already told him that I know you're dead.

"There were two seats on Mark's booking. You told me that yourself."

I nod. "Someone else from the office." I never did get round to asking Denise about that.

"I want you to look in the envelope again," Sadler says.

I frown and smile at the same time. "I have Mark's death certificate here." I wave it in the air. "There's nothing else in the envelope."

"Yes, there is, Tess."

I shake my head, but I peel open the envelope once more, turning it upside down and shaking it. A single piece of paper falls to the floor and skids across to Sadler's feet. It's the same color as Mark's death certificate, and when Sadler reaches for it I catch the sight of the crown at the top.

I snap my eyes shut and scrunch them tight like a child. *If you can't see me, I can't see you.* I hear Jamie's laughter in my head and it sounds so real that my breath catches in my throat.

"Please look at this, Tess," Sadler says.

When I open my eyes, he is holding the piece of paper out for me to take.

I'm cold. So cold, Mark. And even though I don't want to touch the paper or read the words written on it, I reach out and take it in my hands.

"Mark didn't go alone on his trip this time, did he, Tess? It was a special trip. Look at it," he urges.

My teeth are clenched together so hard that my head is throbbing from the pain but I look. I stare at the paper, the replica of Mark's. The same crown at the top, the same writing: *Certified Copy of an Entry of Death.*

"It's a second copy." I shrug. "A spare."

"No, Tess. Read the name."

I shake my head and slam the paper to my lap, turning it over so I can't see it anymore.

"Who was on the plane with Mark?" Sadler asks. "Why did they go on the trip?"

"I don't know," I cry out. A sob shudders through my body. "I want to take a break. Let me see Jamie, then we can continue."

"We'll take a break in a little bit. Right now I want you to tell me who was on the plane with Mark."

Sadler stands up and shuffles around the table. He takes the certificate from my lap and turns it over. "Whose name is written there?" he asks, pointing at the paper.

I gasp as I read the name again. "Jamie," I whisper. *Jamie Edward Clarke. Born April 8, 2010.*

"Mark's company were hosting a special event in Germany for their employees and their families," Sadler explains, his voice calm and loud at the same time. "Jamie was on the plane with Mark. Jamie died too."

I shake my head from side to side. "No. You're wrong. This is a fake. This is what Shelley wants you to think so she can take Jamie away from me."

"That's not true, Tess. Your belief that Shelley wants to take Jamie away is a paranoid delusion. It's a belief that your mind is telling you is real, but is created by your illness. From our talks and looking at your notebook, I also believe the voice you heard on the phone is a hallucination of persecution triggered by Richard Welkin's repeated attempts to contact you and your desire to uncover the truth of Mark's secret project.

"With Shelley, you believe someone is threatening your existence with Jamie, and you're seeing evidence to support this that isn't there, just the same as how you're seeing Jamie. It's an illness, Tess."

"Jamie is alive." I whisper the words aloud, an affirmation for myself as much as for Sadler.

I struggle to my feet, ignoring the pain clenching my stomach and the dizziness pressing down on my head. "JAMIE," I shout. "JAMIE."

"Your mum is here for a reason." Sadler raises his voice, a deep baritone next to my shrill cries. "In cases like this," he says after I fall silent, "evidence that contradicts the delusion is ignored, explained away just as you are doing now. You are burying the facts, making them part of your delusion, just as you've done any time you've found yourself confronted with the truth. It's why you cut yourself off from your mum and your brother, and your friends in Chelmsford. All those in fact who knew Jamie was dead. It's why you've suffered from episodes of isolated amnesia whenever you came too close to the truth."

"No." I shake my head from side to side. "Mum." I turn to face the frail frame of my mother. "Please, I'm begging you, whatever they've told you, whatever they're threatening you with, please—" A sob catches in my throat. "Please tell them they're wrong. You stayed with us after the funeral. You saw Jamie."

Mum nods and for a fleeting second I think she's going to agree with me. "I heard you talking to yourself," she says. "I should've questioned you on it but I knew you were hurting so badly. I didn't think there was any harm in that, but I didn't know you were seeing Jamie. I called the grief charity so you'd have someone to talk to. I should never have left. I'm so sorry."

"I wanted you to go," I mumble. "Jamie was hiding in his room too much. Neither of us could grieve properly with you there."

Mum reaches forward and squeezes my hand. "But Jamie died too."

"Why are you LYING?" I shout. Mum jerks away and shrinks against the chair as if I'm a violent lunatic, but I can't stop. "Why would you say that?"

"Often with hallucinations there's a clue," Sadler continues, his voice now calm as he positions himself back on the armchair opposite me. "A telltale sign that if you look hard enough at the hallucination, then you'll see it for what it is. I want you to do that now please, Tess. Think about the Jamie you've seen since the plane crash. You've said yourself that Jamie was hardly talking to you. Does this seem like the same Jamie you loved before the crash?

"I want you to think back over these past weeks and find that telltale sign, that one thing that will help your mind recognize the hallucination for what it is—a psychosis brought on by your grief."

I shake my head, short side-to-side jerks that blur my eyes. I want to cover my ears with my hands and scream for Jamie but my mother's face is ghostly white and the tears are streaming down her cheeks just as they are mine. "Why are you doing this to me?" I ask her.

She swallows as if about to speak but Sadler holds up his hand.

The death certificate is lying on my lap and I push it to the floor. "These are easy to forge, you know. If you know the right people." I don't know if that's true, but it has to be, doesn't it? It's just a piece of paper. Nothing special at all.

"Tess?" Sadler leans forward so his elbows are resting on his knees.

"There isn't anything. I know in my heart that Jamie . . . that Jamie . . ." The words are there in my head, but they are stuck, like a packet of crisps in a broken vending machine, dangling halfway between out and in, waiting for someone to give the machine a nudge.

Jamie's face floats through my mind. His beautiful eyes are wide and sad, and oh so blue. I can picture him now on the floor of the living room with the PlayStation controller in his hands. His face fixed in concentration, his tongue prodding at the baby tooth at the front, wiggling it back and forth, wondering if today is the day it will fall out.

A wave of sickness hits me. My face must change, because Sadler is nodding and leaning closer, barely perched on the chair anymore. "Follow that train of thought, Tess. Tell me what you see."

"The tooth," I whisper. "Jamie has a wobbly tooth. It's been hanging on by little more than a thread for . . . for months."

A wall of tears builds in my eyes and I can hear Jamie's singsong question in my ears. *"Mummy, if my tooth falls out when I'm in Frankfurt with Daddy, will the tooth fairy give me a pound or a euro?"*

I crouch forward and cover my ears with my hands, muffling the noise in the room but doing nothing to stop the memories I don't want to remember.

All this time Jamie has been pushing the tooth with his tongue, all this time since the plane crash, and the same tooth hasn't fallen out. Darkness and cold flood my body, like jumping into a pitch-black, icy sea. Other memories are breaking free now. I can see myself standing in my slippers on the driveway, waving and grinning at Mark in his gray jumper as he pulls out of the driveway. And there in the back seat with his mess of blond curls, wearing his favorite Liverpool football shirt, is Jamie waving furiously at me.

I see Jamie in his bedroom with his new rucksack open on the bed. The rucksack I couldn't find. *"How cold will it be in Germany?"* he asked, examining a thick jumper as if the answer might be inside the wool.

I remember the rain tapping at the stained-glass windows, the hard wood of the pews. My eyes staring at the worn tiles on the floor, my brother's hand squeezing mine so tight as I fought the urge to keep my gaze down and away from the coffin, so small—too small—sitting beside yours.

"That's it, Tess." Sadler's voice shatters the memory. "That's the sign. Jamie's tooth. You didn't ask him about it, did you?"

I shake my head.

"I think on some level, deep down, you knew Jamie had died that day."

"I didn't," I cry out.

"I've spoken to Denise and Shelley and to your mum." He nods to my mum, pale and quiet and so small in the armchair. "You were so careful not to talk directly to Jamie in their presence. Not until the end when your breakdown worsened and you couldn't keep it in anymore."

Tears fall from my eyes. I'm shivering all over. My stomach hurts. "It doesn't make sense. It can't . . . it can't be true."

"You were supposed to go to Frankfurt with Mark and Jamie. Do you remember? Denise told me she canceled your booking at the last minute. Why didn't you go with them?"

"My passport expired," I whisper. "I didn't check it until a few days before. I was going to go to the passport office and get one the same day but Mark said not to bother. He knew I hated flying. 'A trip for the boys,' he called it. I . . . I was relieved. Oh my baby. My poor sweet baby."

My throat is squeezing shut and I'm crumbling to the floor. I should've been with you. I should've been with my family, and I wasn't. I'm alive and you're not.

Oh, Mark, I've lost you both.

CHAPTER 64

The nurse gave me a sedative. It is Bubble Wrap over my thoughts, but I don't want a cushion. I want oblivion.

"Can I have some morphine?" I mumble to the nurse bustling around my bed and prodding at my wound.

"Are you in pain?" she asks.

"Yes." Everything hurts.

"I'll ask Dr. Sadler when he's back from his break." The nurse in her smart green uniform and mousy brown hair scoops up my chart and scribbles a note before lifting her eyes and giving me a smile that is dripping with pity. I wonder what my notes say—WARNING: CRAZY WOMAN. SEES HER DEAD SON.

Except I didn't just see him, a ghost floating by. I watched *Scooby-Doo* episodes with him. I cooked him dinners. I leaned on the door-frame of the bathroom and listened to him in the bath. I cared for him. I loved him, and he loved me back.

I don't know what to do now, Mark.

"We've put you on antipsychotics, Tess," Sadler explained as I was wheeled back to my room. "The medication, along with our sessions, will take some time to work, but they will work. We will get you better."

I don't want to get better, I thought, closing my eyes and pretending to sleep, pretending not to hear my mother's whispered fears. "Is it . . . is it schizophrenia?"

"No, Mrs. Garfield. Schizophrenia is a lifelong neurological disorder which is often characterized by delusions and hallucinations, but what Tess is suffering from—her hallucination of seeing Jamie, her delusions of being persecuted by an unknown man—have been triggered by Mark and Jamie's deaths.

"Her conscious mind couldn't cope with the loss of both her husband and her son so tragically, and so she began experiencing depression and the start of a psychotic breakdown. It's as though her mind is betraying her, keeping reality away. With the right medication and intense therapy, she can get well again."

I drift off somewhere after that, a no-man's-land between waking and sleep. When I come back to myself I sense Shelley sitting beside me. Her hand is warm on mine and her sweet perfume hangs in the air.

"Hi," I say before opening my eyes.

She stiffens and pulls her hand away.

Oh, Mark, I am a monster, it seems.

"Is it OK that I'm here?" she asks.

I nod and open my eyes. Shelley's face is pale and there are makeup streaks smudged on her face as if she's cried away her mascara.

"Dr. Sadler said you were asking for me."

It takes me a moment to wade through the layers clogging my thoughts to realize Dr. Sadler is the man I thought was a police officer helping me to find Jamie.

"I don't remember."

She shifts position, crossing and uncrossing her legs. "I can go."

"No, please stay. I do want to talk to you. Where am I?"

"You're on a private ward attached to the hospital. It's called Hartfield Ward. It's a private facility that your mum is paying for."

We sit in silence for a moment and I make a fuss of moving the mechanical bed up so I can face her better. I'm buying time, trying to find a way to start a conversation I don't want to have.

"You made a chicken casserole together," I blurt out. "You let Jamie cut the onion with a knife. He told me before we ate dinner. You beat him at FIFA on the PlayStation that afternoon."

She pulls a face. "When?"

I think for a moment. "The second time you came to the house. I was so tired. You came over and looked after Jamie for me and cleaned some of the house."

She nods, causing a spark of hope to pop at the Bubble Wrap in my thoughts, but it's not a nod of agreement, it's one of understanding. "I did come that day. I stayed in the house while you slept and did a bit of tidying. I made chicken casserole. We ate at the table with the candles, just the two of us. I told you about my swimming and Dylan."

"But you stayed over and slept on the sofa?"

"Yes." Shelley nods, and her blond hair jiggles with the movement. "I was worried about you being on your own when you were feeling so depressed."

"You took Jamie swimming the next day and then the two of you went to the supermarket and bought food."

"Oh," she says. "That's why you were so worried when I was back late."

It's my turn to nod.

"There were times early on, like that day, when I felt like you were zoning out," Shelley says. "You talked about Mark but never Jamie—but I didn't know you were hallucinating until much later."

"When?"

She pauses as if considering how much to tell me. "Looking back, there were things you said and did that I should've picked up on. You said to me once that you'd cook for the three of us. I thought I misheard.

"I should've realized when the police came to the house. You told the police operator that Jamie was in the house. The policemen who came round to check on the house told us. They asked to see Jamie's bedroom and I showed them."

"He was asleep."

A wall of tears builds in Shelley's eyes. "The room was empty, Tess. I didn't understand why you were ironing his school shirts that night. I should've tried harder to talk to you about it. You were so sad. I told myself the police operator had misunderstood."

"I don't remember that night. You drugged me with sleeping tablets."

Shelley gasps. "Tess, no. I would never do that. It was your mind's defense mechanism. You shut yourself down and practically collapsed on the stairs. I told the police officers that Jamie had died, but you were so out of it."

"What about the time before, when you stayed over the night of the storm? You made hot chocolates and put something in my drink? I found you in the night singing to Jamie."

"Singing?" Confusion darkens her face. She shakes her head, freeing two teardrops from her eyes. "I . . . I woke up in the middle of the night and thought I heard something. I was on my way to check on you when I went into Jamie's room and sat on the bed. I shouldn't have done it, I'm sorry. I started thinking about Dylan and what toys he'd like to play with if he were here."

"What about the lullaby?" I ask, hearing the tune in my head.

"What lullaby?"

"I heard you sing to him."

She shakes her head. "I was sitting on Jamie's bed when you found me, but I wasn't singing. Think about it, Tess. Jamie isn't real, which means he wasn't in bed, so who would I have been singing to? I thought you were sleepwalking that night. You weren't talking and your eyes kept opening and then closing. I pretty much carried you back to bed."

"Oh" is all I can think to say.

"The beach was when I first saw you seeing him," Shelley says. "You were brushing the air and laughing."

"That was a good day," I mumble.

"I'm so sorry, Tess. I should've done something sooner. Ian thought you should be admitted to hospital when we met in Debenhams. He was angry when I told him I already suspected you might be seeing Jamie. He wanted to tell you right there and then that Jamie had died, but I wouldn't let him. I was trying to protect you. I think . . . I think I was jealous of you too, and that clouded my judgment. When Dylan died, everything was empty, he was just gone. But I could see that you still had Jamie, and even if it wasn't real, to you it was."

Another silence as my mind tries to sift through what I know is true. "I saw Mark. Was that part of my . . . my illness too?"

"I don't know. You didn't see him much, did you?"

"No."

"Maybe it was just like I said—the grief playing tricks on your mind, like it did on mine after Dylan died."

"Mark is dead," I say to myself as much as to Shelley.

She nods. "The passenger manifest showed they boarded the plane. If they'd have turned around and tried to exit the airport then they'd have had to go back through security. Their names would've been written down somewhere."

"I took him to school every day." My voice cracks.

"My friend Mel saw you."

I nod.

"It wasn't the school you went to. It was an office at the end of your lane. It used to be the school, once, a long time ago. But they built a new one."

"I knew that." I frown. Memories of walking Jamie through big blue gates into a modern building with a playground and basketball hoops flicker in my mind.

"Maybe deep down you knew," Shelley says. "If you went to the new school then you'd see other parents and Jamie's old classmates. This way you saw no one."

I swallow hard against a lump cutting into my windpipe. My mouth is dry and my head throbs. I want to close my eyes and be taken away somewhere. Did I know? Deep down in the darkness where I can't reach, did I know Jamie was gone? I think of swimming in the sea and losing sight of him. There was something dark flickering in my thoughts in that moment. I thought I'd lost him. And I had.

"I'm so sorry," Shelley says, squeezing my hand.

"Don't be. You've been a great friend to—" I stop myself in time. Not us, but "me. I thought you were trying to trick me. I thought you were making me think I was imagining things that weren't real. I heard you on the phone after I thought someone had been in the house. You were talking about me."

Shelley doesn't speak and I watch her thinking, remembering. "I was arguing with Tim. I'd just found out he'd had an affair with the woman from the golf club. I didn't want to tell you because you had enough going on.

"I'm so sorry I didn't believe you about that man from the airline," Shelley says. "The police told me about him hanging around. They've spoken to him too and he admitted to being in your garden that night. I should've believed you, but I thought . . ."

"You thought I was crazy."

"No," Shelley says.

"It's OK. I didn't believe me either. I thought you were trying to take Jamie away from me."

"The police told me you thought that, but oh, Tess, I'd never take a child away from their mother. It hurts too much to think about."

Another silence falls between us.

"Here," Shelley says. "I brought you some flowers." She lifts a bouquet of yellow roses from the floor. There are no supermarket tags, just two elastic bands keeping the stems in place.

I make a noise, my eyes shooting to Shelley. "Did you bring me flowers?"

"When?"

"I found tulips by the side door on my birthday . . . I thought . . . I thought—"

"Oh, Tess." Shelley's hands fly to her mouth. "I'm so sorry. I completely forgot about the flowers. I brought them with me, but you weren't in. I didn't want the flowers to wilt in the car from my heaters while I ran some errands. I put them by the side door, thinking I'll get them when I come back. I didn't know you used the side door as the main door. I'm so sorry."

I nod and we fall into silence.

"I'm still trying to figure it all out. So the car that chased me. That wasn't real either? Or the phone call from the man who knew Mark? Sadler said he thinks that's in my head."

"The police took your notebook, Tess. You wrote down the times when you heard that voice, and when you spoke to him. The police checked with the phone company. There were no calls."

"Oh." I close my eyes, blinking away the tears forming in them.

"I guess I owe Ian an apology. I thought he was trying to control me to get Mark's money. But that wasn't real either, was it?"

"Actually," Shelley says, leaning forward, "that was real. Ian did come into the house when you weren't there, and he lied about Mark owing him money. He was the one driving the car that chased you on your way back from the beach. I guess he wanted to scare you so you'd take his help."

A numbness spreads over my body. I can't get my head around what is real and what is not. They're telling me Jamie is dead. They're telling me there was no man with the gravelly voice. But Ian did try to run me off the road, and he did come to the house when I was out and look through your study.

"Why would he do that? Why didn't he just ask me for help?" I ask.

"I'm not sure, but he's admitted it to the police."

"Will anything happen to him?"

"I don't know," Shelley says. "I think he'll be charged with something. Dangerous driving, harassment. Trespassing too. I'm so sorry. This must all be too much. I should let you rest. You're in the right place now, Tess. Dr. Sadler will help you get better."

"What if I don't want to get better?" A single tear traces a line down my cheek. "Jamie is everything to me."

"But you're ill, Tess. You think someone is trying to get you. You thought I was trying to take Jamie away from you." Shelley shifts in her seat and pulls up her handbag. "I . . . I did take something from your house." She peels open the zip of her bag and pulls out the fridge magnet of Jamie, the one I thought had fallen off and been kicked under the fridge. "I'm so sorry. I didn't mean to take it, but I couldn't help myself. I sometimes try to imagine what Dylan would look like now, and when I saw this photo and Jamie's blond hair and blue eyes, I thought it could be what my baby would look like now and I took it. I'm sorry."

Shelley presses the magnet into my hand and I stare at Jamie's face until tears take over my vision.

"I thought because we'd both lost our sons that I could help you. I'm going to take a break from being a grief counselor. Spending time with you has made me realize that I still have a lot of my own grief to work through."

"What would you do to see Dylan again now?" I whisper.

"Anything. Anything in the world."

"And what if you did see him? What if you got him back and someone tried to take him away again and tell you you were crazy. What would you do?"

"I . . . I don't know," she says.

I turn my head to look at Shelley. Tears are falling down her cheeks and she looks like she will crumble to the floor at any moment.

"You can't pick and choose with this kind of illness, Tess," she says, wiping her hands across her face. "The paranoia, the man on the phone. They are part of your illness too."

"You're right," I lie. "Please don't tell Sadler I said that."

Shelley smiles and cups my hand in hers. "It'll get easier."

"Has it got easier for you?" I ask.

Water builds, shimmering green in her eyes. "No."

I nod and close my eyes again, shutting Shelley and her tears out.

"Thank you," I whisper, "for everything you've done for me, Shelley. You've been the perfect friend." The lie comes easily. It's what she wants to hear.

I listen to her sobs and pretend to sleep again.

CHAPTER 65

IAN

I admit to going into Tess's house when she wasn't there. I went to see if she was all right. She didn't answer the door, and I was worried about her, so I used my key and went in. It's hardly breaking and entering if I had a key. It had been my mother's house, after all. I didn't take anything, but while I was there, I wanted to see if I could find Mark's life insurance policy and make it easy for Tess to see it. I thought if she saw it, it might be the kick she needed to get things sorted.

I deeply regret telling Tess that Mark owed me money. I wasn't thinking straight at the funeral. My brother and nephew had just died in the most tragic of circumstances. I think it affected me more than I realized at the time. On top of that, my business partner decided he was going to sell the business and retire. I asked Mark for the money before Christmas and he was going to extend their mortgage or apply for a loan. He was going to help. I'd have done the same for him if I wasn't maxed out.

I needed money, and I couldn't ask Tess for a loan at the funeral. We didn't exactly have a good relationship. I didn't mean to lie to her. I just panicked and it came out. I thought if I told her Mark owed me money, she'd give me some of the life insurance. I knew about the policy. It was written in the will and I knew he'd left everything to his wife and son. I was only asking for a fraction of it to save my business.

I wasn't waiting for Tess when she drove back into the village that Easter Saturday. I just happened to be on my way back from a friend's birthday lunch and thought I'd stop by and see her. I didn't even know it was her car until we turned off the A12 and into the village. I flashed my lights to say hi and she just hit the accelerator. I drove after her to check she was all right, but when she swerved onto the other side of the road I realized I might've scared her by accident. I'd been drinking with lunch. I wasn't over the limit but I might've been on it, and I didn't want to go through the whole Breathalyzer thing, so I just drove home.

I haven't been a good person to Tess, I see that now. I lost Mark too. I think the grief has messed me up more than I realized, but in the end I really was just trying to help her.

I believe that the facts stated in this witness statement are true.

Signed,
Ian Clarke

SHELLEY

Looking back, it's easy to say that I should've seen it earlier. There were signs right from the start. Even on my first visit, there were two bowls of breakfast cereal in the sink. I just thought Tess had changed her mind about what she wanted to eat. It really wasn't obvious, is what I'm trying to say.

The night the police came to the house and Tess told the operator that Jamie was in bed, I thought maybe the police had it muddled. Tess didn't say anything about it when the officers asked. It was me who showed them Jamie's room was empty.

It wasn't until the beach that I was sure Tess was hallucinating. I feel so stupid now, but I didn't want to believe it. Part of me was jealous as well. I know that sounds awful, but it's the truth. Tess still had her son but I didn't have mine. It was all in her head, but to her, Jamie was real. The next time I saw Tess was when we went shopping and she thought she'd lost Jamie.

Ian wanted to tell her in front of everyone—"Jamie isn't real"—but I managed to talk him out of it. I said it would be better to do it at the house. Clearly I was wrong.

I'm not sure what I would've done differently if my judgment wasn't off. My marriage was falling apart; I was dealing with a lot. Normally when I meet grievers I can reason with myself that they've had it easy. They've lost a brother or a parent. I lost my child. I can detach myself from their grief and mine, and help them. But with Tess, she'd lost it all—a husband and a child, and she was so desperately in need of help. I hadn't realized it was Jamie's birthday. I think that was part of the problem. If we'd chosen a different day—or waited until Monday—I think it would've been different, but we didn't. When I opened Tess's car boot and saw the helium balloon in the shape of an eight it almost broke my heart. Tess was skittish the moment she opened the door that day, as if she was expecting something to happen.

It didn't help that Ian waltzed in like he owned the place. Then Tess started accusing us of things. She thought Ian and I were working together. She wasn't making any sense, and Ian was no help. He just kept telling her she'd lost it. When Tess started talking, it was clear she was seeing Jamie. I've replayed that moment with the knife over and over in my head. It was obvious Tess was going for the knife. Ian was closest, and he reached for it too. He had the knife in his hand, but he didn't stab Tess. She ran into the blade. Like I said, it all happened so quickly. Tess pulled the knife out of herself and collapsed on the floor. I covered the wound and Ian called an ambulance. The rest you know.

I believe that the facts stated in this witness statement are true.

Signed,
Shelley Lange

CHAPTER 66

68 DAYS AFTER JAMIE'S BIRTHDAY

Piercing rays of summer sun are dancing through the diamond lattice windowpanes, casting torch beams of light across the cupboards, which hang wonky on their hinges. Sunlight hits the kitchen table, illuminating the white box with the neatly typed writing. *Mrs. Teresa Clarke. Take two tablets daily (with food).*

So much has happened since I last sat at this table with a box of tablets in my hands. So much and nothing at all; but things are different now. I still miss you, Mark. Of course I do. But it's different. Like the way I miss a stage of my life—the dating stage when anything could happen, the baby stage and holding Jamie in my arms. The grief for you is different now. It's in a glass box, like a taxidermy display—a wild animal, beautiful and grotesque, that I want to set free sometimes but can't.

I don't need to hear your voice anymore. I don't need to ask you questions and hear your answers. It wasn't really you anyway. It was my version of you. It wasn't pretend, but it wasn't real either.

You were a wonderful husband and father. We weren't a perfect couple but I think we were as close as two people can get and I loved you. I should never have doubted it, but I have to accept that you've gone now. I have to move on.

Jamie and I are a mirror, and if I'm happy then he's happy. And when he's happy I feel alive. I am nothing without him.

I'll be more careful this time. I won't let anyone in the house when he's here. I can't afford another stay in hospital or the medication they'll force me to take. I can't afford for Jamie to run away again. The man with the gravelly voice on the phone, he wasn't real. He was a delusion. I know this now. I don't need to be scared when he calls me again.

We could move. Find a cottage near the coast, in a different village where nobody knows us. It's not as if money is an issue anymore. It would be so much easier without the sessions with Dr. Sadler and the *"I was just on my way to the pool and thought I'd pop by for a cuppa"* from Shelley. It would be so much easier without the second glances from the villagers I pass on the street, and the silent pauses of worry on the phone with Mum and Sam. But this house with its endless nooks and its gloom is where Jamie is. It's his home, and he is mine. So we'll stay and I'll be more careful this time.

Ian has escaped prosecution. I don't exactly make a reliable witness. He got a police caution. He admitted to lying about you owing him money. I guess he thought that in my state I'd just hand it over and he'd be able to save his company. I know you applied for that loan to help him. You were a good person, Mark.

I feel sorry for Ian sometimes. He really was trying to help and just wanted to save his company. But then I remember the headlights blinding me and I feel only hate for him.

My fingers dance over the foil packaging. Pop, pop, two chalky white tablets fall into the palm of my hand. I hold them in the sunlight just for a moment before closing them in my fist.

"Jamie," I shout up the stairs. "Breakfast time."

There's a pause. A beat of silence that makes my heart thunder in my chest and a familiar pressure squeezing me tight. I don't dare breathe as I listen for movement. What if he's gone again? It took two weeks for him to find his way home after my stay in the hospital. He was distant at first—a flash of blond curls in the tree house, the sound of his laughter from his bedroom. But slowly he came back to me, just as he did before.

The thud of his feet creak on the upstairs floorboards, and I breathe again. Our perfect son.

"It's a nice day," I say as he steps into the kitchen wearing his school uniform, just like always. "How about we go to the beach after school and jump in the waves?"

He nods, and a wide smile stretches across his face, showing the baby tooth teetering at an angle. I drop my gaze and turn quickly, reaching into the cupboard for the Rice Krispies.

"Can we get an ice cream too?" he asks when my back is turned.

"Of course."

"Yesss," he hisses, his voice bouncing with excitement.

I set the cereal on the table beside his bowl and spoon and remember the two chalky tablets cushioned in my hand. I pad to the sink, careful not to knock my stomach on the worktop. My wound is healing slowly. Too slowly, according to the district nurse who came to visit last week. I could tell she'd been briefed. Her eyes kept darting around the room as if she was looking for someone else. She spent forever checking the number of empty medication packets and talking through the correct doses with me. I had to bite my tongue not to tell her to hurry up because I had to collect Jamie from school.

I step to the sink and fill a glass of water. It's cool in my mouth and I gulp it back before pouring the last of it in the sink, where it washes the tablets down the plughole.

I stare out of the window and watch the sun hit the field across the lane. The sky is a perfect celeste blue above the cornstalks, swaying in the summer air, and I force myself to look at it for longer than I want to.

I miss you, Mark, but I have to think about Jamie now. You died and my world stopped, but without Jamie I have no world.

"Ready to go?" Jamie's voice reaches my ears.

"Yes." I turn and smile at our perfect son and his beautiful blue eyes.

ACKNOWLEDGMENTS

Tess and Jamie's story wasn't an easy one to write. Some days it sucked all of my emotions out of me and left me exhausted. I had an idea in my head of how I wanted their story to be and that didn't always transfer to the page. (In fact, I scrapped and rewrote the first half of this book three times.) So my first thank-you (and it's a big one) is to my amazing agent, Tanera Simons, for believing one hundred percent in me and this story and helping me make it what it is today. And to the whole Darley Anderson team behind you—thanks!

A huge thank-you to my editor, Danielle Perez, and the whole Berkley publishing team. Thank you, Danielle, for believing in this story (and me) and for your amazing editorial insights and support. Also, thanks to the Transworld team, especially my awesome editor, Tash Barsby, for her enthusiasm, support, and fantastic editorial input.

I owe such gratitude to my first readers—Maggie Ewings (aka my wonderful mum), Mel Ewings, Pauline Hare, and Rachel Burton. You've been with me on this journey from the very start and your feedback and support means the world to me. Thank you, Rachel, for all of the support you've given me.

A mention should go to some of my family—Steve Tomlin (my dad), Maggie and Mel, Tony Ellingham, and Katherine Cresswell—for all the coffees, chats, and chocolates, and for understanding all of the times I disappeared for weeks on end writing this book.

To Kathryn Jones, my amazing friend and personal proofreader. Thank you for being one of the first to read this story and for letting me witter on endlessly about it during our dog walks. For the kid swaps, play dates, sleepovers and wine, and keeping me sane during long writing days. One day I'll figure out the past/passed conundrum and stop needing to text you.

To all the amazing bloggers who support and cheerlead us authors with such passion—thank you, a million times, thank you! Especially Kaisha at The Writing Garnet, Rachel of Rachel's Random Reads, and Anne Williams of Being Anne—you have my eternal gratitude.

Last, but by no means least, I need to mention my husband, Andrew, and our children, Tommy and Lottie. Thank-you isn't a big enough word for all that you do, and the laughter and fun you bring to my life every day. I love you.

READERS GUIDE

THE PERFECT SON

LAUREN NORTH

READERS GUIDE

Discussion Questions

1. Tess and Shelley are two very different women, and yet a strong friendship develops quickly between the pair. Why do you think Tess was so drawn to Shelley, and Shelley to Tess?

2. Tess's devastation over the loss of her husband seeps into every aspect of her life. Discuss the role of grief in the novel and how Shelley's and Tess's different experiences of grief are displayed.

3. Throughout the novel, Tess speaks to her dead husband, Mark. She asks him questions and hears his answers in her head. Why do you think the author chose to write the novel in this way? What kind of marriage do you think Tess and Mark had?

4. Discuss the role of isolation in the novel. What do you think Tess's experience of grief would've been like if they had never moved house?

5. Tess and her brother-in-law, Ian, have a fraught relationship. Why do you think Ian didn't trust Tess when Mark first introduced them? Why do you think Ian chose to lie to Tess?

6. When Shelley learns the truth she is reluctant to confront Tess. Why do you think that is? Shelley admits to being jealous of Tess. Did you understand why?

7. At what point did you discover or figure out the truth? How did you feel about Tess, as well as the other characters, when you found out? Had you guessed at any point, or were you shocked?

Photo by Laurie Ellingham Author Photos

Lauren North studied psychology before moving to London, where she lived and worked for many years. She now lives with her family in the Suffolk countryside. *The Perfect Son* is her first novel, and she's working on her second.

CONNECT ONLINE

twitter.com/Lauren_C_North
facebook.com/LaurenNorthAuthor